SHADES OF GRAY

Brooke McKinley

Dreamspinner Press

Published by
Dreamspinner Press
4760 Preston Road
Suite 244-149
Frisco, TX 75034
http://www.dreamspinnerpress.com/

Shades of Gray

Cover Art by Paul Richmond http://www.paulrichmondstudio.com

ISBN: 978-1-61581-079-6

Printed in the United States of America
First Edition
October 2009

eBook edition available
eBook ISBN: 978-1-61581-080-2

For my husband, the most supportive
and patient man on the planet.

and

For Holly, who has been along for
the ride from the very beginning.

CHAPTER 1

EIGHTY-TWO, eighty-three, eighty-four. Plop. Plop. Splat. *Don't even want to fucking know what that was. Eighty-five… or shit, was it ninety-five? Son of a bitch! One, two, three…*

Danny Butler was bored. And cold. That always happened when he was in pain, the shakes starting almost as soon as his body registered the hurt. He'd kept it at bay, just on the edge of his consciousness, by concentrating on filling his lungs with smoke. He'd already worked his way through an entire pack of cigarettes and counted the aged ceiling tiles three times. He still hadn't decided if the broken one on the edge should count as two.

Danny tapped the ash from his cigarette, eyes skipping over the red puddle spreading at his feet. The buzzing from the decades-old fluorescent lights overhead was the only sound other than the steady *plop, plop,* which he was trying to ignore.

He'd spent plenty of time in rooms like this. Small, dirty, hopeless. At least this one didn't have a smear of vomit caked on the wall like the last one. But the filthy cinder blocks in front of him held their own vile secrets. Scuff marks from flailing legs and straining arms, dried phlegm that had missed its target, ancient brown stains reminding Danny he wasn't the first man to have shed blood behind these walls. The familiar scent of desperation leaked out slowly, a toxic poison working on the men left to sit here. Last chance, end of the line.

Danny bit down hard on the filter, chattering teeth sounding like ice tinkling against a half-full glass. He risked a glance south at the blood pool growing bigger by the drop. A few dark red chunks floated in the soup, the source of the mysterious splat.

Time to get this show on the road. Send in the clowns.

Danny stood up on careful legs, ran a hand through his sweaty hair. He moved over to the greasy mirror on the far wall and rapped hard against it with his knuckles. "Hey, assholes! What are you waiting for? An engraved invitation?"

Silence. But Danny knew he was being watched, all too familiar with the crawl of judgmental eyes against his skin. He lit his last cigarette with his shiny silver lighter. He drew in a steadying lungful of smoke before he reached down and peeled up his white T-shirt, wincing when the material stuck to the congealed blood below the left side of his rib cage.

"See this? Thinking maybe it could use a fucking bandage." He tried to avoid it, but his eye caught the glint of bone peeking out at him from the gash. "Fuck," he muttered. "Or you could just throw in a needle and thread," he suggested, eyes on the mirror. "Have myself a quilting bee."

No response. He let his shirt fall back with a wet, squishing sound. Then he reached out and slammed his bloody palm against the glass. Souvenir for the next poor schmuck stuck in hell.

THE two men behind the mirror watched Butler without speaking. The taller one took a step forward to get a better look. Up to this point, he'd only seen Danny Butler in photographs or through the gazing end of binoculars. He took in the thick, black hair sticking up in sweaty tufts, the face made pale by a combination of pain and bad lighting, a day or two worth of stubble outlining the shit-eating grin, huge eyes fringed with long, dark lashes, silver glinting from the small hoop in Butler's left ear.

"Jesus," the short man next to him groaned when Butler exposed his wound. "You get a load of that? Can he bleed to death from something like that?"

"No," the tall man said with a shake of his head. "He'd be dead already."

"Oh, that's comforting," Shorty said, rolling his eyes. "Still… don't you think we'd better have it looked at?"

"Later. When I'm done with him."

"Yeah, but—"

The tall man had already let the door slam behind him before the sentence was finished. Miller Sutton didn't need some local cop telling him how to run this investigation. He finally had Danny Butler exactly where he wanted him. He wasn't going to let Officer Friendly fuck it up.

Miller took a quick detour to the bathroom. He always had to take a piss before an interrogation. It was not a fact he'd willingly share with anyone. He did his business, washed his hands, and swiped a palm full of cold water across his face.

He stared at himself in the mirror, scrubbing at the freckles on his nose with two fingers as if he could erase them. He always hated them at times like this; worried they made him look childish, too young to be taken seriously. With a tired sigh he lowered his hand and turned his back on his own reflection.

It used to be this was his favorite part of the job: closing in on a case, trapping someone just frantic enough to save their own ass that they'd help you along. Fighting the good fight and all that happy horseshit. But today he just felt worn out, no anticipation in his gut.

Where'd it go, Miller? Where's that fire in your belly? Get it together. You're one of the good guys, remember?

He couldn't pinpoint when it had started slipping away, when he'd started to see more than an arrest, more than a notch in his career belt, when he looked into someone's eyes across a dirty table in a cramped interrogation room. He wished he could go back to when nothing mattered but the job, when empathy didn't have even the slightest toehold on Miller Sutton.

Maybe he had been doing this for too long. He'd always thought he would become more numb to the crappy state of the human condition as time went on, not less so. Besides, he'd only been at this job for seven years, not nearly long enough for burnout to set in.

Yeah, well, maybe you should have hung it up at five.

But that thought was too depressing to contemplate. He didn't know what the fuck he'd do with his life if not this. Everything set out in neat little boxes, all black and white, exactly how he liked it. Good and evil, right and wrong, innocent and guilty. Stay in the right box and it would all work out in the end.

Enough of this shit! Get in there and nail his ass to the wall. Show Danny Butler what desperate really feels like. Show him if he doesn't do things your way, his hurting days have just begun.

MILLER opened the door, shut it softly behind him. He crossed to the table, pulled out a chair opposite Butler, and sat down without a word. His power had always been in his silence. Never comfortable with coming in and barking out questions, he chose instead to use his quiet nature to work at a suspect. He'd discovered quickly that people weren't easy with silence. Pretty soon they'd be barfing up their life story, splattering Miller with their verbal vomit just to have some noise in the room.

Butler was leaning back in his chair, booted heels propped up on the table.

"Get your feet off the table," Miller said, not looking up from the file he'd spread out in front of him.

Butler took his sweet time about complying, lowering each foot deliberately to the floor. "Yes… sir," he drawled, lip curving up in amusement.

We'll see how funny you think this is in about five minutes, shithook. Miller glanced at the card in his hand. "I see you've been given your Miranda warnings."

"Yeah, where's the lawyer I requested two hours ago?"

Miller shrugged. "Couldn't tell you. Must be on his way."

"Uh-huh," Butler said. "Now why don't I believe that?"

Miller waited him out, praying he would be as over-confident as most of the men who'd sat in that chair before him. He didn't have to wait long.

"Well, get to it." Butler made a beckoning motion with his hand. "Not like I'm going to tell you shit anyway."

Miller swallowed his triumphant smile, flipping through the pages in front of him.

"They must've decided to send in the big dogs," Butler smirked. "Don't think I've met you before. Detective…?"

"Special Agent Sutton."

Butler laughed under his breath. "Should have known. A junior G-man. So they've got the Feds on my ass now. Excellent. I'm moving up in the ranks."

"Says here you've got some experience with the federal system." Miller thumped Butler's file with his index finger. "Done some quality time in Leavenworth, Marion, even a short stint in Super Max."

"What can I say?" Butler shrugged, spread his arms wide. "Wanted to see the world."

"Conspiracy to distribute cocaine, conspiracy to distribute methamphetamine, conspiracy to distribute cocaine again. At least you're consistent."

"Yeah, but I was innocent all those times," Butler said with a lazy smile, gaze floating up to the ceiling.

Cocky son of a bitch. "Oh, really?" Miller gave a cold smile of his own. "Well, this time you're not. Felon in possession of a firearm, Mr. Butler." He made a clucking sound with his tongue. "That's a big no-no. Five years mandatory."

"It wasn't my fucking gun," Butler retorted, tilting his chair back on two legs, his voice bored.

"No good," Miller countered. "Thought you'd know by now, federal judges see right through that one. The gun was in your car when you were arrested. Nobody gives a shit whose it really is. You're on the hook for it, bud."

"As you can see, Sutton, I'm shaking in my boots over here."

Don't let him get to you. It's what he wants. You're holding all the cards here. Danny Butler is nothing. Nothing.

"You ought to be scared. Haven't ever done five years hard time at a stretch, have you? And that's before we add on whatever goodies we find in your house during our search. Be a while before you see the light of day again, Mr. Butler."

"Would you stop with the Mr. Butler shit? It's Danny."

"Fine… Danny."

"And I can call you…?" Danny grinned, Cheshire cat coming out to play.

"Special Agent Sutton will do just fine."

"All right." Danny tipped his chair forward with a bang. He rested his elbows on the table, left forearm and hand streaked with crimson battle paint. "What the fuck do you want, Special Agent Sutton?"

Miller leaned forward, too, until their faces were only a few inches apart. "Roberto Hinestroza's head on a platter," he whispered. "That's what I want."

Danny sat back with a thud. His body slammed into his chair hard enough to force out air and his hand came up to hover over his injured side. "Don't have a clue what you're talking about," he said finally.

Not so cocky now, are you, asshole? Miller could smell blood in the air and not just from Danny's wound. He steepled his hands, rested his chin on his fingers, and waited. He wasn't impressed with Danny's denial, knew he was lying even without the eyes flickering from ceiling to floor to table, never once landing on Miller.

"What makes you think I know Roberto Hinestroza?" Danny asked when the silence grew thick, nervous fingers picking at the dried blood on his arm.

Bingo. "Well, gee, Danny, I don't know. Could it be because you're his number-two man? Been running coke for him since you were old enough to drive?"

"Don't know where you get your information, but I'm not his right-hand man," Danny scoffed.

"You don't want to fuck with me, Danny," Miller warned, voice level, no room for misinterpretation. "I've been investigating Hinestroza for three years now. I eat, sleep, and breathe Hinestroza. I know more about that piece of shit than he knows about himself. And I've had my eye on you all that time."

"Jesus," Danny leered. "I knew I was good-looking, but—"

"Shut up!" *Cool it, Miller. He's working you now. Bring him back to where you want him, let him know who's boss.* "We've been waiting for a reason to arrest you and today you gave us one."

"Running a red light?" Danny waved a dismissive hand. "That's the best you can do?"

"They didn't arrest you for the traffic violation. Arrested you for that Sig Sauer you had in the glove compartment."

"Speaking of my arrest, you gonna get me some medical attention anytime soon?" Danny gestured to his still-leaking side. "This has lawsuit city written all over it."

"That's what happens when you run from the cops."

"He didn't have to drag me back out through that busted window. Cut me all to hell."

Miller gave Danny a blank stare. "He wasn't going to follow you into an abandoned building. Besides, he had orders. I need you breathing to be any good to me at all."

"You're just a prince of a guy," Danny muttered under his breath. "Okay, I'll play along. Let's assume I even know this Roberto Hinestroza, I'm guessing you want me to roll over on him?"

Miller nodded, tapped his top lip with his pen. "Among other things."

Danny leaned his head back and howled. "Oh, man, that's a good one, Special Agent Sutton."

"I'm serious, Danny."

Danny's head snapped down again. "So am I. No—fucking— way."

"We're not going to throw you to the wolves. We can protect—"

"Ummm… the last guy I knew who fell for that line, they found him floating in the river with his tongue ripped out and his dick shoved down his throat. So you'll pardon me if I'm not jumping up and down and squealing like a teenage girl at your offer."

"That's not going to happen this time." *You sure about that, Miller? Because you know as well as he does there's no protecting someone twenty-four seven. Hinestroza wants him bad enough, he'll get him. You willing to make that trade? Yeah... fuck, yeah. What's one low-life drug dealer? Who gives a shit about Butler if he nets me the big fish?* Miller looked down at his hands. Sometimes he made himself sick.

Danny was watching him with knowing eyes, eyes that had been around this block a time or two before. Eyes that knew all the nasty truths hidden behind the pretty exteriors. "Thanks for the reassurance. Might work better if you believed it yourself," he pointed out. "Think I'll take my chances on the five years in prison, if it's all the same to you."

"Thing is, Danny," Miller said, voice all silky menace, "I doubt you'll make it out of those five years alive. Rumor gets around in prison you already ratted on Hinestroza...." He raised his eyebrows. "Not gonna be long before you're out of the picture, so to speak. Why don't you do the right thing for once in your pathetic life and help us out?"

The threat hung heavy in the room. Danny's eyes darkened with the knowledge he was trapped. Miller felt his own body tense up, registering Danny's anger, ready for however Danny tried to run.

"You fucking piece of shit," Danny spit out. "Gonna have me killed if I don't give you what you want? That it?"

"Never said one word about having you killed. It's just that without you being an informant, being protected by the FBI, word's going to get out pretty quick that you were in here talking to us. I'm a powerful guy. But I can't stop what people whisper about on the street."

"Unbelievable. You pricks are unbelievable." Danny pushed back in his chair.

Miller laid his hands flat on the table, gave Danny his beseeching eyes, practiced hundreds of times in his bathroom mirror. One more trick of the trade. "You don't have a choice here, Danny. I'm your best option and we both know it."

"Fuck off," Danny bit out. He got up and walked across the room. "I want out of here!" he yelled at the mirror. "Either charge me or open the goddamn door!"

Miller was up and out of his chair before Danny could say another word. He spun Danny around, shoving him back against the wall beside the mirror, out of the sight line of whoever might be watching. He bumped his chest roughly against Danny's.

"Listen to me, asshole. You're going to do this thing whether you like it or not." Miller's thumb came up to rest a millimeter from Danny's wound.

Danny's eyes went wide, the muscle in his jaw clamping tight as he prepared himself for the pain. Miller had always been a master at honing in on a suspect's weak spot. And once discovered, he had absolutely no compunction about pushing it—hard. Whether it was the sobbing wife out in the waiting room, the adored child destined for the endless foster care roulette, or the actual physical injury that Danny Butler was sporting now, Miller always went for the jugular once he found the vein.

But now, with his face pressed up into Danny's, watching those green eyes watch him, he found he couldn't do it. Didn't have it in him to bring his thumb down and gouge out the answer he wanted.

What the fuck's wrong with you, Miller? Do it. Do it!

He lowered his hand, pushed back slightly to give Danny some breathing room. "What's it gonna be, Danny?"

Danny stared at him with wary eyes, his tongue sneaking out to rub once across his upper lip. "Yeah," he said after an endless moment of silence. "I'll help you." He turned toward the door and looked over his shoulder, voice mocking. "But only because you need it so fucking bad, Sutton."

CHAPTER 2

SUTTON led Danny into the empty hallway, gesturing him toward a wooden bench screwed to the floor with rusted bolts. The whole contraption tilted dangerously, threatening to pitch anyone seated there onto the ground.

Danny sat anyway, his fingers sticking to the splintery wood. He didn't want to picture the combination of bodily fluids that caused the tackiness under his skin. He watched Sutton walk away, surprised there wasn't more swagger in his step. The bastard had gotten what he wanted, hadn't he?

Danny's lips tingled, the tips of his fingers and toes numb. He didn't want to pass out; partly out of pride, partly because he didn't trust Sutton to pick him up off the floor. He tried to put his head between his knees and take deep breaths but his side screamed too loudly to allow that kind of movement.

It's not only the cut that's making you light-headed. It's the thought of how many pieces Hinestroza is going to chop you into when he finds out what you're doing that's really making you sick.

Danny's foot bounced against the floor, fingers drumming a staccato rhythm on the wall. He had never been good at sitting still. Or following orders. Be damned if he would sit on the bench like some dog told to stay. He stood on wobbly legs, feet heavy as lead blocks, and hobbled down the hall in search of Sutton. If he was selling his soul to the Feds, then he expected some help in return. Accepting a death-sentence assignment had to involve a few perks.

He followed the sound of voices around the corner to a small office, where Sutton and a short guy with a bad comb-over were in the middle of an argument. Danny had a fleeting thought of retracing his steps and walking out the front doors. But Sutton would only have to follow the blood—a vampire movie version of the breadcrumb trail.

"Hey," Danny called from the hall, voice unsteady. "I'm not fucking around. I need a doctor."

Sutton turned his head, ran his eyes up and down Danny. "We're working on it," he said, his manner vaguely bored, as though Danny were complaining about a splinter.

Danny leaned against the wall, and then slid down onto his ass, leaving a shiny red streak in his wake. Fuck it, whole place needed a paint job anyway. The cold linoleum bit through his jeans, revving his shivers up into high gear. Sutton and the short guy were giving each other hell, their words floating out to Danny as the volume increased.

"He needs stitches," Sutton said, biting off each word.

"No shit! I tried to tell you that a half hour ago. Take him to the emergency room."

"Why can't one of your officers take him and then bring him back here?"

"Because, Special Agent Sutton, you Feds have taken over this case. He's not my fucking problem anymore. You're so anxious for Mr. Butler, have at him."

"Whenever you two are done fighting over me, I'll be right here, bleeding to death," Danny interjected.

He heard the sharp click of footsteps. Sutton's annoyed face flashed out at him as the door shut with a bang. Danny rested his head against the wall and let his eyelids drift downwards.

"Hey. Hey!" A rough hand shoved his shoulder, snapping him back to consciousness.

He peeled his eyes open. "What?" he asked around a throat full of glass.

"Don't pass out on me," Sutton instructed, taking a cell phone from his pocket.

"I wasn't passed out, I was resting," Danny corrected, not entirely sure if the distinction was true.

"I have to make some calls. Sit tight."

"Easy for you to say. Your ribs aren't sticking out of your skin like toothpicks."

Sutton ignored him, turned his back halfway when his phone call was answered. Danny shifted slightly on the floor, straining to hear.

"It's Sutton. Yeah, I've got him. He's going to need medical attention for—" Sutton paused, listened. "I know. Who should take him? No. No!" A heavy sigh, then Sutton ran a hand across his face. "Yeah, fine. You got someone watching his place? Okay. We'll be there later." He hung up the phone with a snap of his wrist and pivoted to look at Danny.

"Get up. Let's get going."

Danny leveraged himself off the floor, a groan escaping his lips before he could snatch it back. "You taking me yourself?" he asked, running his mouth to cover the pain.

"Looks like it."

"Wow, how'd I rate that?" He followed Sutton down the hall. "Thought you'd get one of your flunkies to handle it."

"I tried that. You're mine to babysit, apparently. Must be my lucky night." Sutton didn't sound pleased and his pace didn't slow on Danny's account; he was already half a hallway's length ahead, his suit-clad legs in a hurry to reach their destination.

Sutton looked good in a suit; Danny would give him that. Danny had always liked men in suits, with their crisp shirts, shiny ties, and polished shoes cracking against the floor. Maybe because growing up in a small town he'd never seen men dressed that way. Seemed like a better world than the one he'd come from. It was sure as hell a step up from the one he lived in now. Men in suits gave the appearance of having made something of themselves, of being in control inside and out—even if it was all an illusion. Those men weren't going to turn their lives into the kind of fucked-up mess Danny's had become.

Danny and Sutton rounded the corner at the end of the hall, dumping them out into the main area of the police station, where officers swarmed like flies. The room was reminiscent of every police station Danny had ever frequented: busy, loud, run-down. The same ever-present fluorescent lights as in the interrogation room, several bulbs flickering and snapping to cast gloomy shadows on the desks below. There were even a few obligatory handcuffed suspects spewing obscenities at unimpressed detectives. Danny could see a corner of the waiting area up ahead, small children crowded onto chairs for the privilege of watching their fathers or mothers paraded in front of them shackled at wrist and ankle. Just setting foot in the place sucked the life out of you.

"Wait here," Sutton commanded as he walked over to a uniformed cop sitting with his hip perched on the edge of a cluttered desk. Danny recognized the cop as the one who'd pulled him out of the window and slapped the cuffs on him, giving Danny's exposed ribs a not-too-gentle nudge with his boot as a parting gift.

The cop didn't seem to like Sutton any more than he had Danny. Whatever Sutton said caused the cop to stand up tall, pushing his body into Sutton's personal territory. Danny wished he had a cigarette so he could sit back and enjoy the show.

"I said get rid of it," Sutton barked. His voice drifted across the room, causing heads to turn from surrounding desks.

"I already did the paperwork, I can't just—"

Sutton leaned forward, hand cupped around his ear. "Am I hearing this right? Are you arguing with me?" One long finger came forward and poked the cop in the chest. "Lose it. I'm not saying it again."

Danny didn't know which man to root for in this fight, considering he wasn't exactly feeling warm and fuzzy toward law enforcement types as a whole. He'd have to put his money on Sutton, though, if it came to blows. The quiet ones always threw the hardest punches.

The cop picked up a sheaf of papers from the desk and held them in front of Sutton's face. He shred them with dramatic flair before letting the pieces flutter to the floor. Sutton looked down, and then stepped away from the mess as though it were a pile of fresh dog shit.

"Come on." Sutton grabbed Danny's upper arm in an iron grip and pulled him toward the main doors.

"What was that about?" Danny asked.

"Your arrest paperwork. I want it to disappear."

Danny snorted. *Well, it's official. I'm fucked.* "That's your big plan? Tear up some paper? Hate to tell you this, Sutton, but that's not going to throw Hinestroza off our scent for a single second."

"Let me worry about the details."

"Why is that not comforting me? Shouldn't—"

"That's him, right there! Right there!" The shriek cut across the din, pulling Danny up short.

"Oh, shit," he breathed, following the sound of the voice to its source.

"What?" Sutton looked in the direction of Danny's gaze. "Is that Amanda?" he asked sharply.

Danny cocked his head. "How'd you know about my ex-wife?"

"Told you already, Danny. I know everything about you," Sutton said, not taking his eyes off the woman in front of them. Only her upper half was visible from where they stood: all glossy auburn hair, vibrant red lipstick, and a skin-tight T-shirt that hugged every curve.

"Danny!" she yelled, waving both hands. "Danny!"

Sutton stepped in front of him, obstructing Amanda's view. "Get rid of her," he demanded as Amanda came barreling past.

"Oh my God, Danny! I've been worried sick. You never called me back after you were pulled over." Amanda belatedly noticed Danny's blood-soaked shirt. Her already strident voice went up an octave or two. "Danny, what happened?"

"I got hurt during the traffic stop, hon. It's nothing," Danny soothed.

"Nothing? You're bleeding!" Amanda focused angry eyes on Sutton. "Is he under arrest?"

"No, ma'am."

"Then why the hell have you kept him here?"

"Amanda—"

"We had to fill out reports, ma'am," Sutton cut in.

"While he was hurt?" She shot Sutton a withering glance. "Typical. Come on, Danny. Let's get you to the hospital."

Sutton moved forward, blocking her progress. "Actually, I'll be taking him. Liability reasons."

"Liability?" Amanda's eyebrows snapped together.

Oh, fuck. Danny was on a first-name basis with that look. Amanda's fuses were blowing faster than an overloaded circuit breaker. And if this dustup escalated to punches, Sutton would definitely be the one going down.

"It means we're taking care of our legal obligations," Sutton explained, his voice patient but the muscle in his jaw a ticking time bomb.

"I know what liability means. Jesus Christ. Don't think because you're taking him to the hospital that means we won't sue your asses!"

"Yes, ma'am," Sutton managed through gritted teeth.

Danny rubbed Amanda's back lightly and said, "Hon, it's okay. Let me get patched up and I'll give you a ring later."

"You'd better call me the minute you get home," Amanda instructed. She jabbed at his chest with a hot-pink nail to let him know she meant business.

"Sure thing," Danny nodded. He and Sutton were quiet as they watched Amanda walk out the door.

"She seems like a handful," Miller remarked once she was gone. His voice was mild enough, but his nose wrinkled up as if he smelled yesterday's garbage.

"You have no idea," Danny said with a laugh, and instantly felt like a bastard. God knew he owed more loyalty to Amanda than to the asshole standing beside him. He cut himself off mid-chuckle.

Sutton sighed, rubbed the back of his neck with one hand. "Make sure you check in with her, like you said. We need to keep this contained. If she gets worried, she'll start making phone calls. We don't want that."

"Fine," Danny said, pushing his way outside. Chill air hit him full in the face. Fall had definitely arrived; not quite six o'clock and it was already dark, the streetlights illuminating small patches of sidewalk, the rest left to drown in shadowy pools. "Shit, when'd it get so cold?" He crossed his arms, feeling the loss of the leather jacket forgotten in the backseat of his car. Probably in some impound lot by now.

"It's not that bad yet," Sutton remarked, tilting his face upward. The slight breeze blew his blond hair off his forehead. His face relaxed for a split second, giving Danny a glimpse of the man behind the badge. Danny was surprised to realize it was a face he might be interested in getting to know better under different circumstances.

Yeah, like circumstances that don't involve Sutton being willing to sell your ass out if it gets him a better shot at Hinestroza.

Sutton returned his eyes to Danny. "I'll bring the car around so you don't have to walk." It was the first time all night he'd given any indication that Danny's injury mattered in the least.

MILLER left Danny sitting on the stone balustrade outside the police station. He didn't worry about him running. There wasn't anywhere he could go that Miller wouldn't find him. Miller's footfalls crackled loudly on the deserted sidewalk, his passage breaking the brittle backs of newly fallen leaves. He could smell the acrid scent of smoke, someone in a nearby home eager to embrace the coming winter. A few lopsided jack-o'-lanterns leered at him from empty porches.

He pulled the dark blue Crown Victoria around to the front of the police station, fumbling in the glove compartment for some cigarettes as Danny limped down the steps, his face a twisted grimace. Miller leaned over and pushed open the passenger door.

He was not in the mood for this. It may have been the local cops who had delivered Danny Butler to his proverbial doorstep, but he didn't feel particularly grateful. He hadn't busted his ass all these years to play nursemaid. It should be some doughnut-eating patrolman's job.

"Can I ride in the back?" Danny asked, leaning down.

"Sure. If you want." Miller shrugged and hauled the door closed again.

Danny climbed into the rear of the car, stretching his long legs out on the seat. "Don't know if I can sit up straight," he explained, leaning back against the door. "Jesus, do all cops drive the same fucking car? No wonder we can spot you a mile away."

"We vary the colors," Miller said, deadpan, eyes on the road.

"Got an extra smoke?"

Miller held the pack over the seat and Danny snatched a cigarette with nimble fingers. "Which hospital?" he asked.

"St. Luke's."

"I usually go to St. Joseph's."

"What, you've got a frequent patron card there or something? They patch up two gunshot wounds, your next one is free?"

"Funny," Danny breathed, his exhaled smoke floating forward to tangle with Miller's mid-air. "For your information, I've never been shot."

"I know." Miller waited a beat. "Knife wound to the right lower back, done with a homemade shank while in Marion. Knife wound to the left thigh, almost bled to death from that one, wouldn't tell the hospital how it happened. And a fractured skull while in Leavenworth. Scar underneath your hair, back of the head."

"Somebody's done their homework," Danny observed, unimpressed. "Want a gold star? And don't forget to add tonight's to the list. Have a feeling it's going to leave a nasty mark."

Miller grunted, rolled down the window to let some fresh air into the smoky interior.

"Hey," Danny said suddenly. "I'm not feeling so great. Think I might be sick."

"For God's sake," Miller muttered, throwing a crumpled McDonald's sack into the back seat. "If you're gonna puke, puke in that."

"Anybody ever tell you that you've got a lousy bedside manner?"

Miller's mouth quirked up, a grin flirting with the corners. "It has been mentioned," he said, catching Danny's eye in the rearview mirror and then looking away quickly.

The last thing Miller wanted was to become friends with Danny Butler. Miller had a mission. He had to remain focused on a single goal: Hinestroza. In order to achieve it, he needed to draw Danny in while at the same time maintaining professional distance. Feelings couldn't enter into the equation. All part of the game.

When did a man's life become a game to you, Miller? He may be a drug dealer, but that's still pretty fucking cold. You got ice in your veins now?

The emergency room was relatively quiet when they arrived. They'd beaten the wee hours' rush, when all the drunks with smashed-bottle lacerations and head trauma from flying through their windshields would come rolling in. The bored front desk clerk handed them a pen and reams of paperwork to fill out, pointing them toward a row of beat-up chairs. The ripped vinyl spewed dirty pieces of foam that clung to the bottoms of their shoes.

Miller would have loved to cut through the red tape, flash his badge and start rapping out orders. But he couldn't risk it. Danny's future breathing prospects would take a nosedive if Hinestroza found out an FBI agent had accompanied him to the hospital.

Miller settled in to wait, something he was fairly good at once he accepted the need for it. Not so Danny, who was driving him nuts with his constant fidgeting, shifting, humming, and clicking of the pen he was using to fill out the hospital forms.

"Jesus," Miller snapped. "Can't you fucking sit still?"

"Apparently not." Danny didn't glance up from his lap where he attempted to balance the papers on his knees and write, while clutching at his side with his free hand.

"Give me the papers," Miller demanded. "I'll fill them out. I have all your information memorized anyway."

Danny passed them over without a fight, tilted his head back, and closed his eyes.

Full Name: Daniel James Butler. Age: 32. *Same as me.* Miller filled in Danny's address and phone number, leaving the section about employment blank. "It asks here about health insurance. I'm assuming you don't have any in your line of work."

Danny didn't respond.

"What about 401k?" Miller prodded. "Pension?"

"Have you thought about a career in stand-up comedy?" Danny asked without opening his eyes. "Seriously. Because you are fucking hilarious."

Miller allowed himself a smile only because Danny wasn't looking, his eyes still shut, the sweep of ebony lashes resting against the tops of his pale cheeks. Miller returned the completed paperwork to the front desk, which earned him a sharp snap of gum from the clerk and not much else.

"I'm starving," Danny commented when Miller sat back down. "Is there anything to eat around here?"

"How the hell should I know?"

Danny's stomach rumbled and Miller threw him a disgusted glance. "You are a pain in the ass," Miller pointed out, but he stood with a sigh and went in search of food. A depleted vending machine in the basement yielded a Coke and a package of peanut butter crackers after stealing the first dollar he fed it. Back upstairs, he tossed Danny the snacks, watching as he ripped into the cellophane package with his teeth.

"Fuck, could these be any staler?" Danny complained around a mouthful of cracker.

Miller took a deep breath, resisting the sudden impulse to smack him in the back of the head. Danny was just downing the last of his drink when a stout woman with a humorless face appeared in the hall, barking out his name. He muttered, "This should be fun," in Miller's direction as he walked away.

Miller collected the crumpled cellophane and half-crushed Coke can Danny had left on his seat and threw them in the overflowing trash can outside the bathrooms. Given the hospital's glacial pace so far, he figured it was a safe bet that he had time to go outside for a much-needed smoke.

"Hey, you!" someone called as he neared the exit. A petite woman in green scrubs, her ponytail askew, plowed through the swinging doors separating the waiting area from the trauma rooms.

"Hey!" she yelled again, advancing on him. "Why didn't you bring him in here earlier? He was this close," she held up her thumb and index finger a centimeter apart, "to needing a blood transfusion. You should have called an ambulance!"

"We got here as soon as we could." Miller raised his hands in mock surrender, pulling on his ass-kissing smile. "Are you the doctor?"

"Yes. Dr. Allen." She didn't offer her hand. Or smile back. "How did he get that gash?"

"What did he say?"

"He said it's a paper cut."

"I don't know what happened."

"Sure you don't," the doctor said, her mouth a thin line. "I'm going to give him sutures. Then you can take him. He'll need antibiotics to avoid infection and he'll have to come back in ten days to get the stitches removed." She cocked an eyebrow at Miller. "And tell him to be more careful shuffling papers in the future."

Dismissed, Miller went outside and had his smoke, the wail of an approaching ambulance promising heartache for a stranger. He could already picture the look on Rachel's face when she smelled the cigarettes on him, but was too tired to care. He lowered himself to the concrete steps, to hell with his suit, and squinted at the night sky—something he didn't do often, always guaranteed to make him homesick. The stars were more visible now that winter was approaching than they ever were during the summer. He wondered if that was a trick of his mind or if the cold air snapped everything into clearer focus.

When he finished his cigarette he wandered back inside, figuring he'd check on Danny's progress. No one stopped him as he pushed through the swinging doors, craning his neck around closed curtains until he found the right room. He could hear a steady tick-tick from the IV drip running clear fluid into Danny's arms via the crook of his elbow. The doctor had gone, leaving behind an ugly row of stitches that poked through Danny's skin like spider's legs.

Miller took a step closer. Danny was unaware of his presence, eyes closed, head turned away. Miller's gaze roamed over Danny's chest, the hard muscles visible beneath the dark hair still matted with dried blood. Danny had a large tattoo on his left shoulder, the yin and yang symbol in all its black and white glory. Not what Miller expected from someone like Danny. Hearts with the word "Mother," prison gang insignia, or even a swastika were more common among Danny's colleagues.

All his life, Miller had preferred looking at people while he himself remained unobserved—from across the school yard, from behind a two-way mirror, from an unmarked surveillance car. From a distance. Although he had mastered the essential skill of pinning a suspect with his eyes, it never felt natural. He always fought against the urge to duck his head and look away. Now, when Danny stirred, bringing a hand up to rub his stubble-laced jaw, Miller drifted behind the curtain and disappeared.

DANNY was feeling no pain. The doctor had ordered morphine in his IV drip along with fluids and antibiotics, smiling slightly at Danny's mumbled, "Bless you," before she had commenced giving him what seemed like a thousand stitches.

Now he rested his head against the cold glass of the passenger window, able to sit up front with Sutton on this ride. The reflections from the lights they passed bounced off Danny's skin, painting his arms all the colors of the city.

"We're here," Sutton said as he pulled up at Danny's apartment.

"Okay." Danny made no move to get out of the car. He was enveloped in a hazy fog, as if he were suspended over his body, watching but not participating. Too bad he didn't do drugs, because morphine might be the way to go.

"Hey, listen to me." Sutton's voice was brusque as he handed Danny a cell phone. "Use this to call me. My number's programmed into it. I'll be calling you on this phone to set up times and places to meet for your debriefings. Got it?"

"Got it," Danny said, palming the phone.

"If you notice anything out of the ordinary, Hinestroza acting suspicious, anything, call. We've got a couple guys watching your place. You'll be fine."

"Uh-huh." Danny wasn't convinced, but he was too damn exhausted to argue about it now. He opened the door and put one foot on the pavement. "See ya around, Sutton." He hesitated. "You have a first name?"

Sutton didn't look at him, both hands clutching the steering wheel. "Miller," he said finally. "My name is Miller."

"Miller?" Danny questioned, rolling the name across his tongue. "What the hell kind of name is that?"

"The one my parents gave me," Sutton replied, putting the car in drive.

"All right." Danny smiled. "See ya around, Miller."

It took him longer than usual to climb the three flights of stairs. He had to pause and rest at each landing. He let himself into his apartment, switching on lights as he moved to the front windows and peered out through the blinds. Miller's car was still there, idling at the curb—the glowing end of his cigarette winked up at Danny, a beacon in the dark.

Unbidden, Danny thought of Miller's burnished gold hair, his somber gray eyes, the whisper of the real man unmasked on the police station steps… his FBI badge. A small rush of heat moved up through Danny's core. Blood swirled in his head, pounding against the backs of his eyes.

He dropped the blinds back into place, went into his bedroom, and lay down with a weary sigh. Resentment over the bargain Miller had forced him into still stung, festering under his skin. But curiosity was creeping up behind the resentment no matter how hard he pushed it away. It had been a long time since he'd had the energy, or will, to be curious about much of anything.

This was going to be trouble. He turned the idea over in his mind and found it didn't frighten him. Trouble was the one thing Danny Butler felt qualified to handle.

CHAPTER 3

IT WAS hard to believe the sun down south was the same one that had shone on Danny during all his boyhood summers in Kansas. He had known it would be hotter in Texas, but he hadn't expected such brutal, relentless heat, forever baking the tender skin of his neck and blistering the backs of his hands.

"Next," he called, waving a green sedan forward into the sunlight where he and Ortiz went to work drying it with their dirty chamois cloths.

"Too bad we didn't get indoor duty, huh?" Ortiz said, squinting at Danny over the hood.

"Fucker never gives me indoor duty," Danny complained. "I think he likes watching me burn."

Ortiz grinned good-naturedly and went back to polishing the car. Danny rubbed large circles with the cloth, his sweat mingling with the water droplets he was trying to remove; it reminded him of those birthday cake candles that would never blow out. He could picture himself trying to dry this same car until doomsday, his own sweat always replacing whatever water he managed to wipe away.

"Hey, kid!" a voice called, low and bottomless—something almost subterranean in the sound.

Danny turned, holding up one hand to shield his eyes from the light reflecting off the black Town Car stopped behind him. The back window was rolled down partway, a slender column of smoke wafting out into the heat-shimmered air.

"Yeah?" he asked, annoyed. Couldn't the idiot see the car-wash line started at the other end of the building?

"Come here."

Danny threw down his rag and walked over to the car, leaning over slightly to peer inside. He couldn't see much, his sun-blind eyes worthless against the dark interior.

"What?" he asked. He'd end up with his pay docked if he didn't get back to work.

A low chuckle from the back seat, the first of a million times that snake's hiss would chill Danny's blood.

"I have a job proposition for you."

"I already have a job," Danny said, pointing back toward the green sedan, but even he could recognize his half-hearted tone.

"Ah... my mistake. I thought you looked like someone interested in more than drying cars for a living." The back window rolled up in near silence.

Danny stood there for a moment, debating what to do. His gut said to walk away, fast. Ortiz was gesturing to him, and he'd be fired within minutes if he didn't go back. But he hated this job, resented this life he'd carved from other people's leftovers. The black car hadn't yet moved. Danny took it as a sign, reached out, and tapped on the window with his index finger.

The window stayed shut, but the door was pushed open by an unseen hand, a rush of frigid air blasting against Danny's feverish cheeks.

"Get in," the voice said, no room for disobedience.

Ortiz was calling his name, but Danny didn't respond. He slipped into the car in one quick movement, the slide of his sweaty back against the cold leather sending icy tendrils tiptoeing up his spine.

Danny pulled the door shut, slowly adjusting to the gloom. A thin face swung in Danny's direction—eyes glittering like dark diamonds, cheeks pockmarked with old scars, one gold-plated tooth playing hide-and-seek behind a ruthless smile.

"I want out," Danny tried to say, scrambling for the door. But it was too late—his future decided in an instant—and the car was pulling away, Ortiz's worried face left behind in the car wash parking lot.

RINGING. Darkness. Danny opened his eyes. Still dark. He fumbled on his nightstand with one hand, fingers closing around the squawking cell phone Miller had given him only hours earlier.

"Hm?" he mumbled into what he hoped was the mouthpiece.

"Danny?" The voice was low and smooth in Danny's ear, like a shot of expensive liquor going down easy. "Danny!" This time louder and impatient. "Are you awake?"

"Christ, Miller, give me a minute," Danny barked back, squinting at his alarm clock. Four a.m. Did the man never sleep?

"Meet me at Loose Park today. There's a bench on the north side of the park near the Rose Garden. Three o'clock." Miller paused. Danny could hear him murmuring to someone in the background, then the sound of a door closing.

Miller has a wife? Or a girlfriend? Or a someone? "You wake your wife up with this call?" Danny asked. "Isn't it weird how people like to sleep in the middle of the night?"

Miller ignored the question and the sarcasm. "Be there. On time."

"Fine. Fine. Should I wear a disguise? Funny hat? Glasses? 'Cause God knows that's probably better than anything you've come up with. Or I could go ahead and shoot myself now, save Hinestroza the trouble."

"Good-bye, Danny."

Danny closed the phone and tossed it to the floor, the movement jarring his side and unleashing the throbbing pain. Propped up on one elbow, he downed two morphine pills dry, the chalky powder stinging against his tongue.

Sleep stole over him in seconds, dragging him down into murky depths as he fell back against his pillow. "God damn it," he moaned when the familiar ring of his phone erupted through the quiet. He snatched it off the table. "Yeah?" he demanded.

"Danny."

The blood froze in his veins. His throat closed up like a clogged drain as he struggled to catch a breath.

"Mr. Hinestroza. What's up?"

"Danny…." Hinestroza chuckled. "You know what's—" a breathy pause between words, "up."

Fuck. How'd he find out so fast? Danny stayed silent; he'd learned the hard way to keep his mouth shut when Hinestroza spoke.

"I heard there was an incident with the police last night," Hinestroza continued.

Danny sat up, flicking on the bedside lamp with one hand, the warm, yellow glow chasing away the monsters in the corners.

"Nothing happened," Danny explained. "I ran a red light."

Hinestroza made a *tsk-tsk* sound. "Very foolish, Danny. We've talked before about your recklessness."

"It was no big deal. I only got a ticket," Danny said, his voice relaxed even as his fingers twisted nervous knots into his sheets. He'd had plenty of practice covering his fear. Learned it early on his daddy's knee, pretending he wasn't scared, pretending to be the boy his daddy wanted. He'd honed it to a fine art while in prison, where showing your terror or insecurity was the quickest way to die.

"Are you sure?" Hinestroza questioned. "Or is there a need for me to come up there and check things out for myself?"

Danny took a deep breath, exhaled with no sound. "You can do what you like, Mr. Hinestroza. I'm always glad to see you in person. But I don't think it's necessary. Like I said, it isn't anything for you to worry about."

"I trust you, Danny," Hinestroza said with brutal force and Danny knew without seeing that Hinestroza's black eyes were blazing.

"I know you do."

Danny had to bite his tongue to keep from filling in the silence on the line, from explaining again or, worse yet, apologizing. He dug his fingernails into his palm and waited. The tension screamed through him, almost forcing words from his mouth before Hinestroza spoke again.

"I'll be in touch before next month. We have that shipment to discuss."

"I remember," Danny said. "It won't be a problem." He waited for the dial tone before closing his phone with shaking fingers.

Sleep had fled the building, no way to turn off the internal engine after that conversation. Danny's mind ran on an endless loop, wondering how much Hinestroza knew, where he was getting his information, how long before some of his men—men Danny had worked with for years—showed up at his door to put a bullet in his brain. *But the bullet won't come until after they have some fun with you.*

Danny calmed himself with the certainty that if Hinestroza knew all the facts he would already be dead. Hinestroza wouldn't have wasted time making small talk. His only call would have been the one that ended with Danny's death.

THE sun's golden rays shone through high, white clouds, light turning amber on Miller's face as it filtered down through the burnt-orange leaves above his head. The breeze was brisk but not cold. Two men sitting on a park bench wouldn't look odd; there were dozens of people walking dogs on the paths, bicyclists streaming by in a rush of air.

Miller saw Danny approaching from a distance, his easy stride unmistakable, unhindered by his injury. He moved gracefully, no hitch in his steps. Miller suffered a moment of envy as he realized that Danny was a man comfortable in his own skin, at home inside his body in a way that Miller had never experienced.

"Hey," Danny said, voice raspy, as he took a seat on the bench.

"You're late," Miller responded in greeting.

Danny grinned as he fished cigarettes out of his pocket. "I did that just to piss you off." He held the pack out to Miller. "Want one?"

"Sure."

Danny passed Miller a cigarette and his lighter, the metal warm from his fingers.

"Hinestroza called me."

Miller snapped the lighter closed and handed it back to Danny.

"What'd he say?"

"He knew about me being pulled over."

"Shit."

"But for right now I think that's all he knows." Danny rested his elbows on the back of the bench and stretched his legs out, crossing them at the ankles.

"You sure?"

"No," Danny admitted.

Miller sighed. "Shit."

"You already said that."

"I thought it bore repeating."

Danny laughed, eyes twinkling like a kid who'd caught his parents cussing and realized they were human after all. Miller jerked his head away, studying a pair of joggers coming around the bend.

"How does Hinestroza run the drugs up here?" Miller asked, clearing his throat.

Danny ran his tongue over his top teeth, took a deep breath. "Just jump right into it, don't you? Not even going to buy me dinner first?"

"Stop fucking around," Miller said, too sharply. He thought he might actually be blushing. He didn't know what the hell was wrong with him. He'd done this dance with informants a hundred times, but today Danny was leading, dancing steps Miller had never learned.

"I don't know any specifics about how he gets the drugs from Colombia to Mexico. He keeps that part of the operation separate."

Miller nodded. That made sense. Hinestroza was too smart to give someone intimate knowledge of his entire smuggling operation.

"Once the drugs are in Mexico City, he has a rotating group of about thirty people who drive them into Texas."

"How does he get the cocaine across the border?"

"In the gas tanks."

"Not terribly innovative."

"No," Danny agreed. "But effective. Most border patrol agents are too lazy to get a mechanic to come take apart the gas tank. And if they do and the drugs are confiscated, the quantities are small enough that it's not going to put a huge dent in the profits. Hinestroza makes sure no car carries more than a hundred pounds of cocaine."

"The gas tank," Miller mused. He'd expected something grander from Hinestroza, but he had to admit the simplicity worked—in large quantities and for a long time.

"You seem surprised."

Miller shrugged. "Maybe."

"Why? You see a lot of drugs come up in more elaborate ways?"

"Oh, yeah." Miller took a drag off his cigarette, debating whether to tell Danny more. Idle conversation served no purpose in the investigation. "We had a case last year where they made bathtubs and toilets out of cocaine and shipped them in eighteen-wheelers."

Danny coughed out a lungful of smoke. "No shit? How the fuck did they manage that?"

"Mixed the cocaine with fiberglass."

"What?" Danny laughed. "Wasn't it hard to separate?"

"That was the problem. They couldn't get all of the fiberglass out, so there were a lot of unhappy customers with noses even bloodier than usual."

Danny's mouth curled up in disgust. "Jesus."

"Probably would have put a dent in your habit, huh?" Miller asked, his voice mild.

"I don't do drugs."

"Right," Miller scoffed.

"I don't do drugs," Danny repeated with more force. "I never have."

Miller looked at him, watching for signs of deception. But Danny maintained eye contact, not fidgeting, not breathing hard. He was telling the truth; Miller would have staked his reputation on it.

"Okay," Miller said, willing to concede the point and move on. "How does Hinestroza get the cocaine out of Texas?"

Danny pulled one foot up onto the bench and rested a wrist across his jean-clad knee. "That's where I come in. Once there's a large enough stash of cocaine in Texas, I go down and collect it. A white guy driving a U-haul doesn't get noticed the way a Mexican guy does." Danny smiled without humor. "Hinestroza knows how to use racism to his advantage."

"Isn't Hinestroza worried about losing the cocaine if you're pulled over?"

"I suppose in theory he is. But I don't get pulled over. I stay right at the speed limit, use my turn signal, don't make crazy lane changes. I dress the part of an average guy, take this out," Danny fiddled with the diamond stud in his ear, "cover the tattoos." He flashed Miller a devilish grin. "I can be pretty charming, too, when I want to be. I never have any trouble."

"But if you did get caught, you'd be going away for a very long time."

"That's a risk Hinestroza is willing to take," Danny noted dryly.

"What happens once you get here?"

"I distribute the cocaine to various dealers. Some stay in this area. Others run it to points east and north. We stay out of the western market."

"Why?"

"Turf wars, mainly. Hinestroza works east of the Mississippi."

"So you don't sell directly?"

"No. I bring the drugs up, distribute them, keep the various dealers in line, do whatever else needs doing, but I don't sell on the street."

Miller wasn't sure why that fact pleased him, why knowing that Danny didn't peddle drugs on grammar school playgrounds filled him with a sense of relief. He acknowledged to himself it was a stupid distinction. Danny was only one step up that particular drug chain.

"I need the names of the dealers who buy cocaine from you."

Danny didn't answer.

"Danny...."

"I thought you wanted Hinestroza."

"We do. But we have to know who else is involved in the operation."

"Why? So you can trap them the same way you trapped me? Follow them around until they jaywalk or litter and then offer them the same shitty deal you gave me?"

"Keep your voice down!"

"I'm not giving you the names."

Miller had to have the names. It wasn't a negotiable point. But this was only the first of many times he and Danny would talk. They'd go over and over this information until they both wanted to bang their heads against a wall. He could wait.

"Fine," he said. "You don't have to tell me today. But what about Amanda? Is she in on the smuggling operation?"

Danny stiffened next to him, throwing his cigarette down and grinding it under his heel. "We're not talking about Amanda. She's not part of this."

Miller's radar went up at Danny's choice of words. "You mean she's not part of the drug business or you're not willing to talk about her part in it?"

"Take your pick," Danny retorted. "She's fucking off limits."

"Danny, if she's involved—"

"She stays out of it," Danny demanded. "I swear to God, I'll walk, right now, if you can't promise me that."

"Why are you so protective of her?"

"She was my wife. Even if it didn't work out, that counts for something." Danny sighed. "Look, this is off the record, okay?"

Miller nodded. Now wasn't the time to mention that as far as he was concerned nothing was off the record if it got him closer to Hinestroza.

"Any involvement Amanda has in this, it's because of me. She shouldn't have to suffer because she married the wrong guy."

"Yeah, but you didn't force her to participate, did you?"

"No," Danny acknowledged. "Nobody forces Amanda to do much of anything. But I don't want her dragged into this."

As a novice, Miller had assumed criminals were different in all ways from the average law-abiding citizen. But over time he had come to realize that drug dealers, murderers, and gang leaders all had people they loved, people they would do almost anything to protect, the same way the successful business man or suburban mom next door looked after their own. Involvement in the criminal world didn't necessarily erase those basic emotions of loyalty and love. It sometimes made Miller uneasy, the knowledge that in fundamental ways men like Danny were more similar to him than they were different. For Miller, life worked better when the lines didn't blur.

"What happened between you and her?" he asked.

Danny gave him a thoughtful look, cupping his hand to light another cigarette. "I'm not the man she thought I was," he said, choosing his words with care.

"What's that supposed to mean? Are you talking about the drugs?"

Danny shifted on the bench, shoving his cigarettes back into his pocket. "I have to get going. I have a meeting with one of the dealers. I can't miss it or it will throw up red flags."

But Miller wasn't quite done yet. "How did you get involved with Hinestroza anyway? How does he recruit people?"

"That," Danny said with a grim smile, "is a story for another day." He started to rise, his feet setting free the loamy scent of freshly turned earth. The smell brought to Miller's mind his childhood days: running free on the farm, the late-setting sun, his mother hollering him home for bed, dirt warm and loose under his feet.

"I'm from western Kansas too," he blurted out. *Where the hell did that come from? Next you'll be giving him your address and social security number.*

"Yeah?" Danny sat back down, raising an eyebrow. "Where?"

"Fowler, in Meade County."

"Atwood," Danny responded. "Up north."

"Yeah," Miller said with a small smile. "I know."

Danny shook his head. "Keep forgetting you're my own personal stalker." He glanced at Miller. "Did your parents have a farm or were you a townie?"

"Farm. Nothing huge. Wheat and soybeans, mainly."

"My dad quit farming about the time I started kindergarten. Couldn't make a living at it anymore. He got a job in town, but we kept the house and a few acres. I always wished we'd sold the whole thing and moved." Danny scuffed his boot against the edge of the sidewalk. "Giving up his land made my dad even meaner than before."

A harried woman walked past pushing two screaming kids in a stroller, the boy in front turning around to pop his brother in the face with a sippy cup.

"You miss it?" Miller asked when the stillness returned.

Danny shrugged. "I couldn't wait to get out of Atwood and I think I'm a city boy at heart. I like how fast everything moves, how not everybody knows your business. But I miss the quiet sometimes. And the way the air smelled." He looked away. "But I left for a reason and that reason is still alive and living in the house where I grew up. Even if I wanted to, going back is not an option." He shredded a dark red leaf between his long fingers. "What about you?"

"I miss the—" Miller made a rolling motion with his hand, "space, I guess. The way the sky always seemed so big and yet it felt almost like you could touch it if you reached high enough." He shrugged, embarrassed to have said so much. "You know?"

"Yeah," Danny said, voice low. "I know."

Miller's gaze snapped to Danny's. They looked at one another without speaking, two men longing for an idealized home, instinctively recognizing the loneliness at their centers. Danny's eyes came to life, darkening as desire swam to the surface, moving past suspicion, cutting ahead of anger. Miller tried to take in a breath and found he couldn't. His insides felt hot and smoky, like he'd swallowed the lit end of his cigarette and was choking on the flame.

What the fuck? Miller wrenched his eyes away, heart beating its way into his throat. He had heard all the rumors about Danny—that he was gay, that he was bisexual, that he liked men but only while in prison, that he liked women but only when drunk out of his mind. But yesterday, when he'd finally met Danny face to face, he had put the gay rumors to rest. Danny didn't fit his perception of a gay man. He was too tough, too cocky, too much like a regular guy. He didn't prance or preen. But Miller couldn't mistake that look in Danny's eyes.

No mistaking what that look did to you, either. But Miller severed that thought on his mental chopping block, locked it in a box labeled DO NOT OPEN in letters three feet high, and threw away the key.

"Gotta run," Danny said, standing again.

"Wait." Miller turned and picked up Danny's leather jacket from the far side of the bench. He thrust it in Danny's direction, not daring to meet his eyes. "Here."

"Oh, hey, thanks. How'd you know I needed this?" Danny pulled the jacket on over his red shirt, the leather matching his raven-wing hair.

Miller wished Danny would just go and leave him in peace, take those all-seeing eyes and walk away. "I searched your car and found it. Thought you could use it in this weather."

"Speaking of my car, am I going to get it back anytime soon?"

"You can pick it up at the impound lot. The one downtown."

"Okay." Danny didn't move, his black combat boots planted on the leaf-littered path.

Miller forced himself to look up. "I'll be in touch," he said, concentrating on a spot in the middle of Danny's forehead.

Danny smiled. "I'll be waiting." He turned and sauntered away, leaving Miller alone in the cool sunlight.

DANNY staggered up the last flight of steps to his apartment, three sacks clutched in his arms, his fingers cramping as they clasped the brown paper in a death grip. Mentally he cursed whoever invented grocery bags without handles. Goddamn morons.

He groaned around the keys clamped between his teeth as the sharp edge of a cereal box rubbed against his still-tender wound. He lurched down the hall and maneuvered one of the sacks between his knees, managing to unlock the door on the second try.

Once he was through the door, he let one of the sacks drop not-so-gently to the floor, too late remembering he'd gotten eggs. He pushed the door shut with his hip, tossed his keys onto the couch, and locked the door behind him. Never used to bother locking his door, but Miller had mentioned it yesterday when he'd called to set up another meeting. As though doors couldn't be kicked in. "If locking my door is the best the FBI has to offer in the way of protection, then I'm seriously hosed," Danny had felt compelled to point out. As usual, Miller had ignored him.

The day was warm for this time of year, the open windows bringing the scents of fall inside, along with weak sunlight that illuminated dust motes hanging heavy in the air. The pungent tang of car exhaust, rotting leaves, the crisp apple smell of autumn, and the musky aroma of cologne all mingled together in Danny's nose.

Danny went still, bile rising in his throat. *Cologne? I don't wear cologne.* He stumbled forward a step, caught himself. He could still detect the faintest hint of fragrance wafting toward him on the breeze blowing from the open windows at the back of the apartment.

Oh, shit! Oh, fuck! They're in here. Okay, calm...breathe... He couldn't go out the front door. By the time he unlocked it they'd be on him. *Get into the kitchen. Go now, asshole. Move! But slowly.*

Danny walked into the kitchen with his bags of groceries, an even pace, humming lightly under his breath. Like everything was normal. Like there wasn't at least one someone in his apartment who was seconds away from blowing his brains out through his forehead.

Danny set the sacks on the counter, moved out of the sight line of the living room. Quickly and quietly, he crossed to the large window next to the refrigerator and peered out at the rusted fire escape. He'd never tried to open this window. Never tried putting his weight on the fire escape, either. But when you have no options, your choices are easy.

One, two, three... do it! He heaved against the frame and the window opened in a screech of flaking paint and groaning wood. He could hear feet pounding toward the kitchen and someone yelling in Spanish as he vaulted onto the fire escape, throwing himself down the steps and pitching forward to miss busting his mouth against the ancient metal by mere centimeters. *Run, don't look back. Run!*

But of course he looked back; how could he not? One floor from the ground he jumped clear of the fire escape and took off at a dead run around the corner, but not before he glanced over his shoulder and saw two men racing down the steps after him. The man in the lead kept coming, but the one behind stopped. Danny would have known that face anywhere; it haunted his dreams almost as often as Hinestroza's did. Madrigal. The man Hinestroza always sent to clean up a mess. The man Danny had known for more than a decade. The man who never left the house without cologne. Madrigal gave Danny a smile made wolfish by too many pointed teeth crowding against thin red lips. He didn't seem bothered that Danny was getting away, saluting Danny rakishly with his silencer-tipped gun. Danny's escape only made the hunt more fun.

Danny winged out of sight, suddenly grateful for all the exercise the guards had made them do in prison. He plowed through the mass of people lining the street for the local farmers' market, for once not bitching about the commotion. Halfway down the block he ducked into a tiny bookstore, weaving his way through the stacks until he was hidden in the back.

He pulled the cell phone from his jacket pocket, sweat running down his face to drip onto the key pad as he hit the button for Miller's number. *Answer, goddamn it! Pick up the fucking phone!*

"Sutton here," Miller answered after the fourth ring.

"They know," Danny panted. "They were in my apartment."

"Where are you?"

"That little bookstore right around the corner from my place." Danny paused to suck in a lungful of air. "On Walnut."

"Are you safe there?" Miller's voice was tight and matter-of-fact.

"Fuck, Miller, I don't know!" Danny flung his hand outward, sending a spray of books toppling to the floor. "Shit!" The woman up front gave Danny a suspicious glance over the rim of her glasses. "Sorry," he called, bending over to gather the books in his arms. "I thought you said I'd be safe in my apartment!" he hissed into the phone cradled between ear and shoulder.

"Stay put, out of sight. I'll be there in ten minutes. When you see my car, come out and get in the front seat. Don't hesitate."

"Don't worry, I wasn't planning on taking the scenic route."

Nine minutes and forty seconds later according to Danny's watch, the blue Crown Victoria pulled up at the curb. Danny walked quickly from the back of the store and crossed the sidewalk in two long steps, unconsciously hunching over and bracing himself for gunshots. He threw himself into the passenger seat and Miller accelerated away in a screech of tires before Danny's door was fully closed.

They drove in silence. Danny's pulse gradually returned to normal, neck-craning backward glances tapering off from every five seconds to once a minute.

"Nobody's following us," Miller assured him when they stopped at a red light.

Danny laughed, a harsh, pained sound. "Well, you told me I'd be fine too. So forgive me if I check things out for myself."

"You okay?" Miller asked, looking at Danny from behind his mirrored shades.

Danny could see his own reflection staring back at him, eyes too wide, hair sticking up at crazy angles. He ran a hand over his head, smoothing down the unruly strands. "Another five seconds, I was dead."

"How'd you get out?"

"Fire escape. Ran like hell. I got lucky."

The light turned green and Miller shifted his gaze back to the road. "Do you know who it was?"

"One of them I didn't recognize. The other was Juan Madrigal."

"Jesus, Danny," Miller breathed.

"His reputation precedes him, I'm guessing."

"I've seen his handiwork a time or two." Miller's voice was grim.

"Yeah, you're not the only one. I've had a ringside seat." Danny turned his head away, closing his eyes against memories he spent every waking hour trying to erase. "Where to now?" He was so tired he thought maybe he could live happily just driving around in this car where he would never have to think about anything again.

"Someplace safe," Miller said. He sounded in control.

"We tried that before."

Miller shook his head. "No. It's going to be different this time." He turned to glance at Danny. "From now on, I'll be the one protecting you."

CHAPTER 4

"IF YOU eat the worm, you get to drink for free."

"What?" Danny raised his eyes from the battered wooden bar, a smile already tugging at his lips.

The girl, who had been watching him from the corner of her eye for the last hour, hopped up onto the stool next to his. Her long hair swung into his face with a blast of pineapple scent, her lightly bronzed skin radiating coconut tanning lotion. She smelled like a pina colada, sticky and sweet.

"I said, if you eat the worm," she pointed to the mammoth bottle of tequila perched behind the bar, "you get the rest of your drinks on the house."

Danny laughed. "No, thanks. I'm not that poor."

"Ah... but I'll bet you're that crazy," she said with a wink.

Danny grinned around his shot glass. "You may have me there."

"My name's Amanda." She offered him slim fingers, cool in his palm. Her thumbnail scraped along his life line when she eased her hand away.

"Danny."

"So, what are you doing in Mexico, Danny?"

"I'm working."

Amanda's eyebrows shot up, her face registering friendly disbelief. "Working?"

"Yep."

"Doing what, exactly?"

"This and that."

Now it was Amanda's turn to smile, her eyes sparkling with untamed ideas. "You're very mysterious."

She had no idea. "What are you doing down here?" Danny asked, steering the conversation to more neutral territory. "Vacation?"

"Yeah, a trip with friends." She nodded her head toward the gaggle of girls crowded at the end of the bar, all of them sneaking glances at Danny when they thought he wasn't looking, waiting for their chance if Amanda couldn't close the deal.

"Hey, you two want anything?" the bartender asked, using a dirty rag to wipe the space in front of Danny's elbow, succeeding more in smearing around the remnants of previously spilled drinks than in actually cleaning anything away.

"Yeah, a couple of tequila shots," Amanda said. "You game?"

Danny didn't need anyone to tell him this was a bad idea. The last thing he wanted was a complication. But there was something about Amanda he liked, something fearless in her eyes, a kind of manic joy he was already drawn to, curious to see if he could capture some of it for himself. She reminded him of the wild girls he'd known in high school who moved too fast and laughed too loud and didn't give a shit what the town thought of them because all they cared about was getting out, getting away. Just like Danny. He could feel the beginning sparks of attraction settling in his fingertips and groin; he wondered if Amanda's neck would taste the way she smelled, if her fruity scent would linger on his tongue. It was all such a bad idea.

"Sure." He smiled, plucking a red rose from the vase on the bar and tucking it behind Amanda's ear. "I'm game."

IT WAS after nine o'clock when Danny finally appeared in the bedroom doorway, his white T-shirt wrinkled and obviously slept-in, his jeans still unfastened at the waist.

"Morning," he mumbled to Miller, who was sitting on the couch, a lukewarm mug of coffee in his hand.

"There's coffee in the kitchen," Miller said. "Some cereal too.

But I'm going to have to run out later for groceries. This place isn't exactly stocked."

After he'd picked up Danny at the bookstore the day before, they'd come directly to this apartment, one of several the FBI kept for just this purpose: hiding witnesses and informants away from the world. Miller had been lucky this one was available; at least it had two bedrooms and was in a decent part of town. There was even a small balcony off the living room. The last time he'd had to babysit someone like this, he'd slept on a lumpy couch for four days. This stint with Danny promised to last a lot longer; he was glad to have a room of his own.

When they'd arrived, Danny hadn't asked any questions. Still shell-shocked, Miller had presumed; because during their short acquaintance, he'd already discovered that silence was not Danny's natural state. Danny's cut had been oozing blood, and he'd taken a wet washcloth and retreated to his bedroom within minutes. Miller had stayed up late flipping channels on the TV, but Danny hadn't reappeared.

Now Danny shuffled into the kitchen, clanking dishes so loudly Miller expected to hear the telltale chime of shattering glass.

"Scoot over," Danny ordered when he returned, waiting until Miller swept his legs off the couch to sit down with his own mug of coffee and a box of Fruit Loops. "Nice cereal selection," he said. "What am I, five?"

"I said I'd go shopping later." Miller took a sip of coffee, studying Danny in quick, sidelong glances. "How's your side?"

"Okay. Think I ripped it open a little when I was running, but it'll be fine."

"Do you need to go back to the doctor?"

"Nah. Stitches will be coming out soon anyway."

Danny munched his way through a handful of cereal. "So, this is where we stay from now on?"

"Yeah." Miller nodded. "You're not setting foot out of here for a while."

Danny groaned. "I'll go crazy cooped up in here!"

"There's a TV. I can bring in movies and books. There's a treadmill so you can get some exercise, and—"

"Whoop-dee-do," Danny said, making a little twirling motion with his index finger.

"The alternative is dead, Danny," Miller reminded him, hanging onto his patience by the thinnest of strings.

"Yeah, and whose fault is that? I told you assholes your shitty plan would never work." Danny set his mug on the floor, tossing the cereal box aside. "How'd he find out about me rolling over anyway? It had to be one of your people." He stood and took a few agitated steps away from the couch. "Someone from the inside had to have told him. What's to stop them from doing it again? Madrigal won't fuck up twice. Then we'll both be dead."

"It wasn't an inside job," Miller said, his voice quiet.

"Then how'd Hinestroza find out?" Danny demanded. "I sure as hell didn't volunteer the information."

Miller stared into his coffee, wishing there were some way to avoid this conversation. When he'd gotten the call last night, he'd momentarily considered ordering someone else to deliver the news. But that would be chickenshit and besides, this was his job. And he always lived up to his responsibilities. "Have you talked to Amanda lately?"

Danny stopped pacing. "Amanda? What does she have to do with it?"

"Have you?"

"Yeah, Miller, I've talked to her. Big fucking deal!"

"What did you tell her?"

"Nothing!"

Miller didn't speak, waiting for Danny to come clean.

Danny sighed, ran a hand through his bed-head hair. "I told her to be careful. I didn't give her any details. Just told her to watch her back. That something might be going down." Danny froze. "Why? Why are you asking me about Amanda?" His panic-tinged eyes told Miller he already knew the answer.

"They got to her, Danny." Miller paused, giving the words their due weight. "Before they went to your apartment, they went to hers."

Danny's face, only newly restored to its usual color, drained of blood, going whiter than it had been in the emergency room. Miller could see him squaring his shoulders, steadying himself. "How bad?" Danny asked, his voice fierce. "How fucking bad?"

Miller stood, took a step in Danny's direction, not sure what he meant to offer: a hand, a shoulder, a pat on the back. "She's alive. But they hurt her. Busted up her face, broke the fingers in her right hand, pulled out a couple of nails—"

A low, animal moan worked its way out of Danny's throat, increasing in intensity as it burst free. His hands came up to cover his face as he took a lurching step backward. "Oh, my God," he choked.

"She's going to be okay, Danny. She's someplace safe."

"Oh, yeah? Safe like you said I was safe, Miller? Safe like that?" Danny kicked hard, sending his half-full coffee mug flying to shatter against the baseboard.

"Hey!" Miller cried as coffee splashed against the bottoms of his jeans. "Calm down!"

"Don't you fucking tell me to calm down! They could have killed her or hurt her worse than they did. I knew I shouldn't have trusted you. You don't give a shit about her or me either. Why wasn't someone watching her?"

"It was an oversight," Miller explained with a calm he didn't feel. "We didn't think they'd go after Amanda. We didn't think she knew anything."

Danny's eyes narrowed. "So you're saying it's my fault? Because I talked to her, told her to be careful, it's my fault now?" He took a step toward Miller. "What about you, Mr. I've-got-it-covered? Maybe you fell down on the job, aren't quite as slick as you'd like to think. Could that be it?"

"Technically all of this is your fault, isn't it, Danny?" Miller shot back. "If you weren't running drugs none of this would have happened. Amanda would be fine instead of her face looking like a kid's art project." The thin string securing Miller's patience disappeared into nothing; his ability to hit the jugular was not lost after all.

"Fuck you!" Danny cried, his face crumpling. He moved forward, arm cocked and aimed at Miller's jaw. A quick spin of Danny's body and Miller had him pinned, Danny's back to his front, Miller's arms wrapped around him tight.

"Stop it!" Miller commanded. "Stop, goddamn it!"

Danny bucked and thrashed in his arms. Their strength was evenly matched and Miller couldn't hold him for much longer. His face was pressed into Danny's neck, the soft, dark hair tickling his skin. He could smell sweat and smoke and a faint whiff of long-ago soap. For the first time in his career it hit him how absurdly intimate it was to hold a suspect this way. Danny's taut muscles flexed under his hands, his ass arched back as he tried to break free, and his stubble-strewn cheek rasped like a rough tongue against Miller's own. Miller released Danny with a stumbling shove, pushing him away.

Jesus Christ. Jesus. Miller ran a shaking hand over his face, breath coming in short gasps. Danny stood across from him, panting, his body visibly relaxing as the anger burned away.

"When did you find out about Amanda?" Danny asked, his voice raw, like tree branches snapping in a winter storm.

Miller stuffed his hands in his pockets. "Last night, late. A neighbor heard her screaming and called the cops. Madrigal was gone by the time they got there. The cops called us from the hospital."

"Where is she? I want to see her."

Miller shook his head. "No. That's not possible. It's too dangerous. We're protecting her, Danny."

"I need to see her, Miller."

"No," Miller repeated. "But you can talk to her on the phone. That's the best I can do."

"Right now," Danny demanded. "I want to talk to her right now."

Miller pulled his cell phone from his back pocket, refusing to acknowledge the tremble in his fingers, and dialed. "Sutton here. He wants to speak with Amanda." Miller passed the phone to Danny, careful that their hands didn't touch.

"AMANDA? You there?" Danny smashed the phone against his ear, as though he could see Amanda if he only got close enough to her voice.

"Danny?" Amanda's speech was thick, like she was talking around a mouthful of cotton or a system full of painkillers. Considering what had been done to her, both were reasonable possibilities. Danny squeezed his eyes shut. "Danny, is that you?"

"Yeah, hon. It's me."

Amanda took a gulping breath and began to weep, unable to form words that Danny could understand. He turned away from Miller, lowering himself to the arm of the couch. "You're okay now," he said. "They're not going to hurt you anymore."

"I didn't want to tell them anything, Danny," Amanda sobbed. "I—"

"I know you didn't."

"They came to the door and said they were worried about you, they thought maybe you were going against Hinestroza. I told them you wouldn't do that. But they barged in anyway, asking me all these questions about you… about how you'd been acting, about that night at the police station, who you'd been with, whether you'd said anything since then. I didn't want to answer, Danny." Amanda let out a wail. "I tried to lie, but they didn't believe me. And then they started hurting me and I… and I—"

"Shhh," Danny calmed her, his free hand clenching into a fist. "I'm sorry. I'm so sorry, honey," he whispered.

"Are they going to come back?" Amanda asked in the smallest voice Danny had ever heard. It scared him. He wasn't used to Amanda being anything less than the loudest one in the room, her sassy mouth taking up all available space.

"No one's going to hurt you again. I promise. The FBI is going to take care of you."

"What about you? Hinestroza isn't going to give up. They'll keep looking for you."

"Don't worry about me. I always land on my feet, right?" He

forced out a strained laugh.

"It's not funny, Danny."

"I know it's not." He paused, keenly aware of Miller standing behind him. "Take care of yourself, okay?"

"I will. They said I can't see you right now." Amanda sounded close to tears again, her voice vibrating.

"No. It's too dangerous. But when this is all over, I'll be there. You hear me?"

"I hear you. Be safe, Danny."

"You, too, honey."

Danny closed the phone with a snap, tossing it over his shoulder to land with a muffled thump on the couch.

"How was she? Did she—" Miller began.

Danny held up a hand. "I don't want to talk right now," he said, enunciating each word carefully. He thought throwing another punch might be in his future if Miller underwent a sudden personality shift and became chatty. But Miller took the not-so-subtle hint and retreated, the sound of running water following him from the kitchen.

Danny fell backward onto the sofa and covered his eyes with his arm. Amanda. With her face wrecked, her bones shattered, her painted fingernails ripped out. Danny could remember exactly how she'd looked on the night they'd met. When her smile was still carefree and her heart not yet broken. When she'd worn a white dress and a crimson flower in her hair and danced barefoot in the street. When they'd both been young and stupid and drunk and Danny had thought wanting men could be limited to the time he spent in a nine by twelve foot cell and Amanda would be the one to save him. But instead he'd destroyed her. Made her a criminal, torn apart her hopes. *Don't forget almost getting her killed.*

One more guilt-ridden entry on the laundry list of his sins.

"I'M BACK," Miller called, shutting the door with his foot.

"Did you get the pizza?"

"Yes," Miller sighed, "I got the pizza. Pepperoni and mushroom, just like you asked. And the beer you wanted. And the bourbon. And the Marlboros. And—"

"I don't need the whole rundown, but thanks." Danny grabbed the greasy pizza box. "What's that?" he asked, pointing at the duffel bag slung over Miller's shoulder.

"That's your stuff." Miller let the bag fall to the floor.

"What do you mean, my stuff?"

"From your apartment. Clothes, mainly."

Danny set down the piece of pizza he'd been about to shove into his mouth. "Um… far be it from me to interfere with the workings of the great FBI, but isn't that a little stupid? To go to my apartment and then come here? Couldn't someone have followed you?"

Miller moved around Danny to the refrigerator, arms burdened with provisions. "Yes, Danny, that would have been stupid. That's why I had someone go to your apartment right after I picked you up yesterday, when we knew Madrigal was long gone, and get your clothes. Then he took the bag back to my office, on the off chance he was followed, and I picked it up today." He shut the refrigerator. "I'm good at my job, Danny. You don't need to worry."

"Let's just hope you're better than the guys who were supposed to be watching my apartment," Danny commented dryly, snagging a beer from the six-pack in Miller's hand. "Want some pizza?"

"Yeah, fine." Miller was knocked off balance by Danny's easy banter. He had expected Danny to remain morose and angry after the conversation with Amanda. But an hour later he had searched Miller out for conversation, still a little distant but close enough to normal that he was able to resume bitching about the lack of food. For all his tough demeanor, it was clear that Danny was a man who couldn't hold a grudge for long—fury and petulance a costume he wore occasionally, but not a permanent ensemble.

It took them only ten minutes to devour the pizza before Danny moved on to a pint of ice cream, while Miller settled in with a beer. There was nothing good on TV but he kept changing channels anyway,

Danny telling him to stop every once in a while so he could make fun of an infomercial or smirk along with canned sitcom laughter.

The air in the apartment was foggy with cigarette smoke, Danny lighting up with a vengeance as he sprawled on the couch.

"Slow down with those," Miller said. "You're gonna run out by tomorrow."

Danny shrugged. "FBI's buying, right?"

Miller shook his head, annoyed, but didn't protest when Danny passed him the pack so he could have a smoke of his own.

"What's the plan now?" Danny asked. "For me?"

"You continue feeding me information. Once we've got everything sewed up tight, we indict Hinestroza. Then you testify against him."

"There are two major problems with that scenario," Danny said, holding up his fingers to illustrate. "One, Hinestroza hardly ever leaves Colombia anymore, so getting him to trial will be next to impossible. And two, he'd blow the courthouse sky high before he'd let me take the witness stand."

"That wouldn't happen. He's not God, Danny," Miller observed.

Danny's eyes were full of fear and memories, his voice harsh as he looked away. "That's what you think."

"Are you ready to tell me how you got hooked up with him?"

"Not really," Danny said, attempting to blow a series of wobbly smoke rings toward the ceiling.

"Well, time's up. I need to know."

"I'll bet you're a fucking barrel of laughs on a Saturday night, Sutton."

"I'm not here for fun. I'm here to nail Hinestroza."

"Like I need reminding," Danny muttered.

"Did you find him or did he find you?"

"Oh, I think it's safe to say he found me." Danny hesitated, eyes focused on something Miller couldn't see. "I was eighteen, living in Dallas, working at this shitty car wash. The kind where you get out of your car and they run it through and then some down-on-their-luck kid dries it for you. That was me, the loser with the chamois rag."

Miller thought back to when he was eighteen, how close he could have been to Danny's situation if his father hadn't pushed him into college, practically forcing him to go, a grown man being dragged like a kindergartener. Without that push, he could easily have ended up like Danny, aimless and adrift with no hope for the future. *Jesus, Miller, why don't you get out the violin and play him a sonata? Danny made his own fucking choices—all of them bad.*

"One day this car pulled up and Hinestroza was inside. He offered me a job. And I got in the car. End of story." But it wasn't the end of the story and Miller knew it. Danny's eyes were jumping faster than feet on fire, his Adam's apple bobbing crazily in his throat.

"I'm going to have to hear the rest of it, Danny, at some point."

"Just… not tonight, okay?" Danny said. "It hasn't been a great couple of days."

"Okay," Miller agreed. "But soon." Not willing to give Danny too much leeway, he was careful to maintain the upper hand.

"Want another beer?" Danny asked, heading into the kitchen. He didn't wait for Miller's reply, came back with two bottles hanging between his fingers. He handed one over and took up his previous position, flopped on the couch, bare feet dangling over the arm.

"What does your wife think of you being stuck here?"

Miller pushed back in the recliner, the footrest popping up with a squawk. "I don't have a wife," he said, eyes on the TV screen.

"Then who were you talking to when you called me the other night?"

Miller never talked about his personal life with informants. Never. It was a rule within the FBI, both spoken and unspoken, and he followed it as though to break it would constitute a personal failure. "That was my fiancée. Rachel."

"Fiancée?" Danny scooted upright on the couch. "When's the wedding?"

"We haven't set a date yet," Miller replied, wishing he'd never opened his damn mouth.

"How long have you been engaged?"

Miller scowled at Danny, who looked back at him blandly, a tiny smile working against Danny's lips. "Five years," Miller mumbled. "We've been engaged for five years."

"Whaaat?" Danny laughed, elongating the word with the remnants of his Kansas drawl. "What's the fucking holdup? Damn, she's a lot more patient than Amanda ever would have been, I'll tell you that."

"How long were you and Amanda engaged?"

Danny shrugged. "A couple of hours."

"A couple of hours," Miller parroted. "Now why doesn't that surprise me?"

"What can I say? I'm a spontaneous kind of guy," Danny grinned with a raise of his eyebrows.

"How'd you meet her?"

"I was down in Mexico, doing a job for Hinestroza. She was there on vacation. I met her in a bar. We danced and drank too much tequila and I woke up the next morning with a ring on my finger and this on my arm." Danny lifted up his right sleeve, revealing a tattoo of barbed wire encircling his bicep. "Apparently Amanda wanted it to be intertwined A's and D's, but thank God I wasn't drunk enough for that."

"You're a big tattoo fan, I take it?"

"Didn't have much choice in the matter, actually. You work for Hinestroza, you get a tattoo. After that it didn't seem like such a big deal to get more. At least he didn't brand me like some of the drug bosses do."

Miller marveled at how nonchalant Danny was, talking of being tattooed or branded as if he were discussing some vaguely unpleasant but inevitable chore—cleaning out a backed-up toilet, maybe, or doing his taxes. "Is a snake still Hinestroza's mark?"

"Yeah. Matches his laugh." Danny tossed his cigarette onto the saucer he was using as an ashtray. "You want to take a look?"

Miller nodded without realizing he was going to, beer bottle poised against his lips as Danny hiked up his shirt, holding the bunched material over his head. He twisted on the couch to give Miller a view of his upper back, a curled-up serpent painted between his shoulder blades. It had the diamond markings of a rattlesnake, but the colors were brilliant jewel tones, dark purple, emerald green, deep ocean blue. Miller's eyes were riveted on the vision of the snake coiled across Danny's tight muscles, the flickering lights from the TV making the colors shimmer and breathe. The tattoo was beautiful, really—unless you knew what it meant.

"Can you see it?" Danny asked, his voice muted through the layers of cotton.

"Yeah, I can see it," Miller replied, husky and low, his stomach pitching forward like an off-balance drunk. He was horrified by his own desire to breach the space between them and lay his hands across Danny's marked skin.

Danny pivoted back around, his shirt inching down in a slow-motion glide as Miller's eyes helplessly followed its descent. Neither of them spoke and the silence wasn't easy; it popped and crackled with possibilities. Miller's eyes swerved back to the TV, his finger stabbing viciously at the remote. He could feel the tension in his face, a furrow etched between his brows, his mouth locked up tight.

He risked a quick glance at Danny, who was watching him with steady eyes, a newly lit cigarette dangling from his lips. Miller felt sweat popping up along his brow, his breathing too rapid for his sedentary position. He reached for his FBI training, switched on his finely tuned ability to disengage, and looked away.

CHAPTER 5

MILLER knew he'd overslept from the strength of the sunlight slanting in through the edges of his blinds to lay warm fingers across his face. Jesus, only two days living with Danny and already he was on deadbeat time. Staying up late drinking beer and smoking, sleeping in past his years-old five-thirty a.m. wake-up call. Judging from the light it had to be close to eight o'clock. *Fucking pathetic, Miller.*

He rolled out of bed with a groan, thankful at least that Danny hadn't broken into the bourbon yet. Even Danny's shaving habits were contagious, it seemed; Miller's hand scrubbed at his whisker-rough cheeks. Miller stretched his arms up toward the ceiling, his back giving off a series of satisfying cracks. He pulled on a pair of jeans, rooting around in the suitcase he hadn't fully unpacked for his old college sweatshirt, "Kansas State University" emblazoned on the front in peeling purple letters.

The living room was deserted, Danny's bedroom door closed. Something wasn't right; Miller felt it almost immediately, the hair on his arms prickling with unease. There was a curious emptiness to the apartment, too silent even if Danny was still asleep. The bathroom was dark, the kitchen quiet. Miller crossed to Danny's door, slapped it with the flat of his hand. No response. "Danny?" Miller called, the metal doorknob cool against his palm. "Danny?"

Danny wasn't in his room, the only sign he'd been there the covers and sheets flung haphazardly across the foot of the bed. Miller backtracked double-time toward the kitchen, glancing out to check the small balcony as he passed. The front door was locked. But the chain, which had been secured when they went to sleep, was hanging free now. A piece of white paper, the back of a take-out pizza menu, was taped to the door.

Miller, had to run out for a minute. Be back soon. Danny.

"Son of a bitch!" Miller cried, racing into his bedroom to throw on tennis shoes. He jammed his loaded gun into the waistband of his jeans and grabbed his cell phone from the clutter on top of his dresser, loose change raining down onto the floor. His keys were gone. The fucker had snuck in while he was sleeping and taken his goddamn keys.

Miller flung open the apartment door, slamming it hard behind him. He took the stairs two at a time and flew out onto the empty sidewalk. He could see his Jeep parked where he'd left it, one block down on the opposite side of the street. So Danny had gone on foot. But where? There were a few shops within walking distance, but on a Sunday morning nothing would be open.

Just pick a direction and start walking. Miller turned left, jogging down the street, eyes straining for a glimpse of that black hair. What the fuck could Danny have been thinking? Out in public, giving away their position, risking his life. Goddamn asshole! Two blocks under his belt and Miller had passed only a lone dog sniffing around a planter filled with dirt and a robe-clad woman making a dash for her morning paper. Miller was about to give up, head back in the opposite direction, when he saw a car idling against the curb, someone standing in the street and leaning into the driver's window. Danny.

Miller bit back hard on the urge to sprint down the street screaming Danny's name, grab him by the scruff of his neck, and drag his sorry ass back to the apartment. Instead, he stuck to the sidewalk, his position concealed by the large oak trees dotting the street at regular intervals, their bare branches pointing gnarled fingers skyward. Miller stopped a few car lengths away from where Danny stood.

The man driving the silver Mercedes didn't look familiar. From what Miller could see he looked about their age, early thirties, medium brown hair, black sunglasses. Smiling at Danny. And Danny was smiling back, one hand resting casually on the roof of the car as he tipped back his dark head and laughed, the deep sound of it trickling away to almost nothing by the time it reached Miller's ears. The man in the car moved his left hand off the steering wheel and held it out the window, where Danny took it in his own, the gesture a mix of high five and handshake. Miller felt a slow burn against his skin, red sparks of fury exploding against his eyelids as the Mercedes purred away, leaving Danny with his hand raised in farewell. Miller was suddenly full of bile, burning and roiling in his gut, the need to spew his anger rising up like vomit thick in his throat. *Stupid asshole! Risking both our lives to hook up with his boyfriend! I can't fucking believe it!* He had been a fool to expect anything more from a man like Danny.

When the Mercedes was out of sight, Danny turned back toward the apartment, only the slightest stutter in his stride when he saw Miller waiting for him on the sidewalk.

"Hey," Danny said. "What are you doing out here?"

"The question is what the fuck are you doing out here?" Miller could feel the veins in his neck bulging, fury a fast-acting poison racing through his blood.

"I had to meet someone." Danny kept walking, forcing Miller into hurrying steps to catch up.

"Yeah, I saw," Miller bit out. "Who was he?"

"A friend."

"I'll bet," Miller sneered.

Danny stopped. "You have something you want to ask me, Miller?" he demanded, his eyes kindling temper fires of their own. "Is there something about me you'd like to know?"

Miller took in a lungful of air. No way was he going near that bait, not even with a ten-foot pole and a gut full of emotion. "You put us in danger! He could easily tell Hinestroza where we are."

"He wouldn't do that."

"No? What if they pull out *his* fingernails? Or slice up that pretty-boy face? Loyalty only goes so far when Madrigal's holding a straight razor against your eye."

"Do you see how many buildings there are around here?" Danny asked, throwing his arms wide. "Griff has no idea which one we're living in or even if we're near here. I didn't tell him shit except to meet me on that corner."

"Griff? Nice fucking name."

"You're not exactly in a position to be making fun of people's names," Danny pointed out. "What is it you're really pissed about?"

"I'm pissed that you're a goddamn idiot, Danny! Putting your life on the line, not to mention mine, so you can meet up with your—" Miller snapped his mouth closed so fast he risked severing his tongue.

"Are you jealous, Miller?" Danny's voice was smooth, his tone hovering somewhere between amusement and seduction.

"Go to hell!" Miller stormed. "What did you need from that guy anyway, huh? Was he bringing you drugs?"

"I already told you I don't do drugs. I'm sick of repeating myself." Danny took off, his long legs chewing up the pavement.

"Don't you fucking walk away from me!" Miller yelled, grasping at the back of Danny's leather jacket. "What the hell did you need from him?"

Danny moved more quickly than Miller expected, twirling out of reach, his hand closing tightly over Miller's arm.

"Back off," Danny growled. "You may have cornered me into rolling over on Hinestroza, but I don't belong to the FBI. I'm my own man, Miller, and I don't answer to you."

"Oh, yeah?" Miller breathed. "Is that what Hinestroza would say, that you're your own man?"

Danny sucked in a whistling breath through bared teeth, nostrils flaring, the muscle in his jaw pulsing in tempo with his heart. They stood chest to chest, only a whisper of breeze passing between them. Miller could see the emerald rims around Danny's leaf-green eyes, the tiny scar above his lip hiding beneath his stubble, the tip of his tongue sliding out to caress the corner of his mouth. They were close enough to fight, close enough to touch… close enough to kiss, and for one heart-stopping, stomach-dropping moment Miller thought that's what Danny meant to do. Danny's face leaned forward for an instant before he stepped away, leaving cold air where his warm body had been.

THE heavy, sharp press of metal against Danny's lower back was comforting, the gun singing its own brand of lullaby to his anxious body. It had been a long time since he'd gone anywhere without a weapon and he'd hated how naked he'd felt the last few days.

He unlocked the apartment door, tossing Miller's keys over his shoulder. Miller snatched them out of midair with a deadly glare. Danny slammed through the apartment to his room, kicking the door shut with an echoing bang. *Fucking Miller. Thinks I need a damn babysitter.* He pulled the Sig Sauer from his waistband, cradling the soothing heft in his palm. Same make and model as the one the cops had taken from his glove compartment. Danny checked the safety, then lifted up his mattress and slid the gun underneath. Not the most creative hiding place, but he had to have easy access or what was the point?

When Danny returned to the living room, Miller was in the shower, the hiss of running water loud in the quiet space. Danny flipped on the TV, grabbed a Coke from the refrigerator, and tossed himself onto the couch. He tried to hold onto his anger, but it was already seeping away like smoke through a clenched fist. Danny relished a good confrontation while it was happening, had never been afraid of expressing his emotions. But, oddly enough, he hated it when people remained angry with him. As a boy he'd always tried to please his father, especially when the old bastard was feeling mean. And as a man he still hadn't managed to outgrow that need for approval.

The shower went silent, the bathroom door opening a crack to let out a small burst of steam. Danny got up and walked to the bathroom, letting the pads of his fingers rest against the door before he pushed it inward a few inches. "Hey," he said quietly, the moist, warm interior like a damp cloud against his face.

Miller was shaving, dressed only in jeans, his face hidden behind a beard of white foam. The circle he'd rubbed into the foggy mirror was already misting over again with lingering steam.

"What?" Miller asked, voice sharp, razor poised to cut a swath down his cheek.

Danny leaned one shoulder against the doorframe, admiring the pull and bunch of Miller's muscles as he shaved, his combination of leanness and strength fascinating to watch. Danny pushed the door open a bit more with his bare foot.

"I didn't mean to freak you out when I left." The closest he could come to an apology.

"You didn't freak me out," Miller said, eyes on the mirror.

"You shouldn't worry about Griff. He's clueless about what's going on. Completely off Hinestroza's radar. Trust me."

"Trust you? That'd be pretty dumb of me, wouldn't it, Danny?"

Man's probably got a point there. "You going somewhere?"

"Yeah. But there will be a car outside keeping an eye on you."

"Where you headed?"

Miller shook off his razor in the water-filled sink, sending an army of tiny hairs marching across the surface. "Out."

Danny rolled his eyes. "You going to see Rachel?"

"None of your fucking business," Miller snapped. Paused. "Why do you think I'm meeting Rachel?"

"Because you're shaving." Danny shrugged. "And it's Sunday, so I doubt you're going to your office." He came farther into the bathroom, made himself comfortable perched on the edge of the double sink nearest the door. "How'd you meet her anyway? I'm guessing it wasn't on a straight tequila night down in Mexico."

Miller took his eyes off his task, stared at Danny. "Before I was assigned here I was in Minneapolis," he said finally. "She's a legal secretary and I met her when I went to her boss's office for a debriefing."

"So she came with you when you were transferred?" Danny asked, rolling Miller's can of shaving cream between his palms.

"Yeah."

"Special Agent Sutton, living in sin," Danny mused. "Not what I'd picture from someone so… law-abiding."

Miller snatched away the shaving cream. "We don't live together. She has her own place."

"Those your rules or hers?"

"It was a mutual decision." Miller pulled the plug on the sink, the drain swallowing the sudsy water with a strangled gurgle. Miller moved his body in a wide arc around Danny's dangling feet and legs, grabbing a white hand towel from the rack on the wall. He swiped the towel across his cheeks. "I've got to get going."

Not so fast, Sutton. Danny reached out a hand, grazing Miller's jaw. "You missed a spot." Miller stiffened up, not moving away but his muscles gone rigid, eyes locked on Danny's. Danny ran his finger gently across Miller's smooth, warm skin. *Shit, he feels good.* Danny held up one finger capped with white foam. "Got it."

Miller kept his gaze on Danny's, his eyes registering a flash of heat, anger following close on its heels, ending with that steely control that reminded Danny of a fortress nearly impossible to breach. *But oh, so damn worth it when you finally do.* Miller threw his towel into the sink, plucked his white T-shirt from the back of the toilet, and pulled it on with vicious stabs of his arms.

"So, Rachel likes you clean shaven?" Danny asked, turning on the tap to wash his finger. No response. "I think you look better stubbly, myself."

Miller didn't stop to put on his sweater, balling it up in his fist as he moved to leave. Danny hopped off the sink, blocking his exit. They stood in the narrow doorway, not enough room for either one to get by without brushing their bodies together. Miller's eyes were like silver bullets. *He knows what I'm doing. And he'd like to kill me for it.* Danny held up his hands, twisting his body out of the way.

"After you," he said with a grin.

IT SHOULD have felt better to hold Rachel in his arms. They hadn't seen each other in almost a week. Between work and then his sudden call to duty with Danny, their time together had shrunk to nothing. But here he stood, Rachel's thin arms wrapped around his neck, and he couldn't get Danny Butler out of his head.

What was that asshole trying to pull in the bathroom? Should have punched that smirk off his face.

"I'm so glad to see you, sweetheart," Rachel sighed into his neck. "Do you know when you're going to be able to come home?"

"No," Miller said, pulling back to look at her open, loving face. "It might be a while."

Rachel's face folded in, a troubled crease appearing between her brows. "Is it dangerous, Miller?"

Of course it's dangerous. I'm in the FBI. "Don't worry. I'm careful." He wondered if this was the same lie all agents told their families, the lie that helped everyone close their eyes at night and sleep in self-imposed ignorance.

Rachel turned toward her small, galley-style kitchen, straightening the magazines on her coffee table as she passed. "Do you want some lunch? I've got chicken salad."

Safe, predictable, good-hearted Rachel. Who always wore pearls and a ponytail, whose hair smelled of green apples, and who, after all this time and all this waiting, still looked at Miller with starlight in her eyes. Miller felt a pang of guilt; he didn't know if the favor of starlit eyes had ever been returned.

He touched your face. And you liked it. Miller took two long steps to Rachel, grabbed her pink sweater with desperate hands, pushed her backward onto the couch, and fell on top of her with a frantic body.

"Miller," Rachel gasped as he drove her down into the cushions. "Miller, what are you doing?"

Miller smiled, hoping like hell it didn't look as pained as it felt. "Undressing you." Rachel's lip gloss tasted sweet and tacky against his lips, her body too pliant beneath him.

Rachel laughed, the sound short and embarrassed. "Let's go in the bedroom." She wiggled out from under his weight, pulling him by the hand. "Come on."

They collapsed onto her fluffy white bedspread in a tangled heap. She yelped a little when he yanked her ponytail loose to release her hair to his grasping hands.

"I didn't shower this morning," she panted.

"I don't care," he whispered.

Rachel sat up, her sweater hiked above her breasts to reveal a lacy pink bra. "Just... just let me hop in real quick, okay? I'll be right back."

Miller turned over on his back, pressing his thumbs against his closed eyes as Rachel's weight lifted off the bed. He suddenly wished he'd gone anyplace but here.

DANNY heard the muffled sound of the apartment door opening and closing. He glanced at his watch, the face glowing silver in the moonlight. Seven o'clock. He craned his neck to look back through the gauzy curtains at a tall shadow etched against the wall.

"Danny?" the shadow called. "Danny?"

"I'm on the balcony."

Miller poked his head through the open sliding glass door. "What the hell are you doing out here? Someone could see you!"

Danny smiled and took a swig of newly opened bourbon before answering. "It's pitch-dark, Miller, if you haven't noticed. And I turned off all the lights inside. Nobody can see shit. Come on out." Danny pointed to the empty deck chair next to his, ducking down slightly as though hiding from enemy fire. "But if you're worried, I can run inside for my camouflage paint."

"Shut up, asshole," Miller grumbled, pulling the deck chair away from the railing with a screech of metal against wood.

Danny laughed. "We're making progress, I see. I'm 'asshole' now instead of 'Danny'."

Miller grunted, zipping up his jacket.

"Here." Danny passed him the bottle of bourbon. Miller held it between his hands, contemplating it, before he raised it to his lips and took a deep swallow. He leaned over to pass it back and Danny caught the scent of woman on his skin. Danny grabbed the bottle, his throat tightening as he turned away to inhale the fresh breeze blowing from the west. *Knowing in your head what Miller has been doing the last few hours and actually smelling sex on him... turns out those are two different things, aren't they, Danny?*

Miller rested his elbows on his knees and gave Danny a sideways glance. "Your friend Griffin Gentry has a record," he said slowly. "I ran his plates."

"Kudos on the detective work." Danny cradled the bottle between his knees while he lit a cigarette behind his cupped hand, setting the pack and his lighter on the small table in front of him so Miller could reach them if he wanted.

"Aggravated assault," Miller continued. "He was your cellmate at Leavenworth."

"Right again." Danny took a gulp of bourbon. "Is there a point to this?"

"We're picking him up tonight. We're taking him out of circulation for the time being. He's a loose end, Danny, and I shouldn't have to tell you that Madrigal's made a career out of finding loose ends."

Danny sat up straight. "You don't have any grounds for arresting Griff."

"We're not arresting him. But he can't be anyplace where Hinestroza can reach him. It's too big a risk for him and for us." Miller paused. "Is there anybody else Hinestroza can use against you? Someone besides Griffin or Amanda? Another friend... or lover?" Miller stumbled over the word. "Anyone?"

"No," Danny said. "I travel light. After Amanda, I swore I wasn't going to bring anybody else into this life and I've kept my word."

Miller reached out his hand for the bottle. "What really happened between you two?"

Danny leaned back, resting his feet on the balcony railing. "I thought you knew everything about me, Sutton."

"I do."

Danny waited until Miller met his eyes. "Then you should already know I like men. That's what happened to Amanda and me. I'm gay, Miller." There it was, finally out in the open, what they'd both been dancing around since the moment they'd met.

"That's what I'd heard, but I wasn't sure...." Miller's voice drifted away, eyes following close behind.

"Why? Because I don't skip down the street and wear eyeliner?"

Danny mocked.

"No!" Miller protested, strongly enough that Danny knew he'd struck close to the truth. "Just, with you having been married—"

"Lots of gay men get married, Miller. It doesn't make them straight."

"I guess that's true enough," Miller admitted, his voice noncommittal. "But why'd you marry her in the first place?"

Danny blew out a shaky breath. He knew his reasons for marrying Amanda would never be good enough to balance out the hurt he'd caused. "I was lonely. I hadn't faced up to the fact I was gay yet, not completely. But after Amanda I made a promise to myself that I'd never deny it again." He looked at Miller. "Speaking of tying the eternal knot, why haven't you and Rachel taken the plunge?"

Miller shrugged, fingers fiddling with the bourbon bottle's label. "Time's just never been right. I was transferred, then she was looking for a job down here, and my work never slows down."

"You realize how lame that sounds, don't you?"

Miller surprised him by laughing, though most of the humor was missing. "There just doesn't seem to be any hurry."

If that isn't a damning indictment... poor fucking Rachel. "Well, Miller," he drawled around his cigarette, "seems you have a problem with moving too slow and I have one with moving too fast."

His observation hung between them, as heavy and loaded with intent as a blanket of storm clouds. He could feel Miller watching him and he rolled his head in Miller's direction, but those smoke-colored eyes proved impossible to read in the inky air.

"Here," Danny whispered, holding out the bourbon again. Miller took it from his grasp, his long fingers running smooth across Danny's as, for that single moment, he accepted what was being offered.

MILLER knew it was past midnight from the angle of the moonlight sliding through the cracks in his blinds to spread chill shadows across his skin. His body was tired, but his mind was restless, refusing to allow him the safe harbor of sleep.

He considered getting up to watch TV, maybe make a sandwich and check out the Late Show. Or he could read. He had a paperback in his suitcase he'd been trying to get through for the last three months. And God knew he had 302 reports of his conversations with Danny that needed typing, his laptop sitting neglected on top of his dresser. Or….

Miller closed his eyes, conjuring up visions of Rachel from earlier today. Her milky-white skin always looked so pure and untouched. Her smell, flowery and clean when she'd come out of the shower. He drew his knees up a little, moved his thighs apart. His fingertips whispered over the sheet. He remembered how soft she was, her small breasts carrying an unexpected weight in his hands, her nipples pale pink under his tongue.

He lifted the sheet away, running a palm underneath the waistband of his boxers, easing them down. He tried to conjure up a picture of Rachel writhing beneath him, crying out, but the image wouldn't form. Instead, he saw a man's hand, sneaking forward to run smooth against his jaw, the touch of that single finger sending white-hot sparks cascading into his belly like a Roman candle exploding beneath his skin.

I'll bet Danny is loud in bed. He probably moans, and whispers, and groans out his pleasure.

Miller's hand froze, his eyes flying open in the dark. What the hell was he doing? Thinking about Danny when his hand was on his dick—the dick that was getting harder with every vision of that thick, black hair, that full mouth, the poised-to-strike snake rippling across that chiseled back. Shit.

Miller drew in a steadying breath and forced his mind blank. He could do this; he could do this without thinking of Danny. He ran his palms up the inside of his thighs, fingers twining through the coarse hair, hand fisting around his hardness, stroking slowly, his thumb brushing the tip to make use of the wetness already leaking down.

He squeezed his eyes shut, gripped the sheet hard with his unoccupied hand, teeth grinding together violently. He opened his mind just a crack—allowed himself to think about women he'd known, women he'd had, women he'd wanted.

But when Miller came, hips bucking up off the bed in a violent shudder, it was with Danny's face behind his eyelids and Danny's name against his lips.

CHAPTER 6

DAMN, if Atwood could see him now. Danny "always been a fuck up, always will be" Butler, in a two-thousand-dollar monkey suit, sipping expensive champagne. Granted, the tuxedo was on loan and Danny's everyday life was more McDonald's than filet mignon, but still, not bad... not bad at all.

"Danny." A strong hand closed over Danny's shoulder, claw-like in its boniness. "You enjoying yourself?"

Danny smiled, the happy "I-live-to-kiss-your-ass" smile. "Having a great time, Mr. Hinestroza."

"Good, good." Hinestroza plucked a fresh flute of champagne from the tray of a passing waiter. "Where's Amanda?"

"She couldn't make it." Danny paused. "We're having some marriage trouble, actually."

Hinestroza frowned. "I'm sorry to hear that, Danny. I hope your personal situation with Amanda won't make our continued use of her services a problem."

"No. She's still on board for now," Danny said carefully, not wanting to commit Amanda to anything long-term, but not wanting her to be seen as disposable, either.

Hinestroza pointed with his champagne flute toward the couple being photographed under a loggia of red roses. "My Lily, doesn't she make a lovely bride?"

Shit... how to play this one? Too enthusiastic and he'd be looking at a broken kneecap for perving on Hinestroza's daughter. Too nonchalant and it'd be a busted jaw for insulting her beauty. "She does, Mr. Hinestroza. You should be very proud."

Double clap on the back letting Danny know he'd answered just right. Call me fucking Goldilocks, Danny thought with an internal grimace. But part of him felt a sense of accomplishment, happy to have won Hinestroza's approval even for something as silly as a comment about his pretty daughter. The odd combination of fear and loyalty that Hinestroza always produced churned in Danny's blood. It would be so much easier if Danny could simply hate him.

"Monday morning, it's back to business," Hinestroza reminded him with a wink, moving off into the crowd.

"Sure thing," Danny called after him, waiting until Hinestroza disappeared to down the rest of his champagne in one long swallow.

Danny climbed the stone stairs leading to the overhanging veranda; no way to get close to the tables of food with people standing three deep in line. He could just make out the tip of a winged ice sculpture, unable to discern if it was swan or angel. From the edge of the veranda the ocean was visible, the endless blue fading to tattered pink on the edges as the sun dipped below the horizon. Much to his surprise, Danny had discovered a soft spot for the ocean, the sound, the smell, the vastness. All leading him to the certainty that his life—and every shitty, destined-to-burn-in-hell choice he'd made—didn't matter much in the end. The notion was comforting in some perverse way.

Hinestroza and his wife, Maria, had joined their youngest daughter and her new husband under the roses. Hinestroza smiled widely, no trace of cruelty today, as the photographer positioned the family this way and that for picture after picture.

"Papa, Papa," Hinestroza's granddaughter called, weaving between guests to reach her grandfather. She laughed as Hinestroza lifted her easily and tossed her three-year-old weight toward the sky.

Danny watched as she patted Hinestroza's scarred cheeks, whispering into his ear, one finger twirling through his black hair that was just this year showing its first signs of gray. She was not afraid. She didn't know fear in her grandfather's arms, had no concept of the agony he caused. To her, Roberto Hinestroza would always be a good man—the man who let her dance on his feet at her aunt Lily's wedding, who sneaked her extra pieces of cake when her mother wasn't looking, who believed she could do no wrong.

Danny turned away, his eye snagged by the man standing near the set of French doors, a sly grin easing out from around his upturned glass when he spied Danny.

Fuck, fuck, fuck.

"Danny," Madrigal said, slinking over to where Danny stood, the grin replaced by an amused, indulgent little smile.

"Juan."

"Classy party."

"Yes."

"Must be nice to be sprung," Madrigal commented. "I've heard Leavenworth is no picnic."

Danny shrugged. "I survived." He scanned the crowd for anyone he recognized, anyone who could provide an excuse for his departure.

"You know who I was thinking about the other day?" Madrigal asked, his voice casual but his eyes gleaming eerie, golden fire— anticipating the pleasure of inflicting pain.

Don't say it, Danny thought frantically. Don't you dare say his fucking name to me. I'll kill you. I'll rip your throat out with my bare hands, I'll—

"Ortiz," Madrigal continued. "Remember him?"

Danny ground his jaw together, heedless of the skin clenched between, too late tasting the salty tang of blood oozing from his tooth-torn cheek. "Yeah," he managed, finally, in a strangled voice. "I remember him."

Madrigal shook his head, eyebrows coming together in mock concern. "Too bad what happened to him. Had to be an awful way to go out."

Danny could feel sweat beading on his brow, his gut going loose with terror and memories, his breathing turning labored while spots bloomed like blood spatters against his eyes.

"Fuck you!" Danny lashed out, his fury blunted by the hand he was forced to bring up, steadying himself against the iron railing. The scar on his thigh throbbed with remembered pain, as though the razor had only just this minute pierced his flesh.

"Pull yourself together, Danny. Shouldn't you be over it by now?" Madrigal laughed, cruel and pitying. "It was such a long time ago."

"JESUS, who pissed in your cornflakes?" Danny asked, tugging on his running shoes.

Miller looked up from his coffee, a scowl writ large across his face. "What?" he barked.

Danny rolled his eyes. "You've been sitting there glaring at your breakfast for the last half hour, grunting at everything I say like a fucking caveman."

Miller ignored him, went back to staring into his cereal bowl. Danny couldn't figure out what was wrong. Last night on the balcony he had felt friendship taking hold, desire tangible in the air as the boundaries between them eased, giving Danny a taste of the real Miller. And, like the bourbon they'd been drinking, it made him thirsty for more. But this morning Miller was closed tight as a steel trap, his whole body stiff with resistance.

"Suit yourself," Danny sighed. "I'm getting on the treadmill."

Growing up, Danny had always kept in shape by helping his old man, taking care of the horses, mending fences, general upkeep. None of that stopped when the bulk of the land was sold, and those daily chores kept Danny lean and strong. Prison and fear had kept his body in top form since then. Behind bars, the boredom was mind-numbing; Danny had never passed up a chance to run in the yard or lift weights when it was offered. Staying fast and packing a hard punch were skills he needed both in prison and out. He wasn't going to let being trapped in this apartment become an excuse for slacking off. Being able to outrun Madrigal was still at the forefront of his mind.

Five miles on the treadmill, two hundred sit-ups, two hundred push-ups, same routine every morning. Although he had to forego the sit-ups for now while his side was healing. Most days, Miller holed up in his room, ear attached to his cell phone, while Danny worked out. But today he stayed put at the small table against the wall, shoving his cereal bowl out of the way to open his laptop, typing from handwritten notes on a yellow legal pad.

"See you went to the Danny Butler school of typing," Danny panted, raising his voice to be heard over the whir of the treadmill.

"Huh?" Miller said without looking up.

"Hunt and peck." Danny demonstrated by tapping his index fingers mid-air.

"Yeah," Miller agreed, glancing down at his hands. "Not very efficient, but it gets the job done."

Not much, but at least we're progressing beyond the one-word answers.

Danny finished his run with a hard quarter mile sprint, moving to the floor for his push-ups.

"How did… a guy from… the ass-end… of Kansas… wind up in… the FBI?" Danny asked between deep breaths of carpet dust.

"Watch it," Miller replied. "Atwood isn't exactly doing Kansas proud, you know."

"I'm not arguing." Danny stood up. "I'm the first to admit Atwood is a shit hole." He grabbed a bottle of water from the refrigerator, turning the chair across from Miller backward and straddling it as he guzzled down the water. "So?"

"So, what?" Miller blew out an exasperated breath.

"Sooooo," Danny drew out the word with a grin. "How'd you end up in the FBI?"

"It's not a very interesting story."

"Does it look like there's anywhere else I need to be?" Danny asked with raised eyebrows.

Miller shifted his eyes away, his neck disappearing into his shoulders. He looked very young suddenly, shy and embarrassed, the tough, controlled shell slipping away. Danny wondered if he was the first person to ever really want to hear this story, the tale of how Miller Sutton made something of himself. Something burst into life below Danny's breastbone—tenderness, maybe? It had been so long since he had felt much beyond fear, guilt, and the basic need to survive that he wasn't even sure how to name the emotion.

"Seriously, Miller," he said. "I want to know."

Miller glanced at him, closing his laptop with one hand. "My mom died when I was nine—"

"How?"

Miller looked away for a moment. "Cancer."

Danny ran his tongue across his front teeth, made a small clicking sound with his mouth. "That must have been tough."

"Yeah, it was. My dad never really got over it. Still hasn't. After she was gone… he just… it's like he gave up. He became an old man overnight."

Danny couldn't imagine his father giving a shit if his mother died, other than to wonder who was going to make his dinner or iron his shirts. He'd be more pissed about the inconvenience than anything else.

"But he made sure I finished high school," Miller continued. "And when the time came, he insisted I go to college too. That had always been my mom's dream, that at least one of us get an education."

"K-State," Danny supplied.

"How'd you—?"

"Your sweatshirt yesterday."

"Oh." Miller nodded. "Yeah, K-State. I never thought I'd be the one to end up in college. But my older brother Scott got a girl knocked up, so he couldn't go. It probably should have been my sister Junie who went; she was always the best student. But she got married right out of high school, too, and sort of gave up on that dream. I was the only one left." He shrugged. "So I went."

"Bet they're all really proud of you now."

Miller looked up at the ceiling, tipping his chair back on two legs. "I suppose they are. But we don't have much in common anymore. Junie's got four kids and a husband to worry about, and Scott works the line at a plastics factory. And my dad just stays on the farm, pretty much refuses to leave. It's like… they gave me this chance to be something more, but now I'm not really part of the same family."

He dropped his chair back to level with a thud, avoiding Danny's eyes.

"What was college like?" Danny asked.

"It was okay, I guess. I had to study a lot to stay afloat. I've never had book smarts the way some people do."

"I always liked school." Danny smiled at Miller's dubious expression. "Don't look so surprised."

"So why didn't you go to college?"

"Never crossed my mind. Nobody in my family ever has. And when I turned eighteen and graduated, the only thought in my head was getting as far away from Atwood as I could."

"What's the story there?" Miller asked, idly stirring his mushy cereal with a spoon.

Danny's body tensed up; he fucking hated thinking about his father. "Probably nothing different than a thousand other kids. My dad and I don't exactly get along." Danny kept his voice bland but Miller flashed keen eyes on him, watching him for a long moment after he stopped speaking.

"How so?"

Danny squirmed in his chair. "He has a wicked temper. He wasn't afraid to use his belt on me, or whatever else he had handy. His mouth was a pretty effective weapon too. He always made it very clear exactly how he felt about me. He could never quite put his finger on how I was different. Shit, I didn't even know myself when I was a kid. But it didn't stop him from trying to beat the difference out of me. And then he caught me with a neighbor kid. A boy my age."

"Doing what?" Miller asked, eyes not quite meeting Danny's.

"Just messing around. Pretty innocent shit, in the scheme of things. But it confirmed everything my dad ever suspected about me. He kicked me out that day. Haven't seen him since. Anyway, I thought we were talking about you getting into the FBI." Danny tossed his empty water bottle over Miller's head where it landed with a rattling bang in the kitchen garbage can.

"Like I said, there's not much to tell. I'd always thought about being a cop. When I was a senior in college they had this seminar about jobs in law enforcement and I picked up a brochure about the FBI."

"And...." Danny prompted when Miller failed to continue.

"And I joined the local police force in Wichita after graduation, worked there for two years, and then applied to the FBI. I got in and went to Quantico. My first assignment was in Minneapolis and then I got transferred here."

"Do you like the job?"

Miller's slight hesitation told Danny more than any words he might choose to say. "For the most part," Miller answered. "After 9/11 we all got stuck on terrorism duty for a while and I didn't like that so much. I like the drug cases a lot better."

"Why?"

"The terrorism cases, I was never sure who I was working against. I prefer having a specific target."

"Like Hinestroza."

"Yeah, like your lovely boss, Hinestroza."

"He's not a complete monster, you know." Danny felt that familiar pang of loyalty rising up, that need to defend Hinestroza from outside attack, similar to the strange phenomenon that allowed a person to say something nasty about their own spouse but forbade anyone else from opening their mouth to agree.

Miller gaped at him. "How can you sit there and say that with a straight face, Danny? Who do you think gives Madrigal his orders? They're ruthless men. They sell drugs to little kids and kill people without a second thought."

"But he has a family who loves him," Danny said, his eyes on the table. "That's more than I've got. He must do something right."

"You think that makes him a good man? The fact that he's got a wife and kids who love him? They don't even know who he is!"

"No, it doesn't make him a good man. But it does mean he's not all bad."

"He's brainwashed you," Miller said with disgust.

Danny thought about that for a moment. "Maybe, a little. And maybe there's more than one side to a person. You know, I've known a lot of cops in my time, Miller, and you all suffer from tunnel vision. You can only see one way of doing things, one way of looking at the world." Danny eased out of the chair, peeling off his sweaty T-shirt. "It must make life awfully boring."

"What are you doing?" Miller asked, his voice pulled thin.

Danny knew the power of his body, had learned hard lessons about how to use it. He hung his T-shirt around his neck, arms flexing as he gripped the ends. "Gonna hit the shower," he explained.

Miller's eyes ran down Danny's torso, bobbing back up like a yo-yo on a string. His face remained blank but his fingers clutched convulsively at the edge of the table.

"It's about time for those stitches to come out," Miller commented around his clenched jaw.

Danny looked down. He'd almost forgotten about the injury since it had stopped itching a few days ago. "Yeah, it's been ten days today, I think."

Miller grabbed his cell phone. "Let me make some calls, see if we can get you to a doctor."

CHRIST, you'd think he was trying to arrange a manned spaceflight instead of having some stitches removed. Miller had been on the phone most of the day attempting to coordinate Danny's trip to the hospital. Finally, after half a dozen calls, they'd decided on a plan of attack: Miller would take Danny to St. Luke's, where he'd be whisked into a trauma room and whisked back out again. But within minutes that plan had been scrapped by the higher-ups as too risky. Now Miller was trying to arrange a house call from a doctor, but the U.S. Attorney's office was worried that plan could open up a doctor to bribery.

"Oh, for God's sake," Miller sighed into the phone, pushing away the plate of Chinese food they'd had delivered a half hour ago. "There's got to be someone who can take out a handful of damn stitches."

Miller could hear Danny laughing from the kitchen.

"It's not funny," Miller called, trying to sound stern.

"It's pretty fucking funny," Danny disagreed, ambling into the living room with a couple of beers. He put one down in front of Miller. "The FBI can't figure out how to get my stitches out? I can solve that problem in five seconds flat."

"What? Fine, call me back," Miller said into the phone, tossing it down in irritation. He turned to Danny, twisting the cap on his beer. "Oh, yeah? How's that."

"Wait," Danny commanded, moving into his bedroom. He came out seconds later, something small hidden in his hand. "Here's your answer," he said, holding out his palm.

Miller looked at the Swiss Army knife. "How's that my answer?"

Danny flicked the knife with his fingers, revealing a tiny pair of scissors and miniature tweezers. "Get to work, Sutton," he said with a grin.

"What?" Miller choked a little on his beer. "I'm not a doctor."

"Please," Danny scoffed. "You grew up in the country, right?"

"Right," Miller agreed cautiously.

"Well, so did I and I know I've done plenty of things more disgusting than taking out a few stitches. Slaughtering a pig ring a bell?"

"What if it gets infected?" Miller asked, stalling for time.

"The wound's healed, Miller," Danny said patiently. "That's why the stitches are coming out in the first place. Listen, you really want to spend half the night waiting around for some half-assed plan to get me to the hospital? Then, once we get there, we'll have to sit around for the other half of the night killing time until a doctor can see me." Danny held out the knife. "This can be done in ten minutes. I'd do it myself, but my arm won't bend that way."

Miller stared at Danny's hand, the long fingers cupping the knife. He imagined pulling those black threads from Danny's skin, how close he'd be to Danny's bare chest. *You don't have to do this, Miller. What are you trying to prove? That you can? Didn't manage that last night in bed, did you? Couldn't exactly keep him out of your head. He's playing a game, but you don't have to. Get back on the phone and call a doctor.*

"Fine, give me the knife," Miller said, rising to the challenge he saw in Danny's eyes. Too late he remembered how he'd never been able to back down as a kid when Scott called his bluff, Scott using that knowledge to drive Miller to dumber and dumber heights. Once Scott had challenged him to see how long he could keep a lighter against his palm. Probably would have burned a hole clean through his hand, but Junie had walked in and screamed the house down. He still had the scar. Taking a dare didn't always work out so well for Miller Sutton in the long run.

"Over here," Danny motioned, switching on the nearby table lamp as he lowered himself to the sofa. He yanked off his black sweater, the material ruffling his hair and unleashing the cowlick in front. His white T-shirt came next, revealing the row of stitches and the downy mat of hair covering his chest, trailing off over his stomach where it disappeared into a thin line inside his jeans.

Miller cut his eyes away, pretending to study his fingernails as heat bloomed in his cheeks, his neck stiff and prickly with warmth.

"Ready?" Danny asked, raising his left arm so Miller could get to the wound.

Miller nodded. He knelt on the floor in front of Danny, eyes trained on the ladder of black knots. So fucking careful not to look anywhere else. "Here goes nothing," he muttered, laying one hand gingerly on Danny's side.

Danny flinched backward, sucking in a strangled laugh. "Cold," he explained with a smile.

"Oh, sorry, beer bottle." Miller rubbed his hand against his thigh, bringing warmth to his fingertips. "Better?" he asked as he replaced his hand, Danny's skin hot and silky under his fingers.

"Yeah."

Miller held the tiny scissors, snipping tentatively at each stitch.

"It doesn't hurt," Danny reassured him.

Never had a space been so quiet. Miller could hear nothing but the sound of Danny's breathing, the faint metallic snap of the scissors, his own heart galloping in his chest.

"I'm going to start pulling them now," Miller warned. He wished Danny would crack a joke, start running his mouth the way he usually did. Anything to cut the smothering silence that was sucking up all the air in the room and making it impossible for him to breathe.

Miller began with the topmost stitch, plucking with the tweezers, pulling it out in one quick, smooth stroke. He could feel Danny's eyes on him as he worked.

"You're good at that," Danny said quietly.

"You've had a lot of stitches?" Miller asked, hoping to break the intimacy of the act he was performing.

"My fair share. The ones in my head were the worst."

Miller worked steadily down the row until he was tugging at the last stitch, his eyes drawn to the angry red line left in their absence.

"Okay," he said, his voice low. "You're done."

Neither of them moved. Miller's steadying hand remained glued to Danny's side, his eyes still fascinated with Danny's newest scar. He wanted to touch it. God, he didn't know what was wrong with him, but for the first time in his life he was incapable of restraining his impulses, his body's urges growing stronger than his iron will.

He leaned forward, running a finger gently down the red welt, tracing its path on Danny's tender flesh. He could smell Danny the way he had when they'd wrestled earlier in the week, that newly familiar scent of smoke and soap and sweat. It was the best thing Miller had ever smelled; he wanted to bury his face in Danny's skin and just breathe, let it fill him up.

Miller looked up. Danny's eyes were serious on his, not daring him anymore, not mocking, just watching. Those eyes worked their way under Miller's defenses, uncovering things he had spent a lifetime trying to hide.

"Danny," he whispered. He didn't know what he was asking for, but it seemed Danny did because he shifted on the couch, bringing one knee around to encompass Miller between his legs. Danny lifted his hand and passed his finger along Miller's jaw line, the same path as yesterday but this time not stopping, bringing his thumb forward to slide across Miller's lower lip.

"I want to kiss you," Danny breathed. He moved forward, his mouth a heartbeat from Miller's. "Can I?"

Miller moaned, a strained, growling noise breaking free of his seized-up windpipe. He couldn't bring himself to say the word, but his body answered for him, rocking toward Danny, his protesting mind drowned out by his body's rising chorus of *yes, yes, yes.* Danny kept his hands on the sofa, balancing there as he brought his mouth down, drew Miller's bottom lip slowly between his own.

Miller tried to keep his eyes open; it would feel less like surrender, less like passion if he didn't close his eyes. But his eyelids fluttered down of their own accord, his mouth opening under Danny's, the kisses soft and quiet, experimenting, tasting. He felt one of Danny's hands come up, cupping the back of his head, Danny's fingers raking through his hair, pulling him forward. Miller went with it, swaying into Danny, bringing his own hands up to rest on Danny's waist.

Even with the gentleness of the kisses, there was no pretending it was a woman's mouth against his. Danny's stubble scraped like fine sandpaper against his chin, the hand cradling his head large and strong. Miller could taste beer and Chinese spices on Danny's lips, nothing he hadn't sampled from a woman's mouth before, but it was different this time, something in the taste of Danny himself that was fundamentally male.

Danny pulled back slightly. Miller could feel him breathing against his lips but he didn't open his eyes. His tongue sneaked out of his mouth, licking his own lip just as Danny pushed forward again. Open mouths met and Danny groaned, his tongue slipping against Miller's, gaining entry, running hot and strong over Miller's teeth, against the inside of his cheek, the roof of his mouth, wrapping around Miller's tongue and sucking lightly. Miller's hands left their resting place, coming up to bookend Danny's face. His thumbs stroked against the stubble, his tongue forging a path between Danny lips. The kiss was not gentle anymore.

Danny's legs tightened on Miller's waist, the muscles in his thighs holding him prisoner. Miller twisted his torso, moving himself forward, and he felt Danny's hardness against his hip. He suddenly felt like he had as a boy when his mother had taken him to the park and he'd fallen off the swing, landing spread-eagled on the ground, all the air bursting from his lungs in one huge whoosh.

Miller's jeans were tourniquet-tight between his legs, his hips straining to thrust forward against Danny's stomach, his breathing torn and broken as it whistled from his throat. The hand Danny had threaded through Miller's hair clenched violently, the stinging tug against his scalp unfurling fiery tendrils to race down his spine as Danny forced their bodies closer.

Miller wrenched his face away, chest heaving, sweat prickling on his forehead. Danny's cheeks were flushed, his mouth open, one finger still drawing lazy figure eights against the nape of Miller's neck. The eyes Danny laid on him were stunned and vulnerable, scaring Miller more than if Danny had lunged at him and ripped off his clothes.

Miller stumbled backward, falling down on his hands, backing away on all fours. He scrambled to his feet, holding his arms out in front of him when Danny stood.

"I… we… I—"

"Miller," Danny said gently.

"I'm not gay, Danny," he burst out, running a hand across his kiss-swollen mouth.

"Are you sure?" Danny's voice was not accusing, just asking.

"I'm sure! I'm not like you!"

Danny's face closed, his eyes taking on that aloof, cocky look Miller had first seen in the interrogation room. "Oh, yeah?" Danny breathed. "'Cause what you had pressed into my stomach just now? That wasn't screaming 'let's be friends'."

"I… I didn't—" Miller shook his head.

"Is that your only objection? That you're not gay?" Danny asked, moving toward him. "Because if it is, I think we can take care of it pretty quickly."

"No, goddamn it," Miller said, anger fueling his words as he slipped behind the numbing comfort of his job. "It's not my only fucking objection. I'm an FBI agent, Danny, and you're a criminal informant on my case!"

Danny's eyes narrowed. "Is it the criminal part that really sticks in your craw? Or the fag part? Or the breaking-the-fucking-rules-for-once-in-your-by-the-book-life part?"

Miller slapped his hand down hard on the table. "I'm not that kind of man. I'm not going to risk my case or my career, not on someone like you!"

Danny flinched, fielding the verbal blow like a punch. "It must be nice to always be so damn sure about yourself," he spit out. "To always know you've got the moral advantage in every fucking situation. Too bad life isn't as black and white as you like to pretend. I'll bet you've ruined plenty of people's lives playing your little FBI games. It's not only guys like me, the ones pulling the triggers, who are guilty of that."

Miller cocked his head like an animal sensing a distant threat… or an investigator hearing the confession just behind the words. *Back up a minute. What was that? No violent crimes on his record. Never heard rumors about it on the street.*

"You've pulled the trigger?" Miller asked softly. "Have you killed someone, Danny?"

Danny took a deep breath, the storm of anger replaced by the weight of old ghosts hanging their heavy shadows in his eyes. "Yeah, I've killed someone. But not in the way you think."

"Danny, what—"

Danny turned away, his voice distant, talking to a stranger now. Miller was just another man with a badge. "Anyway, it doesn't matter. It was such a long time ago."

CHAPTER 7

"He said he killed someone."

"What?"

"He said he killed someone," Miller repeated, keeping his voice low. Danny was in the shower; Miller could hear drumming water even with the door closed, but this conversation was private. "He said it wasn't in the way I thought. I don't know if that means he wasn't directly responsible or if he just meant it wasn't a shooting. We were talking about pulling the trigger at the time," he explained.

"How did the subject come up?" Miller could practically hear Colin's mental gears whirring.

"It's a long story." *And one I'm never going to tell you.*

"Well, it's news to me," Colin said. "I've never gotten any information about Butler committing murder."

That's what Miller had figured. Colin Riggs had been on the drug task force for fifteen years, and if there was a rumor out there, he'd heard it.

"Did he give you any more to go on? A name, maybe?"

Miller let out a short laugh. "No. He didn't exactly talk his way into a murder conviction."

"Yeah, stupid question," Colin conceded. "I'll ask around, but don't hold your breath."

"Okay, listen, there's something else—"

The bathroom door opened, Danny riding out a wave of steam and not even glancing in Miller's direction as he stalked to his bedroom. At least today he was wearing a shirt.

"I can't talk right now," Miller said. "Can you meet me later?"

"Sure. Give me a couple hours. How about The Quaff around five? We can grab a beer before I head home."

"See you then."

Five o'clock couldn't arrive fast enough for Miller. He was exhausted from trying to ignore Danny in an eight-hundred-square-foot space, Danny's presence eating away at him even through a closed door. As hard as it was for Miller to admit, he missed the camaraderie he'd been starting to feel with Danny, the easiness in his presence that felt dangerously close to friendship. But that path was dark and uncharted, nowhere Miller wanted to travel. He preferred to stay on the well-lit road of professional distance.

But you miss the sound of his voice—his real voice, not the guarded one he uses with you now.

Miller crossed over to Danny's door, pounding out his frustration with a rough fist. "Danny? I need to talk to you."

"What?"

"Get out here," he commanded, refusing the indignity of talking through the door.

Danny brushed past Miller to throw himself on the couch. "Well?" he sneered, arching a brow.

Miller took a seat in the recliner. "What were you talking about the other night? About having killed someone?"

Danny raised bored eyes to Miller's. "Nothing."

"Danny, don't bullshit me, I—"

"I'm not a fucking moron, Miller. You've made it crystal clear what your role is here. FBI Agent Extraordinaire, right?" Danny smirked. "I'd have to be pretty goddamn stupid to tell you anything more."

Miller blew out an impatient breath. "Fine. You don't want to talk about that, then let's talk about Hinestroza. How'd you get involved with him?"

"I already told you."

"No," Miller corrected. "You told me the watered-down version. Now I want the whole story."

Danny stood up. "This requires a beer." He didn't offer to get one for Miller, but Miller still anticipated the favor. He pulled his arm back self-consciously when Danny returned with only a single bottle clutched in his hand.

"You told me you were working in a car wash, right?"

"Yeah, they recruit from car washes a lot. They must know how shitty that job is; guys are desperate to do just about anything else."

"Did he recruit other kids when he got you?"

Danny looked away, taking a long swallow from his beer. "No," he said finally.

Miller waited but Danny didn't offer any additional information. He wasn't lying, exactly, but there was something going unsaid. Miller would have put money on it.

"So what happened after you got in the car?"

"I was in back with Hinestroza. There was a driver up front. We went to an old warehouse in a rundown part of town. They pulled the car inside. And Hinestroza explained what my job would be. It was obvious I didn't have the option of saying no."

"What exactly did he say?"

Danny stared at his hands. "I told Hinestroza maybe I'd changed my mind about a job. But he said now I knew where the warehouse was, so there was no going back. I was in. I was eighteen. I was scared." Danny smiled, sad and wistful. "And it turns out I was good at the job."

Miller imagined Danny, young and terrified, caught in a trap with no way to see himself clear. Is that all it came down to sometimes? One bad choice to ruin a life?

"What did he have you doing at first?"

"Just petty shit." Danny shrugged. "Delivering small amounts to dealers, helping load and unload trucks. Nothing that involved giving me control over lots of cash or drugs. He didn't trust me yet."

"What kind of money did you make?"

"Not much, but more than the slave wages at the car wash. He upped it slowly but steadily until I had a nice apartment, a new car.

Where else was I going to find a job that paid that well?"

"He seduced you with the money."

"Yeah, and the responsibility. The fact that he started trusting me, having faith in my abilities. He's a smart guy, Miller. He could tell how much I needed someone to be proud of me and he used it."

Miller caught Danny's gaze; he felt compassion for the boy Danny had been, the man he'd been forced to become.

"Who'd you work with?"

Danny's eyes danced away. "Another kid."

"What was his name?"

Danny hesitated. "I can't remember."

"Is he still in the operation?"

"No."

"What happened to him?"

"I don't know." The lie played smoothly off Danny's tongue, but Miller caught it anyway, the telltale flush on Danny's neck proving he'd be a shitty poker player.

"What aren't you telling me here, Danny?" Miller pressed, leaning forward with his elbows on his knees.

"It's none of your fucking business."

"Everything about Hinestroza is my business."

"No," Danny said, his voice firm. "I won't talk about it. Not with an FBI agent."

"You don't have any privacy anymore, Danny. Whatever you know, it's my information. And I want it."

"Bullshit. You don't get open access to me, Miller. I'll tell you exactly what you need to know to nail Hinestroza and not one damn thing more." He paused, gave Miller a sly, sideways grin. "But maybe you want to make a trade? Tit for tat? You tell me something about you, something private, then maybe I'll talk."

Miller sat back, eyes cool on Danny's, choking down the disappointment he felt that they had returned to game playing. *Games are fine, Miller. It's all part of the job. Just don't tell him anything too personal. Play by your own rules.*

"Okay," he said with a calm he didn't feel. "What do you want to know?"

"How about the real story behind why you became a cop? What about that? What are you hiding from behind that badge?" Danny shot his questions out rapid-fire and Miller realized that Danny had been storing this ammunition, waiting for the opportunity to use it. Whatever he'd meant about killing someone, he was definitely skilled at aiming his shots.

"Danny, I don't—"

"Or what about Rachel? And don't give me any crap about not having time to get married. I can't believe she falls for that line."

"I don't have to listen to this shit," Miller retorted, jerking out of the recliner. Danny stood with him, the two of them facing off, Danny's eyes blistering with resentment.

"Paybacks are hell, aren't they?" he mocked, reaching out and clasping Miller's forearm when he tried to move away. "Hold on. I've got one more question for you. Remember when you stuck your tongue down my throat and then tried to pretend you didn't like it? At least I don't lie to myself about who I am. I know I'm a queer with a felony record. But who the fuck are you, Miller?"

"Shut your goddamn mouth," Miller growled, pivoting away from Danny and his arrow-tipped words that found festering homes in all Miller's weak places.

COLIN RIGGS was the closest thing to a friend that Miller had, besides Rachel, of course. And that was pretty fucking sad, when Miller thought about it, considering he hardly ever saw Colin outside of work and they never discussed anything other than the job.

Miller spotted Colin across the crowded bar, his prematurely gray hair glowing silver in the neon lights against the wall. Colin was in his early forties, a career FBI man with a wife and three kids he hardly ever talked about. He kept his personal life separate from the job.

"Hi," Colin grinned when Miller sat next to him at the bar, gesturing with one hand for a beer. "How are you doing?"

"Fine. Hate this babysitting duty, though."

"Yeah," Colin nodded. "It always sucks." He waited until the bartender deposited Miller's beer before continuing. "I asked a few contacts about Butler. Nobody's heard shit."

"I'm not surprised. There's something there, but he's not budging."

"What else did you want to talk about?"

Now that Miller was here, sitting next to Colin, he found the topic harder to breach, wasn't sure how to initiate the conversation without giving too much away. "You've done a lot of hand-holding with informants, right?"

"Oh, yeah. Anne always gets so pissed when I'm stuck in an apartment for weeks on end, hardly ever get to come home." Colin took a pull from his beer. "Why? This one really getting to you?"

"Yeah." Miller drummed an offbeat rhythm with his fingers. "You ever become friends with someone you're watching?"

Colin turned on his bar stool to give Miller an appraising look. "It's happened. But it's never a good idea. That distance is there for a reason. I had one guy I was babysitting, my first assignment. We were holed up together for three months. I was young and green and thought we were friends. He ended up selling me out and I almost got killed. But it can work the other way too. I know someone whose informant got murdered and he was a wreck for months. It never pays to make friends with them. They're a tool of the job and you have to think of them that way. Nothing more."

"I know," Miller sighed. "It's just—"

"Believe me, I understand," Colin interrupted. "You go into it already knowing almost everything about them. You start seeing their human side, start believing you're friends. And it's just the two of you, day after day. It's natural to want to talk. It's a fine line, and not everybody has the chops to handle it. There's nothing wrong with chatting, shooting the shit. But don't let it go farther than that. Nothing personal exchanged. Don't let him inside your head."

Miller smiled ruefully into his beer bottle. He could just imagine what Colin would say if he knew all the secrets Miller had already given away—about his past, about Rachel, about the job.

Not to mention kissing him while he was half naked.

Miller tossed his head upward like a horse shooing away a pesky fly, trying to throw off the relentless internal voice.

"You want me to switch you out?" Colin asked, dropping peanuts into his mouth one by one from his closed fist. "I can get someone else to watch Butler."

Miller knew what his answer should be, yet he found himself shaking his head. "No. It's fine. This is my case. I'm going to see it through."

Colin smiled. "I knew you'd say that. You're one stubborn son of a bitch, Sutton." He motioned for another beer. "Hey, you know who you might want to take a crack at, as far as the Butler-killing-someone angle goes? That Griffin Gentry guy. He was Butler's cellmate, right? He might know the story."

At the mention of Griffin's name Miller's stomach flipped into a knot, his beer backing up into his throat. He remembered the smile Griffin had given Danny. And the one Danny had given back, laughing easily with the man in the Mercedes. A man who, after all the time he'd spent learning about Danny, Miller hadn't recognized. That single fact ignited Miller's blood, like a match to lighter fluid, the resulting inferno burning wild and out of control. Danny's life was his domain and no strangers belonged there.

"Yeah," Miller said, clearing his throat around his pinched voice. "That's not a bad idea, actually. I might try to talk to him sometime this week."

"Just call Sakata. He's got him stashed at the apartment north of the river."

"Will do."

It was full dark by the time Miller left the bar, since he'd stayed behind for one more beer after Colin took off for home and dinner duty. The air was chill and leaden with the promise of rain. Miller pulled up the collar on his jacket, stuffed his hands into his pockets, and headed north into the wind, toward his car parked three blocks away.

The gun at his hip promising safety, he took a shortcut through a dark alley that was empty except for some fast-food wrappers swirling against his feet in the buffeting wind. Miller knew Colin was right: grooming an informant was always a delicate job. Trust had to be established to get the information, yet distance had to be maintained to retain the power structure. Miller had never had a problem in the past. He'd always been able to manage just the right degree of familiarity to swoop in and pull out the secrets he needed without involving his own emotions. But with Danny... with Danny, it was different.

Miller tried to tell himself it was simply a factor of how long he'd been watching Danny: almost nine months now, much longer than he'd ever spent investigating a previous informant. That in itself fostered its own kind of intimacy. Miller was privy to information about Danny that only those closest to him would ever know, if anyone did. He knew Danny liked Mexican food and Marlboros in the hard pack. That he preferred baseball to football and sometimes rode a motorcycle. He knew that Danny and Amanda had divorced almost two years ago but that Danny still took her to dinner at least once a month and always let her pick the restaurant. He knew that Danny had type O Positive blood, the green of his eyes was real, and that he was exactly six feet, one inch tall. That Danny wasn't a morning person, usually stayed up past midnight, and drank a single cup of black coffee every morning. He knew that men sometimes visited Danny in his apartment, but they never stayed the night.

And now you know how he tastes. You know how his skin feels under your hands.

Miller stopped walking, closed his eyes, and tried his old trick of turning his mind into a blank, white sheet.

You liked kissing him. It felt... honest... and right. You wanted to keep going. You wanted to undress him. You wanted to touch him, you wanted to—

"Damn it," Miller hissed. This was insanity; this was not his life—the life he'd built so carefully, brick by brick. Miller Sutton was not gay. He did not want to have sex with another man. A man who was a convicted criminal. A scum-of-the-earth drug dealer. A man who was used to casual fucks and would think nothing of adding Miller's name to his list of one-night stands.

That's not fair. Or true. You saw his eyes, the way he looked at you after the kiss. Those weren't one-night-stand eyes. There was nothing casual about it, Miller. For either of you.

"God, stop it!" Miller cried, swinging out violently, his fist connecting with the concrete wall in a cracking thud. He drew in a shuddering breath, the impact sending a merciful flash of white light traveling up his arm to wipe out everything else in his head. He cradled his ruined knuckles, blinking back the tears hovering against his lashes. He should go see Rachel. She'd fix his hand, comfort him, he could spend the night with her....

But when he got to his car, he turned away from Rachel's place. He was tired and just wanted to go home. He wanted to go home and see Danny.

IT TOOK Miller two weeks and seven jewelry stores to pick out the ring. It shouldn't have been such a production; Rachel had made it clear she wanted a round solitaire on a gold band. Traditional, elegant, simple. But he couldn't seem to make the final decision, always wondering if there would be something better in the next store he'd enter. Eventually he was forced to choose simply because he didn't have any more time to spend hunting. The FBI wasn't too keen on hearing "engagement ring shopping" as an excuse for dereliction of duties.

Miller's palms were sweating and he wiped them absently on the cushions of Rachel's pale green sofa. God, how did people ever do this? He felt like he was having a panic attack, his stomach contracting in a painful ball, his mouth dry as dust.

"Here, sweetie," Rachel said, returning from the kitchen with two glasses of wine. She handed one to Miller and curled up next to him. "What did you want to talk to me about?"

"Rachel, I...." Miller cleared his throat. Rachel was looking at

him with a smile in her eyes to match the one on her lips. She knew what he was going to ask, was just waiting for him to say the words. They'd been dating a year now, and he was well aware Rachel had been anxious for this moment for at least half that time.

As for Miller himself, he'd known on their first date that Rachel was good wife material, as his brother Scott would say. From the beginning, Rachel had been supportive of Miller's career but not overly enamored of it. Not like so many of the women he met in bars whose eyes went shiny like they'd discovered a hidden cache of jewels when they found out he was an FBI agent. Women who, after a few too many margaritas, started making jokes about his "gun" and hinting about the handcuffs in his pocket. They always made him feel awkward and embarrassed and he couldn't escape them fast enough.

"Miller?" Rachel questioned, laying one slim hand on his arm. "What is it?"

No way was he getting down on one knee. He pulled the black velvet box from his pocket, took a steadying breath. "Rachel, will you marry me?" he asked, his eyes shifting from her face to the ring and back again.

"Miller," Rachel sighed, a smile breaking free that was wide enough to show her back molars. "Yes," she exclaimed. "Yes!" She threw her arms around his neck, dragging him forward, laughing and crying against his cheek.

"Careful," Miller warned, pulling back to wipe her tears with his thumb. "Don't knock your ring into the wine."

Rachel glanced down at the diamond, seeming to notice it for the first time. "Oh, it's gorgeous. Just what I had in mind." She held out a trembling finger. "Put it on me?"

Miller nodded. He plucked the diamond from its velvet bed, the ring looking impossibly small and delicate in his hand, and slid it onto Rachel's finger. They both stared at it, the stone picking up the lights of the room and throwing them back in shiny pinpoints.

"Miller, I'm so happy," Rachel said.

Miller kissed her softly on her parted lips. He wanted to say it back, so much. But he couldn't. Because even now, even at this moment that he'd thought would finally give him everything he needed, the little voice in his head was still whispering, insistent and unrelenting, "Is this it? Can this really be all there is?"

The voice was not fooled at all by the diamond ring on Rachel's finger.

DANNY was mildly drunk, the only thing keeping him from a rip-roaring bender being the fact that there was only the single bottle of bourbon left in the apartment. He didn't want to drink it all in case Miller came back and needed some himself.

Can't believe you're worried about him. After the things he said to you…. But the truth hurts, doesn't it, Danny?

That last voice was not his own but his father's, the old man's constant refrain when Danny was growing up. Say something nasty, something designed to cut a child straight to their soul, then follow it up with, "Truth hurts, don't it, Danny?" His father always had a special knack for sinking the knife in to the hilt. He felt a stab of guilt that he'd run away and left his mother alone with the old man, abandoning her to bear the weight of his father's anger on her weak shoulders.

"Here's to you, you old fucking bastard," Danny whispered, raising the bottle toward the silver sliver of moon flirting from behind its veil of wispy clouds.

Danny understood why Miller had said what he did. He recognized Miller's struggle, body and mind torn in different directions. But understanding didn't make the words sting any less. It had been a long time since someone had been able to hurt him that way. But coming so close on the heels of that kiss…. That kiss had opened a door in Danny he'd thought was closed forever.

Lust was nothing new to Danny. He'd never been a man to deny his body. But desire, that was unfamiliar; wanting more than just to satisfy his basic needs with another man's flesh, instead wanting to stroke and soothe and discover. That was virgin territory, and the fear was almost as strong as the wanting. Down the path of that kiss lay darkness and uncertainty, but maybe that was all right with him. He couldn't remember what safe felt like anyway.

Leave it to you, Danny, to feel... something... for the one man in the world you'd have to be an absolute fool to trust.

"Hey." A gruff voice floated from over Danny's shoulder, causing him to make a startled grab for the bottle that threatened to slip from between his knees.

"Shit." He exhaled. "You scared me."

"Sorry." Miller hesitated, only his head braving the trip onto the balcony.

"You can come on out." Danny motioned with his free hand. "I won't throw you over."

"Gee, thanks," Miller said, deadpan. "How can I resist an invitation like that?" But he stepped onto the balcony, taking the seat next to Danny's.

They sat in silence as Miller lit up a cigarette. He didn't ask for Danny's lighter, instead fishing his own book of matches from his pocket.

"You want some?" Danny asked, holding out the bourbon, his voice coming out angrier than he felt.

"Okay," Miller said, tone wary.

"How was Rachel?"

Miller tightened up next to him. "I didn't go see Rachel."

"No? Then where were you?"

"Working."

"I thought I was your job."

"You are."

Danny laughed in spite of himself. "Jesus, this reminds me of being in prison. Never could get a fucking straight answer there, either."

Miller didn't respond right away, taking a pull from the bottle before passing it back. "What was prison like?" he asked, eyes on the stars.

"About what you'd expect," Danny said, lighting up his own smoke. "Tough, scary, boring as hell. The food is the nastiest you'll find anywhere and the company's in the same league. But I can survive there, better than you might imagine."

"How?"

Danny thought about the question before answering. "You have to have a certain attitude with the guards: respectful but not too friendly. If the guards like you, but the other inmates don't think you're a suck-up, you get a lot of leeway. And my second time in I had Amanda around to send me things I could barter—cigarettes, stamps, porn. Having something to trade makes all the difference."

"What happened when you ran out of that stuff?"

Danny pondered how much to tell and figured he didn't have anything to gain by lying. "I have a pretty face, Miller," he said evenly. "And I know how to use it."

Miller inhaled a sharp breath, glanced at him and then just as quickly away. "Was it always… consensual?"

Danny's laughter was tinged with bitterness. "That's not exactly the term I'd use. But yeah, most of the time it was."

"Most of the time?" Miller spoke as though the words were being dragged out of him, his voice only one step up from a whisper.

Danny closed his eyes. He'd gotten past all this. He had. He'd worked hard to put it behind him and move on. But it would be a lie to say he'd forgotten, or that he ever would. He still remembered the sounds and the smells, the cut on his cheek from having his face pressed to the floor, and the eggplant-hued bruises they'd left on his arms that took a month to heal.

"It was prison, Miller, not fucking Bible study," he said, swallowing past the tremor he heard in his voice.

"Jesus, Danny."

"Don't you dare feel sorry for me. I survived in there. A lot of men don't. I made it out alive. And I'm okay. That's what matters."

Miller looked at Danny, nodded once, his lips a thin line. "Was it in Leavenworth?"

"No." Danny shook his head, his lips trembling around his cigarette. "My first stint. Marion."

"You were just a kid then," Miller said, his voice soft.

"Yeah. Twenty-two. Wasn't a kid anymore by the time I got out." Danny gulped down bourbon, backhanding the excess that trickled from the corner of his mouth. "This is depressing me. Let's talk about something else," he choked.

"What can we talk about after that?" Miller asked, his own voice rough and strained. "The weather? Football? What to have for breakfast?"

Danny smiled. "All right. Maybe we don't need to talk tonight. Let's just drink." He passed the bottle to Miller, his eye snagged by the blood smeared across Miller's fingers.

"Christ, Miller, what happened to your hand?" Danny sat forward, trying to get a better look in the weak, milky-white moonlight. He reached out, his finger passing gently over the bruised and swollen knuckles. He wished things between them were different so he could hold Miller's hand, use his mouth to kiss away the hurt.

Miller didn't answer, just tipped his head back and slugged down a throat full of liquor. Danny could see the scratches on Miller's knuckles and knew you didn't get abrasions like that from hitting a person. Miller's fist had gotten up close and personal with something hard and inanimate; Miller looking to punish himself, not someone else.

Danny slouched back in his seat with a sigh. "Are we ever going to talk about what happened the other night?" he asked. "Or are we going to keep talking around that kiss?"

He heard Miller suck in a breath, stomp his half-finished cigarette under his shoe. "It was a mistake."

"I thought mistakes were supposed to feel wrong."

Miller twisted his neck in Danny's direction, their eyes meeting above the glow of Danny's cigarette. It would be so easy, Danny thought, so easy to lean forward and kiss him again. To lick the smoke from his tongue, watch lust dampen the confusion in his eyes, and show him that being with someone like Danny wasn't all bad. But Danny wasn't willing to risk it, to risk bearing the brunt of all Miller's fears. So he took a swallow of bourbon instead and tipped his face to the stars.

THE screaming woke Miller out of his alcohol coma. Danny's voice shouted loud and hoarse from the room next door, and adrenaline surged so fast and powerful through Miller's body it threatened to blow off the top of his head and turn him into a human geyser.

"Fuck, fuck," he cried, rolling out of bed. He hit the floor on wobbly legs, sprinting across the room to grab his gun from the dresser. His shin knocked hard against the bed frame, the sharp throb a distant second to his fear.

He was out of his room and into Danny's in a matter of seconds, gun drawn, safety off, not sure what he expected to find. But Danny was alone, legs tangled in his sheets, head thrashing against his pillow.

"Oh, no, please," Danny moaned. "God, don't... don't!"

Miller hunched over, one hand on his knee, drew in a deep breath. Fuck, he'd about had a heart attack over a damn nightmare. Shit.

"Danny," Miller called, still bent at the waist. "Danny, wake up."

Danny didn't hear him, his body twisting violently on the bed, legs thumping against the mattress. "Don't," he cried again, a strangled sob. "Oh, my God, Ortiz. Please."

Miller crossed to the bed and looked down at Danny. "Danny. Danny! Wake up." He leaned over, put a hand on Danny's bare shoulder, and gave him a little shake. "Wake up."

Danny's hands flew up, one smacking hard against Miller's arm, clutching desperately, finding Miller's good hand and grabbing on. "It's okay," Miller whispered. "It's okay, Danny. You were dreaming."

Danny's eyes opened as he swam up from sleep, confused and scared. "Miller?"

"Yeah, it's me." Miller smiled. "Go back to sleep. It was just a dream."

Danny's eyes drifted closed, his face still tense with fear. Miller lowered himself to sit on the edge of the bed, waiting and watching until Danny's breathing evened out, his face growing calm in the moonlight.

Miller carefully untangled his fingers and smoothed the sheet over Danny's bare chest. He stood and brushed the hair off Danny's forehead with one hand, the strands as soft against his fingers as the stubble on Danny's cheeks had been rough when they'd kissed.

"Good night," Miller whispered. "Don't pull that shit again. Scared me to death."

Miller left his door ajar so he would hear if Danny needed him. He put his gun back on top of his dresser, next to the cell phone that beckoned him with thoughts of duty and responsibility. Miller stared at the phone. He didn't want to make the call. He didn't want to know.

Do your fucking job, Miller. The one they pay you for.

He grabbed the phone, punched in the number he knew by heart, and listened to the distant ringing in his ear.

"Sutton here. Sorry to wake you. I've got a possible name on the Butler murder." Miller pinched the bridge of his nose, hard. "Try Ortiz," he said and hung up the phone.

CHAPTER 8

IT MADE Danny nervous when there was a knock on the door. He hadn't always been that way, but just like he no longer answered his door armed only with a smile, he couldn't get past that sharp stab of alarm when someone came looking for him. The constant anxiety, even in the face of the most mundane of activities, was a part of his new career he had not anticipated.

He tugged on his jeans, the worn denim sticking to his shower-slick skin. He didn't bother with a shirt, shoving his gun into his waistband like second nature. He pressed his back to the wall beside the front door, the way Madrigal had shown him, ready if it was kicked open by a hostile leg.

"Who is it?" he called.

The peephole in the center of his door might as well have been invisible. He'd stood on the other side of a door not long ago and watched Madrigal use that particular pathway to blow someone's brains out through their curious eye. No peepholes for Danny after that.

"Danny, it's me. Ortiz."

Danny opened the door and found Ortiz's wide, familiar face grinning at him.

"Hey, man." Danny smiled, giving Ortiz a quick, one-armed hug. "Come on in."

Ortiz gave a low whistle as he crossed the threshold. His eyes roamed around the spacious living room, taking in the clean, white walls and the new furniture. "Nice place," he commented.

"Thanks. You want a drink?"

"Sure. Soda or something is fine."

Danny pointed him toward a set of bar stools pushed under the overhanging counter. There was a rectangular cut-out in the wall above, giving a view into the tiny kitchen. Danny grabbed two Cokes from the refrigerator, passing one through to Ortiz before resting a hip on the kitchen side of the counter. "It's good to see you."

"You too. It's been a while," Ortiz said.

Danny had only talked to Ortiz a half-dozen times in the year since he'd left the car wash. Once, just a week after he started working for Hinestroza, Ortiz had dropped by Danny's old apartment, wanting to make sure he was okay. The most recent time had been a month ago, when Ortiz had called late at night, drunk, asking Danny for a job.

"How are things at the car wash?"

"Terrible." Ortiz shook his head. "That asshole hasn't given me a raise since you left. Still working for less than minimum wage."

"That's against the law," Danny pointed out.

"Yeah, well, so is being an illegal. He knows I'm not going to complain."

Danny had been surprised when he'd first found out Ortiz was an illegal alien. He spoke with a heavy accent but his English was good. Better than a lot of the rednecks Danny had grown up with, that was for sure. Danny had assumed Ortiz had gone to school in the States. But he'd learned at home; Ortiz's mother spoke English and she had made sure all six of her children were fluent in case they ever got the chance to cross the border.

"There's got to be somewhere else you can work."

Ortiz shook his head again, flipping the tab on his soda can back and forth so hard it snapped off in his fingers. "What about your job? How's that going?"

"Fine," Danny said, turning away to grab a bag of pretzels. He tore it open using teeth and hands and tossed it down on the counter.

"I know you said you didn't have any work for me, that time I asked." Ortiz looked embarrassed, his eyes focused on the counter. "I'm sorry about that, calling you drunk...."

"No big deal."

"But I'm desperate, man. I need more money. Isn't there any way you can get me a job?"

Danny set down his can with a hollow pop. "Do you even know what I do, Ortiz?"

Ortiz looked up and met Danny's eyes. "I got a pretty good idea. Hard to miss that gun in your waistband."

"You want to get mixed up in this life?"

Ortiz gestured over his shoulder with a thumb. Danny's gaze followed to his clean, white living room. "Doesn't look so bad," Ortiz noted.

How could Danny possibly make him understand? Sure, he had money now, and responsibility and people who relied on him. But he also had drugs and guns and fear gnawing away at him day after day.

"It's not the kind of life you want. Trust me. There are better ways to make money."

"How, Danny? How?" Ortiz burst out. "I'm hardly sending anything home as it is. I've been looking for better paying work for over a year now. There's nothing. Please, I'm begging you. Just tell them to give me a chance. I'll work hard. You won't be sorry. Please."

Danny knew Ortiz had a wife and baby back in Mexico, even though he was only a year older than Danny himself. He hadn't seen his daughter since two weeks after she was born, but his wife sent pictures when she could. His little girl was almost three now and wouldn't recognize her father if she passed him on the street.

"Ortiz...."

"If I can make some more money, maybe my wife can come to the States. Right now, we're barely making it. Half the time they don't have enough to eat. They're living with my mother, eleven people in a two-room shack. Please, Danny." Ortiz ducked his head, but not before Danny caught the sheen of tears in his dark eyes.

"It's ugly, this work I'm involved in," Danny told him, his voice soft.

"Uglier than my daughter getting bitten by rats when she's sleeping on the floor at night? Uglier than my wife having to make

*shoes for her out of old pieces of tire and duct tape? Uglier than that?"
Ortiz asked, angry.*

*The right thing to do, for everyone, would be to say no to Ortiz's
request. He would be furious; he might never speak to Danny again.
But eventually he'd find a job that paid more or he'd go back to
Mexico. Either option was better than following in Danny's footsteps.*

*Ortiz was the only friend Danny had in Texas, the first person
he'd met when he'd stepped off the bus from Atwood—Dallas was as
far from home as his money could take him. Danny had walked twelve
blocks that day with a stained duffel bag slung over his shoulder,
sweating through his long-sleeved shirt, before he'd come across the
car wash and stopped to ask the kid drying cars if he knew a cheap
place to eat. That kid had been Ortiz. He'd shown Danny a restaurant
that sold tacos for fifty cents and helped him get a job at the car wash
and a craphole apartment down the street from his own. Danny owed
him; he owed him more than to get him entangled with Hinestroza.*

*But Danny was nineteen years old and he was lonely. He wanted
to have a friend again. He thought maybe he wouldn't be so fucking
scared all the time if he could work with someone who didn't make his
blood freeze, someone he could trust.*

*"Okay," he said, looking at Ortiz's pleading eyes. "I'll talk to my
boss. I'll see what I can do."*

ONE of the first lessons Miller had learned at the FBI Academy was
not to make value judgments about the person you were interviewing.
Recording impressions, drawing conclusions: those things were
acceptable. But when you let personal feelings enter the equation, it
clouded your ability to accurately assess the information you were
receiving. Sitting across from a suspect who had raped and killed a six-
year-old girl? You were not allowed to despise him. Hatred stops the
flow between suspect and interrogator. Neutrality was the order of the
day. But here Miller was, having barely spoken five words to Griffin
Gentry, and already he hated his guts.

The man was just what Miller had expected: tough, cocky, and over-confident. His attitude worked well with his handsome face, although it pained Miller to acknowledge it. His thick brown hair covered one sapphire-blue eye, the muscles in his arms flexing as he reached for a cigarette, his mouth full like Danny's but not as soft. Everything about him came with a harder edge. Just being in the same room with Griffin, the man whom Danny had smiled at with such familiarity, started Miller's blood on a slow simmer.

Half an hour earlier, Miller had left Danny sprawled on the living room couch, bitching about having to eat take-out again and thumbing through a magazine. For the last two days Miller had waited for Danny to mention his nightmare, to bring up the name Ortiz, but Danny didn't appear to remember, which only made the guilt whispering around the edges of Miller's mind that much stronger.

When Miller had said he was leaving, Danny had given him a long look, muttering, "Give Rachel a hug from me," as the door closed. Miller had considered telling Danny he wasn't going to see Rachel, but reminded himself that was information Danny didn't have any right to know.

On the drive north, Miller had prepped for this meeting. He was going to talk to Griffin Gentry for one reason and one reason only: to find out what, if anything, the guy knew about Danny's admission of murder. Griffin's relationship with Danny, past and present, wasn't relevant and Miller would not allow himself to tread that ground.

"Mr. Gentry, I'm here to ask you some questions about Danny Butler," Miller said, pulling out the chair across from Griffin. They were seated at a small table in the living room of the apartment where Griffin was being hidden away. It was similar to the one Danny and Miller were sharing, only smaller and slightly shabbier. Special Agent Sakata had taken the opportunity to escape for a while now that Miller was there, saying he'd be back within the hour.

Griffin gave Miller a half-smile around his cigarette, flicking the hair from his eye with a slight toss of his head. "Call me Griff."

Miller ignored him. "You and Danny were cellmates in Leavenworth." Griff didn't answer. "Well?" Miller demanded, already losing patience.

"Was that a question?" Griff asked. His voice was rough, full of gravel, like he suffered from a permanent sore throat. "'Cause I'm assuming you already know the answer or you wouldn't be here."

Smart-mouth fucker. "Did Danny ever mention the name Ortiz to you?"

"No."

"Are you sure."

"Yeah. Why?"

Miller tapped his pen against the legal pad on the table. "Danny told me he killed someone."

That got Griff's attention. He ground out his cigarette. "Nuh-uh. Never happened. Danny wouldn't kill someone. He couldn't."

"He said he did," Miller replied.

"I don't give a shit what he said. I know him, and he doesn't have it in him."

"How well do you know him?"

Griff's eyes narrowed. "What do you mean?"

What, your resolve not to broach this subject is going to last all of five minutes? Don't go there, Miller. It's nothing you need to know for the investigation, it's not— "Danny's gay. You were cellmates...." Miller let his assumption hang in the empty air.

Griff tapped a fresh cigarette from the pack on the table. "Since when is Danny's sex life, or mine, of interest to the FBI?" he asked, eyebrows raised.

He's right, Miller. If Sakata was sitting here, too, would you be asking this question? I'm guessing the answer to that is a big fucking "no."

"What is it you want to know, exactly?" Griff's voice was amused, indulgent. "Whether we were lovers?"

Miller fought hard against the visions trying to form in his brain, mental pictures of Danny and this man, touching....

Griff smiled, his eyes coming to rest on Miller's hand, the one clenched into a fist so tight his nails were cutting into the fleshy pad of his palm. Miller forced himself to relax, his hand smoothing out on the tabletop. "I want to know how well you know him," Miller repeated.

"We were cellmates for twenty-two months," Griff said. "So we got pretty close. What else is there to do in prison but talk?" He didn't continue, watching Miller with cunning eyes.

"So you weren't…." Relief seeped into Miller, filling him up like a dry sponge taking on water, cooling the burning in his blood.

Griff grinned. "I think you misunderstood me. As it happens, Danny and I discovered we were good at more than talking. In Leavenworth and afterwards too." He wagged a finger in Miller's direction, like a teacher chastising the errant schoolboy. "But that's as much detail as you're getting. I don't kiss and tell."

Miller gritted his teeth, the fiery sting of Griff's words making him want to reach across the table and smash his fist into that pretty face, bust open those lips that had kissed Danny's more than once and probably never called it a mistake.

"Why did it end?" Miller chewed off each word like biting through a stick.

"Does Danny know you're here, asking me these questions? He'd probably answer them himself." Griff paused to blow smoke in Miller's face. "If you had the guts to ask him."

Miller reached over and snatched the cigarette from Griff's fingers, crushing it out on the table.

Griff laughed, not intimidated at all. "How do you know it's over between Danny and me?"

"Because I've watched Danny for the last nine months and I never once saw your face," Miller said, satisfaction he didn't even attempt to disguise punctuating every word.

Griff shrugged. "You'd have to ask Danny why it ended. He's the only one who can answer that particular question."

"Why did he meet you that morning on the street corner? What did you bring him?"

"Nothing," Griff said, shaking his head. "He just wanted to see me." He was good; he didn't give a single thing away. Miller couldn't tell if he was hearing the truth or a lie.

"And he never mentioned the name Ortiz to you?"

"No. I already told you. Is that who he said he killed?"

"No. He didn't give a name or any details."

"You're wasting your time. It never happened." Griff graced Miller with a dismissive smile. "And if you knew Danny half as well as you think you do, I wouldn't have to tell you that."

"WHAT the hell are you doing?" Danny asked, waving away smoke with one hand. "You're gonna set off the fire alarm."

"You said you were sick of take-out." Miller kept his back turned, facing the stove with a brandished spatula.

Danny finished pulling on his shirt, smoothing back his damp hair with one hand. "When did you get home?"

"Couple of minutes ago. Figured you'd be starving."

"I am." Danny moved up behind him, peeking over his shoulder. "What the fuck is that?"

"Grilled ham and cheese."

Danny waited a beat. "Is it supposed to be black like that?"

"Shut up, dumbass," Miller said, elbowing him backward. "If you don't want yours, you can order pizza again."

Danny groaned. "I never thought I'd say this, but I think I could live happily without ever eating another slice. Living here has put me over my lifetime quota."

"Yeah, me too," Miller agreed. "Grab some plates."

Danny set the table with two plates, paper napkins and a couple of beers. "Want chips?" he asked.

"Sure," Miller nodded, sliding blackened sandwiches onto each plate.

Danny took a bite of his sandwich, the cheese and ham overpowered by the flavor of scorched bread. But he didn't mind; he was actually thankful for the smoky, ozone stench in the kitchen. It spared him having to catch the scent of Rachel.

"Did you have a nice break from this place?" he asked, washing down a mouthful with a swallow of cold beer.

Miller poked at his sandwich with one finger. "I wasn't taking a break."

"What were you doing?"

"Work stuff," Miller said, taking a hesitant bite of his own creation.

Yeah, I'll bet. "Still, it must be nice to get out," Danny said. He watched Miller chew. "Do you think we could leave tonight? Just for a little while?"

Miller's head snapped up. "No! Are you nuts?"

"It's dark. Couldn't we just take a walk around the block? I'm losing it here, Miller."

"What if Madrigal—"

"You really think he's cruising random city streets at night hoping to spot me?" Danny laughed. "That's not his style. It would be beneath him. He'll wait until he knows exactly where I am."

Miller shook his head. "It's too risky. Besides, it's freezing out there. And they said it might rain."

"Are you sure you're really from rural Kansas?" Danny asked skeptically.

"What? Yes. Why—"

"Because if you think this wimpy-ass weather is cold, I seriously doubt you've lived through a winter on the plains."

"Smartass," Miller mumbled, a little grin inching its way across his face.

Danny smiled back. "You know I'll keep nagging you all night if you don't say yes."

"Jesus," Miller sighed. "We're only going around the block one time."

Danny nodded his agreement. "I just need to get out of here, even if it's only for twenty minutes."

"Ten minutes," Miller corrected.

"Okay," Danny grinned. "Ten minutes."

When they were done choking down their sandwiches, Danny rinsed the dishes, saying he'd finish washing them later. Miller shook his head in disgust at Danny's excitement, but pulled on his coat and brown stocking cap without another word.

"Your cool factor just plummeted," Danny said, pointing at the hat.

"I don't give a shit about my 'cool' factor," Miller retorted, shoving his feet into boots. "I care about keeping my head dry."

"Fair enough." Danny smiled, flipping up the collar on his jacket.

Danny wouldn't admit it, but Miller was right: the night air was cold, their breath escaping in cloudy bursts like a pair of miniature steam engines. But after a block of fast walking, Danny could feel heat bubbling up through his skin, his hands stuffed inside his jacket pockets taking on a thin sheen of sweat.

It wasn't raining yet, but Danny could sense the moisture hanging above them, biding its time. They passed a row of houses still decked out in Halloween finery, gossamer cobwebs covering the bushes out front, orange lights twinkling around door frames, and a glow-in-the-dark skeleton beckoning from a porch swing.

"I used to love Halloween," Miller said, almost to himself.

"Yeah? I was never that excited about it."

"My mom was good with sewing costumes. One year I was an Indian and she made me a giant headdress. That was my favorite." Miller smiled at Danny in the dark.

"We lived so far out in the middle of nowhere and I never had anyone to trick-or-treat with, anyway. So most years we skipped it."

"Was it hard, being an only child?"

"Yeah, especially with my dad. I think he might have been easier on me if he'd had another kid, someone else he could pin his hopes on. Someone who wouldn't disappoint him."

"Was it just you being, you know, gay, that made him so hard on you?"

"I have no idea." The conversation tossed Danny back to childhood, where his strongest memories were of being beaten, the old man's belt flying through the air with a whistling snap, the buckle unerringly finding bare flesh. Sharp boot points rousting him out of bed, his body landing with a thump on cold floorboards where the kicks found their mark with ease. "He's not exactly the sort of guy you can sit down with for a heart-to-heart," Danny explained, his mouth twisting up with bitter memories.

"Did your mom ever stand up for you?"

Danny huffed out an angry laugh. "Hell, no. She just stood back and let him beat the shit out of me. I'm sure she was scared too. But still...."

"You were her kid," Miller finished quietly.

"Yeah."

When Miller turned to look at Danny, an errant raindrop landed in the middle of his forehead. Danny brushed it away from Miller's cold skin, felt the rough edge of ice under his fingers. "It's gonna start sleeting, I think."

"Told you this walk was stupid," Miller pointed out, picking up the pace.

They were a block from the apartment, the rain gathering force, when Danny heard the footsteps behind them. Just a soft crunch of leaves, but he knew what to listen for. Miller stiffened next to him, his hand coming up to bump against Danny's arm.

"Danny," Miller whispered, "there's—"

But Danny didn't wait to hear the rest. He'd been taking care of himself for years now, the idea of placing his safety in another man's hands as alien as a walk on the moon. He reached down, pulled the Sig Sauer from his waistband in one fluid movement, and pivoted, arms outstretched, gun pointed directly at the head of the man behind them.

"Don't fucking move," Danny commanded, his voice as icy as the rain spattering against his face.

"Whaaaa," the man moaned, his face frozen, eyes and mouth large O's of surprise. His leashed dog leapt crazy circles around his legs.

"Danny!" Miller hissed. "Danny! What are you doing?"

"Who are you? Why are you following us?" Danny demanded, even though his sinking stomach had already alerted him to his mistake.

"I wasn't, I didn't... I'm walking my dog," the man cried, thin rain rivulets running off his bald head and down the sides of his face.

"Danny!" Miller said again, putting a steady hand on Danny's arm. "Put the gun down, now!"

Danny's elbows didn't want to move, locked with the flow of adrenaline. He pulled his hands back toward his chest slowly, his eyes still trained on the man with the dog.

Now that the gun wasn't pointed in his face, the dog walker was gaining some courage. "What the hell is going on?" he yelled at Miller.

"I'm sorry, sir," Miller said, pulling out his badge. "FBI. We're very sorry for the mix-up."

"You could have killed me!" the man said, his voice shaking, using anger to hide his humiliation. "I'm going to report this!"

They watched him scurry away, pulling his reluctant dog behind him.

"What the fuck was that, Danny?" Miller cried, as soon as the man was out of earshot. "Where the hell did you get that gun?" He made a grab for Danny's arm, but Danny pushed him away. Nobody put their hands on him without permission, not even Miller.

"You want to get into a fist fight out here?" Danny asked. "Because you try to grab me again and that's what's going to happen."

"We need to get back to the apartment," Miller said, his voice pulsing with fury. He waited for Danny to pass him on the sidewalk but didn't try to touch him.

IF MILLER had ever been this angry in his life, he couldn't remember it. It had never happened to him before, but the mythical red haze descended over his eyes, clouding his vision as he stomped up the stairs to the apartment. He waited just long enough to close and lock the door behind them before he rounded on Danny.

"I asked you where you got that gun." His voice was deadly and low.

Danny didn't look up from where he was leaning against the wall, bent over with fingers working at the laces on his boots, icy beads of rain gathered in his hair like diamonds.

"Did Griff bring it to you?" Miller asked, taking a step closer, his hands balled into fists.

Danny shrugged, giving him a bland look. "I needed protection. So I asked him to bring me a gun. Griff and I, we watch each other's backs."

Miller's barked out a venomous laugh he didn't recognize as his own. "Is that what they're calling it these days?"

Danny's eyes blazed. "Fuck you," he said, tearing off his jacket and throwing it with violent aim.

Miller arched backward, water splattering his face as the leather missile sailed past. "Give me the goddamn gun, Danny."

"No."

"Give. It. To. Me."

"No," Danny repeated. "I've been taking care of myself for years now. I've saved myself from situations you probably can't imagine in your worst nightmares. I need protection."

"You're a convicted felon. You can't have a gun."

"Are you serious? At this point, I'm not too worried about technicalities. I'm worried about staying alive."

"If you were so worried, you should have talked to me," Miller said, coming around the couch to stand in front of Danny. "I'm the one who's protecting you. Not your fucking boyfriend!" He spit out the word like rotten food in his mouth.

You're mine, Danny. Not his. Mine.

Danny took a step away from the wall, his face a centimeter from Miller's. "You volunteering to take his place then, Miller? Didn't think you were interested, seeing as how you're not gay. Right?" Danny asked, voice smooth.

"Right," Miller said, his jaw grinding together until his teeth ached.

"That's what I thought." Danny pulled off his remaining boot with one hand. "Hate to break it to you, but having you as the sole barrier between Madrigal and me isn't that comforting. I still need the gun."

"No, you don't!"

Danny whipped his face up into Miller's, his green eyes wild. "What about when you're out fucking Rachel?" he cried. "Who's going to protect me then?"

Miller jerked backward, feeling Danny's words like a slap.

"You think I'm so stupid I can't tell what you've been doing? Think I can't fucking smell her all over you?" Danny shouted.

Miller was done playing, done with whatever trap Danny was trying to push him into. "Give me that gun!" He reached both arms behind Danny, grasping for the weapon, their hands scrabbling against each other. He winced as his sore knuckles slammed against Danny's defensive fingers.

"Like today, for example," Danny panted from between gritted teeth, hands still battling Miller's at the small of his back, their chests pressed together. "What if Madrigal had shown up while you were out screwing around with Rachel? What then?"

"I wasn't with Rachel," Miller yelled. "I don't want to fuck Rachel. I want to—" Miller choked on his words, pushing himself away from Danny.

They stared at each other in silence, both of them breathing hard.

Danny's jaw was still tight with anger, but his eyes were gentle when he spoke. "Being with her isn't going to make it go away, Miller. It isn't going to stop that hunger, that wanting. Believe me, I know. I married my Rachel, remember?"

"Shut up!" Miller cried, wanting to close Danny's mouth, stop any more painful truths from spewing out. He shoved Danny into the wall, pinning him between his arms, bringing his mouth down hard. The lips under his were cold, but Danny's tongue sizzled with heat. Miller pushed his way inside, Danny's mouth opening wide and accepting, inviting him in. Danny's tongue ran across the roof of his mouth, back to front, making Miller shiver and gasp.

"Ah, God," he moaned, taking a shuddering breath against Danny's lips. He didn't know who he was talking to or what he was asking for. He lifted his hands off the wall, resting them on Danny's wet face, whisking rain drops onto the floor as he combed his fingers through the thick, dark hair.

It felt just as good this time, just as right—the combination of soft lips and rough stubble, the hands grasping his hips strong and demanding, the deep voice murmuring into his mouth, the taste of desire easing his jealousy, the balm of friendship blunting the jagged edge of his anger.

Miller pulled himself away, not wanting to stop but not sure how to go forward. He looked down, his eyes drawn to Danny's chest where his rain-wet T-shirt stuck to his skin. The outline of Danny's muscles was visible against the thin material, his chest hair dark and matted underneath.

Miller's hand rose, wanting to explore, but he checked its forward progress, fingers hovering. Danny looked down, then back up, his eyes hot and heavy-lidded.

"It's all right," he whispered. "You can touch me." Danny grasped the bottom of his T-shirt, easing it over his head and letting it drop from his fingers to form a white puddle on the floor. Miller sucked in air violently as his palm came up against Danny's bare stomach, the skin cold and damp against his fingers. Miller's other hand joined the first, spreading wide across Danny's torso, his thumbs carving a path between Danny's ribcage. He could feel the hard ridges of muscle tightening under his fingers and Danny's heart thundering under his hand.

"Yes," Danny whispered as Miller's fingers moved higher, his thumbs brushing across Danny's nipples. "Fuck yes, just like that...."

Miller tried to hold back, to go slow, to stay in control, but the feel of Danny, the sound of his voice, husky and slurred, and the smell of his skin combined to push him over the edge—falling from the precipice he'd been balancing on since the moment he'd met Danny Butler.

Without warning he grabbed Danny's arms, spinning him to face the wall, pushing up behind him roughly.

"Miller, what... uh... Jesus," Danny groaned, his hands flexing on the smooth walls as Miller ran his tongue down his back, following the curves of the snake coiled between Danny's shoulder blades. Miller licked the colors, blue, purple, and green passing beneath his tongue. Only at that moment did he acknowledge to himself how much he'd been aching to do this, to claim Danny's marked back as his own.

Miller slid his arms around to the front of Danny's body, his fingers hooking into Danny's collarbone, his chin nestled in Danny's neck, spearing the hoop in Danny's ear with the tip of his tongue and tugging gently against the cold metal. Miller could feel Danny's gun pressed into his stomach and reached between them, plucking it from its resting place.

Danny spun around, his head knocking against Miller's as he turned to him with wary eyes.

"It's in the way," Miller explained. He moved away from Danny, setting the gun on the table, placing his own next to it. Not giving the weapon back but not taking it away, either. Calling a truce.

"Come here," Danny commanded, and the sex in his voice made Miller's spinal cord vibrate like a plucked wire.

As soon as Miller was in touching distance, Danny lashed out, grabbing Miller's sweater in both hands and wrenching it over his head, heedless of wool catching on nose and ears. They struggled with Miller's undershirt, four hands making the simple task complicated, the material ripping as Danny pulled it free.

The feel of Danny's bare chest against his own wasn't something Miller had spent time contemplating, not like thoughts of kissing Danny or driving into his body. But the sensation was so different from holding a woman, so much better, that for a moment Miller forgot how to breathe. All Danny's unforgiving muscles rubbed against his own. The hair on Danny's chest tickled and teased Miller's skin. There was nothing fragile on Danny, nothing delicate, every inch of him the definition of a man.

Danny's mouth covered his, his teeth nipping against Miller's lower lip, his tongue following behind and easing the welcome sting. Danny's hands pushed between their bodies, tearing at Miller's jeans, pulling the buttons through the well-worn holes with shaking fingers.

"Danny, I—" Miller breathed.

"Do you want to stop?" Danny whispered.

"No." And it was the truth. There wasn't one part of Miller that wanted to turn back; even that voice in his head hushed into momentary silence.

"We can go slow. We don't have to do anything you aren't ready for." Danny brushed his fingers against Miller's jaw.

Miller nodded, not sure what slow meant to Danny and too fucking terrified to ask.

Danny smiled, his shuffling feet edging Miller backward toward the sofa. "Right now I want to taste you," he said, still quiet. Miller felt the words all the way through his body. "Take you in my mouth. Is that all right?"

Miller couldn't answer; his vocal cords were frozen, his neck muscles throbbed with anticipation, and his whole body was threatening to fly apart from the lust expanding in his chest. Even with his senses reeling out of control, he noticed that Danny had asked if he could do more, the same way he had before their first kiss. Miller wondered if it was because of what had happened to him in prison; if Danny was forever haunted by memories of those times he wasn't given the option of refusing. The thought made Miller's throat ache and he pressed Danny against his body, kissing him wet and deep, not separating until the need to gasp in a lungful of air was stronger than the pleasure.

Miller's calves bumped against the sofa, Danny bending with him as he sat, his tongue following the vein on Miller's neck. A slow, sexy grin spread across Danny's face as he climbed Miller's body, straddling him, his hands tangling in Miller's hair as they kissed. Miller wound 's hands around to grab Danny's ass, pushing off with his feet to pivot sideways, taking Danny down on the sofa underneath him.

Their jeans and shorts were shoved down in tandem, tangling around their knees, the friction as they rubbed together making Miller groan against Danny's neck.

"Roll over," Danny whispered. "I want to look at you."

Miller rolled onto his side, facing Danny, his eyes following Danny's down the length of their bodies. He watched as Danny touched him, lightly at first, just a finger up and down, then taking Miller in his fist with slow strokes, the rhythm increasing as Miller lifted his hips.

"Christ, Danny," Miller said breathlessly, sucking the smooth flesh of Danny's neck.

Miller reached his own hand between them and found Danny, hot and smooth under his fingers. Danny moaned against his shoulder, his face turned into the sofa as Miller dragged the rough pad of his thumb over the tip of his cock.

"Shit... that feels so good," Danny gasped, lifting his head to watch Miller's hand pumping.

Having Danny in his hand was different from touching himself, but recognizable too. Miller knew what felt good, knew Danny's hand on his meant he wanted more pressure, knew what Danny's increased breathing signaled. It felt like walking familiar land even though it was nowhere he'd traveled before.

"Oh, Jesus... yes." Danny spread his thighs as much as he could within the confines of a narrow couch and knee-high jeans. Miller felt a surge of accomplishment, proud of the fact Danny wanted him this way—his green eyes losing focus, his back arching as Miller increased the tempo.

"I can't... fuck, Miller, I can't hold back," Danny groaned. His fingers dug into Miller's arm. Miller watched, mesmerized by the way Danny bit his own bottom lip as he came, the tender flesh sacrificed to his pleasure.

Danny opened his eyes, giving a lazy smile as he ran a hand through Miller's hair. "Your turn," he murmured, ducking his head to roll one of Miller's nipples between his lips, moving down Miller's body with a trailing tongue.

"Ow, fuck!" Miller exclaimed as Danny's knee came to rest on his swollen hand.

"Shit, sorry." Danny paused for a moment and then picked up Miller's hand, giving the sore knuckles a tender kiss.

Miller couldn't look away, watching as Danny released his hand and moved lower. Danny took Miller's cock in his palm and brought his mouth down to close over the tip, tongue swirling. Miller laced his hand through Danny's hair, not holding him there, not wanting Danny to feel forced, but simply touching, loving the softness of those short strands against his fingers.

He groaned as Danny took him in deep, a sound he'd never heard from his own mouth before bubbling up from somewhere deeper than his lungs. It took them a minute to find their rhythm, Danny's hand pumping too slowly at first. But Miller put his hand over Danny's to speed things up, moaning as Danny's tongue found the right spot.

Miller looked down and knew that if he lived to be a hundred years old, this—Danny's eyes raised to his, Danny's mouth covering him, his lips wet and shiny, Danny's naked chest cradled between his legs—would always be the most erotic moment of his life.

Miller's toes curled downward, the nubby fabric of the couch rubbing against his feet. "I'm going to come," he whispered, warning Danny the way he always did with Rachel, but Danny didn't back away. Miller jackknifed forward as his orgasm ripped out of him, Danny's eyes dark and glittering on Miller's as he swallowed. The knowledge of what Danny was doing caused Miller's hips to buck involuntarily, a throaty moan accompanying the movement. It felt like more than sex to Miller, more than release. It felt like the answer to every question he'd never dared to ask himself.

Danny lingered for a moment, licking him clean, kissing his thighs and stomach, gentling his trembling flesh. He dropped one last kiss on Miller's shoulder as he maneuvered into the space between Miller's body and the back of the sofa. Miller closed his eyes, listening to Danny's steady breaths, feeling the warmth of Danny's hand on top of his own.

What the fuck are you doing, Miller? One good blow job, that's 'l it's going to take to ruin your career?

Miller brought his free hand up to cover his face, turning his head away from Danny. He tried to concentrate on the pleasure he'd felt, both giving and receiving, but his internal voice had disengaged its mute button and would not be silenced.

You keep this up, the life you know, it's going to be over. For what? For something you don't even know if you want? For something that can never last? He's going to go back to his life. And you'll go back to yours... what's left of it, anyway, after this disaster.

The sofa cushions dipped underneath his back as Danny shifted his weight. "What's wrong?" he asked, his lips pressing soft kisses against Miller's arm.

"Danny, I can't...." Miller hated how weak his voice sounded, how reedy and close to tears. He pushed himself upright, yanking up his jeans with one hand. He looked over his shoulder at Danny, who was watching him with no judgment in his eyes, his dark hair tousled like a little boy's.

Miller leaned forward, elbows on knees, and rested his head in his hands. He wanted his old life back, the one where he was sure about who he was and where he was headed. The one where he could keep a lid on the doubts and fears that had been trailing him around every corner of his life for as long as he could remember. The life where he was going to marry Rachel and have three kids and that house in the suburbs. The one where he knew the difference between right and wrong and was sure about who was good and who was evil. The one where he'd never met a man with black hair and green eyes and a jeweled snake painted across his back, a man who pushed into all Miller's private spaces and made himself at home.

Danny put one hand on Miller's back, his thumb stroking a slow half circle. "What do you want, Miller? What do you want to happen here?"

Miller could smell Danny on his fingers. He dropped his hands from his face with a weary sigh. "I want to be the man I was before I met you."

Danny swung his legs over the edge of the couch, hiking up his own jeans as he moved. He sat next to Miller without speaking, their bare shoulders touching. Miller risked a glance at Danny's face, prepared for anger and steeling himself for scorn, but Danny was looking at him with compassionate eyes, telling him without words that it was all right. And for the very first time in his life, Miller felt understood—felt that someone was seeing him all the way through and not turning away.

Danny cupped Miller's jaw in his hand, that simple touch making his stomach cartwheel to the floor. "It's too late for that. It's too late to go back," Danny said, gentle but firm. "Now you have to decide the man you want to be from here on out."

CHAPTER 9

MILLER hated college. He felt disloyal even thinking the thought; it was no secret what his family had sacrificed to get him there. But he didn't fit in, and after two and a half years, he knew he never would. Kansas State University was hardly upper-crust, privileged, Ivy League ground, but it might as well have been to Miller, who'd grown up on a desolate farm where the nearest town boasted a whopping 400 residents.

Driving into Manhattan the first day of freshman orientation, his father at the wheel of his rusted-out pickup and Miller in the middle where the broken spring cut into his back, it felt as if they'd landed on Mars. The noise in the small city made him want to cover his ears like a little boy, the sheer volume of people and the speed at which they moved hurting his eyes. His father had given him a slap on the back when they'd dropped him in front of the dormitory, telling him, "Good luck, boy," before hopping back in the truck. Junie had been slightly more emotional, hugging him close and saying she'd see him at Thanksgiving. Then they'd driven away, leaving him standing on the sidewalk with his thrift-store backpack and a threadbare suitcase that had been his mother's.

From the very first, college had seemed dangerous, like he was navigating a series of land mines. He felt pried into; his personal space felt invaded, the way everyone wanted to talk all the time. Miller's fellow students were full of rabid curiosity, always asking questions about his past and what he planned to do when he graduated. Professors wanted to know his opinions on books, current events, and philosophy. He soon learned that grunting and ducking his head was not an option unless he wanted to end up back in Fowler with his tail between his legs, facing a furious father who had somehow tied Miller's success in college to the memory of his lost wife. Over time, he got better about talking, could answer a question in class without feeling the prickly heat of embarrassment staining his cheeks, and could make small talk in the library without hiding behind a textbook. But he was always careful about what he said, forever thinking out his answer before he spoke.

He made a few friends, but more on the order of drinking buddies, guys to catch a basketball game with, no one destined to weather a lifelong friendship. He learned from the other boys, though, how to pretend he liked the overcrowded bars packed with too many people drinking too much, how to walk around campus with his head up, waving to students he recognized, how to smoke a joint without choking and make crude jokes about girls he'd slept with once or twice. Girls he met out at the local bars and then followed back to their rooms or apartments for fumbling, drunken sex. The sex always felt good enough during, though never "mind-blowing," as Scott had once described it. But afterwards, walking back to his own place, he was always lonelier and more confused than he'd been the night before. He learned to live with constantly feeling like a stranger in his own life, inside his own body, and the little voice in his head stayed mercifully quiet.

He never asked himself what exactly he was hiding from, what he was so terrified might be revealed. That was an answer he had no interest in hearing.

MILLER loved the FBI Academy. From the first day he arrived at Quantico, he felt safe. No one cared about his inner thoughts, about discovering who Miller was. They cared about making him a good agent, teaching him tricks and techniques for success, molding him into a man who believed he was acting on the side of the good and righteous, and it turned out to be a perfect fit.

He was expected to remain neutral in the interrogation room, to coax a suspect into talking using a variety of methods, gain their trust if possible—more information was revealed that way. But if not, he could be a hard-ass with the best of them, dish out a little dose of fear. Outside the interrogation room, Miller was to remember he was one of the good guys. The bad guys were the enemy, and he was a barrier between them and the rest of society. He wasn't to let empathy sway him—these people were getting what they deserved.

Being a good agent required compartmentalization, and Miller was gifted at locking away parts of himself. Things he didn't want to examine were shuffled to the back of his mind and never thought of again. His mental filing system had been serving him his entire life and never more so than in his early days as an agent.

He was damn good at his job. He felt confident, even living in a city with all its bright lights and overcrowded sidewalks, shielded somehow by his new "us versus them" mentality. He was able to walk into an interrogation room and remain professional and objective with the men sitting across the table. He was able to get them to open up, tell their darkest secrets, believe Miller was there to listen and might help them cut a deal, and then he could walk away at the end of the day, go have a few beers and laugh about what scum-sucking pieces of shit they all were. And he slept just fine at night.

He received commendations from his bosses for his ability to uncover the truth, to instinctively recognize when a suspect was withholding or outright lying. But about five years in, a funny thing started happening to him—the better he got at ferreting out the truth, the more often that little voice in his head started clamoring to be heard. It wanted to ask questions Miller had spent thirty years avoiding. He'd get up in the morning and look in the mirror, and he'd hear his own internal voice, the interrogation room one, smooth and slick, turning its intuitive powers on him. He managed to drown it out, choke it down, most of the time, but the effort wore on him, leaving him exhausted and disillusioned too.

He started feeling sick when he lied to a suspect, making them believe things were going to work out all right in the end, when in truth, they were going down hard and the ride would be ugly as hell. He began wanting to lunge across the table and smack the ones who smarted off to him, daring to challenge his authority. He was slipping, and he knew it. He thought maybe he could get it back if he could just silence that voice, that fucking voice... the voice that had gained its strength from how good Miller was at his job, how skilled he was at uncovering lies. His ability to take cover inside his FBI skin unraveled *in direct proportion to his talent as an agent. It was a Catch-22 of which his dreaded English professor would have been proud.*

The job Miller had chosen because it felt safe and insulated—free from self-reflection, its parameters and goals clearly defined with no room for errors or individuality—ended up feeding the doubts Miller had been trying to starve into silence.

He was hanging on, though—some days with two strong hands, other days by his bitten-to-the-quick fingernails. And then he'd gotten the call, the nod from above he'd been waiting for: the go-ahead to begin surveillance on Danny Butler.

DANNY was slamming around in the kitchen. Miller smiled into his pillow as he listened to the sounds of Danny starting his day, a sideways glance at the bedside clock showing 9:03 in the morning. The man couldn't make a pot of coffee or pour a bowl of cereal without it turning into a production. In spite of the noise, Miller liked knowing Danny was out there performing his morning rituals.

Then why don't you get your lazy ass out of bed and go see him?

They'd parted company in the living room last night, Danny leaving Miller where he sat, closing his bedroom door softly behind him. When Miller had finally leveraged himself up with a defeated sigh, he'd noticed Danny's gun was missing from the table. He hadn't wanted to argue about it anymore, his anger burned out of him, leaving only exhaustion behind. He'd brushed his teeth and fallen into bed, welcoming sleep so he wouldn't have to chase his thoughts around inside his head.

And now he was scared to face Danny. Scared of where they would go from here. Danny was right; there was no going back. But Miller didn't see a clear way forward, either. He should call Colin, tell him he wanted off the Butler babysitting duty, and have another agent sent over to take his place. But what if they assigned some rookie, a newbie who'd make a stupid mistake and get Danny killed? Or Miller could stay. But he knew what staying meant. There was no way he and Danny could be in this apartment together and not touch, not kiss, not continue what they'd started. Miller had willpower, but he wasn't an idiot.

First thing you've got to do is get out of this room. Go talk to him. You've had his dick in your hand and your tongue in his mouth, and you can't sit down and eat a bowl of cereal with him?

Miller pulled on some jeans and a clean T-shirt and ran a hand through his hair. Danny was still in the kitchen, shirtless, his back to Miller as he crammed a filter into the ancient coffee maker on the counter. One glance at him and Miller felt the pins and needles of anticipation. The desire to touch, the need to taste Danny's skin was obviously not sated, because Miller's tongue was longing to make that journey again.

"Hey," Miller said, his voice a tangle of sleep and lust.

"Shit!" Danny exclaimed. As he pivoted, the spoon he was holding turned to pepper the floor with coffee crystals. "You scared me. Is that the first thing they teach you at the FBI Academy, how to lurk in doorways?"

Miller smiled. "I think it was the third lesson." He pulled out a chair and sat down. Danny leaned back against the counter, watching him with careful eyes.

"How'd you sleep?" Danny asked.

"Good. You?"

"Pretty good." Danny dipped into the coffee again, dumping the new spoonful into the machine. The comforting gurgle of promised caffeine filled the kitchen.

"Miller—" Danny began.

"We need to start thinking about what you're going to do after this," Miller said swiftly. "They're going to be starting the ball rolling for the Witness Protection Program, and it helps if you have some ideas about the kind of work you might like to do." Miller looked down at the table, away from the disappointment he saw in Danny's eyes.

"Okay," Danny said. "I guess drug runner is out as a future career option."

"You're kidding, right?" Miller asked, eyes snapping to Danny's.

Danny shrugged, taking two mugs from the cabinet above the sink. "It's about all I'm qualified to do. And I'm good at it."

"You don't seriously want to go back to that life, do you?"

Danny didn't answer right away. "I don't know. I don't think so. But there were parts of it I liked. I'd be lying if I said there weren't."

"Like what?" Miller asked. He didn't even try to keep the disbelief from his voice.

"The money. And this sounds weird, considering how Hinestroza runs my life, but the independence. No clock to punch, no one telling me to be at work at a certain time. My time was my own, for the most part." Danny stopped to fill the mugs with coffee, the steam rising up into his face. "And I liked being good at something, being someone Hinestroza relied on. Working on some blue-collar assembly line isn't going to afford me the same benefits."

"No, but there is the 'no one trying to kill you or arrest you' part that might be a nice change," Miller pointed out, taking his coffee from Danny's outstretched hand.

"I guess," Danny said. He didn't sound convinced.

"I don't understand you," Miller said, exasperation making his voice harsh. "I thought you'd be glad to be leaving that life behind. To be moving on to something better."

"Better is relative, though, isn't it? I mean, sure I get a 'new' life. One where I don't know a fucking soul in the world, where I've got to work some menial labor job because that's all I'm qualified for. A life where I never get to see Amanda again, or Griff, or… anybody I care about, and I'm watching my back until the day I die. Honestly, it doesn't sound like a real treat."

"But you'll be alive, Danny," Miller said.

"Yeah," Danny sighed, his tongue running along his lower lip. "I'll be alive."

The silence in the room felt heavy, that thick-with-implications quiet that Miller felt so often when he and Danny were together. He watched as Danny set down his coffee mug, took a purposeful step in his direction. "Miller," he said, trying again.

The cell phone in Miller's pocket sprang to life, the jangling ring startling him, making his hand jump against the table. He checked the caller ID. Colin. "I have to take this call."

"Fine," Danny nodded, looking away. "Fine."

Miller walked into the living room before flipping open the phone. "Hello?"

"Hey, Miller. How's it going?"

"The usual." Miller slipped on his coat and shoved his feet into tennis shoes. "What's up?" He pulled open the sliding glass door and stepped out onto the balcony, shutting the door behind him. It was frigid outside, the day gray and bleak. The icy rain of the night before had ended, but snowflakes were floating down, not sticking to the pavement yet, but catching on tree branches and grass, snagging on Miller's hair as they tumbled to earth.

"We've checked all the unsolved murders in this area. Don't think we've got any matches on an Ortiz. There are some John Does out there, but none of Hispanic descent. We've got one unidentified Hispanic woman, but that's it."

"Huh," Miller grunted, pinching the phone between his ear and shoulder so he could light a cigarette. "I don't think it's a woman."

"Why not?"

"Don't know, really. Just a hunch."

"You want me to have them keep looking?"

Miller raised his eyes to the sky, let snowflakes gather on his lashes, blurring his vision. "Yeah," he said. "Tell them to try Texas. Near Dallas. That's where he was up until about ten years ago."

"You got it." Colin paused. "You still holding up okay there?"

"Yeah. I'm fine," Miller said, exhaling a plume of cigarette smoke into the frosty morning air. He didn't know if it was true, but he couldn't afford to have that conversation with Colin. "When are we getting him down to the Marshal's office for the Witness Protection interview?"

"I have a call in to the U.S. Attorney's office. I'll let you know when I hear back. Call if you need anything," Colin instructed.

Miller hung up the phone, tucking it back into his pocket. His hands were stiff with cold, the snow falling harder now, a thin layer coating the cement floor of the balcony. He started to open the door and head back inside but pulled up short when he saw Danny standing on the far side of the sofa, watching him.

Miller looked through the glass, looked into those green eyes. He knew what he wanted. He just didn't know how to go about getting it without losing everything he already had. His job would be gone if anyone found out, his idea of himself in pieces on the floor, and his relationship with Rachel compromised in every possible way.

You still think you're ever going to marry Rachel? Or any woman? After what you feel when another man touches you? Stop kidding yourself, Miller.

He tossed his cigarette down in the dusting of snow and stubbed it out with his foot. He knew if he did this, if he followed where his body wanted to lead, he wasn't going to be able to hide anymore. He was going to have to start answering those questions he'd been ducking all his life.

Maybe it's about time. Maybe it's about time you started answering some fucking questions of your own.

But what was the point of doing this, becoming lovers with Danny Butler? Did his body have that much control over him? Could lust drive him this far off the path he'd chosen for himself?

But it wasn't just lust, and he damn well knew it. He liked being around Danny. Liked the way he sounded and the way he smelled and the way he made Miller feel… like someone finally understood him. Like he finally had a friend.

Maybe it would all work out fine. No one would ever have to know. It would be their secret, something they shared while they were stuck together in this apartment. It would end when Danny testified and they could both enjoy it while it lasted. No need to make it more than it was.

Are you out of your mind? What the hell are you talking about? You honestly think—

But Miller silenced the voice by action. He opened the door.

DANNY waited in the kitchen until he heard the sliding glass door close. He took a sip of coffee, wincing at the bitter taste. He didn't even really like the stuff, but he'd started drinking it when he was sixteen because it made him feel grown up. And now he needed the caffeine, just like he needed the nicotine—he'd started smoking at fifteen for the same reason.

He figured Miller was talking to Rachel; otherwise why would he be out on the balcony? Or maybe the conversation was about him. Maybe Miller was making arrangements to leave, have someone else take over this job. The thought made Danny's hand clench around the coffee mug. He couldn't imagine sharing this small space with anyone but Miller, couldn't imagine someone else stepping in to take his place.

Danny left his mug on the counter, poking his head into the living room to find Miller still outside, his hair dusted with white. It was early for the first snowfall, but Danny wasn't complaining. He wouldn't have to drive in it and he loved the way the snow always made everything so quiet and clean, like the whole city was starting over.

Danny watched as Miller tipped his head back, eyes on the sky. Danny could see his lips move, but only the faintest murmur carried through the glass door. Miller spoke again and then tucked his phone into his pocket, turning toward the door and Danny, who couldn't pull his eyes away. He'd never wanted someone the way he wanted Miller, had never been so scared about what it all meant. He'd thought he was done with caring about people, with hurting them because he was lonely and needed to feel connected, even if it only lasted a little while. After Ortiz and Amanda he'd had enough, had promised himself never again.

Pretty soon you're going to be gone from here, anyway. Disappeared into the wide world. No more Danny Butler. So what's the harm? What's the harm in pushing forward?

But Danny knew what the harm was. He knew exactly what Miller had meant the night before when he'd said he wanted to be the man he was before he met Danny. Danny didn't have anything to lose, but Miller had a career at stake and a woman who loved him. What could Danny offer to compete with that, except a few weeks of rolling around on a bed? Was he going to end Miller's career, force him into admissions about himself he wasn't ready to make, leave him without even Rachel for comfort?

Why the fuck are you always worrying about him? You should be more worried about yourself. You're the one with your life on the line. You wouldn't have to testify if Miller's boss knew about last night. Hinestroza would probably be amused by the poetic justice of you sacrificing an FBI agent's career on his behalf. That might be just the kind of offering he'd need to welcome you back into the fold. No indictment with his name on it, and an FBI agent ruined. He'd love it, Danny, you know he would.

The voice was sneering and cocky, Danny's interrogation-room voice, the one he used on cops and lawyers, the one that had grown quieter with each day he'd spent near Miller Sutton. That voice had served him well for a long span of years; it had kept him alive and kept him strong. But it was an intruder in this private space he'd created with Miller, and he hated hearing it again, back at full volume, proving it wasn't gone but had only been waiting for an opportunity to remind him of the man he'd been for so long.

Danny imagined what it would be like to betray Miller. It would mean not having to worry about Madrigal finding him and handing down his own brand of torturous justice. Danny could step back into his old life, work for Hinestroza again. He pictured the look on Miller's face when he found out what Danny had done, all the warmth gone from those familiar gray eyes. It would mean proving all Miller's preconceived notions right, solidifying his belief that he'd be a fool to take a risk on someone like Danny.

Danny had spent his life making shitty, spur-of-the-moment decisions: getting into the car with Hinestroza; being lonely enough to say yes to Ortiz; marrying a beautiful girl with a red flower in her hair. And look where those decisions had led. His own young self, so full of dreams, was a criminal now, forever branded; Amanda, bitter and broken; and Ortiz... dead on a dirty warehouse floor. Danny looked down and then back up into Miller's eyes, still staring at him from the other side of the door, one hand pressed against the glass. And Danny realized maybe Miller wasn't the only one with a decision to make about the man he wanted to be from here on out.

Miller opened the door. Cold air swirling with snow followed him into the warm apartment and raced across the room to smack against Danny's face. Miller stood across from him, shucking off his coat after a long beat of stillness, white flakes melting in his hair.

Danny knew this was the moment, that whatever was done now could not be undone. They would both have to live with whatever decision was reached. This was the moment when it would all really begin or it was the moment when it would finally end.

"Danny…." Miller's voice cracked. He glanced away, his eyes bouncing from floor to wall to ceiling and then returning to Danny, locking on tight. "Danny… I…." His face looked so fragile; one wrong move and he'd break like a thin sheet of glass or an early morning cobweb or a dream. It made Danny want to be careful, his passion overwhelmed by tenderness.

"I'm right here, Miller," he said softly. "I'm standing right in front of you."

This time, Miller didn't hesitate. He charged around the sofa barrier, his body ramming up hard against Danny's, his hands spreading wide across Danny's bare back. Danny shivered, smiling into Miller's seeking mouth. "You and your cold hands."

"Sorry." Miller's slow smile made goose bumps blossom on Danny's skin. He eased his hands off Danny's back and brought them up to cradle Danny's face. Danny held Miller the same way, eyes closed, foreheads touching, breathing in unison.

"I don't know what I'm doing," Miller whispered, his words wobbly and drunk with uncertainty.

Danny's heart clenched. He knew that Miller was talking about more than just the physical; he understood how hard it was for Miller to let go of his need to control the future. "It's okay," he whispered back, fingers trailing down Miller's face. "We'll figure it out. It'll be okay."

He lifted his mouth to Miller's, outlining Miller's lips with his tongue. Before Miller, it had been a long time since he had kissed anyone. Kissing wasn't on the top of his priority list with the men he occasionally brought home for an hour or two. With those men, he was looking to satisfy his most basic needs; he wasn't searching for anything more intimate, didn't care about faking a connection he knew wasn't there.

But Miller's mouth was the part of him Danny found he craved the most. He loved the smoky flavor of his tongue, the way those lips Miller held so serious and stiff in real life turned swollen and soft when Danny sucked them between his own. Miller stuck his index fingers through Danny's belt loops, tugging him toward the sofa.

Danny shook his head. "Bed," he murmured against Miller's lips, walking backward into his own room and bringing Miller along with him.

All their clothes came off this time, no legs hampered by constricting jeans, their bodies not restricted by unaccommodating furniture. Danny pulled Miller down next to him on the bed. He thought maybe he shouldn't stare, had a fleeting worry that Miller might be shy, but he couldn't stop himself. He had to see.

Miller was beautiful; there was no other way to describe him. All long legs, lean muscle, and golden skin. His eyes cloudy and deep and full of secrets, and his hair ever so faintly brushed by the sun.

Miller put pressure on Danny's shoulder, easing him down onto his body, Danny moving his hips to line everything up right. They lay that way for a moment, arms outstretched, every inch of their bodies touching, joined together from feet to hands. Danny sighed into Miller's neck as they rocked against each other.

He propped himself up on his elbows, then dipped his head and licked the base of Miller's throat, felt the blood pulsing under Miller's skin. He ran his tongue up over the rumbling he heard, meeting Miller's groan as it escaped his mouth, swallowing it with his own.

"Do you want to fuck me?" Danny whispered. He understood the impact of his question, his words falling like stones into a shadowy lake—on the surface things return to normal, but in the deep the landscape is forever altered.

Miller's hands flexed on Danny's waist, the gray of his eyes taken hostage by his dilated pupils, his ribcage pounding against Danny's. "Yes," he said, rough and hoarse. "God, yes." He paused. "But I don't have anything."

Danny smiled. He scooted his body off Miller's, hating to leave the warmth behind, and reached for his wallet on the unsteady bedside table. "I've only got one," he said, pulling out the foil square between index and middle fingers.

Miller laughed, a hand coming up to tug gently on Danny's earring. "Who the fuck does that in real life? Carries one in their wallet?"

"Me, asshole. And aren't you glad I do?"

"Yes," Miller admitted, his eyes sparkling. "Now come here."

Danny left the condom on the table and rolled his body into Miller's, their mouths coming together. Danny's leg curved over Miller's hip as he stroked a hand down Miller's side, dipping into the hollow of his waist.

Danny had never been to bed with a man who hadn't had long practice at touching another man's body, the role of teacher one Danny was unaccustomed to performing. But he discovered he liked showing Miller the way. And it turned out Miller was teaching him, too, somehow making this act, which Danny had done so many times before, seem fresh and newly discovered, like something they'd created all on their own.

Miller's tongue found Danny's tattoo again, slithering along the snake, the welcome weight of his body pressing Danny into the mattress.

"I've always hated that thing," Danny said with a muted laugh. "But you might make me change my mind."

He felt Miller smile against his skin. "I love looking at it." He paused, and Danny could feel a flare of heat from Miller's cheek pressed against his back. "You're the fucking sexiest thing I've ever seen, Danny," he whispered, his fingers still caressing the painted skin.

Danny groaned. It wasn't the words that caused the reaction, but the fact that Miller felt free enough to say them. But Miller wasn't done, his voice scraping rough along Danny's back. "I get hard just watching you walk across the room."

Danny sucked in a strangled gulp of air, not able to fill his lungs.

"Show me," he breathed. "Show me how hard you get."

It happened fast. Miller ripped into foil with his teeth, lotion from the jar by Danny's bed rubbed on with shaking hands, Danny down on knees and elbows. He felt Miller hesitate, right on the brink.

"It's all right," Danny reassured him, his voice low. "I'm ready. You won't hurt me."

But whatever Danny had expected it wasn't this, Miller barely pushing in at first, sliding so slow and smooth, coughing out a gasping wail as he entered Danny's body. Nothing in Danny's life had ever felt so goddamn good, so inevitable, so right. He turned his face into the pillow and moaned deep in his throat.

"No," Miller said, startling him into raising his head, turning to glance at Miller over his shoulder. "No," Miller repeated, his eyes on fire. "I want to hear you. I want to hear the sounds you make."

"Jesus... Miller," Danny groaned, right on the edge of coming from words alone.

Miller pulled out as slowly as he'd pushed in. He thrust forward hard this time, all the way, Danny's back arching as he pressed himself against Miller. "Fuck, yes," Danny moaned, not holding back. And Miller wasn't holding back, either, grunting with each thrust, his fingers biting into Danny's hips, his hands clutching hard enough that Danny knew they would leave purple finger shadows behind when it was over. But Danny didn't mind being Miller's anchor; he liked knowing he was the one giving Miller something he so desperately needed and had never found anywhere else.

Miller shifted his weight, entering Danny at a new angle, plunging deep. Danny cried out, a choked, sobbing sound, his hands knotting in the sheets. "Oh, Christ, Miller, yes... right there, right there."

Miller pounded into him, releasing one hand's grip to stroke Danny in his fist. Danny didn't know if he could stand it, the pleasure almost at the point of pain. The sensations overwhelmed his body, swamping his senses—the spicy cinnamon scent of Miller's skin, Miller's rough palm working against him, Miller's guttural groans as he moved inside him, filling him up, cool drops of sweat falling from

Miller's face onto his burning back.

Danny's orgasm hit him like a crack of thunder, the sensation both unexpected and anticipated, a sudden clenching of his body, reverberating outwards and stealing his breath. His head fell down onto the bed, mouth open and gasping for air as he let it all go in Miller's hand.

Miller thrust forward once more and shouted out Danny's name, surging forward to rest his face against Danny's heaving back. Crushed between Miller's deadweight and his own laboring lungs, Danny could barely take in a breath. But he didn't want to move from this spot, didn't want to leave this moment with Miller still inside him, his heavy exhales stirring the hair at Danny's neck. Miller finally released his grip on Danny's hip, his hand crawling upward to capture Danny's own, their fingers lacing together easily.

Danny was already half-asleep when Miller slid off his body. He heard the faint snap of latex as Miller took care of the condom, and then Miller was back against him, rolling them both onto their sides. Miller pushed one leg between his, brought an arm around to find his hand again, and kissed his shoulder as they settled into sleep.

Danny closed his eyes. He felt safe and protected, strong and brave. It was only the two of them now, enclosed in their own little world. Anonymous men in a nondescript apartment, snow falling heavily against the windows, already muting the tenor of the city. The occasional car passing below released only the faintest whisper, the only sound the hushed murmur of their breathing.

HINESTROZA answered on the third ring. "Hello?" he demanded, static and impatience marring his deep voice.

Madrigal had thought he wouldn't be there and had moved on to the next task on his agenda while the phone rang in his ear. With a rough snort the white powder was up his nose, making him cough lightly into the receiver. "I have a lead on Danny."

"What is it?"

Madrigal glanced out the window at the snow piling up against the curb. "I paid off some flunky clerk at the police station downtown to let me take a look at the recent reports. I figured Danny couldn't stay out of trouble for long. Turns out I was right. Some concerned citizen out walking his dog last night was accosted by two men. One had a gun, the other flashed a badge and said he was an FBI agent. The dog walker thought he was lying, but I'm guessing he wasn't."

"Any descriptions?"

"No, he couldn't read the name on the badge and the FBI guy was wearing a hat. He remembered the man with the gun had an earring, though, and black hair."

Hinestroza laughed. "I told Danny I hated that earring."

"Tomorrow I'll start nosing around the neighborhood. Shouldn't take me more than a few days to figure out where they are. In the meantime, I had the clerk pull the report. We don't want anybody giving the FBI a heads-up." Madrigal paused, wiped his bloody nose on the back of his hand. "What do you want me to do with the agent?"

"I don't care," Hinestroza said. "Something quick is fine. But with Danny… I want to make sure Danny appreciates how very deeply he has disappointed me. You understand?"

"I understand." Madrigal smiled. "It won't be a problem." He used his fingers to carve Danny's initials in the frosty glass. He liked the snow; it wiped away his tracks. He could go anywhere he wanted, and by morning there would be no evidence of his passing.

CHAPTER 10

"*WHAT the hell do you think you're doing?*" *Danny demanded, his voice coming out louder than he intended, anger echoing off his vocal cords.*

"*What do you mean?*" *Ortiz's eyes pinballed in his head, hands shaking as he folded his arms across his chest.*

"*I saw you,*" *Danny hissed.* "*I saw you with him.*"

"*Who?*"

Danny bit down on his exasperation. "*What do you mean, who? You see anyone else around here?*" *He jerked his head toward the table behind Ortiz where Madrigal watched their exchange with bland boredom.*

"*We were just hanging out,*" *Ortiz said too quickly.* "*Waiting for you.*"

"*Then what's that white stuff around your nose, Ortiz?*"

Ortiz's hand flew upward, rubbing hard against his skin. He wouldn't look Danny in the eye.

"*How long have you been snorting coke?*"

"*I don't know.*" *Ortiz shrugged, his manner that of a teenager caught in a lie, snappish and dismissive.*

Danny spat out his disgust on the stained concrete floor. "*Jesus.*"

"*What's the big fucking deal? Madrigal does it all the time.*"

"*So what?*" *Danny lowered his voice.* "*You want to end up like him?*"

"*He's doing okay,*" *Ortiz said.*

"*He kills people for a living and he can't go more than a couple of hours without a nosebleed!"*

"Hey!" Madrigal called from his seat at the table. "Watch your fucking mouth, Danny." But he sounded amused, letting Danny know by the tone of his voice how very little he thought of him, Danny a mere mouse to Madrigal's big, bad wolf.

Danny kept his gaze pinned on Ortiz. "Come on, I'll take you home. He can finish up here."

Ortiz looked at Danny, his eyes empty and distant. "No, you go on. Madrigal can give me a ride after we're done unloading."

"Ortiz, wait—" But he was already moving away, back into the dark depths of the warehouse.

Danny should have known he was using; the signs had been right in front of him for months now. Ortiz always hyper and agitated, calling Danny in the middle of the night, wanting to talk. He constantly complained about being short on cash, hitting Danny up for money whenever he could. But Danny had made himself blind to the evidence, hadn't wanted to believe. He'd just been glad Ortiz was talking again, finally opening his mouth instead of staring straight ahead with nothing to say. He hadn't wanted to question the reason behind the change.

Ever since Ortiz's daughter had died the previous winter, he'd been vacant, barely registering as alive. His daughter and wife had still been living in the two-room shack when she got pneumonia. She hadn't lived to celebrate her fifth birthday, Ortiz's dream of giving them a better life buried in an unmarked grave he would probably never see. His wife blamed him, convinced that if he'd worked harder and sent more money home, their daughter would still be alive, and maybe she was right.

Ortiz stopped caring after that. The job he'd taken to save his family became just one more shackle he couldn't escape, one more debt he was going to have to pay. And now he was hanging around Madrigal, his thin body hunched over a rickety card table, snorting white powder up his nose.

Danny stood on the threshold, debating with himself. Should he go in, drag Ortiz out? Or should he let him make his own decisions? He was a grown man, after all. In the end, Danny turned and walked away—left his friend to journey deeper into the shadow lands and did not one damn thing to block his way.

MILLER woke before Danny, the absolute quiet startling him out of sleep. His leg, pressed between Danny's, was numb, and he withdrew it slowly, straightening it out against the cool sheets, wiggling his toes and cringing at the sting of newly awakened flesh. Danny was still spooned against his body, his breathing deep and even. Miller ran two fingers down either side of his spine, the bones beneath Danny's skin laid out like a string of pearls.

Well, you did it, Miller... had sex with another man. You've crossed that great divide. Definitely no going back. And you finally understand what Scott was talking about all those years ago, about sex being "mind-blowing."

It all made sense to Miller now, the way people were so obsessed with sex, why they killed and died over it, thought and dreamed of it. Up until now he'd never understood, hadn't truly appreciated his body's capacity for pleasure. Something in the mysterious combination of Danny and him burned hotter and brighter than anything he'd ever imagined. When he'd had sex with Danny it had felt like the path he was always supposed to have taken had suddenly been revealed to him; a fork in the road that up until that moment had been overgrown and hidden was now clearly visible.

Miller propped himself up on one elbow and watched Danny sleep. He looked young and innocent despite the tattoos and scars, his full mouth curving up slightly, his face relaxed. He was sexy even in slumber, and Miller gave in to the urge to touch him, nuzzling against his ear, kissing the soft corner of his mouth.

Danny came around by inches, his long body stretching against the bed as he turned onto his back, his eyes lighting up when they landed on Miller. "Hey, you," he whispered, running a warm hand along Miller's jaw.

"Hey," Miller murmured in response, wanting to preserve the quiet, not wanting to disturb the lazy green of Danny's eyes. They studied each other for a silent minute. Miller waited for the rush of awkwardness, the claustrophobic certainty that this had all been a mistake, but it didn't come. Instead there was simply the knowledge that, for the first time in recent memory, he was happy.

"You doing all right?" Danny asked, his voice a caress.

"Yeah." Miller smiled. "I'm doing fine."

Danny smiled back, a sweet, boyish smile that made Miller's heart trampoline into his throat. "Is it still snowing?"

Miller craned his neck to look out the window, swirling white the only visible landmark. "Still coming down hard."

"Guess we'd better stay in bed, then," Danny said, low and suggestive. "Although you're going to have to venture out at least once."

"Why?"

"We need food and… other necessities." Danny's eyes flickered to the torn foil wrapper on the bedside table. "I only had the one, remember?"

Miller groaned, flopping down onto his back.

"Well, I guess you don't *have* to go out." Danny leaned over him with a smile. "We can just skip the sex."

"Fuck that," Miller growled. "I'm going."

Danny laughed, lowering his head, his tongue coming quietly into Miller's mouth. "Just so you know," he said, pulling back slightly, "I'm clean. After prison I started getting tested regularly."

Miller already knew; he'd seen Danny's medical records. But having sex without a condom seemed like making a pledge, promising a part of himself to Danny that he couldn't deliver. "Okay," he said. "But for now I think we should still use something."

"Yeah," Danny agreed; he didn't seem upset.

"I should probably head out before the snow gets worse." But he didn't make a move to leave, instead wrapping one arm around Danny, his hand finding the old scar on Danny's lower back, the skin raised and velvety under his fingers. "You got this one in Marion, right?"

Shades of Gray | 137

Danny nodded.

"How?"

Danny took a deep breath, eyes on a spot above Miller's head. "The first time they came after me, I fought back. Stupid in hindsight, considering there were four of them and only one of me. I knew I couldn't win, but I wanted to go down trying." He gave a sad, haunted smile. "They did what they wanted anyway, then knifed me in the back as a reminder not to fight again."

Miller closed his eyes. He didn't want to imagine Danny used that way, those men taking the intimate act he and Danny had just done together and turning it into something so ugly and hurtful. When he opened his eyes Danny was still looking away, his jaw clenched. "I'm sorry, Danny," he whispered, the weight of sorrow heavy behind his eyelids.

Danny turned his angry gaze downward. "I told you before not to feel sorry for me."

"It's not pity," Miller said. "I just wish it hadn't happened to you. There's a difference." He kissed Danny softly, moving his arm up Danny's back, hand settling in Danny's hair. "How'd you get this one?" he asked when they broke away, his fingers sifting through the black strands for the silky battle scar he knew was there.

"That one's from Leavenworth. I got in a fight in the kitchen with another guy and he hit me in the face. That's how I got this little one above my lip too," Danny pointed. "Then he popped me in the back of the head with part of a wooden chair. No real damage, but it bled like hell."

"He fractured your skull," Miller reminded him.

Danny seemed unimpressed with his own injury. "It wasn't that bad."

"What was the fight about?"

"In prison the fights don't have to be *about* anything. Probably he was just having a shitty day."

Miller's free hand moved down Danny's torso, sliding over his stomach, heading toward his leg. He could feel Danny tensing up before his hand reached its destination. He ran a finger across the horizontal scar on Danny's inner thigh. Danny flinched at the touch.

"It doesn't still hurt, does it?" Miller whispered.

"No." Danny's voice was as pinched as his face.

"How'd you get it?"

Danny shook his head, his lips pressed together tight. "I don't talk about that one." Miller heard the *not even to you* without it being spoken.

The scar was older than the others, the white line paler and more settled into Danny's skin. Instinctively Miller knew the injury had something to do with Ortiz, was tied somehow to Danny's claim of having killed someone a long time ago.

Push him, Miller. His defenses are down. He'll tell you. Push him.

Miller the FBI agent needed the answers. But Miller the man didn't want to ask the questions—didn't want to invite the cop and the criminal into the domain of Miller and Danny.

When Miller was a little boy, his mother would tell stories to Junie at night, fairy tales about princes on white horses rescuing the fair maiden in the tower or saving her from the gnarled hands of the evil witch. Scott thought the stories were stupid and never stuck around to listen. But Miller always curled up next to Junie on her pink sheets to hear their mother spin her tales. It wasn't the stories themselves he had found so fascinating, except for the ones where dragons spouted fire and had teeth like splintered needles. It was his mother's voice he'd loved and the spell she'd seemed to effortlessly weave, like a glimmering cloud all around them in the dim bedroom, creating a world that was safe and enchanted, where every ending was happily ever after. When she'd died the spell had been broken, and he had never found anyone who could cast it again. Until now, until Danny. What they had together, right in this moment, felt like magic, and Miller didn't want to be the one to break the spell.

MILLER had been on hold for ten minutes, the tooth-rotting sweetness of elevator music blasting into his ear. He took a swig from his nearly empty beer bottle, the remains of the early dinner he and Danny had shared spread out on the table. With his free hand he carried dishes to the sink, giving them a half-hearted rinse while he waited.

"Um… you still there?" The clerk sounded harried; he'd probably been hoping Miller had given up by now.

"Yeah."

"No, I don't see anything like that. No reports from that precinct fitting the description you gave me."

"You sure?" Miller demanded.

"Uh, yeah, yeah," the clerk stammered. "I'm sure."

The man's nervousness didn't raise Miller's eyebrows. He was used to the powers of his FBI badge.

The bathroom door opened and Danny stepped out, naked except for the white towel at his waist, the damp turning his hair midnight black. He smiled at Miller as he walked to his bedroom, his back sparkling with water droplets.

"Okay. Well, if a report like that comes in, I want you to call me." Miller gave the clerk his name again and his office phone number before hanging up.

He could hear Danny singing in the bedroom, belting out some off-key tune; might have been the Rolling Stones, but it was hard to tell. Abandoning the idea of cleaning up, he watched from the doorway as Danny rooted around in the dresser for clothes, his personal concert continuing unabated.

Miller smiled, resting one shoulder against the doorjamb. "Between your singing and the elevator music I was just listening to, I'm thinking I should get hazard pay."

Danny grinned in his direction. "Any reports from our dog-walker friend?"

Miller shook his head. "No." He paused. "Your back's still wet."

Danny's hot gaze landed on him. "You want to take care of that for me?"

Miller shoved away from the door, moving forward until they

were almost touching. "I don't have a towel."

Danny's eyes made a slow-motion trek down and then back up again. "Guess you'll have to use this one."

Miller yanked the towel from Danny's waist, causing Danny to stumble forward, their chests bumping together. Danny didn't move as Miller reached behind to dry his wet shoulders, the towel moving lower until Miller let it fall to the floor, his hands continuing the journey southward.

"Lean back," he whispered, his tongue gliding across Danny's lips. "Against the wall."

Danny did it without question, his naked body moving backward as Miller went down on his knees. Miller ran his hands up Danny's thighs, the skin damp and warm, the coarse hair curling against his fingers, the scent of Danny's body soapy and strong. He let his tongue play follow-the-leader behind his hands, up Danny's thigh, across his stomach, and down the other leg. With one finger, he stroked down the length of Danny's cock as lightly as he could, barely touching, smoothing away the wetness at the tip. Danny's head hit the wall with a thump, and Miller smiled.

"Jesus, Miller," Danny moaned. "What the hell are you waiting for?"

"Haven't you ever heard of delayed gratification?" he asked, his voice a low rumble against Danny's upper thigh.

Danny looked down at him and gave his hair a good-natured tug. "Haven't you ever heard of a cock tease?"

Miller laughed, taking Danny into his mouth before the chuckle died in his throat. "Ah, fuck," Danny managed. His hand spasmed against Miller's scalp, yanking hard. "God, that's so good."

If someone had told Miller a month ago that he'd willingly be on his knees in front of another man, loving the taste, reveling in the sounds, he'd have laughed in their face right before he shattered their nose. And yet here he was, and it felt like where he belonged. He'd tried this for the first time on that snowy afternoon three days ago. He'd been scared, worried, and excited when he'd first taken Danny into his mouth. He knew that this act, having Danny against his tongue, was something no straight man would ever do or at least would never admit to doing.

It had been surprisingly hard work that first time, his shoulder screaming by the end as he bent over Danny on the bed, his jaw aching, his gag reflex kicking in when he took Danny too deep. He'd never realized how much work it was, and he'd been hit with a sudden flash of empathy for the drunken girls he'd known in college who'd spent long minutes on their knees. But beyond the effort there was pleasure, too; hot embers burning under his skin as he watched Danny's reactions, heard him moaning. All of it filled Miller with the desire to give Danny everything he wanted.

And already he was better at it, only days later; more confident, looser, learning what Danny liked, what made him groan down deep in his throat the way that caused Miller's cock to twitch in response. It was more now than just a longing to please Danny; having Danny in his mouth was what pleased him too.

Danny spread his legs, allowing Miller room to stroke, to work a finger behind. Danny was panting hard, huffing out each breath as Miller sucked, tongue flicking over the slit, drawing Danny in as far as he could. Danny's hips made little jerking movements as he lost control.

Danny breathed out a sound, something between a sigh and a moan, and passed a thumb across Miller's eyebrow. Miller looked up at him through lowered lashes. He knew Danny was close to coming, could feel it in the tightening around his finger. Danny's tongue curled over his top lip as he heaved in air, his hands clenching convulsively against the wall. "Oh, Christ, Miller," he groaned, his eyes going liquid and dark as he spurted into Miller's mouth. The hot spray coated Miller's throat; the thought of moving back or spitting it out never crossed his mind.

He rested his head against Danny's stomach, Danny's fingers playing lightly in his hair. Miller's knees cracked as he stood and leaned his body into Danny's, pinning him to the wall with his weight. Danny reached between their bodies to stroke Miller through his jeans. "I like tasting me in your mouth," Danny whispered as they kissed.

Miller moaned. Danny's hair was still wet under his fingers, his hips grinding forward as Danny sucked hard against his tongue. He loved it when Danny talked that way. It made him feel powerful and wanted, like his touch ignited some secret part of Danny that belonged only to him.

Danny pulled Miller's shirt from his jeans, working his fingers against the soft skin of his lower back, pushing under his waistband. "You're overdressed," he murmured into Miller's neck.

They set about remedying that, and Miller was down to his shorts when his cell phone rang, a muffled jangling from the pile of clothes on the floor.

"Ignore it," Danny said, lips on Miller's nipple.

"Fuck, can't," Miller groaned. "Don't go anywhere."

Danny laughed, throwing himself backward onto the bed, head propped on one bent arm as he watched Miller answer the call.

"Hello?"

"Miller, it's Colin." His voice was serious, nothing remotely friendly in the tone.

"What's going on?" Ice cubes barreled into Miller's stomach, smothering the lust fire burning there.

"We got a complaint in at the Bureau. A man out walking his dog in that neighborhood a few nights ago said he was threatened by two men. One claimed to be an FBI agent, the other had a gun." Silence on the line. "You know anything about that?"

Miller sunk onto the bed, resting his forehead in one hand. "Yeah, that was us," he said wearily. "Danny and me."

"What the fuck, Miller?" Colin exploded. "You know protocol! You should have reported it the second it happened!"

"It wasn't that big of a deal."

"*Not that big of a deal?* He had a gun!"

This was it; all his years of training and loyalty to his job ramming up hard against a few weeks of Danny Butler.

"No, Danny didn't have a gun," Miller said. His brain might be tripping over the words, but his tongue didn't appear to have a similar problem. "It was a can of mace I'd given him because he was nervous when I left the apartment. The guy walking his dog overreacted."

"A can of mace?"

"Yeah."

"Uh-huh," Colin said slowly, waiting for Miller to jump into the silence. But Miller was a master at that old game. He could lock his lips with the best of them.

"He shouldn't have been outside in the first place, Miller."

"I know, but he was going stir-crazy. I'm allowed to use my discretion, right?"

"Right."

"Well, I thought letting him take a quick walk around the block after dark was better than him losing it in here and heading out on his own at some point."

"It still should have been reported," Colin reminded him again, but his hurricane voice had died down to a blustery wind.

"I know. I'll get something on file tomorrow."

"The dog walker made a complaint at the local police station too."

Miller scrunched up his brow. "I checked there today, they said there wasn't any report."

"Trying to cover your tracks?"

"No," Miller said honestly. "I just didn't want any information getting out that could be traced back to us. I figured he hadn't reported it to the Bureau yet or I'd have heard."

"Maybe he meant he was planning on reporting it to the local police." Miller could hear the scratch of pen against paper. "I'll double-check."

"Okay."

Colin sighed. "I'm only going to ask you this one more time. Do I need to pull you off this case?"

Miller looked over his shoulder at Danny, laid out naked on the bed, his green eyes worried, his lips red and swollen from Miller's stubble. "No," he said, not taking his eyes off Danny. "No."

"Next time I won't ask," Colin warned. "I'll pull you. Got it?"

"Got it," Miller replied. He tossed the phone aside, kneading his forehead with stiff fingers.

They'd managed to keep the real world at bay for seventy-two hours; that was all. Three days with no talk of Rachel or Danny's plans or where they were going from here. Talking around the future, the consequences, and the way their bodies fit together just right. But now reality was back, stronger than ever, like a neglected dog nipping at their heels, refusing to be ignored.

The bed shifted under Miller as Danny moved closer, his lips pressing into the juncture of Miller's neck and shoulder, tongue stroking lightly. He knew it was Danny's way of saying thank you, recognizing Miller's sacrifice on his behalf.

"I need to do the dishes," he said, easing away from Danny's touch. He felt old all of a sudden, worn down.

"Miller...."

He pulled on his jeans, not bothering to fasten them. "Just... let me do the dishes, Danny. Okay?" Miller always craved space when he was upset, time to battle his own demons. Rachel never could accept that, always pushing him to talk, wanting to "work through it together," when all he wanted was to be left alone.

But Danny only nodded and let him retreat to the kitchen to soothe himself with a mindless task, calm himself with the repetition of rinse and dry.

"PHONE," Danny mumbled, his mouth pressed against the warm smoothness of Miller's chest. "Phone," he said again, louder, using the arm stretched across Miller's body to shake him awake.

"Hm... what?"

"Phone."

"Shit." Miller scooted out from under Danny, who, even more than half-asleep, was not able to stop himself from admiring Miller's muscles as he shoved himself upright, his body illuminated by the faint glow from the kitchen.

Danny rolled over, easing his way back into sleep when the sharp crack of Miller's voice knocked him into full consciousness.

"What?" Miller said, his voice humming with anxiety. Danny sat up, rubbing his face with one hand. "Okay," Miller agreed with whoever was on the other end of the line. "Okay. I'll call you when we're clear."

Miller grabbed his jeans from the floor. "We have to go, Danny. Now."

Danny moved off the bed, grabbing his own pants, yanking them on with hurried hands. "What? Why?"

"Madrigal knows where we are. Or he's pretty damn close."

"Fuck," Danny said, the air snatched from his lungs with an icy hand.

They dressed in silence, keeping the room dark. Danny took his gun from the top dresser drawer and stuck it in his waistband. "Do we take anything?" he asked.

Miller threw Danny's duffel onto the bed. "Whatever you can pack in ten seconds," he said.

Danny tossed in a couple pairs of jeans, a handful of T-shirts and underwear, and his wallet. "Done."

"Grab the condoms," Miller said, pointing to the bedside table.

Danny never thought he'd laugh in a situation like this, with fear snapping fiercely through his blood. "What?" he asked with a strangled chuckle.

"They'll come afterwards and clean the place out. I can't have them finding that stuff."

Danny followed Miller into the living room, waiting by the front door while Miller grabbed his jacket from the back of a kitchen chair and snatched his keys and wallet from the counter. "Let's go."

The hallway was dim and quiet when they eased out the door. Miller pointed with his gun toward the stairs, motioning for Danny to follow behind. The adrenaline was pumping now, Danny's hand squeezing his own weapon, blood rushing in his ears. They made it outside without passing a soul—not surprising since it was three in the morning—but thankfully not bumping into Madrigal hiding behind a corner, either.

"This way," Miller whispered once they were on the street, gesturing toward his Jeep four cars down. They hugged the building, keeping away from the streetlights and making friends with the shadows.

"Give me your keys," Danny said when they reached the Jeep.

"What? No," Miller protested.

"I'm a good driver, Miller," Danny said, as patiently as he could. "I've been in a lot of tight situations. You want me driving."

"I can drive the car, Danny," Miller scoffed, unlocking the doors.

"I'm not saying you can't. I'm saying I can drive it better." He could see Miller was going to argue with him, not believing the incident would escalate now that they'd escaped the apartment unscathed. But Danny knew better; Madrigal was closing in.

"Right now," Danny said, low and urgent. "Give me the fucking keys." Something in his voice convinced Miller, because he tossed the key ring into Danny's outstretched hand. Danny moved to the driver's door and pulled it open. He heard it then, so quiet it might have been his imagination, the faint click of a car door opening down the block. But it had been real, and he knew who was coming.

"Get in," Danny hissed, watching as Miller dove into the car, a bullet whistling through the space his head had just occupied.

"Shit!" Danny threw himself behind the wheel, pulling the car out into the deserted street with a screech of tires, fumbling on the dashboard for the lights.

"He's behind us," Miller said, craning his neck to look out the back window. Danny could see headlights in his rearview mirror as Madrigal's car pulled out into the street.

"Put on your seat belt," Danny said, his voice even. "Once you're strapped in, hold the wheel so I can put on mine."

Miller did what Danny asked, not questioning his instructions, steering one-handed as Danny pulled the seat belt over his lap. Danny glanced once in Miller's direction. "You ready for this?" he asked, voice grim.

Miller nodded, eyes grave on Danny's.

"Okay," Danny replied. "Hold on." He allowed himself one moment of pure terror, panic flowing through his veins like poison, freezing his heart to the point he thought it might shatter inside his chest.

You fuck this up, Danny, and you die. And just behind that thought, one even worse. *You fuck this up, Danny, and **he** dies.*

He pushed the fear away, tightening his whole body against it the same way he had as a child when he'd heard his father's heavy tread on the stairs, the old man's brass belt buckle whacking against the walls to give Danny advance notice of exactly what he had coming; the same way he had when he'd been pulled over with a U-Haul full of cocaine and talked his way out of a search and a one-way ticket to life in prison; the same way he'd walked into the yard at Marion and faced men who had only a single thought in their minds when it came to Danny Butler. Danny was no stranger to the metallic taste of terror. He knew how to be brave.

He jammed his foot against the accelerator and the Jeep surged forward. Danny thanked God the bulk of the snow had melted and the roads were clear. He spun the wheel hard to the left, taking a side street at the last moment, not wanting to give Madrigal any advance warning. The car skidded hard, Danny going with the momentum, the back end fishtailing as he completed the turn.

"Still there," Miller said, his eyes on the side view mirror.

"Is he alone?"

"I think so." Miller twisted in his seat, taking aim with his gun. "I'm going for his tires."

"Fuck that. Go for his head." Danny's voice was cold and detached, all his fire directed toward survival.

"I can't get a clear shot. He's ducking down."

Madrigal obviously didn't have the same reservations, because the back window of the Jeep exploded inward, spraying Danny's neck with rough pebbles of safety glass.

"Fuck!" Miller shouted, one hand coming up to cover his face.

"You okay?" Danny asked hoarsely, looking out of the corner of his eye.

"Yeah. Fuck," Miller said again, wiping away the thin trail of blood leaking down his face. "Where are you going?" Miller asked as Danny made a hard right, barreling past dark storefronts, blasting through red lights on mercifully empty streets.

"Highway."

"No!" Miller exclaimed. "Too much traffic."

"Not this time of night. How good a shot are you?"

"Good," Miller replied.

"We can get up a lot more speed on the highway. It'll be harder for him to get off a decent shot. Can you hit a tire if I slow down enough?" Danny could feel Miller watching him. "Do you trust me?" he asked, eyes on the road.

"Yes."

"Can you hit a tire?"

"Yes."

Danny nodded, flexing his hands on the wheel. "All right, then."

He took the entrance ramp to the highway at one hundred and fifteen miles an hour, blowing past a semi, veering around the cluster of cars going sixty. A quick glance in the rearview mirror showed Madrigal still on his tail.

Danny stuck to the far right lane, slowly easing off the accelerator. Miller pivoted in his seat, balancing his arms on the back of the seat as he aimed out the nonexistent back window. He fired, five shots in rapid succession, the echo in Danny's head drowned out by the sudden explosion as a bullet found its target. Danny slammed his foot back onto the gas, heading for the approaching exit. He could hear the ear-splitting squeal of tires on pavement, Madrigal's car weaving drunkenly across the highway as he fought for control. Danny took the exit, the Jeep bouncing over the low hill. Danny's neck snapped forward at the impact, his teeth rattling as his jaw locked down hard.

They drove in silence for several minutes, Danny constantly

checking the rearview mirror to make sure they weren't followed.

"Maybe he's dead," Miller said finally.

"He's not dead."

"How do you know?"

Danny shrugged, gripping the wheel with iron hands to stop the shaking. "I doubt he even wrecked. He's like one of those horror movie villains, impossible to kill. We'll see him again."

MILLER directed Danny to a parking lot near the airport, the Jeep mingling with five thousand other cars. From there they took a cab downtown, neither one of them talking during the ride. Miller felt numb, his neck pounding with a dull ache. He noticed Danny rubbing his hands, his fingers probably cramped up from clutching the steering wheel in a death grip.

Miller had the cab drop them off at a bus stop and they took a cross-town ride to a string of cheap motels. Miller picked the one that looked least likely to rent rooms by the hour. He went into the front office while Danny waited outside. Better if two men weren't seen checking in together; he didn't want to give Madrigal any leads. Key in hand, he led the way to the ground floor room and they went in, Danny locking the door and pulling the chain behind them.

Danny leaned against the door, watching Miller in the darkness, only a sliver of light coming in through the musty-smelling drapes. Miller suddenly felt flooded with sadness, homesick with wanting for the apartment, the place where they'd felt safe. He knew how close they'd come to dying. He'd heard the bullet singing past his face.

But together he and Danny had cheated Madrigal of his prize. Danny had been fearless in the car, his face a mask of calm, his voice strong. In that car Miller had realized for the first time exactly what Danny meant when he said he'd been taking care of himself for years now. He didn't need Miller to do that job. He was as capable of saving Miller as Miller was of saving him. But somehow the knowledge that Danny didn't need him that way made Miller more protective, more determined that no one was going to hurt Danny, not ever again.

"I'm sorry," Danny said into the stillness, his voice cracking. "If we hadn't gone on that walk...."

"It's not your fault." Miller's voice was rough, his words tumbling out like loose gravel.

"You could have died."

"But I didn't. And you didn't, either." Miller took two steps closer. "We're safe, Danny. We're together and we're safe."

Danny reached out, grabbing fistfuls of Miller's coat, hauling him forward. They slammed back against the door, Miller's hands pulling hard in Danny's hair, not worrying about hurting or being hurt; pain just meant they were alive. Danny's mouth was frantic on his, a wild thing without a clear purpose except to lick and bite and suck whatever it could reach. His teeth nipped violently, not backing off even when Miller growled low in his throat.

Danny tore Miller's jeans down, fingers eager and demanding, moving off Miller to help rip away his own jeans, snatching at Miller's shirt, his hands pinching as they moved upward.

"Turn around, turn around," Miller chanted. He couldn't wait, not one fucking second, had to be inside him, *now, now, now....*

Danny turned to face the door, bracing himself with his hands, moans falling from his lips in a rush of sound. Miller started to push forward, stopped. "I don't... do we need something?" he panted.

"Just do it... do it, Miller!" Danny cried. "Fuck me!"

Miller did what Danny asked, spit into his hand and rammed home in one deep thrust. Danny pushed back against him, his fist pounding out a ragged rhythm on the door. He was the tightest, hottest thing Miller had ever dreamed of, taking whatever Miller gave him, not pulling away.

"God, yes, Danny," Miller growled through bared teeth, his pace fast and brutal. "God, yes." He licked the smear of blood on Danny's neck, glass shrapnel rough under his tongue.

"Come on, baby... come on, that's it," Danny moaned, urging him on. Danny threw back his head, their mouths connecting as Miller reached around and took him, firm, in his fist. They came at almost the same moment. The heat of Danny's release pouring into Miller's hand sent him spiraling over the edge, groaning Danny's name.

Danny leaned his forehead on the door, his gasping breaths filling the silence. Miller put his lips against Danny's neck to search out the vein pulsing with life, his hand easing under Danny's shirt to lie against his pumping heart. Danny was alive, his blood was flowing, his lungs were filling, and his body was holding Miller, tight and warm. Danny was alive.

And right now, that was the only thing that mattered.

CHAPTER 11

"DANNY... Danny?"

"Hmmm, what?" Danny barely glanced up from his plate. His mind was a million miles away, but if pressed, he wouldn't be able to name a single thought inside his head.

"I was thinking, when my supervised release is over next year, maybe we could get a place together."

Danny's head bobbed up to find Griff observing him with neutral eyes. Someone who didn't know him would think he didn't care at all about Danny's answer. But Danny knew better. He caught the little muscle jumping at the corner of Griff's mouth, the way it always did when he was nervous. Danny had seen that particular twitch more than a few times in the months they'd spent behind bars, when trouble came at them from all directions.

"Well, what do you think?" Griff prodded, when Danny failed to respond.

"I'm married."

Griff snorted out a laugh. "Since when? Last I heard, you were separated. You honestly think you and Amanda are going to try again?"

"No," Danny admitted.

"Then what's the problem?"

"What about you? You really willing to give up all the women you haven't slept with yet?"

"Don't make this about me," Griff said, his voice gone quiet. A sure sign he was getting pissed. "I'm ready to give up women, and the rest of the men too. What are you ready for, Danny?"

Danny had known this conversation was coming, ever since Griff had gotten out of Leavenworth six months ago. They'd been seeing a lot of each other, even though it was a violation of their terms of supervised release. Having Griff around was comforting to Danny, made him feel less alone in the wake of Amanda's leaving, taking herself and all her familiar habits to a new apartment across the city. But comforting was one thing... and making a life together was something else entirely.

"It's too dangerous," Danny said. "I don't want you to get involved in my work."

Griff leaned back, tossing his hair out of his eye. "Why don't you give me a reason that isn't complete bullshit? How about that?"

"It's not bullshit!"

"Danny, you know the life I've had. You know the crap I've been mixed up in. There's nothing you can put in my way that I haven't seen before. I can handle it."

"I just—" Danny cut his eyes away, watching two girls at the bar smooth on lipstick, giggling to each other behind their cupped hands. "I just don't think we're right for each other. I don't think we have what it takes. Not in the long run."

Danny would always be grateful to Griff for being his friend, for watching his back in Leavenworth, for never judging him. But he couldn't tell Griff that without risking a fist in the face. Those were words no man in love wanted to hear—no matter how heartfelt, those sentiments would only sound like pity.

Griff finished his cigarette, eyes on the table. Danny twirled his now-cold pasta around and around his fork without taking a single bite.

"Okay," Griff said. "You want to end this, then?"

"Not the friendship. But the rest of it... yeah, we probably should."

Griff grabbed his half-empty pack of cigarettes, yanking his jacket off the back of his chair as he stood. "Don't be a stranger, Danny."

Danny tried to smile. "I won't." He held out his hand and Griff took it in his own, sliding his palm smoothly across Danny's, the way they always did. "I'm sorry, Griff."

"Me too."

Danny finished his beer after Griff left, but his plate of food went back to the kitchen uneaten. The romantic part of Danny—that hidden kernel that not even years of living under his father and Hinestroza had killed—wished he could fall in love with Griff. He didn't know if his capacity to love had been stunted, buried beneath the need for survival for so long it had forgotten how to breathe, or whether it was simply Griff himself who failed to evoke stronger feelings. But he understood how dangerous it would be to truly love someone, the power that would give Hinestroza. As lonely as he was, he couldn't help but feel thankful he'd never experienced that rush of emotion for Griff, or anyone else. Danny's life was not his own; every move that mattered was dictated by outside forces. Danny's soul-deep love for another human being was the last remaining trump card Hinestroza didn't hold.

MILLER woke up wrapped around Danny, his head on Danny's chest, their legs twisted together beneath the sheets. Miller had never been a cuddler; he didn't like anyone touching him while he slept. Rachel teased him about it, but he sensed her undercurrent of hurt, stung by the fact that he didn't want her too close while his body rested. But sleeping with Danny, that turned out to be different. Danny followed him around the bed like a heat-seeking missile, some part of his body always in contact with Miller's: foot, hand, full-body press. And the funny thing was, if he woke up and Danny wasn't touching him, he solved that problem immediately, curling around Danny's back, drawing Danny onto his shoulder, searching for a free hand. Danny managed to break all of his rules, both big and small, inserting his own game plan into every facet of Miller's life.

Miller rolled onto his side of the bed, squinting at the time on his cell phone. He'd called Colin last night after Danny had fallen into exhausted sleep and made arrangements for him to bring a car over this morning. He only had about ten minutes before Colin showed up at the door. Miller threw on his clothes from yesterday, the only ones he had, and went out to wait in the parking lot. The last thing he needed was for

Colin to catch an eyeful of the lone bed in the motel room, or Danny lying naked across it.

The morning was cold. Miller was grateful to the shining sun both for the warmth of the rays and the necessity of slipping on his mirrored shades. He didn't want to face Colin unarmored. He shoved his hands in his pockets and leaned back against the aging wall of the motel, his coat scraping loose tiny bits of pink stucco to scatter at his feet. He was pretty sure Colin didn't believe him about the gun, and his job was riding on how he handled the situation from this point on. If Colin pulled him off the case, it would send a clear signal that he didn't have what it took to move up through the ranks.

Last night you thought Danny being alive was the only thing that mattered.

But last night things had been simple. Fear distilled everything down to its fundamental essence—Danny breathing, Danny in his arms, Danny alive. But this morning, in the sunlight, the terror of their narrow escape was receding and other concerns were crowding in around his feelings for Danny—Rachel, his career, Danny's past, both their futures. Without that blinding fear of death and the relief of outrunning it, real life was asserting its place in the lineup of what mattered.

It wasn't even an issue of how much Miller was willing to give up or what he was willing to sacrifice, not really. Because the simple fact was that staying with Danny was not possible. There was no way to keep Danny safe here much longer. He needed to move into the next phase, obtain his new identity, start preparing to testify, begin his transformation into a different man. Danny was heading into a world where Miller could not follow.

And isn't that lucky for you? Now you don't have to make any tough choices. Can just ride your dirty little secret until the end of the line, you chicken shit.

Colin arrived five minutes early, driving the dark blue Crown Victoria that Miller knew so well. He got out of the car with cups of coffee in his hands, kicking the door shut with his foot.

"Morning," he said to Miller, passing him a cup.

"Thanks." The cardboard was hot against his hands, the coffee steaming into the air as Miller removed the lid for a tentative sip.

"I've got another one in the car for Butler."

"He's still asleep."

Colin nodded, perching one hip on the hood of the car. "There are skid marks all over the highway where you said you shot out Juan Madrigal's tire. And we found the car in the median about a quarter mile down. But it was empty."

"Shit," Miller sighed.

"We can move you guys to another apartment today."

"No."

"No?" Colin raised his eyebrows.

"If we're in an FBI apartment, there will be too many people who can be bribed. It's safer if we just move from motel to motel every couple of days. You and I will be the only ones who know where Danny's staying."

"Speaking of bribes, it was the clerk you talked to at the police station who gave Madrigal the dog walker's report. For a lousy two hundred bucks."

"Son of a bitch!"

"After I talked to you the first time yesterday, I confirmed that a report had been filed at the police station, so I went down there to talk to the clerk. He denied knowing anything about it. But I leaned on him and eventually he broke."

"See?" Miller exclaimed, throwing out an arm. "It's not safe for too many people to know where Danny's located."

"You can trust our people, Miller."

"Anybody can be bribed, Colin. Or threatened."

Colin ran a weary hand over his face. "Okay. We'll do it this way. For the time being."

Miller nodded, risking a bigger gulp of hot coffee.

"I heard back from the U.S. Attorney's Office. Patterson's handling the Hinestroza case. She said she wants to meet with us later this week."

"Why? Shouldn't we meet with the Marshal's Office first?"

Colin shrugged. "Who knows? It's going to be a high-profile case. She probably wants to make sure all her ducks are in a row. I'll let you know the date and time once I have the details."

"Fine."

Colin stared at Miller through his sunglasses. "So, that can of mace thing? That was pretty lame."

"What do you mean?"

"Miller… come on."

"It was mace, Colin."

Colin pinched the bridge of his nose, closing his eyes for a moment. "I get the feeling something's not exactly kosher with this case."

"I already said the walk was a mistake. What else—"

"It's not the walk I'm worried about."

Miller kicked at a small pile of loose gravel on the edge of the parking lot, a few tired weeds hanging onto life between the asphalt cracks. "There's no reason to worry," he said, wanting to end the conversation. "Do you need a ride somewhere?"

"No." Colin gestured toward a cab idling at the far end of the street. "That's mine. Here," he said, as he opened the car door and grabbed the extra cup of coffee. "Let me know when you change motels."

"Okay."

"I'll call you tomorrow." Colin shielded his eyes with one hand as he squinted at Miller in the sunlight. "Be careful."

"Yeah. We will."

The bed was empty when Miller let himself back into the motel room, the sound of the toilet flushing carrying out into the seedy little room. The sooner they moved out of this crap-hole, the better.

"Is that coffee?" Danny asked hopefully, emerging from the bathroom in his boxers, scratching his chest with one hand.

"Yeah."

"Where'd you get it?"

"Colin brought it when he dropped off a car for us."

Danny took a sip through the tiny hole in the lid of the cup. "Ah, it's the good stuff," he said with approval. "Who's Colin? Your boss?"

"Not exactly." Miller shrugged out of his coat. "But he is my supervisor on this case."

"Is he the one you lied to yesterday? About the gun?" Danny asked, eyes on Miller over his tilted cup.

Miller nodded, exhaling a weary sigh.

"He a good guy?"

"Yes, he's a really good guy." Miller looked down at the floor.

Danny reached forward and took his hand. "Come on," he said gently.

"Where are we going?"

"Back to bed. It's cold in here. The heater in this dump doesn't work for shit."

Miller didn't protest, just kicked off his shoes and climbed under the covers, back resting against the wall next to Danny.

Danny laid his foot on top of Miller's. "You know what sounds good right now?"

"What?"

"Pancakes."

Miller made a face, wrinkling up his nose in the age-old expression of distaste.

"You don't like pancakes?"

"Not really."

"Who the hell doesn't like pancakes?" Danny asked, leaning forward to peer into Miller's face with his eyebrows cocked.

Miller shrugged. "I just don't like sweet stuff for breakfast."

"Please don't tell me you're secretly a wheat germ, granola type guy."

He laughed, shoving Danny's shoulder with his own. "I wouldn't go that far."

"What's your favorite food? I mean, if you could have anything you wanted for dinner, what would it be?"

Miller turned to look at Danny, his dark head resting against the uniform white of the wall. "Why do you want to know—"

"You always say you know everything about me. Right?"

"Right."

"Well, now I'm returning the favor. Just humor me, okay?" Danny brushed his fingers through the hair at Miller's temple.

"Okay." Miller smiled, leaning into Danny's hand without even thinking about it. "Chicken-fried steak with mashed potatoes and homemade gravy."

Danny grinned. "You are from Kansas."

"Yep."

They sipped their coffee, Danny's toes rubbing against the top of Miller's foot.

"What's the plan? Is this our new home sweet home?"

"Not for long. We're going to be on the move for a while, until they get you out of here. You should have your Witness Protection Program interview by next week."

Danny was quiet, running one finger around the lid of his cup.

"What?" Miller asked.

"Nothing." Danny shook his head. "I'm not looking forward to it, that's all."

"We've got to get you someplace safer, Danny. You can't stay around here."

"I know." Danny raised his eyes to Miller's. "So that'll be it, then?"

Miller knew what he was asking. The end seemed close now, more immediate than it had even twenty-four hours ago. Once the Marshal's Office took over, Danny would be whisked away to points unknown. The FBI wouldn't be privy to where he'd gone, Miller cut out of the loop that would encircle Danny's new life. Maybe when

Danny testified, Miller would catch a glimpse of him in a courthouse hallway, hold his eye across a room. That was the most he could hope for. He would never get the chance to know the man Danny would become.

"Yeah, that'll be it," Miller said, his voice low.

"No more Danny Butler."

"You'll be Danny somebody. They like you to keep your first name."

"That's not what I meant, Miller."

"I know it's not." Miller traced the vein on the back of Danny's hand with one finger, listened to Danny's slow breathing next to him, the warmth from Danny's thigh seeping through his jeans. He wanted to memorize this moment, for when it was all over.

"What about Amanda? Am I going to be able to talk to her again before I go?"

"That's not up to us anymore. She went to her sister's in Indiana."

"Wait." Danny shifted to face Miller. "I thought you said the FBI would be protecting her!"

"We were. But she didn't want to stay here, said either we charge her with something or she was leaving."

"God, she can be a pain in the ass sometimes." Danny sighed. "I would have liked to have said good-bye to her. I doubt I'll ever see her again."

"Can't you call up there?"

"I can try. But her sister was never my biggest fan."

Miller smoothed the blanket over his lap, picking at the fluffy pieces of lint scattered across its surface. "How'd Amanda find out you were gay?"

"She probably suspected for a long time. But then when Griff got out of Leavenworth, he was hanging around a lot. She put two and two together."

The muscle in Miller's jaw hardened, like a walnut under the skin, as he remembered those cool blue eyes reminding him he didn't know Danny as well as he thought he did.

Know him a lot better now, you prick.

"So you were cheating on her."

"Yeah." Danny scrubbed at his face with both hands, his coffee cup balanced between his knees. "I was a shitty husband."

Miller wasn't going to disagree, although given his performance as a fiancé he didn't have much room to talk. "I'm surprised you guys never had kids. You were married long enough."

"Five years. But I was in prison for some of that. And neither one of us was that thrilled with the idea of kids, thank God. I hate to think how bad we'd have fucked one up." Danny gave Miller a sideways glance, his bottom lip hooked between his teeth. "What about you and Rachel? Kids on the agenda?"

"That's the plan." Miller's voice sounded tired, not able to kick up any enthusiasm behind his words. It would be fair to say that, since he'd met Danny, he had barely given a passing thought to Rachel, even on the afternoon he'd spent at her apartment. He felt guilty that he didn't feel guiltier, that his desire for Danny surpassed his loyalty to a woman who had never intentionally done anything to hurt him and probably never would. Speaking about Rachel with Danny now, after they were lovers, bringing her into this room they shared, made real the damage Miller was doing... to her, to Danny, to himself. He didn't want Danny and Rachel to mingle, in his life or in his mind. The results were too confusing—his thoughts so jumbled in his head he wasn't even sure which one of them he was betraying.

"WHERE are you going?"

Miller grabbed his car keys from the scarred top of the dresser, long fingers of wood missing from the surface. "To get us some dinner. I'm going to swing by my place, too, for some clothes. And I need a suit for later in the week."

Danny hopped off the bed where he'd been watching the news, tossing the remote over his shoulder. "I'm coming with you."

"Danny...."

"I think it's safer if we stick together as much as we can," Danny said, pulling on his boots.

"All right," Miller nodded. "Come on."

It was barely past five thirty and already dark, their headlights cutting golden swaths across the faces of pedestrians crossing on the busy downtown corners, everyone in such a rush to get home.

"I was wondering," Miller said, tapping his index fingers against the wheel. "Is there anywhere Madrigal hangs out here? A base camp? Maybe we should stop waiting for him to find us."

"No. He doesn't put down roots. He only lands somewhere when he's doing a job, finds a warehouse or an abandoned building and goes to work, then gets out." Danny leaned back against the headrest. "He likes those types of places because there's never anyone around to hear the screaming."

"He ever use the same place twice?"

"I seriously doubt it. Last time he was here he used an abandoned house on the Paseo, but there are dozens of those, no reason to risk coming back to the same place. The time before that it was a warehouse in the West Bottoms." Danny craned his neck to look out the window as they pulled into the lot of a four-story brick building. "This your apartment?"

"Yeah."

"I love the way they're restoring all these old buildings."

"This one used to be a paper mill," Miller said, stepping out into the parking lot. "We can take the fire escape."

Danny's boots clanked against the metal steps as they worked their way up to the top floor. Miller unlocked the heavy door and pointed Danny toward the apartment at the end of the hall. The building was quiet, the only noise the faint murmur of TV laughter creeping out from under the door of Miller's nearest neighbor.

Miller's apartment was cold and dark and already had that peculiar odor of space left too long without human company. Miller flipped a switch near the door and a floor lamp in the living room winked into life. Silver ductwork glinted in the fifteen-foot ceilings, crumbly old red brick exposed on three walls, the fourth lined with tall windows. The floors were gleaming glossy oak, a few throw rugs warming up their cold shine.

"You keep your place neat," Danny said, eyes roaming over the uncluttered surfaces, the even stack of magazines on the dark wood coffee table, the carefully arranged books on the narrow shelves against the far wall.

Miller looked around like he was seeing his apartment for the first time. "I'm never home," he explained. He pointed with a thumb toward a dark doorway. "I'm going to go pack up some stuff."

"Okay."

Danny wandered over to the bookshelves, drawn by a single framed photograph. It was in a silver frame, the photograph itself faded with age, one corner marred by a bend in the paper. It showed three children—two boys and a girl—and a woman, strands of blonde hair blowing across her laughing face. She had a slight gap between her front teeth and Danny smiled when he saw it, that lone imperfection making her more beautiful somehow. They were all sitting on a porch swing, Miller on his mother's lap, Junie next to them, her head resting on her mother's shoulder. And Scott on the opposite end, looking bored and sulky. Miller had two scabbed-over knees, his hair a mass of gold, thick and straight and falling into his eyes even then. He was leaning back against his mother's chest, covering the hand she had around his belly with his own. Danny guessed he was about seven, right on the cusp of being too old for his mother's lap, maybe the last summer he could sit there without risking ridicule.

Danny couldn't remember ever sitting on his mother's lap. She was always busy, flitting around like a hummingbird, scared to light anywhere for too long in case his father came in and caught her being unproductive. She didn't have time for kisses or books or bedtime stories, all her energy channeled into keeping one step ahead of his father's demands.

"That's my mom," Miller said over Danny's shoulder, his pointing finger stopping just short of touching her face.

"I figured. She was beautiful." Danny turned to Miller. "You look like her."

Miller flashed him a sad smile, full of a child's need. "She had the nicest voice. Low for a woman, smooth. I don't know how she managed it with three kids, but she never yelled."

Danny put the photograph back on the shelf, careful with it, setting it down gently. And then he walked Miller slowly backward, into the wall, easing his mouth down, fingers threading through Miller's hair.

"Danny," Miller breathed between kisses, his tongue playing against Danny's. "We need to go."

"Why?"

"I don't know, I—"

"That's not a good enough reason," Danny teased. "I have something in mind." He rotated his hips forward, smiling when Miller moaned into his mouth. "Let's go in your bedroom." Danny pulled back a little, hands working at the buttons on Miller's shirt. "I want to make love with you in your bed. So next time you sleep here, you'll smell me on your sheets and remember."

Miller's eyes clouded over, dark night eclipsing the clear gray. "I won't need the sheets to remember, Danny," he whispered. He pushed up Danny's T-shirt with his hands, thumbs brushing across Danny's nipples. Danny's chest muscles tightened, trails of liquid heat streaming down into his belly.

Their mouths came together, not as frantic as the night before, gentleness behind the joining of tongues and lips. Danny moved down Miller's throat, back up to blow hot breaths in his ear, laughing softly as Miller squirmed and groaned.

"You're always so ticklish right there," Danny murmured. "Gets you every time."

Miller stiffened against him, his hands on Danny's hips suddenly pushing backward, away from him. "What—" Danny's question died in his throat when he caught the expression on Miller's face, shock and shame dancing a slow waltz across his features. Danny knew without looking what caused it, not surprised at all when he turned his head and saw the woman in the doorway, key ring held in her frozen hand, her big eyes blinking in slow motion, not believing what they were seeing.

"Rachel," Miller choked out, moving around Danny toward the door.

Danny pulled down his T-shirt, smoothed back his hair. But there was no way to fix it. No way to pretend what Rachel had seen was anything other than what it was. Miller's shirt was still half unbuttoned, his hair rumpled from Danny's fingers, his lips swollen with stubble burn—badges of lust even a blind man could recognize.

"Miller, what's going on?" Rachel's voice was so quiet Danny could barely hear it. She obviously wasn't the type to chuck pots at Miller's head or slap the shit out of him the way Amanda had with Danny when she'd found out. "I saw your lights on when I drove by on my way home from work, so I thought I'd come see if you were here, and… and…." Her words drifted away, eyes racing between Danny and Miller, tears pouring out on a sudden gust of comprehension, making her gasp and retch, one hand curled around the doorknob for balance.

A cruel, numb part of Danny, developed and nurtured through years of hard living, wondered what Miller saw in Rachel. She was pretty in a nondescript kind of way, her light brown hair pulled back in a ponytail, a string of pearls hanging just above the neckline of her pale yellow sweater. There was nothing sexy about her, nothing exciting, every feature bland and average and safe.

Yeah, but she doesn't have a felony rap sheet or a shadowy past or a dick, Danny. Three marks squarely in her favor if Miller wants a normal life, right? And let's be honest, what can you really give him that she can't? Besides the obvious. I mean, once you've got your new life, how long before you're in trouble again? A month? Two at the outside? That way of life is in your blood now, you know it is. You really want to drag him down with you? Make him give all this up… for what? For you? Talk about a bum deal.

Danny turned away, walked to the far window and leaned his forehead against the cold glass. He could hear Miller murmuring behind him, Rachel's sobs punctuated by wails of grief, trying to make sense of something she would never understand. He wondered what Miller was telling her, what lies he was trying to force-feed her, because Danny knew Miller would never tell her the truth. That would mean admitting something about himself he couldn't even say to the man who shared his bed.

Danny could see a couple in the apartment across the street, crammed together in the tiny kitchen, the woman laughing as she tried to reach something on a high shelf. Two windows down, he spied a lone man, only the back of his head visible above his recliner, the channels on his TV surfing by at rapid speed. It reminded Danny of nights he used to drive around after dark, his loneliness making it impossible for him to stay still, and he'd look into the lighted windows of the houses he passed, catching brief hints of the lives inside. He knew many of those homes were filled with the same troubles that haunted men the whole world over: marriages ending, illnesses beginning, dreams shattering, but he liked to pretend that he was a silent witness to peace, the cozy interiors full of people who had found their way to happiness.

But Danny was learning that finding what made you happy was only the beginning of the journey—figuring out how to keep it often proved to be the unreachable destination.

"SO THAT was Rachel," Danny said when the motel door closed behind them. It was the first either one of them had spoken since they'd left the apartment ten minutes after Rachel had, still crying when she'd staggered out to her car.

Miller didn't answer, sat heavily on the edge of the bed. He would never forget the way she'd looked at him, her eyes drowning in sorrow. It would have been easier if she'd been angry, called him names, or thrown his ring back in his face. But that wasn't Rachel's way. She got her point across using guilt and regret.

"What did you tell her?" Danny asked, leaning back against the dresser, kicking off his boots with a thud.

"I don't know," Miller sighed. "Nothing she believed."

"Do you want her to believe it?"

"What's that supposed to mean?"

"Is that what you want?" Danny's voice was mild, unfazed by Miller's glare. "To step back into that life you had, the one where you were going to marry Rachel?" Danny kept his eyes glued to Miller's, not letting him look away.

"It doesn't matter. I don't know if I can step back into that life."

"I'm not talking about 'can', Miller. I'm talking about what you want."

Miller pressed his lips together, shaking his head in denial, his fingers tying crazy knots in his lap.

"How long have you been fighting it?" Danny asked, his voice quiet. "Fighting who you really are?"

Miller lay back on the bed, covering his eyes with one arm. *That's one of those questions it's about time you answered, don't you think?*

He heard the sound of Danny's jacket landing on a chair, felt the bed dip when Danny stretched out next to him. "You can talk to me, Miller," Danny said, his finger stroking along Miller's jaw. "How long?"

Miller opened his mouth, choking back a sob he hadn't known was waiting there. "I don't know," he whispered. "My whole life, probably."

"That's a hard secret to keep. Especially from yourself." Danny's lips were soft against Miller's hand, his long body curving against Miller's side. "Did your mom know?"

Miller shrugged. "If she did, she never said anything. But I think maybe she suspected. She was always more careful with me somehow, like she was avoiding something painful, stepping lightly."

"What about your dad?"

"I don't think so. I doubt it. It wouldn't have occurred to him... that he might have a son who was...." He let his voice fade, not able to say the word. Another sob slammed against the back of his teeth. He'd never known he was such a coward. "Danny?"

"*Hmm?*" His warm fingers still trailed over Miller's jaw, soft and soothing.

"How did you know... about me?"

"I didn't, not at first."

"When?"

"I had an inkling that day on the park bench. Something in the way you looked at me. I was so goddamn attracted to you." Miller could hear the smile in Danny's voice. "And the way you stared at me then, I thought maybe… maybe you were feeling it too."

Miller blew out a shuddering breath. "I felt it. I didn't want to, but I did."

"Look at me," Danny whispered, pulling on Miller's arm. "Look at me."

Miller withdrew his arm, turning his head when Danny put gentle pressure against his cheek. "There's nothing wrong with you, Miller. It's like having blond hair or freckles." His smile was tender and crooked as his finger brushed across Miller's nose. "It's just who you are."

"Nobody's ashamed of having freckles, Danny."

Danny's eyes flared, his hand yanking hard in Miller's hair. "You don't have to be ashamed. That's a choice you're making."

"I can't accept it the way you can." Miller looked up at the ceiling, tears battling against his eyelids.

Danny flipped onto his back, both of them staring at the ceiling as if it were a sea of stars instead of dingy white plaster clustered with stains. "You'll never be happy with her," Danny said finally.

Miller wanted to be angry, to ask Danny what the fuck he knew about it anyway, but he couldn't muster the energy. It was hard to be self-righteous when your bluff was called. "I know," he said instead.

Danny rolled on top of him and cradled Miller's face between his hands. "I hated seeing her there. With you." His voice was fierce. "I hated it."

Miller hooked his legs around Danny's, arching his hips up, holding Danny prisoner with his body. "Now you know how I feel about Griff," he said between clenched teeth.

Danny's head jerked back. "What?"

"I met him. And it made me crazy, thinking about you and

him…." Miller captured Danny's earring between his lips.

Danny's breath stuttered in his chest as Miller's tongue snaked behind his earlobe. "When did you meet him?"

"A few weeks ago. Wanted to see if he knew anything about Hinestroza." That was as close as he could come to telling Danny the truth. He didn't have the courage to be honest about Ortiz or to let Danny know how dangerous it had felt to sit across from Griff, how Miller had thought maybe he could kill him if he said the wrong thing—made Miller visualize too clearly what Griff and Danny had done together in bed. How ever since, Miller wondered if he, who had never been with a man before Danny, could possibly compete with someone like Griff, who oozed sex out of every pore.

Miller pushed off with his leg, using his weight to flip them over and pin Danny against the mattress. Danny moaned, low and sensual, as Miller licked his way up his body. "Did he ever make you feel this good?" Miller growled, lips curving over Danny's stomach, tongue running through the hair on his chest as Danny's white T-shirt bunched up under his arms.

Jealousy wasn't an emotion Miller was familiar with; he hadn't mastered tricks for handling it or learned secrets of containment the way he had with other unpleasant feelings. He wasn't used to the harsh scrape of pain when he heard Griff's name, like being whipped on the inside. He couldn't seem to clamp down on the uncertainty quickly enough, wasn't able to stop himself from wondering what exactly Danny had felt for that man, what he still felt, whether Miller was only getting what was left over.

Danny's eyes were foggy with lust, his throat vibrating under Miller's mouth as he groaned when Miller stroked him through his jeans, fast and rough. "Did he ever make you come as hard as I did last night?" Miller demanded. He could hear the insecurity behind his words but didn't know how to hide it, his hand digging into Danny's thigh. "Did he?"

Miller waited for Danny to say something smartass, talk dirty, maybe. But Danny just stared at him with wide eyes, searching his face. "Did he?" Miller asked again, his voice cracking.

Danny brought one hand up, passing his fingers over Miller's mouth. "Shhh," he soothed. "It's all right, Miller. There's no reason for you to be jealous." He pressed against Miller's lower lip with his thumb, his eyes gentle. "I never loved him."

"Danny," Miller moaned, burying his face in Danny's neck. He knew what Danny was telling him, wished he could say something back, something that Danny would be able to hold onto when he left. But in the end Miller had to be content to tell Danny without words, rocking inside him, his body whispering all the things he could not say.

THE shards of light coming in through the curtains cut across Danny's face as he slept, the shadows playing on his skin. He was the most gorgeous thing Miller had ever seen, like a Greek god or an ancient statue in some museum. Miller kissed his bare shoulder, running his tongue along the protruding bone.

Colin had called ten minutes ago, waking Miller out of a sound sleep but not disturbing Danny. They'd found Ortiz, or thought they had. No fingerprints or dental records, but a neighbor had identified him when his body was discovered eleven years ago in an abandoned warehouse outside Dallas. Tortured and shot in the stomach, left to bleed to death on the concrete floor. Even with all his injuries, the medical examiner had said in her report that it probably took a long time for him to die. No suspects, although Ortiz's neighbor thought he was involved with drugs. The local police found cocaine in his apartment when they searched it, a fairly big stash. No fingerprints at the warehouse, no physical evidence, just lots and lots of blood.

Danny hadn't had any more bad dreams, not since Miller had been sleeping beside him. His demons were resting now. But come morning Miller was going to have to drag them out from their gloomy hiding places, force them into the light. No more stalling, no more excuses. He had to know the truth. Miller almost hoped the truth would be something he could not bear, answers so horrible they would transform Danny before his eyes, turn him into a monster and not a man, not the man Miller wanted so damn much. He recognized his own desperation—searching for anything that would make it easier for him to let Danny go.

CHAPTER 12

THEY cut off Ortiz's thumb first, just to ensure they had Danny's undivided attention.

Danny had known something was wrong the minute Madrigal picked him up for the hastily arranged meeting with Hinestroza, who was in town for a few days. Madrigal had been too eager when he'd appeared on Danny's doorstep, humming with anticipation, giving Danny sidelong glances filled with smirking glee. The dull press of worry had escalated to the sharp edge of panic when they'd reached the warehouse and Madrigal had marched Danny inside, his hand biting into Danny's bicep as he shoved him into a cold, metal folding chair.

Ortiz was already seated, his ankles duct-taped to the narrow chair legs, his torso bound with a thick black cord, his eyes taking up all the room in his face. Hinestroza was sitting behind a long, narrow table, his face serious, hands clasped as though he were about to begin an important business meeting. Another man, one of Madrigal's assistants, stood next to Hinestroza's chair.

"Mr. Hinestroza, what—" Danny choked out.

"Danny—"

"What's going on?" Danny turned to look at Ortiz. "What happened?"

"Danny." Hinestroza's voice was icy with reprimand; he did not like being interrupted.

"Mr. Hinestroza, whatever's going on, I can explain it. I can—"

"You can explain the cocaine that was stolen from the last shipment?" Hinestroza's eyebrows went up. "Well, then, I'd be very interested to hear about that, Danny."

Danny's stomach contracted into a tiny ball, terror worming its way into every cell of his body. "Ortiz," he moaned. "What the fuck did you do?"

"Danny. Danny!" Hinestroza snapped, but Danny was too frightened to acknowledge him, his brain trying frantically to come up with a lie, something that would stop this before it was too late. Out of the corner of his eye he saw Hinestroza motion to Madrigal, who stepped forward, grasping Ortiz's wrist with strong fingers.

"Wait!" Danny cried, eyes skidding from Ortiz to Madrigal to Hinestroza and back again. His blood was pounding in his ears. He couldn't hear, couldn't focus, didn't know if he should watch or look away, didn't know whether to beg or fight.

Ortiz was trying to resist, pulling back his arm as Madrigal dragged it slowly forward. Madrigal slammed Ortiz's arm down onto the table, his straight razor flicked open with an expert hand.

"Mr. Hinestroza, wait, maybe it's a mistake, maybe he can explain—"

Madrigal's voice was hollow in Danny's ears, as if he was speaking from the other end of a tunnel, his words coming to Danny from a long distance. "Lay your fucking hand flat, Ortiz, or I'll cut the whole thing off."

The blade whispered through the air, the metallic clank when it connected overpowered by Ortiz's scream, high and desperate—not a human sound, more like an animal caught in a trap, the fear spiraling higher with each breath. His blood flew out in a shimmering arc, fat, dark drops sliding over the edge of the table onto the dirty floor.

Someone was moaning, a harsh, keening cry. Danny didn't even realize it was his own voice until Hinestroza called his name, jerking him back to reality. Danny turned his head in what felt like slow motion, made stupid by shock, his eyes bulging out of their sockets.

"Your friend here, the one you recommended for a job, he's been stealing from me," Hinestroza informed him once Danny met his eyes.

Danny licked his lips, trying to work up some spit. He could see Ortiz next to him, cradling his ravaged hand. "He's addicted, Mr. Hinestroza," Danny managed, his words made almost unintelligible by *his shaking body. "He wouldn't have done it otherwise."*

Hinestroza laughed. "I don't care if he has to snort it every ten seconds to stay alive, Danny. That cocaine was mine!" He slammed his fist into the table. "And no one steals from me." His voice was quiet now, gentle. "You know that."

"But he's worked with us for a long time. More than two years. Can't you give him another chance? Let him work off what he owes?"

"So the next person will think they can steal from me and walk away missing only a thumb?" Hinestroza shook his head, almost as if he were truly sorry. "No, Danny. I can't do that." He made an impatient motion with his hand.

Madrigal stepped up next to Ortiz again, brandishing the razor. "What do you think?" he asked conversationally, looking at Danny with lively eyes. "An ear?" Madrigal ran the razor against Ortiz's ear, opening up a red river of blood. He moved the razor around to Ortiz's face, pulling his head back by a handful of hair. "Or maybe take off this nose? The one that likes to snort up Mr. Hinestroza's cocaine."

Danny and Ortiz screamed at the same time—long, echoing wails. Danny came up out of his chair, his cries ragged and wild. "Please, no, don't! God... don't!"

"Sit the fuck down!" Madrigal commanded, pointing the razor in Danny's direction.

"Wait... now, wait," Hinestroza said, holding up both palms. "Sit down, Danny. And let's talk about this."

Danny sank into his chair, his legs jittering against the seat. Maybe they could still get out of this. Maybe Ortiz didn't have to die this way. Maybe...

"I didn't realize you felt so strongly about Ortiz."

Danny nodded, his head bobbing up and down like one of those dolls they passed out at baseball games. "Yes. He's a good friend. Please, Mr. Hinestroza."

Hinestroza pursed his lips, tapping them with his unlit cigar. "The bottom line is, someone stole from me, Danny. That can't go unpunished." He put the cigar in his mouth, lighting it with a gold lighter from his pocket. He took a few deep inhales, chomping contentedly on the end. "But I'm willing to make a deal, because you've always been such a good employee."

"Anything," Danny agreed. "If you want to take some of my wages, too, or something like that, that's fine. No problem. I'll—"

"You take his place," Hinestroza said, his voice fierce, eyes burning into Danny's.

Danny didn't understand, his brain not able to make sense of the words. "Wh-wh-what?" he stammered.

Hinestroza shrugged, pointing with his cigar to Ortiz. "He stole from me. Someone has to pay, Danny. Otherwise I get a reputation as a man who doesn't protect what's his. And that only leads to trouble. I understand that you don't want your friend to die. It's actually very noble of you. But you'll have to take his punishment instead."

The tears fell hard now, running down Danny's cheeks and splattering against his jeans. He was beyond the point of feeling shame or embarrassment for his weeping, terror the only emotion in his repertoire. "Mr. Hinestroza, I... isn't there some other way?"

"No. That's your only choice. Make it." Hinestroza's voice was as cold and unforgiving as the razor in Madrigal's hand.

"Danny," Ortiz groaned, his voice alive with anguish. "Danny." But Danny refused to look at him. He didn't want to hear whatever he was going to say, didn't want to read the pleading in his eyes.

Because Danny already knew what his answer would be. He knew exactly the limits of his own bravery, knew precisely where his ability to sacrifice himself ended. And he knew he couldn't do it. Couldn't fall on the sword meant for Ortiz. Danny was going to let him die.

"Well?" Hinestroza demanded. He wanted Danny to say it out loud. Hinestroza understood the power of guilt, understood that Danny would choose to live but would never take another easy breath, would be forever haunted by the man he did not save.

"No," Danny whispered, strangling on his grief.

"No, what?"

"No... I won't take his place."

Hinestroza leaned forward across the desk. "Fine. Then stop your *whining and let Madrigal do his job." He pushed back his chair with a screech of metal on concrete, his cigar clamped between his teeth. "I'll be out in the car," he told Madrigal. He pointed at Danny, "You stay here and watch."*

In the end, Madrigal took Ortiz's ear next, the one closest to where Danny sat so he could see. Danny closed his eyes, but Madrigal threatened to cut out his eyeballs if he did it again. "Mr. Hinestroza told you to watch." So Danny watched. With each new body part or chunk of flesh that littered the blood-soaked floor, Ortiz's cries grew softer, but he would not die.

Danny had long since emptied his stomach onto his lap and down the front of his shirt, his breathing coming in ragged gasps, his eyes rolling back in his head as they tried to escape the sight. Danny cast his mind out, away from the stench of fresh blood and the wails of the dying. He could taste the vomit in his throat, feel it caked around his mouth. Danny sent up a prayer that he could be struck dead alongside Ortiz. But, like all of Danny's prayers, this one went unanswered—he kept right on breathing, right on seeing.

Danny didn't even recognize Ortiz anymore; he was just blood and gaping wounds. Danny wished they were seated closer so he could hold his hand, so Ortiz would know he wasn't alone.

Danny remembered the day he'd met Ortiz, how he'd smiled so wide when Danny had walked up to the car wash, smelly and scared. Ortiz had not hesitated, had accepted Danny as his friend and helped him without question. Danny remembered how they would sit outside on their lunch break and eat cheap tacos, and Ortiz would tell stories about his wife. How he'd loved her since the day they'd met as seven-year-old children. He was never embarrassed to admit his feelings; he always spoke with pride.

Danny wished he could turn back time, press the rewind button on his life and say "No—fuck, no," when Ortiz came to his apartment asking for a job. He wished he had done more to stop Ortiz from sliding into darkness after his daughter died. He wished he'd had the courage to save his friend.

Finally, even Madrigal grew tired, looking with disgust at his ruined clothes, flinging the bloody razor onto the table. "What do you think, Danny? Think he's had enough?"

"Please," Danny croaked. It seemed to be the only thing he could say, the only word his brain could dredge up. "Please."

Madrigal pushed Ortiz's head with the flat of his palm. "Hey, asshole, you still alive?"

Ortiz let out a low whimper, gurgling and wet, and Danny's stomach heaved in response. God help him, he wanted Ortiz to hurry up and die; he wanted it to be finished. Madrigal kicked over the chair, and Danny winced at the hollow thud as Ortiz's head bounced against the floor. Ortiz was looking at Danny from between bloody strands of hair, his remaining eye filmy and dark. Madrigal pulled out his gun and held it tight against Ortiz's head.

"Nah," he smiled. "Too quick." He moved the gun lower, pressed the barrel into Ortiz's stomach.

Danny thought all his tears were gone, but he sobbed out Ortiz's name, weeping behind his hands. When Madrigal fired the shot, Ortiz's body jumped against the floor.

"I'm going outside for a smoke," Madrigal said, his voice easy, satisfied with a job well-done. "You wait here."

Danny stayed with Ortiz until he died, crooning a wordless tune, telling Ortiz he was sorry, even though he doubted Ortiz could hear him. Danny hoped he had escaped to somewhere far away—a place beyond the pain, a place where his daughter waited. Danny didn't bother asking for forgiveness. He couldn't see the point of wasting his breath begging for something he did not deserve.

MILLER was ready. He'd climbed out of bed early, showered and shaved in the cramped and steamy bathroom. He tried not to think. He wanted to disappear inside his professional shell, his mind focused solely on the goal of discovering the truth about Ortiz. He pulled on navy slacks and a white dress shirt, stopped short of wearing a tie. With one hand he smoothed back his damp hair and gazed at himself in the mirror. He looked like an FBI agent, hard and detached, a man he hardly recognized anymore.

You're going to walk out there and break him now? Is that the kind of bastard you are, Miller? After what he said to you last night about never loving Griff? You know what he was telling you, what those words meant. And you're going to turn around and push him this way?

But Miller couldn't find out what he needed to know if he didn't wear the mask. And he had to admit there was a sense of relief that came with stepping behind the façade again, putting himself beyond Danny's reach. He'd never been so drawn to another human being in his entire life, and had never been so frightened by someone's power over him.

Danny was still asleep, sprawled across the bed, hugging a pillow now that Miller had vacated his spot. Miller sat down in the chair near the window and waited, his elbows balanced on his knees, hands clasped. He'd picked this time and method deliberately, knew Danny would be vulnerable when he first woke up, naked physically and mentally against Miller's surprise attack. No matter what the outcome, Miller would not blame Danny if he hated him after this.

And maybe that's your goal, huh? It's a lot easier for you when the other person's the first to walk away, isn't it?

Miller wasn't sure how long he sat there watching Danny sleep, the tattoo on his back calling Miller closer. He wondered if he would ever get the chance to touch it again. A sliver of sun had poked through the break in the curtains, warm on Miller's neck, when Danny finally woke up, rolling over with a jaw-popping yawn.

"Hey," he greeted Miller with a puzzled smile. "What time is it? Why are you all dressed up?"

Miller took a deep breath, kept his face neutral, his voice even. "I know about Alejandro Ortiz."

Danny recoiled, like he'd touched an electric current, his body arching away from Miller. "What did you say?" he choked out.

"I need you to tell me what happened. How did he die, Danny? Is he the one you were talking about when you said you killed someone a long time ago? What did you mean by that?" Miller was relentless in his questions, not letting up, not giving Danny any time to think.

"It's none of your goddamn business." Danny leaped off the bed, grabbing his boxer shorts from the floor and tugging them on. His eyes were wild, and Miller was transported back to that moment weeks ago in the interrogation room when he'd thought Danny was going to try to run. Miller stood quickly, putting his body between Danny and the door.

"We can talk about it here or I can take you down to headquarters and you can talk to Colin." Miller might have been speaking to a complete stranger, Danny a suspect facing him in an impersonal interrogation room, instead of across the bed they'd shared only the night before.

Danny's head whipped around. "Fuck you, Miller," he spat. "Why don't we do that, then? Head on down there, and while I'm at it I can tell him all about how you had your dick up my ass last night."

Now it was Miller's turn to take a step back, the breath freezing in his lungs. Danny barked out a bitter laugh. "It's not much fun being ambushed, is it?"

"You wouldn't do that," Miller said with more certainty than he felt.

"Try me." Danny's eyes were ice cold, brutal self-preservation rising to the occasion.

"Answer the questions, Danny."

Danny's brow furrowed, his mouth twisting up. "How'd you find out about him anyway?"

"You had a nightmare one night, at the apartment. You were calling his name. I had Colin start trying to track him down."

Danny looked away, the muscles in his throat leaping under his skin. "Why didn't you say something?" he asked finally.

"Because you wouldn't have told me. I had to do my job."

Danny glared at Miller with narrowed eyes. "Is that what you've been doing with me all this time, your *job*?"

"What? No! I just… I need to know. I need to know the truth."

"And what if the story isn't what you expect? What if I did kill him? Are you going to have me arrested, charged with murder?" Danny took a step closer. "You fucked me, kept right on fucking me, thinking maybe I killed a man in cold blood?"

Suddenly Miller felt like the one who'd been broken, his heart laid open in front of him. He couldn't do it, didn't have it in him to play the FBI agent to Danny's criminal. Not anymore. But the realization came too late; Danny was already watching him with wary, distant eyes.

"I know you didn't kill him." As he spoke the words he realized they were true. He didn't believe, would never believe, that Danny was a killer.

"You don't know shit!" Danny cried furiously. "You want to hear this story? Pull up a chair, grab some popcorn—you're in for a treat."

"Danny...."

"Oh, don't stop me now, Miller. You went to such trouble to get the answers, right?"

Miller didn't respond, wondered how the tables had gotten so turned, how he'd ended up the one in the spotlight instead of shining it on Danny.

"Well, Special Agent Sutton, have at it." Danny spread his arms wide with a challenging raise of his eyebrows.

"Danny, you don't have—"

Danny took him by surprise, rushing forward to slam him into the wall. Miller's head cracked against the plaster, his arms pinned beneath Danny's weight.

"What do you want to know?" Danny shouted, one shaking fist aimed and ready to fly. This Danny was not someone Miller recognized, his face hard and determined, his eyes crackling with disdain. Miller flinched, bracing for the impact, but the punch never came. Danny let his arm fall. He pushed roughly away from Miller, muttering, "Fuck," under his breath.

Danny retreated to the far side of the room and leaned against the wall, arms crossed over his chest. "What do you want to know?" he repeated.

Miller took a steadying breath, his eyes level on Danny's,

searching for the man he knew—the man he'd sent running for cover. "Who was Ortiz?"

"He was the first person I met in Texas. He was just a couple of years older than me. We—"

"Were you lovers?" Miller asked quietly.

"Does that question fall under the heading of personal or business?" Danny smirked. "Not that you probably give a shit anymore, but we were just friends. We worked at the car wash together."

"So Hinestroza recruited you both?"

Danny shook his head. "No. Only me. But Ortiz was desperate for money. He had a family back in Mexico, so after I'd been working with Hinestroza for a while, he came and asked me for a job. I said no at first, but eventually I talked to Hinestroza and he took Ortiz into the operation." Danny gave Miller a bland stare. "Shouldn't you be taking notes? Or do you have a tape recorder hidden around here somewhere? Maybe wearing a wire under your fancy shirt?"

Miller ignored him, talking past the sharp twist of his heart. "What happened then?"

"He got hooked on coke. Started using with Madrigal. The problem was, Madrigal could afford his habit and Ortiz couldn't." Danny sighed, rubbing his face with both hands. "He stole some cocaine from a shipment."

"Ah, Jesus," Miller sighed.

Danny's eyes flew to his, sad and angry. "They took us to a warehouse and Hinestroza ordered him killed. Madrigal tortured him." Danny blew out a trembling breath. "Then he shot him in the stomach and left him to die."

Miller clenched his fists until his knuckles screamed. He knew what Danny was leaving out from his matter-of-fact recitation. Colin had read him the medical examiner's report over the phone. Ortiz had endured the unthinkable before he'd finally died. Miller didn't need the details to imagine what Danny had been forced to see and hear. No wonder he still had nightmares.

"You didn't kill him, Danny," Miller said, as gently as he could.

"Yes, I did." Danny's voice was flat.

"Just because you helped him get a job doesn't mean you're responsible—"

Danny held up his index finger in a mocking wave. "You haven't heard the best part yet." He paused, the muscle in his jaw thumping under his skin. "I could have saved him, but I didn't."

Miller walked around the bed and sat on the edge closest to Danny. He didn't reach out and touch him, but he wanted to. "Tell me."

Danny made a gagging noise in his throat, swallowing back misery like a bitter pill. "Hinestroza said he wouldn't kill Ortiz if I took his place."

Danny's eyes were far away, glistening with the liquid sheen of unshed tears. Miller's heart broke watching him, splintering into a thousand pieces inside his chest.

"Jesus, Danny," Miller whispered. "You couldn't have saved him. Hinestroza would have killed him anyway, after you."

"You don't know the first damn thing about it," Danny spit out. "Hinestroza isn't a liar. He never has been. If he says he's going to do something, he does it. Whether it's killing you for stealing or sparing you because someone else took your punishment. He doesn't go back on his word, not ever."

"You didn't kill him," Miller repeated. "No one would have chosen to take his place."

"Bullshit," Danny said. "What would you have done? Would you have let him die that way?"

"I… shit, Danny, I don't know." Miller threw up his hands in frustration. "Probably."

"Well, that's the difference between us then. Because my answer wasn't 'probably', it was 'yes', a no-hesitation 'yes'." Danny's voice broke and he sagged back against the wall.

"I don't believe that," Miller said. "I think you agonized over your decision then, just like you've probably agonized over it every day since." He stood up, moving toward Danny but still not touching him. "I know you, Danny. You're not as hard as you pretend."

"You don't know me," Danny sneered. "You have no idea what I'm capable of. When we first started... this," Danny motioned back and forth between their bodies, "I thought about using it to save myself. I considered it. Don't fool yourself about the kind of man I am."

Anger flared inside Miller at Danny's words, blindsided by the knowledge that Danny had teetered right on the edge of betraying him.

But how's that any different from what you're doing to him right now, Miller? There are all types of betrayal. At least he didn't go through with it... unlike you.

"I'm still the same man you met in that interrogation room. The one you thought was a piece of shit. Nothing's changed." Danny's voice was steady, but his eyes were broken.

Miller took the final step, pressing against Danny, holding his face, forcing Danny to meet his gaze. He could feel the violence in Danny's body, the urge to shove rising up beneath him. "Yes, it has. Everything's changed," Miller said, emphasizing each word. "Including you. Including me."

"No, we haven't." Danny pushed against Miller, sending him stumbling backward. "Look at us right now. Miller the FBI agent getting his answers, and Danny the criminal with a lifetime of bad deeds behind him. That's all we'll ever be."

Miller was not a talker; he'd always been uncomfortable with words, constantly struggling to find the right thing to say. But with Danny, conversation came easily. Miller felt heard when he spoke. But now that old insecurity, that inability to put together the right words, hit him hard at the exact moment when Danny needed him to fix what was broken between them—what Miller had broken when he'd diminished what they felt for each other, reduced Danny to a function of his job.

"That's not true. That's not who we are when we're together." Miller's voice was shaking, but he did not look away. "I'm sorry, Danny. For Ortiz. And for what I did. I... I got scared."

Every muscle in Danny's body contracted, fighting Miller's words, a sobbing moan escaping as his eyes tried to run where Miller could not reach them. "I should hate you," he whispered. "I want to hate you."

"Danny," Miller murmured, pulling Danny forward, enfolding him tightly in his arms. Danny grabbed on with all his strength, pressing himself against Miller's body, his back heaving under Miller's hands.

Danny's breath was hitching in his chest, and Miller pulled back a little. He ran his hand down Danny's bare leg, pushing his fingers up under the edge of Danny's boxer shorts to touch the scar on his thigh. Danny sucked in a breath, his hand coming down to shove Miller away.

"How'd you get it?" Miller whispered.

"Who wants to know?" Danny replied, his voice rusty with tears. "The FBI agent?"

Miller closed his eyes. He wished he could go back and start the morning over, come at Danny in a gentler, more honest way. "No. Just me. Just Miller."

Danny looked past him, over his shoulder. "Madrigal did it... afterwards. With his trusty razor. It was a message from Hinestroza. A way of telling me not to fuck up like that again, bringing someone who couldn't be trusted into the fold. And the scar was to remind me of what I'd done—that I'd chosen my life over Ortiz's."

The desire to murder another human being had never been so wild in Miller's blood. He wanted five minutes alone in a room with Madrigal and Hinestroza, wanted to make them both suffer the way they'd made Danny suffer all these years.

Miller slid down Danny's body onto his knees, pushing up Danny's shorts with his hands to expose the thin, white line. He ran his fingers across it slowly, Danny trembling under his touch. Miller lowered his head and licked the scar with the tip of his tongue, light and soft.

"Miller," Danny sighed, his voice weary and sad. He pushed out and away, trying to escape. "Don't... please."

"It's okay. It doesn't have to mean what he wanted it to mean. We can change it, make it something different. Just like we did with the snake on your back."

"There's no changing it. There's no making it better." Danny pulled his leg out from under Miller. "It's a piece of who I am. You can't erase all the ugly parts of me, the parts that don't fit who you want me to be."

Miller stood, tucking his hands into his pockets. "That's not what I'm trying to do." Never had he been this crushed by sadness, not even when his mother died—it felt like a steel vice around his chest, smothering him with sorrow.

"Don't fucking lie to me. I can always tell when you're lying."

Danny was right—of course he was. Hadn't Miller wished, more than once, that he could feel for Rachel what he felt for Danny? That Rachel could be the first person he thought of when he woke up in the morning and the last person he wanted to touch before he fell asleep at night? Or that at least Danny could be a different kind of man, one who was upstanding and honest, a man who hadn't spent most of his life in the shadows?

"I don't know what to say," Miller admitted, his shoulders slumped in defeat. "I'm so fucking confused. About you and me and us. I don't even know who I am anymore. Or what it is I really want."

Danny refused to look at him, his jaw closed and hard, eyes on the floor.

"Danny…." Miller spoke through tears gathering heavy and thick in his throat. Even without the possibility of a future together, the idea of it ending this way between them brought pain he could not bear. Danny responded to the ache in his voice automatically, his gaze coming up to land on Miller's, anger in a losing battle with compassion, one hand reaching out. Miller marveled at his own selfishness, seeking comfort and reassurance from the person he had just wounded, taking for himself what Danny probably could not afford to give.

But Miller claimed it anyway, let himself be drawn close with Danny's whispered, "Come here." Danny ran his thumb under Miller's eye, kissed him softly, the way he had the very first time.

They held each other for a quiet moment, and then Danny's hands moved down Miller's torso, slipping between their bodies to tug gently at his waistband. Miller scrabbled at the buttons on his shirt, wanting to rid himself of his clothes, the markers of his job. There was an urgency as they came together, a desire to erase the memories of the morning, but there was a somberness, too, a recognition of what this meant for both of them.

When they were stripped bare, Danny lay back on the bed and Miller crawled up beside him. They pressed together, Danny's back to Miller's front, not moving, just holding. Miller could feel Danny's heart beating under his hand, Danny's dark hair sliding against his cheek.

Miller leaned forward to kiss the hollow where Danny's neck and shoulder met, his mouth tracing along the bone, then behind, dipping down to meet the serpent's tongue with his own. Danny was shuddering against him, his breath coming faster as Miller reached around and took Danny in his hand, wetness leaking out onto his fingers.

Danny tipped his head backward until their mouths met, Miller's tongue tender on Danny's, consolation for all the harsh words they'd hurled at each other. Danny bit Miller's chin lightly, smiling against his skin. "I miss the stubble," he whispered.

"I'll let it grow."

Danny started to turn over, but Miller held him still. "No, this way. Just like this." He rolled away and grabbed lotion from the bedside table, coming back to spoon against Danny's body as he smoothed it on. Danny drew his top leg up toward his chest when Miller positioned himself, rubbing against him, sliding in just a little then backing away, over and over until Danny was moaning low in his throat, pushing back against Miller, his face flushed.

Miller thrust forward slowly, and Danny opened up for him, drawing him in deeper. He wondered if he would ever get used to how good it felt to be inside Danny, how they fit together in all the right ways, their bodies not concerned with doubts or divisions or what tomorrow might bring, the union of their flesh the only topic on the agenda.

Miller propped himself up on one elbow, fighting to keep his eyes open; he wanted to see the way Danny's face went soft and peaceful with each thrust, his tongue catching between his teeth as he moved with Miller, rocking his hips. Miller was struck by the sudden wish that Danny would call him 'baby', the way he had that night against the door, but he couldn't bring himself to voice the desire.

Danny turned to look at Miller, holding his eyes as Miller slid forward, groaning as he sank deep, and clenching hot and firm around him. Danny's unwavering gaze left Miller feeling exposed and unveiled, the depth of his emotion for Danny rising up in him with unstoppable force, making him almost sick with longing, wrenching words from his mouth.

"Danny, I—it's more than this for me," Miller said urgently, their lips almost touching, desperate for Danny to hear beyond his words. He clutched Danny's hip, fingers sinking into his skin. "It's more than just this."

Danny stopped moving, pulling Miller's hand up to his mouth to kiss his knuckles, run his tongue along Miller's palm. "I know," he whispered. The tears that Danny had been holding back all morning were overflowing now, running down the sides of his face to form uneven pools on the dingy, white sheets.

Miller exhaled a trembling breath and caught Danny's tears in his hand. They made love silently except for their low moans and the sounds of their bodies joining together. Miller thrust steady and strong, wanting to make it good for Danny, wanting him to feel loved. Danny came quietly with a deep wavering sigh, spilling over into his own hand. Miller wasn't far behind, his own tears wetting Danny's collarbone as he fell forward, his body shaking against Danny's warm skin.

Even through his grief, Danny offered what Miller needed, reaching a gentle hand up to stroke his hair, murmuring, "*Shhh…* Miller. It's all right," into his ear. And Miller knew that, deserving or not, he had been forgiven.

CHAPTER 13

DANNY'S clothes no longer fit him; they belonged to a man twenty pounds heavier and a whole lifetime younger. Fifteen months in Marion had shed Danny of a lot of things, the least important of which was weight.

"Hey, Butler, time to go." The guard motioned him forward, snickering at the way Danny's jeans rode low on his hips, one wrong move away from forming a puddle around his ankles.

Danny kept a hand hovering near his waistband just in case, the other clutching a plastic grocery sack filled with his prison loot—two letters from his mother, heavy with recriminations and "how could you do this to us, Danny?"s, a half-filled tube of toothpaste, and twenty-one dollars, the sum total of his prison account.

"See ya around, Butler," the guard said as Danny eased out into the bright freedom. His brief trips to the yard hadn't prepared him for the sun again, the way it burned hot circles into his closed eyelids and left shimmering imprints behind to mar his vision.

"Thanks," Danny muttered. He felt scared suddenly, although escaping from this place had been the single thought on his mind during every day he'd spent inside. He wasn't sure where to go or what to do; he couldn't afford even a bus ticket back to Texas.

He had heard nothing from Hinestroza since the day he was arrested, sold out by a dealer busted with the cocaine he'd just picked up from Danny. The Feds had leaned hard on Danny, offered him deals too good to be true, and tossed out threats like confetti. But he didn't give in, refusing to name a single name. His case had landed on the desk of an over-worked public defender, weary and cynical. She'd washed her hands of him when he wouldn't take a plea.

"*Danny!*" *a voice called from across the street, where a stocky man in dark sunglasses slouched against a black car.*

"*Yeah?*" *Danny asked, not moving any closer.*

"*Get in. I'm giving you a ride.*"

"*Who are you?*"

"*Just get in the car. We're not gonna talk about it out here.*"

Danny hesitated, looking up and down the street. The man took a few steps in his direction. "Mr. Hinestroza sent me," he said under his breath.

Danny crossed to the car and got into the backseat, sliding across the soft leather with a satisfied sigh. "Mr. Hinestroza's here?" he asked, addressing the driver's thick neck.

"*No. He's in Dallas.*"

"*You're driving me all the way to Texas?*"

"*How else were you planning to get there?*"

It took them eleven hours to reach Dallas, driving almost without stopping except for short breaks for gas and food. The driver, who never told Danny his name, seemed content with silence. And for once, Danny didn't mind. He slept almost the whole way, the first time in over a year he'd been able to close his eyes without fear. He woke only to eat, stuffing down sacks full of greasy hamburgers and too-salty French fries—trying desperately to fill up the hollow space carved out of him in prison.

It was near sunset when they drove into downtown Dallas, the fading orange-pink of the sun reflecting off the glass skyscrapers. The driver pulled up in front of a swanky hotel, waving away the eager valet.

"*He's in room 1215. He's expecting you.*" *The driver leaned one arm on the seatback to peer at Danny over the top of his sunglasses.*

Danny scooted his way out of the car, his body screaming in protest after being bent in half for so long. He felt like an idiot carrying his plastic bag through the lobby, but didn't want to leave it behind.

The elevator was mirrored on three sides, affording Danny a too-close view of his gaunt frame, the deep purple circles under his eyes giving him a haunted look. He licked his palm and smoothed down his hair the best he could, cringing when he caught a whiff of himself. He definitely needed a shower.

He knocked on the dark wood-paneled door of room 1215. He heard the shushing sound of feet on carpet and the door swung inward, Madrigal grinning at him from the other side.

"Hi, Danny."

Danny brushed past him into the room, the hairs on the back of his neck bristling when their bodies shared the same space. He could never see the man without his thigh throbbing, the reminder always performing its intended job.

"Danny." Hinestroza was standing against the windows, the early evening light blooming behind him, casting his face into shadow.

"Mr. Hinestroza." Danny supposed he should be worried, but knew that if Hinestroza meant him harm, it would have come to him in prison.

Hinestroza moved forward, stopping inches from Danny's chest, his dark eyes pulling at Danny's—drinking in his secrets, sipping Danny's pain like wine.

"You've had a hard time, Danny," he said. "But you're out now. And I'm very proud of you." He enfolded Danny in his arms, hugging him with strong, thumping pats against his back.

It took Danny a moment to react, to put his own arms around Hinestroza. They had known each other for more than five years, and until today had not so much as shaken hands. What started as a tentative laying of arms across Hinestroza's back became a comforting embrace. It had been a long time since anyone had touched Danny without violence or indifference. Had been so long since anyone cared whether he was alive or dead.

Danny squeezed his eyes shut, swallowing past the urge to cry. He let Hinestroza go reluctantly and took an awkward step backward, swiping self-consciously at his nose.

"Why don't you take a shower? Then we can go to dinner. Talk."

"Okay," Danny nodded. "But I don't have anything else to wear."

"I picked up some shit from your apartment," Madrigal interjected. "Doesn't look like it's your size anymore, though. You look like hell, Danny," he added with a wink.

"Shut your mouth," Hinestroza commanded, snapping his fingers with a warning pop. Danny couldn't bite back the smile coaxed from his lips as he watched Madrigal's face grow dark with embarrassment.

"You were at my apartment?" Danny asked belatedly.

"I sent Madrigal there to get you a change of clothes."

"But I thought... with prison and everything, I thought I wouldn't have an apartment anymore."

"I paid for it while you were away. It's exactly how you left it." Hinestroza patted Danny's cheek, the way his own father never had. "You do for me, Danny, and I do for you. That's the way it works."

How was it possible to loathe and love someone all at the same time? To know they were responsible for the cesspool of your life and yet live for their approval? To know they were capable of the most evil acts and still find the humanity buried underneath? It wasn't only fear that kept Danny bound to Hinestroza. It would have been less painful if it were. But there was loyalty, too, a fierce need in Danny to make Hinestroza proud. It shamed Danny to know it, but didn't diminish the yearning.

"Go on. Get cleaned up." Hinestroza smiled his cold smile, but there was a flare of admiration in his eyes, just for Danny. "We're going to a nice restaurant. You need some real food."

"Thank you," Danny said, and he meant it. He'd been so alone when he'd stepped beyond the prison walls with not a single place in the world to go. And now he had his old apartment back and someone to eat dinner with and a place where he belonged. Hinestroza bought Danny cheap. But the truth was, he could have had him for less.

"GODDAMN it," Miller laughed. "Stop doing that!"

"What?" Danny murmured, his tongue stealing into Miller's ear. "This... or this?"

Miller bucked his shoulder, shoving Danny onto his side of the bed, both of them buried beneath the covers, head to toe.

Danny grinned. "You know what this reminds me of, being in bed like this?" His breath floated hot into the air as he talked, their combined exhales steaming up the quilted cave.

"What?"

"When I was a little kid, I used to build forts in my bed. I'd use a whole bunch of pillows and a blanket and sometimes my mom would give me a snack to take under there, too, cookies or a brownie. Although that was always risky, because my old man would beat my ass if he found out I'd been eating in bed."

"We used to build forts outside sometimes." Miller smiled, his skin glowing like a rainbow from the light shining through the patterned bedspread.

"Getting the fort ready was always more fun than actually being in it. I'd get in there, but then I'd be lonely—no one to talk to, no one to share it with." Danny twined a lock of Miller's hair around his finger. "I like it better this way… with you."

Miller stared at Danny, his eyes unreadable in the dim light. Then he pressed forward against Danny's mouth, palming the back of Danny's head as they kissed. Danny pushed back the covers with one hand, the warm air in the room feeling almost cold when it hit his over-heated cheeks. They'd moved to a new motel two days ago, a nicer place where the thermostat actually worked.

They'd been careful since their fight, stepping lightly for fear of re-opening wounds. They hadn't revisited Danny's revelations about Ortiz, pretended their tears had never fallen. But the aftermath pressed heavy against them, that morning still alive in all the words they did not say.

Danny nipped Miller's lower lip to get his attention, smiling when Miller groaned softly in response. "We ever going to get out of bed today?"

"I have to soon. I've got that meeting with the Assistant U.S. Attorney at one."

Danny pulled his hand away too quickly, snagging at Miller's hair. "Sorry." Danny flopped over onto his back, tucking one arm behind his head.

"What's wrong?" Miller asked, leaning over, his eyes coated with a dull sheen of worry.

"Just thinking about what's coming," Danny sighed, pulling against his bottom lip with his thumb and index finger. He turned his head to look at Miller. "When I testify, will I be behind a screen or something?"

Miller shook his head. "There's no point. Hinestroza knows who the witness is against him. It'll be a closed courtroom, so there's no harm in having you on the witness stand." Miller paused. "Why?"

"I wish I didn't have to look at him when I testify."

"He won't be able to hurt you, Danny. He can't get to you."

Danny didn't answer, shifting his eyes back to where his feet drew restless circles under the sheet.

"This isn't about you being scared, is it?"

"I'm scared shitless, Miller, don't get me wrong. But, no, that wasn't what I was talking about."

"Then what?" Miller was trying hard to sound understanding, but Danny could hear the impatience trickling into his words.

"I hate letting Hinestroza down. I hate throwing all the faith he had in me back in his face." Danny closed his eyes, not wanting to witness Miller's changing expression.

"What the hell?" Miller exclaimed. "How can you still care about that man, about what he thinks or what happens to him? After what he did to Ortiz? After what he did to you?"

"Hinestroza didn't kill Ortiz, Madrigal did."

"Danny...." Miller's voice gusted out on a wave of disbelief.

Danny was aware how his words must sound, like the ravings of a crazy man, and he wondered briefly if he should censor himself. But he didn't want to pretend, not with Miller. He wanted to reveal all the complicated, messy parts of him that would never go away.

"I know Hinestroza ordered him killed, Miller. I'm not an idiot.

But he had his reasons for doing it. They may have been cruel and hard, but at least they were reasons. Madrigal killed him because it was fun."

"You think Ortiz stealing some cocaine is a good enough reason to justify being tortured to death?"

"No, of course not. But Hinestroza doesn't care about fair. He cares about results. About making sure people don't cross him or underestimate him. Violence is the way he communicates."

"But that's not justice, Danny, that's just depravity."

Danny exhaled a bitter laugh. "Justice? What the fuck is that? What does that word even mean? Is that what you guys hand out? Where's the justice in sending a twenty-two-year-old kid to a maximum security prison for selling a little cocaine? Tossing him in there to be fought over and ripped apart like a scrap of meat? You think my punishment fit my crime, Miller?"

Danny watched as Miller swallowed hard, his Adam's apple squeezing into a rigid lump in his throat. "We're not talking about you. We're talking about Hinestroza, and I can't fucking believe you're defending him!" Miller's voice rose with each word.

"I've known him for a long time," Danny said, his own voice thrumming with feeling. "You only concentrate on what's bad about him. But I see more than that. The truth is, I'm probably more like him than I am like you."

Miller jerked away, maneuvering to sit on the side of the bed, lowering his head into his hands. "I don't understand how you can even say something like that, Danny. He made you a criminal. He forced that life on you."

Danny knee-walked over to Miller's back, sliding his legs around Miller's hips to hold him from behind. "You're always so quick to think people are all one way, Miller. It's more complicated than that." Danny ran his mouth up Miller's bare spine, his lips thumping over the notches of bone. "Hinestroza may have opened the door, but I walked right through and never searched very hard for a detour sign."

Miller blew out a deep breath, his fingers stroking across Danny's calves. "Is this how you punish yourself?" Miller asked finally. "Make it all your fault instead of giving him his portion of the blame?"

Danny tried to draw back, but Miller gripped his legs tight, not allowing him to escape. "Maybe," Danny choked out. "Maybe that's what I'm doing. But he protected me for a lot of years. He was the closest thing I had to a family. And no, I don't need you to tell me how fucked-up that is." He rested his forehead on Miller's back. "I know he deserves to go to prison. I just don't want to be the one to send him there."

"You're goddamn right he deserves it," Miller said viciously. "Deserves worse. And if I play even the smallest part in making that happen, I'll be a happy man."

Danny didn't reply. Miller had never seen the way Hinestroza's daughters and granddaughter adored him, the way his wife's face lit up when he walked into a room. Miller had never stepped out of prison lonely and scared and found Hinestroza on the other side, waiting with words of praise and comfort. All Miller could see was Ortiz. But Danny knew more than one person was responsible for Ortiz's death, that his own hands would never be washed clean.

Miller lowered Danny's legs gently to the floor. "I'd better start getting ready," he said, fingers picking at the sheet. "Don't want to be late to the meeting."

"How long?" Danny asked, his voice hoarse. "How long do we have before I go?"

Miller's answer was muffled, speaking through half-closed lips. "A week. Maybe less."

A week. Maybe less. Danny tried to imagine waking up in a distant city without Miller by his side, his sheets smelling like detergent instead of sex and Miller's cinnamon skin. He pictured coming home at night to a dark apartment and watching TV alone, always wondering where Miller was and if he was happy.

Danny wanted to be the kind of man who hoped for something better, who believed deep down that life was going to start passing out gifts it had been stingy with so far. He wanted to hope that he and Miller could find a way to be together. But this was real life, and men like him didn't get happy endings. He wanted to leave Miller better than he'd found him, though, wanted Miller to understand what he meant to him.

"This is the best, most real thing that's ever happened to me," Danny said quietly. "I've spent my whole life jumping from one bad choice to the next. Choosing this, with you, is probably the only decision I've ever been proud of making." He pressed himself closer to Miller's back, wrapping his arms around his waist. "I'll never be sorry."

Miller's whole body caved under, his hands coming up to grasp Danny's as they leaned against each other. Danny wanted to howl and rage like a wounded animal, demand that they find a way to make it work. But there was no point in that. Danny had learned early that sometimes there was nothing to do but suffer through.

MILLER pulled at his tie, making sure it was straight and not hanging too low, before he turned away from his reflection. Danny was lounging in a chair near the window and he ran his eyes up and down Miller slowly, letting loose with a wolfish whistle.

"Shut up," Miller said, slipping on his black overcoat.

"What?" Danny smiled. "You look handsome."

Miller felt his cheeks warming. "Thanks," he said, fighting back the urge to look at the floor. "But you've seen me in a suit before."

"I know. Thought you looked good then too." Danny managed to wink and smirk at the same time as he stood. "Even though I wanted to kick your ass." He paused, grabbing his leather jacket from the chair. "Are you sure it's okay if I go with you?"

"Yes. I don't want you staying here alone. Colin said we'll go in through the judges' underground entrance at the courthouse, so there's no risk anyone will see you. He should be here any minute."

As if on cue, Miller heard the light tapping of a horn. He glanced out the window and saw Colin parked in a dark green sedan with tinted windows. "He's here." Miller let the curtain drop back into place. "You ready?"

"Yes," Danny replied. He looked calm, in control, Miller's Danny retreating behind a wall of indifference. Miller didn't blame him.

Danny was stepping back out into the world; he couldn't afford to walk unprotected, not even with Miller by his side.

"Hi," Colin called as they approached the car.

Miller pointed Danny toward the backseat, taking the front passenger seat for himself. "Let's do this," he said, closing his door.

Colin swiveled around, reaching over the back of the seat with his right hand. "Colin Riggs."

"Danny Butler." Danny leaned forward to shake hands and the scent of his skin wafted into Miller's nose.

Colin pivoted in his seat, putting the car in drive. He glanced at Miller. "You forget to shave today?" He seemed amused, smiling with one corner of his mouth.

"Huh?" Miller ran a hand over his stubbly jaw. "Yeah, I guess," he mumbled, Danny's smile burning a hole into the back of his neck.

The federal courthouse always made Miller's stomach knot in anticipation, even when he wasn't there to take the stand. The courthouse represented the most dreaded sort of battleground, one where words were the weapons of choice. Defense attorneys lived to pick Miller's words apart, to force him to stumble over facts, to twist his version of the truth into a lie. He could never step through the doors without bracing himself for war.

Their footsteps echoed across the cavernous rotunda, two pairs of dress shoes clicking with purpose and Danny's thudding boot-steps bringing up the rear. The glass walls of the entry hall stretched three stories high, sunlight slanting in to illuminate the giant cast-iron sculpture in the middle of the room. It was a collection of five slender columns, tipped with a variety of sharp implements, what appeared to be spears or screws. When Miller had first seen them, he'd thought they resembled instruments of torture. Even with his feet firmly planted in the prosecution camp, he imagined the sculpture, titled *Sentinels of Justice*, was not all that comforting to defendants awaiting trial.

They escorted Danny to a small conference room inside the U.S. Attorney's main office. It was empty save for a table and two chairs and a stack of legal books piled high. Danny flipped through one with a raised eyebrow. "Real page-turner," he muttered, throwing himself into a chair.

"We'll be back soon," Miller said, telling Danny with his eyes that it would be all right, but he wasn't sure if Danny received the message.

Assistant U.S. Attorney Patterson kept them waiting in the lobby for ten minutes. It was an old routine that Miller was used to—the prosecutors forever having to prove their superiority even though they were all supposed to be playing for the same team.

Tanya Patterson was seated behind her desk when they were ushered into her office, her cocoa-colored skin complemented by a crisp, cream suit. She gave them a thin-lipped smile, but Miller didn't take it personally. What she lacked in warm fuzzies she made up for in being a relentless prosecutor, well-prepared in the courtroom and not easily intimidated. Miller knew she'd take on Hinestroza with guns blazing.

"Sit down, sit down," she said, waving them toward two burgundy leather chairs opposite her desk. When they'd made themselves comfortable, she crossed her hands on her blotter. "We've got a problem with this case," she stated matter-of-factly.

"What kind of problem?" Goosebumps broke out on Miller's arms. Instinctively he knew it was bad, dread coiling hot inside his gut.

"We can't get Hinestroza into the country for trial."

Miller stared at her. "I thought that was all taken care of. I was told not to worry about that end of it, that it was being handled."

"It was being handled, before your witness shot his mouth off to his ex-wife and Hinestroza found out what was going on. Now he's not setting foot in the country. He's staying put down in Colombia. Or if he is making trips up here, we're not getting so much as a whisper about it through the usual channels." She sighed. "Of course, if would could get our hands on the cell phone records faster, it might help. As it is, by the time we figure out where he's been, he's already somewhere else."

"We do the best we can with the phone records. You know that." Miller protested. "It's not Danny's fault!"

"Tanya," Colin interjected. "What's the bottom line here? Are you trying Hinestroza or not?"

"I'd love to," Patterson said, "believe me. But if there's no warm body in the defendant's chair, then there's no trial."

"So, what happens now?" Miller demanded. "Danny's just going to have to wait to start his new life until we can get Hinestroza up here?"

Patterson shifted her eyes to her white-tipped fingernails. "No. Chances are there's never going to be a trial." She looked up at Miller. "We're cutting Mr. Butler loose."

Miller blinked slowly, Patterson swimming across his line of vision. He heard her words but couldn't process their meaning. "What? What about the Witness Protection Program?"

"You both know the drill. There's no Witness Protection Program if you're not a witness. He's no longer eligible."

Miller shot forward in his chair, slamming one hand down on the desk. "They'll kill him!" he exclaimed. "They're going to kill him!"

"You know how the system works, Miller," Patterson said, her condescending lawyer voice scraping across his skin like sandpaper.

And the hell of it was, he did know. He'd seen similar scenarios play out dozens of times. Witnesses protected until the day the verdict came down, then cast into the wind as if murders couldn't be ordered from behind an electrified fence. Men coerced into taking a plea and then told too late the Witness Protection Program wasn't available to them. It had never bothered Miller in the past. He used his witnesses to get the information he needed and then forgot about them when the trial was over. Sacrificing your way up the criminal totem pole to reach the highest offender was how the game was played, and everyone understood the rules. But that was before now, before Danny.

Miller surged to his feet, jerking away when Colin reached for his arm. "I forced him into this deal! I didn't give him any goddamn choice because we needed a witness, a good witness. And we got him. We got him because I promised him he'd be safe. And now we're just throwing him back out there? That's what we're going to do?"

"Listen." Patterson pushed back from her desk with both hands, her rolling chair squeaking across the floor. "It's not a good situation. I admit it. But we don't have any choice. We can't protect him indefinitely. And frankly, Miller, I think you're forgetting that it's Mr. Butler's own criminal record that got him into this predicament in the first place. He's hardly a choir boy."

"I don't give a shit if he's Jack the Ripper; we cut him loose and he's dead the next day!" Miller yelled. "Have you seen what Hinestroza does to people who cross him? Do you have any fucking idea?"

"You had better watch yourself, Special Agent Sutton," Patterson said, her voice dropping to freezer level. "I'm willing to take a pass on prosecuting Mr. Butler's gun charge since he agreed to help us out. Please make sure he understands, though, that if he gets into trouble again, that gun charge will be pursued."

Miller gaped at her. "Are you kidding me? I'm supposed to walk out there and tell him, 'Sorry, deal's off. Good luck staying alive. And, by the way, you should be thanking us because we're not prosecuting your ass on the gun charge'?"

"Miller, calm down," Colin said, moving into his sight line, trying to catch his eye.

"Don't tell me to calm down!" Miller raged. "I gave him my word that he would be safe! He risked his life and now—" Miller's voice broke and Colin cut his eyes away, discomfort etched in every line of his face.

"Fuck this," Miller muttered, shoving out through the door.

He tore up the hallway separating him from Danny, enveloped in a swirling tornado of fury, buffeted on all sides by guilt and shame and the awful knowledge that his own zeal for Hinestroza's blood had led to this moment. He'd been so damn anxious to nail Hinestroza that he'd ignored Danny's human face, manipulated him and threatened him and bent Danny to his will.

And how's that any different from what Hinestroza's been doing to him for the last decade? You may be on opposite sides of the law, but your methods for breaking Danny look awfully similar.

Miller wanted to return to that cold interrogation room where the coppery tang of Danny's blood clogged the air, where Danny had stood against him, so cocky and arrogant, and whisper in Danny's ear, *Don't give in. Don't believe a word I say. Fight me. Fight me.* Because Danny had been right. There was no justice here.

THE list of potentially relevant features of criminal behavior is long; the fact that they can occur in multiple combinations means that the list of possible permutations of factors is virtually endless. The appropriate relationships among these different factors are exceedingly difficult to establish, for they are often context specific.

Danny slammed shut the *Federal Sentencing Guidelines*, the sound punctuated by the conference room door banging open.

"Hey," he said, glancing up as Miller and Colin entered the room. He tapped the cover of the *Guidelines*. "This shit is so boring. No wonder lawyers are such assholes, having to read this crap all day. You should—" The rest of Danny's sentence died in his throat when he looked at Miller's face, cloudy with rage, his eyes unable to meet Danny's, his jaw muscles tight as steel.

"What's going on?" Danny asked, rising to his feet.

"There isn't going to be any trial." Miller's voice slammed hard against the walls of the room, his hands balling into fists as he spoke.

Danny moved around the table, closer to Miller. "Okay," he said. "Why not? What does that mean?"

"We're having trouble getting Hinestroza into the country," Colin said. "And without him here—"

"You know, he told me that," Miller interrupted. "Danny told me weeks ago that we'd never get Hinestroza here. And I told him not to worry about it. I told him we had it covered." Miller barked out something that might have been a laugh.

"Miller," Danny said, reaching out to touch his arm. He could see Colin watching, his eyes darting between them, and let his hand fall.

"Without him here we can't go forward." Miller closed his eyes, scrubbing at his face with one palm. "And if there's no trial, then you aren't a witness. And if you're not a witness, then there's no Witness Protection Program."

Miller's words sunk in slowly, each one piling up on top of the last, leaving Danny buried under. "So I'm on my own," he said. It was not a question. And he was not surprised. He believed in Miller, but he didn't believe in this—the system or justice or that twelve people in a jury box and the judge behind the bench always came up with the right answer.

"We can keep you in protective custody for three more days," Colin told him. "To give us a little time to try and come up with a plan. But yeah, after that, you're on your own."

"Jesus!" Miller exclaimed, turning away from Danny.

"Miller, there's something else." Colin spoke to his back. "According to Patterson, there are rumors floating around that you're on Madrigal's hit list now too. Apparently he took the tire incident personally."

Danny's whole body froze, each inhale burning into his lungs like acid. He'd known Miller was in danger while they were together. Madrigal wouldn't hesitate to cut down whoever stood between him and Danny. But he'd thought Miller would be out of Madrigal's path once Danny was gone, safe to move on with his life, to once again stride tall and confident through these halls.

"We're going to have to talk about getting you somewhere safe," Colin continued when Miller didn't answer.

"So we cut Danny loose, but we protect our own. Is that how it works?"

"Miller, he's right. Don't worry about me," Danny said urgently. "Worry about yourself. Madrigal won't give up."

"And what about you, Danny? Where the hell are you going to go that he won't be able to find you?"

"I don't know." Danny shrugged. "I'll figure something out. I always do." He fought hard to hide the fault line opening beneath his words.

They rode back to the motel without speaking, Miller looking out the passenger window and refusing eye contact. The air was so thick with tension it made Danny's neck muscles ache, relentless, oppressive fingers pinching down his spine.

When they pulled up to the motel, Miller threw open the car door, storming away before Colin was fully stopped. Danny moved more slowly, an icy north wind swirling around him as he stepped out.

"Danny."

"Yeah?" He stuck his head back into the warm interior.

"I'm sorry," Colin said. His words were sincere, but his eyes already marked Danny as a dead man.

Danny nodded, shutting the door with a sharp click. He let himself into the motel room and locked the door behind him, throwing his jacket on top of Miller's already-shed overcoat and tie. Miller was pacing in the small space at the foot of the bed, his long frame traveling the same ten feet over and over, desperation pulsing off him like heat waves on a summer sidewalk.

"Why aren't you screaming at me?" Miller asked angrily, his eyes blazing with guilt. "Why aren't you telling me what an asshole I am, huh? Because you were right all along, Danny. You were right!"

"Yeah, I was right." Danny sat down on the bed with a sigh.

"We're going to figure something out," Miller said. "Do you hear me?"

Danny laughed—a tired, hollow sound. There was nothing to figure out. They were both hunted men now, and Danny couldn't live if anything happened to Miller. If Miller died, Danny died. If Miller suffered, Danny suffered. Danny's heart was no longer his own. Hinestroza finally possessed the key to Danny's undying cooperation— and he didn't even know it. Gallows humor at its sickening best.

Miller ripped at his shirt with one hand. "I'm going to take a shower. Then we can get some food and talk about this." He rubbed the back of his hand against Danny's cheek. "Okay?"

"Okay," Danny said. His fake smile bounced back at him from the mirror on the wall.

He waited until he heard the water running and then he got up and crossed to the mirror, studying his face in the glass. They could run, together or separately, but Danny wanted more for Miller than life on the run, always dreading what was coming around the next bend, never sleeping easy. Danny knew the price of fear and he would not allow Miller to pay it.

This is your chance, Danny. Finally, your chance to save someone you care about. To save the person you love most in the world. The only person you've ever loved.

Danny was no martyr. He could feel tiny pinpricks of terror bursting into larger life until they took up all the space in his body. But there was a rightness to this decision that he could not deny. Danny had been waiting a long time for Ortiz to call in his marker, to ask Danny to step up to the plate he'd run from the first time around. And now here it was: a chance to make up for what he'd done to Ortiz; a chance to make a choice that benefited someone else, for once, instead of himself; a chance to save Miller and give him back his life; a chance to be the kind of man Miller deserved.

Danny picked up Miller's cell phone, tossed onto the dresser along with his wallet and keys. He opened the wallet with one hand, running his finger over Miller's driver's license picture. Miller's face was somber, not even attempting a smile for the camera. Danny wanted Miller to be happy; he wanted him to live without looking over his shoulder.

It took him two tries to dial the number he'd had memorized for a decade, his fingers shaking against the tiny buttons on the keypad. He held the phone to his ear, the ringing sounding far away as he stared at himself in the mirror. He looked at peace; he looked already gone.

Someone picked up on the other end, a deep voice rumbling over the distance between them. Danny took a shuddering breath. "Mr. Hinestroza? It's me. It's Danny."

CHAPTER 14

"DANNY."

Danny heard the surprise in Hinestroza's voice, the slight upswing at the end of his name. He could imagine Hinestroza leaning back in his chair, eyebrows raised in curiosity. He would find Danny contacting him this way nothing if not intriguing. Hinestroza was always amused by a good surprise, secure in his ability to savor the last laugh.

Danny tried to speak, his voice failing to move past a throat clogged with fate and fear. The silence stretched out painfully, a rubber band of possibilities pulled taut, waiting to explode into meaning.

"Mr. Hinestroza," he finally managed. "I want… I want to make a deal."

Hinestroza chuckled, his tongue clicking out a faint *tsk-tsk* against the roof of his mouth. "Danny. I don't need to make a deal with you."

"Yes, you do," Danny corrected him, struggling to keep his voice strong. "I've been pretty hard to catch so far. Madrigal's already let me get away twice."

Hinestroza was silent for a moment. "I'll humor you. What kind of deal do you have in mind?"

"A trade."

"A trade? Enlighten me."

"The FBI agent who's been protecting me. The rumor is that Madrigal is planning on killing him too. I want you to tell Madrigal to let him go."

"I don't care about the FBI agent. He was only ever incidental in getting to you."

"But you can call Madrigal off, right? I mean, if you tell him not to kill the agent, he doesn't get killed. You have the final say."

Hinestroza's lighter clicked into life, the sound of small puffs floating into the receiver. "Why are you willing to do this for some FBI agent?" he asked, disdain clear in his tone.

"That's not important," Danny said, closing his eyes. "What's important is that I'll let Madrigal come get me. I'll go without a fight." He clenched his fist. "Please." He would beg if he had to, get down on his knees and plead, whatever it took. Begging was such a small price to pay when measured against Miller's life.

"Are you setting me up, Danny?" Hinestroza asked, his voice smooth in Danny's ear.

"What good would that do me? If I lure Madrigal into a trap, you'll have someone else on my trail the next day."

Danny could hear Hinestroza weighing the wisdom of his words. "Where are you?"

"Do we have a deal?" Danny countered.

"I always knew you were a brave man." Hinestroza paused. "Yes. We have a deal. Your FBI agent is safe. And you go with Madrigal. No tricks, no resisting."

"Yes," Danny agreed, nodding as though Hinestroza could see him, relief an anesthetic in his blood. Miller was safe; Miller would live. "I'm at the Best Western Motel off I-35 and 43rd Street, room 132. I'll be waiting."

"Good-bye, Danny."

Danny flipped the phone closed. He didn't need anyone to tell him how sick it was that he felt a momentary pang of sadness, wishing Hinestroza had been sorrier to say good-bye.

MILLER stayed in the shower a long time, until the hot water was running lukewarm, the steamy clouds of vapor dissipating against his wrinkled fingertips. He'd told Danny they would figure something out, but he had no idea what or how. Danny could run. But how far would he get? Miller could run with him, but how much was he willing to leave behind? A life with Danny… that was what Miller wanted. But if he was being candid with himself, he wanted that life on his terms—stable, honest, safe. But he couldn't have those things and have Danny too.

He dried himself off with the scratchy motel towel, hardly bigger than a washcloth and thin as paper. He pulled on jeans and a black T-shirt, leaning on the sink to stare into the mirror. They would come up with a plan. They would find a way. Because if they didn't… if they didn't, Danny would die.

Miller shivered slightly when he moved out of the damp humidity of the bathroom. Danny was seated where he'd left him on the end of the bed. He'd put his leather jacket back on, his combat boots still on his feet.

"Are you cold?" Miller asked, rubbing his hair with the towel. "Or are you coming with me to get the food?"

Danny didn't answer, his head swinging slowly in Miller's direction. His eyes were big and bright, swimming in a too-pale face. Miller wanted to hold him and tell him it would all be okay, that Danny shouldn't be scared, but he didn't want to lie.

Danny pushed off the bed, moving steadily toward Miller, stopping when their bodies were pressed together, his eyes roaming over Miller's face. He ran a finger across Miller's eyebrow, down his cheek, rubbing against the stubble, tickling across Miller's lower lip like a blind man memorizing a beloved landscape. Danny smiled a little, his mouth trembling as he brought his other hand up to frame Miller's face, stopping Miller's questions with his mouth, murmuring sounds that weren't words against Miller's lips, his tongue soothing and stroking. Danny closed his eyes, resting their foreheads together.

"I stayed to tell you that you're safe now," Danny whispered. "You don't need to worry anymore."

A pure, clean shot of terror catapulted into Miller's chest. His heart tripped over itself, slamming hard against his ribs. "Danny, what are you talking—"

His head snapped up as a series of knocks rang out at the door—

hard against the wood, but something jaunty in the rhythm, as though the person on the other side was singing a tune with their fist.

"Wait here," Miller breathed, starting to ease around Danny's body in the direction of the door. Danny put a staying hand against his chest, stopping his forward progress.

"It's all right," Danny said. "I know who it is."

"What? You told someone where we were? Who is it?" Miller demanded.

Danny stared at him for a moment, running one hand along Miller's jaw. Then he turned away, flinging the door open before Miller could make a move to stop him.

"Hello, Danny." The voice from the doorway cut like a cold blade, Miller's stomach dropping through the floor at the sound. And then the face came into view, the dark hair slicked back, the pointy white teeth framed by a leering smile. Juan Madrigal. And he already had his hand on Danny's arm, pulling him out of the room.

Miller lurched for his gun, snatched it off the dresser, thumbed the safety off, cocked it, and aimed in less than a second. "Freeze!" Miller yelled. "Don't move!"

No one reacted the way he expected. Danny watched Miller with sad and sorry eyes, but he didn't seem afraid or even surprised. And Madrigal only smiled wider at Miller's gun, his own brought up against Danny's side, the hand on Danny's arm tightening as he looked from Danny to Miller and back again.

"I thought you said no tricks, Danny," Madrigal commented.

"Put the gun down, Miller," Danny said, his voice even.

"What?" Miller barked, his fingers not moving from the trigger. "What the fuck are you talking about?"

"It's not loaded. I took the bullets out of the magazine."

Miller stared at Danny, not taking his eyes away even as Madrigal spoke. "You are one lucky man. You're off my 'to-do' list, thanks to Danny here." Madrigal thumped the side of Danny's head hard with the butt of his gun. Danny stumbled sideways at the impact and Miller stepped forward to steady him.

"Uh-uh." Madrigal swung the gun in Miller's direction. "Back off." Madrigal jerked hard on Danny's arm, pulling him closer to pat him down with a rough hand, fingers sliding under his shirt to check for a wire. "Let's go, asshole," he said when he was satisfied Danny was clean.

"Danny!" Miller cried.

"Let me go, Miller," Danny said, his voice low. "It's all right. You're safe now. He won't come after you. I promise." His boots scraped over the threshold as Madrigal dragged him backward.

"Don't think about following us," Madrigal said. "I'll start shooting him. Bullets are pretty good at removing body parts, one by one." He winked at Miller, shoving his gun hard against the front of Danny's jeans.

Miller was waiting for someone to jump out from behind the curtain, announce that this was all a joke; waiting for Danny's hand on his shoulder in the dark hours of the night, reminding him it was just a dream, soothing him back to sleep. But the chill wind gusting in through the door, the black gun against Danny's body, and the spicy scent of Madrigal's cologne all told Miller this was reality. *This was happening.* Danny had made it happen.

Miller's body gave birth to a vast and impotent rage, none of his usual tricks retaining any of their remembered power. The gun in his hand was useless and silent, the strength of his limbs pointless with nowhere to strike, and the hot fury in his brain not knowing which way to burn.

He followed them out into the parking lot, stumbling along behind, not close enough to touch but close enough to drown in the anguish spilling off Danny in great, swamping waves, his eyes begging Miller to go back, to let go… let go. Madrigal shoved Danny into the passenger seat of his car, the tinted windows swallowing him in a single gulp. Madrigal stepped around the front of the car to fold himself behind the wheel. He didn't even look at Miller, the blond man shouting hoarsely in the parking lot of no more interest than a pebble under his foot or a leaf dancing in the wind.

"Danny!" Miller screamed. "Danny!" But there was no one to hear. Danny was gone, disappearing as if he had never been.

"SO, WHAT does FBI-boy have that Ortiz didn't?" Madrigal asked around his cigarette. "Or is that a stupid question?" He snorted out a noseful of smoke, impressed with his own humor.

Danny didn't respond, testing the side of his head with delicate fingers, wincing at the rising lump.

"I mean, you were happy enough to let Ortiz die. But not some guy you met a month ago?" Madrigal took his eyes off the road, glancing at Danny's face. "Don't worry about that knot on your head. Pretty soon it's going to seem like a hangnail."

Danny looked out the window at bare trees whipping by and lawns turned brown and dormant. He wished he could have died in the spring, when everything was green.

They didn't drive far, pulling into a cracked driveway less than ten minutes later. The asphalt heaved upward in ragged chunks, giving way to weeds and dirt. "Get out," Madrigal instructed, stopping the car next to a house with plywood-covered windows, its once-white paint reduced to gray flakes that dotted the grass like dandruff.

The block was quiet, most of the houses abandoned—the kind of neighborhood where people kept their eyes straight ahead when they drove by, not wanting to see. Madrigal marched Danny up the back steps and shoved him through the boarded-up door that had already been kicked open, sharp splinters of wood littering the stoop.

Danny stopped in the gutted kitchen, empty squares visible on the filthy linoleum where a refrigerator and stove had once stood. The walls were pockmarked at irregular intervals with gaping holes, as though a giant had passed through, smashing in plaster with his fisted hands. Two metal folding chairs were the only furniture in the room and Danny coughed out a startled laugh, unable to help himself. "You carry those around in your trunk just for times like this?"

Madrigal popped him in the face with the gun and blood gushed out of Danny's temple, hot and slick. "You know me, smartass, always prepared," Madrigal said. "A regular Boy Scout. Now take off your jacket and sit the fuck down."

Danny tossed his jacket onto the floor and sat, blinking back the blood clinging to his lashes. "What's the other chair for? I thought you liked to move around while you worked." Madrigal didn't answer. He removed a cord from a black bag on the counter and tied Danny's torso to the chair.

"The chair's for me, Danny," came a voice from the doorway, a voice Danny would know anywhere, the sound as familiar as his own breathing. Danny looked up, finding Hinestroza's coal black eyes from behind a sea of red.

MILLER stood frozen in the parking lot. He wanted to move but didn't know how. It reminded him of when he'd been stunned by a Taser gun at the academy, his brain issuing commands his body simply could not follow.

He's going to die, Miller. He's going to die if you don't get your ass in gear.

He sprinted back to the motel room, his feet sliding out from under him as he charged inside, his hands pawing frantically across the dresser top, fingers clutching at his cell phone. Colin answered on the second ring, his voice cut off by Miller's harsh words. "Madrigal has Danny. They're gone."

"What?"

"We need an APB out on a black Honda Accord, Missouri license number GHT 4783."

"Got it," Colin said, not wasting time with pointless questions.

"Call Patterson. Find out who her source was on Madrigal. We need to find out if they know anything more. Where Madrigal's been staying, where he's planning on going. Anything."

"I'll call you back. Stay where you are, Miller. I'm on my way."

Miller slid his phone into his back pocket, catching a glimpse of his white, strained face in the mirror. How could Danny have done it? How could he have thought that this was ever what Miller wanted? How could he not understand that his death wouldn't free Miller but would be a weight Miller could never shoulder, a burden that would crush him?

Without wanting to, Miller's mind skipped to the police report on Ortiz, the details of how he'd died, how he'd suffered. "Fuck!" Miller sobbed out, his terror translating into destruction. His arms swept across the dresser, sending the TV crashing to the floor with a sharp pop of glass; the mirror was wrenched off the wall and smashed against the dresser top; chairs were heaved sideways, curtains were ripped halfway off their rods. And still Miller had a surplus of grief and anger left to spend.

Get it together. You can't help him like this. You have to be smart. You have to be calm. Help him, goddamn it!

Miller gasped in breaths, his head hanging low. He felt untethered, as if the strings connecting him to Danny were being snipped one by one. The phone in his pocket broke the silence.

"What?"

"Patterson's contact doesn't know much." Colin's voice was strained, high with tension. "Just that Madrigal was scoping out abandoned houses earlier this week."

"Where?"

There was a too-long pause. "He didn't know, Miller. The most he could guess was somewhere on the East side."

Last time he was here he used an abandoned house on the Paseo, Danny's voice whispered in his ear. "I'm going," Miller said, already moving out the door, grabbing his gun as he left.

"Miller, wait! I'm—"

But he couldn't wait. Madrigal wasn't going to stop and allow him time to catch up. If he wanted to save Danny, he would have to do it alone.

HINESTROZA took the chair directly across from Danny, crossing his legs to balance one ankle atop his knee, careful not to mar the crease in his dark gray slacks.

"What… what are you doing here? The FBI said they couldn't get you into the country."

Hinestroza laughed. "I go where I please, Danny, you should know that by now. The FBI doesn't frighten me." He pointed at Danny with his unlit cigar. "I had to come up. The big shipment arrived this week and you weren't available to oversee it. You left me… how do they say it," he twirled his cigar in a small circle, "in the lurch. And I had to make sure Madrigal didn't fall down on the job for a third time."

They both turned their heads at the metallic clanking from the counter as Madrigal laid out his instruments. Danny could see the razor and a pair of pliers and—proof that an old dog can learn new tricks—a set of gleaming brass knuckles, all of it making Madrigal's gun look so benign in comparison.

"Danny," Hinestroza said softly, snagging his attention again. "I wish it hadn't come to this."

"Me too," Danny whispered. Why did having Hinestroza sit across from him make this so much more difficult? It would be easier if it ended in a blaze of hatred, Madrigal's golden eyes the sole focus for Danny's anger. But Danny's feelings for Hinestroza were too complicated for such single-minded emotion. Rage stewed in a melting-pot mix with respect and fear and the humiliating, aching need to be loved. Hinestroza's presence made Danny feel weak when he so desperately needed to be strong—made him want to seek forgiveness and be granted absolution without even understanding the exact nature of his sin.

"I'm sorry," he said. "I never wanted to testify against you."

"But you were going to do it."

"They threatened me. I didn't think I had a choice."

"There are always choices."

"Yes, there are." Danny thought of Miller, breathing free and out in the world. Some choices were worth whatever price life demanded in payment.

"I always liked you, Danny," Hinestroza said. "I understand the feeling is probably not mutual"—he flashed his icy smile—"but I wanted you to know."

Danny nodded and Hinestroza nodded in return. "Let's get this over with," he said.

Madrigal stepped in front of Danny, blocking Hinestroza from view. He had the pliers in his hand. "When I used these on your wife, she screamed like a cat in heat. Let's see how you do, Danny."

Danny cast his eyes up to the ceiling. He remembered how Miller had looked on the day they'd met, so hard and untouchable in the interrogation room... how scared he'd been when Danny had kissed him, his lips warm and soft... how Miller hadn't hesitated when he'd come into Danny's arms that snowy day in the apartment... how from the very beginning it had been about more than sex for both of them. He remembered that Miller was alive.

And the end might not come quickly. But it would come.

FORTY-SIX minutes. That's the head start Madrigal had. Miller tried not to think about how much damage could be inflicted on a human body in that length of time. Maybe they'd argued first. Maybe it had taken Madrigal a while to get started. Maybe....

Yeah, Miller, and maybe they're playing poker and having a beer. Find him!

He'd driven up and down the entire length of the Paseo, slowing down in front of each abandoned house, craning his neck for a glimpse of the black Accord. He'd ignored his ringing phone, every bit of his attention focused on searching, on finding. He pulled his car over to the curb and took steadying breaths, his hands shaking against the wheel. Forty-seven minutes. Now what?

Now you turn around and do it again, because what choice do you have?

"Please," he whispered, tears backing up thick and heavy in his throat, making it impossible to swallow. "Please, help me." He didn't even know who he was talking to, whether it was God or Danny or the indifferent winter air. Miller couldn't remember the last time he'd prayed, but he wanted to get down on his knees and promise everything he had, offer up whatever sacrifice God demanded. He understood the desperation that led people to make deals with the devil.

Forty-eight minutes. Miller pulled the car into a squealing U-turn, steering with one hand as he leaned into the passenger seat to peer at each house. There was a row of five decrepit houses, all of them neglected for years. Miller slammed on his brakes as he passed the second one, as something peeking out from the back of the house caught his eye. There it was: a flash of black hiding where the driveway curved behind the house.

Miller's stomach shrank into a knot, his hands flexing on the wheel. He turned right at the next side street and parked against the curb. He checked his gun, reloaded from the bullets he kept in the glove compartment. He came at the house from the back, picking his way through yards crowded with trash and debris, broken glass crunching beneath his feet. Miller jumped lightly over the ramshackle chain-link fence surrounding the house, skirting his way around the car to check the license plate. GHT 4783. Madrigal's car.

There was no time for relief or fear. Danny was dying inside that house. Miller's brain reverted to agent-mode automatically, noting facts with the ticking accuracy of a computer: only one car, kicked-in back door, no drag marks in the dirt—Danny had been upright when they'd entered the house—eye-level window on the side of the house missing half its plywood patch. Miller moved around the corner of the house, careful to stick to the clumps of dead grass, where his footsteps made no sound. He pressed himself up against the exterior, taking a deep breath and risking a quick look inside. The window opened into an empty room, the wood floors coated with a thick paste of dust and grime, the walls decorated by a graffiti artist's multicolored spray cans.

The room led into the kitchen and Miller could see Danny tied to a chair, blood running from his hand onto the floor in thin streams, his elbow bent backward, snapped like a twig. His head was hanging forward, bloody and swollen. Miller put a hand up against the side of the house, heaving in air, fighting back the black spots swarming across his vision. What do you do when the person you love most in the world is dying right in front of you, being taken apart piece by piece before your eyes?

You fucking suck it up and get in there, asshole!

Miller glanced inside once more, noting Madrigal's position next to Danny. He didn't have a gun in his hands, but Miller could see one tucked into his waistband within easy reach. Another set of legs was visible, seated in a folding chair, but Miller didn't have a clear view of who was there or what sort of weapon they might be holding. It didn't matter. He had to go in. There was no time to stop and call Colin. It was a moot point anyway; by the time he arrived, it would be over, one way or the other.

Miller cocked his gun and then crept around to the back door again. He climbed the steps on silent feet. A deep voice floated out through the cracked doorframe. "I've had enough. Finish it."

"But I barely started," a voice Miller recognized as Madrigal's protested. He sounded like a whiny child being denied a long-promised treat.

"I said finish it!"

Miller didn't take time to think, instead counting on his years of training to guide him through. He burst into the room, the door exploding inward and slamming against the wall, the knob burying itself in the mealy plaster. "Don't move," he yelled, his rock-steady gun hand trained on Madrigal. "Or I'll blow your fucking head off!"

Madrigal froze, both hands rising slowly in the air. But Miller had to fight his trigger finger, which wanted—with almost undeniable force—to pull back, fire bullet after bullet into Madrigal's body. Miller willed his finger to stop moving, glancing at the man seated in the folding chair across from Danny. Hinestroza. Miller refused to show his surprise, not wanting to give away a single advantage. "Get your hands behind your head, right now!"

Hinestroza complied. He didn't seem agitated in any way, his movements relaxed. Miller moved to Danny's side, reaching down with one hand to yank the restraining cord off his body. "Danny," he said urgently, not taking his eyes off Madrigal. "Danny, can you hear me?"

Danny moaned, a low, desperate sound, his head rolling forward on a limp neck, a loose-hanging flap of skin near his ear giving Miller a glimpse of muscle underneath. Danny's eyes shifted upward, the pupils so dilated that his green eyes looked black. But those eyes recognized him, Miller was sure. He rested a hand on Danny's shoulder briefly.

This was do-or-die time. He couldn't hold Madrigal for long. Not with these odds. Any second now Madrigal was going to make a move; he couldn't afford not to.

"Turn around," Miller commanded. "Put your hands flat on the counter."

Madrigal turned, but too quickly, one hand grasping the pliers, throwing them hard at Miller's head. He ducked and the pliers winged past in a blast of air, landing with a thud in the corner. Miller only lost his concentration for a moment, but that was all Madrigal needed, his arm shifting behind his body to grab his gun. Miller straightened, taking aim as Madrigal's gun centered on his own head. It was a race to see who was going to get off the first shot, but before either trigger could be pulled, Danny launched out of his chair, bursting forward with a ragged scream, throwing himself at Madrigal.

"Danny!" Miller yelled, pulling his gun up short as Danny dove into his line of fire, driving Madrigal backward. Time stopped moving as Madrigal and Danny wrestled for control of the gun, Madrigal's two good hands against Danny's one undamaged arm—brute strength against a decade of pent-up vengeance waiting for its moment. Miller couldn't get a clear shot without risking Danny and he didn't dare move away from Hinestroza. This was Danny's fight now.

The seconds spun out into eternity, the bright bang of a gunshot slamming everything back into focus. Danny wrenched free, his momentum toppling him backward, pulling Madrigal down with him, and the gun spun wildly across the kitchen floor. Danny pushed himself across the floor with his heels and single working elbow, Madrigal tangled around his legs, trying to climb over Danny's body to reach the gun.

Miller moved around the chair in an attempt to grab the gun, or at least kick it away, his own weapon still pointed at Hinestroza. He pulled his foot back to make contact as Danny threw his arm over his head, hand scrabbling on the floor, fingers finding and tightening on their goal. He brought the gun up between his bent knees and aimed at Madrigal's head.

He didn't give a warning the way Miller had. He didn't hesitate. He bared his bloody teeth and blew Madrigal's brains out against the worn plaster walls—bullet meeting skull, proving that it was possible to kill Madrigal after all.

It took Miller a moment to move, for his professional instincts to take precedence over the shock. He crossed to Hinestroza and tied him to his chair, taking pleasure in wrenching the cord tighter than he needed to, watching Hinestroza's mouth curl up in displeasure as the soiled cord left a thin red line against his snowy-white shirt front.

Danny shoved Madrigal's body off his legs with frantic kicks. He backed away, scooting up to a sitting position against the wall, the gun hanging loosely from his fingers.

"Danny?" Miller said, squatting down in front of him, trying to catch Danny's wildly rolling eyes. His face was such a field of blood that Miller couldn't tell what damage he'd suffered. "Can you get up?" He held out his hand and Danny covered it with his own palm, a small sobbing noise escaping him as Miller pulled him upright.

"I'm going to call—" Miller looked at the wall where Danny had been leaning. It was splashed with bright red, streaking down to pool on the grimy baseboards. "Danny." Miller's voice didn't sound like his own, high and panicky. "Is that your blood?"

Danny looked confused, glancing from the wall to his own body. "I… I think he shot me," he managed finally.

"Oh, Jesus, Danny," Miller moaned, wondering how he could have missed the blood on Danny's shirt, his left shoulder soaked dark red, his T-shirt ragged and torn. "Oh, Christ."

Danny let go of Miller's hand, slumping back down onto the floor, sliding sideways, his head coming to rest against the worn linoleum.

Miller dialed 911 with shaking hands, his voice ragged and barely coherent as he spoke to the emergency operator. He let the phone fall when he was done, lowering himself down next to Danny. "Please, Danny," he breathed. "Please hold on." He hoped he hadn't exhausted all of God's good wishes earlier, hoped God hadn't had enough of this sordid mess and turned His back on them with a disgusted sigh. Miller knelt on the floor and used his palms to stanch the bleeding. He tried not to think, tried to concentrate only on Danny's warm skin, refusing to feel it growing colder, looking away from Danny's life bubbling up between his fingers.

MILLER rubbed his hands together, Danny's blood worked into every line of his palms, embedded in black half-moons under his fingernails. Colin had suggested—twice—that Miller find a bathroom and clean up, but he'd ignored the advice, scared to wash any of Danny away.

They'd been waiting at the hospital for more than two hours. Everyone in the emergency room gave them a wide berth, staying far away from the bloody, broken man who watched the trauma room's swinging doors with unblinking eyes.

Miller had ridden with Danny in the ambulance, Colin following behind in his car. Danny had been unconscious most of the way, waking once, briefly, as they'd neared the hospital. His eyes had found Miller's amid the chaos of needles sticking into his skin, the oxygen mask breathing life into his body. Miller hadn't given him a chance to speak, had leaned over and whispered fiercely in Danny's ear, "You don't remember anything, Danny. You don't remember."

"Miller. Miller?"

"Huh? What?" Miller didn't take his eyes off the doors hiding Danny from view.

"What exactly happened back there?" Colin asked.

Miller had already given him the abbreviated version as he'd watched Danny being loaded onto a stretcher at the scene. He knew what Colin was doing. Testing Miller's recollections, looking for holes. It came with the job.

"I found the house. Madrigal had Danny tied to a chair. I went in and Madrigal went for his gun. We fought over it. Danny got hit when the gun fired. I managed to get the weapon away from Madrigal and I shot him." Miller bit out each sentence, adding no more details than he'd given the first time around.

He could feel Colin watching him. "Nobody else was there?"

"No."

Silence. "Then what happened to Madrigal's car?"

Miller's breath froze in his throat, but he shrugged easily, eyes still on the doors. "It's a bad neighborhood. Cars don't stay put for long."

Colin sighed. "Miller."

"Do we have to talk about this right now?" All Miller's fear spilled over into anger at Colin. "Jesus Christ!"

"We're going to have to debrief you. And Butler too—"

Miller stopped listening. A doctor came through the swinging doors, pulling a surgical cap off his head wearily, his eyes searching the sea of waiting faces. "Agent Sutton?" he called.

Miller shot out of his seat like a carnival act, transformed into a human cannonball. He couldn't stop himself from invading the doctor's personal space, crowding too close, pushing for answers. "How is he? Is he going to make it?"

"Mr. Butler is almost out of surgery now; they're closing him up. We were able to remove the bullet from his shoulder successfully. He's also—"

"Is he going to make it?" Miller repeated.

The doctor held up one hand, asking Miller for patience he did not have. "He has extensive injuries. A fractured humerus and a dislocated elbow, a severe facial laceration near his left ear. We brought in our plastic surgeon to suture that wound. He's missing all the fingernails on his left hand. He has a concussion from blunt head trauma and significant kidney damage. He was hit in the right kidney multiple times with something harder than a fist."

"Brass knuckles," Miller said, low.

The doctor didn't appear shocked. Working the emergency room in this part of town meant he'd probably seen it all before. "That would account for the damage. It's still touch-and-go as to whether he'll lose the kidney. He is in serious but stable condition. We anticipate—"

"Is he going to make it?" Miller cried.

The doctor looked at him—two men used to having the upper hand staring each other down. Then he nodded slowly. "Yes, he's going to make it. With his gunshot wound and other injuries, the risk of infection is high. But barring serious complications, he should eventually make a complete recovery."

"Thank you," Miller whispered, every muscle in his body melting with relief after hours of holding himself stiff with tension. He could feel the hot scald of tears on his cheeks and he didn't care, didn't care that Colin was standing next to him, that the true nature of his relationship with Danny was being revealed. The life he'd known was over, regardless, thrown away in that filthy, blood-spattered kitchen. His moral compass had been broken in an instant. And already Miller was learning the cost of making his very own deal with the devil.

CHAPTER 15

"SO, WHAT happens now?"

Miller ignored Hinestroza, shifting his weight as the linoleum bit into his knees, his hands aching from pressing so tightly against Danny's wound.

"I assume I'll be arrested."

"Damn right," Miller said, not even sparing Hinestroza a glance.

"And then Danny will have to testify against me." Hinestroza hummed lightly in his throat, a sound calculated to catch Miller's attention. "Our deal will be off... and he'll always be a hunted man. Putting me in prison doesn't stop anything, you know. My people will keep looking for him."

"Don't even try to pull that shit with me!" Miller snarled. "I'm not falling for it, asshole."

"I'm not trying to pull anything... Agent." Hinestroza let the silence hang. "You are the FBI agent, aren't you?" he asked when Miller didn't rush to fill the gap.

Miller raised his eyes to Hinestroza's. He could feel the man's magnetism, his control, saw how easy it would have been for him to exert it over a lonely, eighteen-year-old boy. "Yes, I'm the FBI agent."

Hinestroza nodded, looking from Miller to Danny. "He cares about you very much. He was willing to die for you."

Miller turned back to Danny, blood spreading out beneath him in a deep red blanket. Hinestroza's unasked question hung heavy in the air... what are you willing to do for him, Miller? How far are you willing to go?

"It's a shame," Hinestroza continued. "All his suffering for

nothing. He's back in the same place he was a few days ago."

"Shut the fuck up!" Miller cried, Hinestroza's words buzzing in his ears like relentless mosquitoes. "Shut up!"

The sound of Danny's labored breathing filled the room. Miller tried to focus only on Danny's survival, but his mind kept shifting to the world beyond the kitchen. Hinestroza belonged in prison. He deserved to be locked up; it was the right thing, and a month ago, Miller would not have hesitated. It was still the right thing now, and all Danny's talk of Hinestroza's wife and daughters who loved him did not negate the trail of human wreckage he'd left behind as he passed through life. Prison was designed for men like Hinestroza, and his incarceration would be justice. A justice Miller could count on, believe in—one he could practically taste.

This moment was what he'd spent three years working toward: three years of sleepless nights, canceled dates with Rachel, memorized facts about Hinestroza's life and then Danny's too. He'd lived to see this day—Hinestroza in custody with a solid, believable witness against him. And now they had more than drug charges; attempted murder was on the table. He would go away forever, no question. Hinestroza owed a debt to the world that should be paid.

But how much more could Danny endure? How much more could be expected of him? Wasn't Danny owed something too?

Miller felt the answer in his gut, a sharp, nagging trap that his mind kept falling into no matter how hard he tried to steer his way around the idea. He could let Hinestroza walk away, let him disappear into his dark world again. But if that happened, what about the man who would take Danny's place in Hinestroza's life? Because there would be another Danny and another Madrigal, another Ortiz and another Amanda. If Hinestroza went free, how many more lives would be ruined because of it, how many more bodies left behind on dirty floors? But how did Miller measure Danny's life against the lives of strangers? How could men he had never met even begin to compare with the one man who meant everything?

Miller sucked in a lungful of fetid, blood-tinged air, preparing himself to say the words from which there would be no retreat, no possible way back. He raised his eyes to Hinestroza's. "If I let you walk out of here, you forget he exists. Danny, Amanda, his family, anyone connected to him... they're all safe. Forever." Miller's voice was low and fierce.

Hinestroza nodded, demonstrating his cleverness yet again. No triumph showed in his face, his expression blank, giving away nothing that might goad Miller into changing his mind.

"And you stay gone. Don't ever get caught. You understand me? This is all over for him—right here and right now. It's done."

"Yes, I understand."

Miller took a deep breath. "Danny told me you're a man of your word. That you never go back on a deal."

"That's true."

Miller stood quickly, not wanting to take his hands off Danny's wound for more than a moment, each heartbeat sending out fresh waves of blood. "Then go," he said, jerking the cord off Hinestroza's body. "Go! They're looking for that car, so you can't drive it for long."

Hinestroza stood, plucking Madrigal's keys from the counter where they lay next to the soiled brass knuckles. He stopped at the door and looked over his shoulder at Miller, his eyes falling to where Danny lay on the floor. He opened his mouth, but whatever he planned to say went unheard, upstaged by the wail of an ambulance cutting through the still air.

"Get the hell out of here!" Miller cried.

Hinestroza pushed the door open with his foot, leaving it shifting slightly in the breeze. Miller listened for the car engine, the crunch of wheels over the uprooted asphalt of the driveway. Danny sighed, a light, airy sound, his eyelashes fluttering against his pale cheeks.

Miller pressed harder on Danny's shoulder, willing the blood to stop flowing. But he felt insubstantial, as if he were floating weightless above his own life. The Miller Sutton he'd thought he was had turned out to be a different man entirely, his concept of himself shredded down to the stark, white bone... and he didn't know if he could live with what remained.

DANNY opened his eyes, squinting against the nauseating roll of fluorescent lights blurring by above his head. "Where'm I?" he mumbled.

A pretty nurse with an upturned nose leaned over him. She smelled like pink bubblegum and had a single freckle near her left eye. Her girlish presence was comforting, and Danny relaxed against the bed.

"You're on your way to ICU, Mr. Butler. You came out of surgery just fine."

"Where's Miller?"

"Who?"

But Danny didn't answer, suddenly scared to have spoken Miller's name out loud. He didn't know what was safe, what could be said and what needed to be locked away. *You don't remember anything, Danny. You don't remember.*

The nurse pushed his bed around a corner, punching a button on the wall with her hip, a set of swinging doors opening with a muffled hiss of air.

"Danny!" a voice called, staying the nurse's progress through the doors into ICU.

Danny turned his head slowly, the effort taking more energy than lifting a fifty-pound weight. Miller was near the wall, moving closer, his face white and tense, his hands wearing uneven gloves of blood.

"Miller," Danny whispered, his lips so dry the word came out as a dying man's rasp. He tried to smile, though he felt like weeping.

Miller came to stand beside him, smoothing the hair off his forehead with stained fingers. "You're going to be okay," he said. He glanced up at the nurse. "Can I come in with him?"

"No," Colin said, appearing at Miller's side. Danny hadn't noticed him before. "Not until the investigation into what happened is closed."

"What are you talking about?" Miller snapped. "I want to see him!"

"Miller, I can't let you talk to him. Not until you've both been fully debriefed and the investigation is over. You know how it works."

"Fuck how it works!" Miller cried, his hand clenching on the bed's side rail when the nurse tried to push forward.

"Sir," she said, "I need to get him into ICU."

"It's okay," Danny said, fighting a losing battle with the darkness dragging him under, his whole body sinking deep. He looked at Miller through half-mast eyes. He could see love in Miller's face, but it was doing battle with guilt, fighting hard against anger and regret, and Danny couldn't tell which emotion would emerge the victor. He closed his eyes; he didn't want to see any more. "My debriefing will be short," he mumbled to Colin. "I don't remember anything."

"OKAY, Miller, let's go over it one more time."

Miller sighed, pushing back in his chair to stretch his legs, his mouth coated with a paste of smoke and stale coffee. His teeth felt like they were sprouting fuzz. "We've already been over it five times today," he reminded them.

The man next to Colin didn't look up from his legal pad. "And we'll go over it ten more times if that's what I decide to do. Got it?"

Miller realized he'd used virtually those same words countless times in the interrogation room, the same dismissive demeanor, the sour curling of the mouth that told a suspect more about what he thought of them than any spoken insult ever could. No wonder they had all hated him. Even Danny had hated him at first.

He'd been trapped in this room eight hours a day for the last three days. His only company had been Colin and Special Agent Ryan Nash from internal affairs—a prick of the highest order. Miller had repeated ad nauseam the details of what had happened in the kitchen of that abandoned house, walked them through his exact movements at least two dozen times already, Colin playing the part of Danny, Nash standing in for Madrigal.

"Okay," Nash said, flipping back a few pages in his legal pad.

"How did you know where Juan Madrigal had taken Mr. Butler?"

"I didn't know. I made an educated guess based on information from AUSA Patterson and a few things Danny had told me about Madrigal's pattern."

"So you just got lucky?" Nash asked, his tone skeptical.

"Yeah, I got lucky." *Fucking luckiest moment of my life.* Miller looked from Nash to Colin. "What? You guys think I was in on this with Madrigal or something?" He shook his head, blowing out a disgusted billow of smoke. "Jesus."

"Nobody thinks that, Miller," Colin said calmly. Nash didn't look as convinced, his sharp eyes cutting Miller no slack.

"And from the street you spotted the car Madrigal had been driving?" Nash raised his eyebrows.

"Yes." Fuck him. Miller wasn't going to give him one more word than he needed.

"Who was in the house when you went in?"

"Madrigal and Danny."

"That's it?"

"Yes."

Nash jumped ahead in the questions, a trick Miller knew well, trying to throw the suspect off his practiced pace. "If you had control of Madrigal's weapon, why did you shoot him?"

"Because he ignored my commands. He was still trying to grab for the gun. I had no choice but to fire the weapon."

The door to the interrogation room opened and a young agent who looked like he was being strangled by his tie poked his head into the stale air. "Agent Nash? I need to speak with you for a minute."

"Fine." Nash heaved himself out of his chair, his slight belly giving away his position in internal affairs. No on-the-job agent would allow themselves that kind of indulgence. Agents prided themselves on being different from out-of-shape local cops—one more way to show off their extra rungs on the ladder.

When the door closed behind Nash, Colin turned to Miller,

leaning toward him across the table. "I know you're lying, Miller. And he knows it too. Level with me. Maybe I can help you."

"I don't need any help," Miller replied.

"I don't think you're the one who shot Madrigal and I don't think the three of you were the only ones in that house."

Miller didn't rise to the bait, his eyes level and blank on Colin's. Colin blew out a breath, tapping his fingers restlessly on the tabletop. "Let's say, hypothetically, Danny was the one who shot Madrigal. Why are you covering for him? It would be a clear case of self-defense."

"Okay, let's go down that hypothetical path," Miller shot back. "So, no murder charge against Danny. But what's to stop Patterson from resurrecting the gun charge, from when we arrested him? I'd bet that, according to Patterson, killing someone would definitely qualify as the 'trouble' Danny was supposed to stay out of."

"She wouldn't do that," Colin scoffed.

"Are you sure?" Miller demanded. "You willing to guarantee that?"

Colin stared down at the table, maybe remembering that day in Patterson's office when she'd thrown Danny to the wolves without a second thought. "No," he said. "I can't guarantee it."

"That's what I thought." Miller paused. "Which is why it's a good thing I was the one who shot Madrigal."

Colin's mouth thinned, the faint lines around his eyes growing deeper. Miller was testing his patience, trading on their friendship for his own benefit. He could see the strain in Colin's face, tension etched there from going out of his way to rein in Nash. Miller knew Colin would probably pay a professional price for his loyalty.

You're a real piece of shit, Miller, you know that? For the time it took to draw in a breath he considered coming out with the truth, letting the chips fall where they may. But that would only be a way to relieve his own conscience, and Danny would be the one left hanging.

"Who else was in there, Miller?" Colin demanded. "Was it Hinestroza?"

"You think I'd just let him get away if I had him in my sights?"

"I don't know what to think anymore."

"He wasn't there."

"I hope not. Because I hate to think we let someone like that get away. Let him go when we could have contained him. That would be a sad and sorry day in my book."

"Mine too," Miller said wearily. It felt like the first time in three days he wasn't telling a lie.

DANNY'S whole world was pain, agony so strong he could smell it on his skin, feel it beating behind his closed eyelids. Every few hours, never often enough, a nurse would come in with drugs that were sucked down eagerly by Danny's starving veins. They kept him flying under the pain for a little while, but too soon he'd smack against the ceiling of hurt, groaning into the empty room.

His only visitors were Colin and some big, meaty agent with flinty blue eyes. Danny couldn't seem to hold the man's name in his head. They asked him question after question, although the doctor only let them stay for an hour at a time, twice a day. Colin's voice was always low and soothing, his eyes full of apologies he didn't voice. The other one was angry; Danny knew from the way his hands kept curling into fists that he'd like to smack Danny around, and probably would have if he thought he could get away with it.

Danny told them he didn't remember anything after Madrigal pulled out the first fingernail. He said he and Madrigal were alone in the house. No matter how many ways they came at the questions, his answer was always the same: I don't remember. But he *did* remember most of it, at least up until he was shot. He could picture Hinestroza's dark, glittering eyes, his gold tooth the brightest spot in that gloomy kitchen; he could still taste the flood of blood when he'd bitten through his own tongue as Madrigal had taken his second fingernail. He remembered looking up, dazed and confused, into Miller's face and feeling no joy—knowing only sorrow because the one good thing he'd tried to do in his life, saving Miller, had not worked. Miller had been there, in danger, and Danny had failed again.

Danny felt raw inside and out. He knew he should be relieved at the way things had turned out, but he couldn't seem to move past the guilt and fear. He understood what Miller had done for him. He couldn't picture any scenario in which Hinestroza had walked out of that kitchen without Miller's consent. Every time Danny thought of what Miller had sacrificed, it was like sandpaper on his heart, scraping rough against a bleeding wound. He wished Miller hadn't done it. When Hinestroza had left that kitchen, he'd taken more than his own freedom with him. Danny knew how strongly Miller valued his belief in right and wrong. He could only imagine the toll letting Hinestroza go would take on Miller's soul. If Miller had let Hinestroza walk, the part of Miller that believed in his own goodness, his rightness, was gone, and Danny couldn't stop thinking about all that had been lost.

"Danny?"

Danny's eyes shifted toward the voice, found Griff standing in the gap of the slightly open door, his face nervous and worried.

"Griff?"

"Yeah, it's me," Griff said, venturing all the way into the room. "Fuck, Danny, look at you," he breathed.

"I'm trying not to," Danny joked, his voice hoarse. "How'd you know I was here?"

"They released me from protective custody yesterday. Agent Sakata, the one who'd been staying with me, told me what happened."

"Thanks for coming."

"Where else would I be?" Griff smiled. "It's not every day I get the chance to see handsome Danny Butler laid out like this. Might be the only time in my life I'm better-looking."

Danny laughed, the movement sending red fire up through his shoulder and down into his kidney, killing the smile on his lips.

"Shit, Danny." Griff's face was pinched. "What can I do?"

"I'm okay," Danny wheezed. "I'm due for some painkillers soon." He paused. "Can you stay for a while?"

"Yeah, absolutely." Griff pulled over a large chair covered in faded blue upholstery, tossing his hair off his face as he sat. He touched

Danny's hand through the bed rails, holding it in his own, careful to avoid the weeping bandages over Danny's fingertips. "Go to sleep," he said. "I'm not going anywhere."

Danny was glad to have someone sitting beside him. It wasn't so scary falling asleep now that he wasn't alone. And having Griff there was so uncomplicated, Danny's feelings for him crystal clear. Thinking about Griff didn't add to Danny's torment; hearing his voice didn't tear at Danny's wounds; seeing his face didn't remind Danny of all the things he had ruined.

MILLER had been sitting in his Jeep with the heater running for over thirty minutes. The last time he'd seen this car, he and Danny had been trying to outrun Madrigal, the back windshield disappearing in a bullet's wrath. The window had been repaired since then, the glass swept away, but Miller imagined he could still smell Danny against the leather seat, and God knew he remembered the way Danny had felt in his arms when they'd finally made it to that motel room.

Miller cracked the driver's side window, letting in a hint of bitter winter air and allowing his cigarette smoke to escape. The early evening sky glowed pink behind the hospital's dark brick walls, the cotton-candy clouds wispy against the setting sun. Miller folded one leg up to rest his foot on the seat and leaned his head back, closing his eyes with a sigh. Sleep had not been finding him lately. He could feel exhaustion all the way through his body, settling somewhere beyond the flesh.

He'd made it through those hours of waiting to hear about Danny's condition by imagining the moment they would be together again, alone, just Danny and Miller. But that moment had never come. One hour had turned into one day, one day rolling into twelve. Almost two weeks since he'd seen Danny's face. And now the scene Miller had pictured so clearly in his mind in the hospital emergency room, being reunited with Danny, would no longer come into focus, like some wonky television screen cursed with so much static that the image refused to gel.

Miller was scared—not terrified the way he'd been when

Madrigal took Danny, nothing that specific or immediate. But saddled with a kind of low-level dread, a pervasive feeling that things were not right and might never be again.

He opened his eyes, returning them to the line of revolving doors at the front of the hospital. It took another fifteen minutes before Griff Gentry emerged, pulling the collar of his jacket up against the wind, cupping his hand to light a cigarette before making the trip across the parking lot.

Miller got out of the Jeep, meeting up with Griff as he stepped into the lot, the streetlights blinking on above them. "Griff," Miller said, his voice coming out hard and angry, although he'd promised himself he wouldn't allow jealousy a seat at this meeting. But he hated knowing Griff was seeing Danny when he couldn't, hated that Griff was the one to offer Danny comfort. Danny's words about never loving Griff sounded hollow when faced with the flesh-and-blood man.

Griff's steps slowed as he recognized Miller. "Agent Sutton," he drawled, coming to a full stop.

"Have you been in with Danny?"

"Yeah."

"How's he doing?"

"Why don't you go see for yourself?" Griff said, flicking ash onto the pavement.

Miller looked away, stomping down the urge to do battle with Griff's handsome face. He wanted to do better than replay the script they'd followed during their first meeting, acting like dogs marking their territory. He owed Danny more than that. And the bottom line was that, if not for Griff, Danny would be suffering all alone. Miller made an effort to temper the rough edges from his voice. "They won't let me see him. An agent I work with told me you've been here most every day."

Griff studied him for a long moment, awareness flashing through his clear blue eyes. "He's getting better. But it's slow going. His shoulder was infected, but they got that under control. They had to take his kidney three days ago."

Miller's stomach contracted, a steady beat of sorrow taking up residence in his chest. "Christ," he breathed, his voice unsteady.

"It's been rough. He's not talking much. He sleeps most of the time."

"When's he getting out?"

"They're not sure. Maybe tomorrow, maybe the day after."

Miller shoved his hands into the front pockets of his jeans. "Where's he going to go?"

"My place," Griff said. "He doesn't have anyplace else, and someone's got to take care of him for a while." Like Miller's anger, the cockiness was retreating from Griff's voice. He sounded tired and sad, and Miller realized with an anguished jolt that, whatever Danny's feelings, on Griff's end it had been love and probably still was.

"Will you tell him... will you tell him I was here, that I'm thinking about him?"

Griff paused, looking away for a moment, his face stiff with reluctance. "Yeah, I'll do that," he said when he turned back. "For Danny."

Miller nodded, shamed a little by Griff's words. He'd thought the man had no redeeming qualities when they'd first met, couldn't imagine what Danny had ever seen in him beyond his face. But Griff was putting what Danny needed above his own desires, letting Miller breach a space he coveted for himself. Miller didn't know if he'd have it in him to do the same if he were in Griff's shoes. "Tell him I'll call him once the FBI investigation is over. It shouldn't be too much longer."

"Okay." Griff stood there for a moment, rolling on the balls of his feet. "Listen, I've got to go." He pointed toward the lot.

"Sure, sure." Miller stepped out of his path. "Thanks."

Griff nodded, moving away. Miller stood in the lot as darkness crept in, watching the hospital windows light up. He wondered which room was Danny's, if he had any idea of how much Miller missed him, how strongly he was wanted. It cut Miller's soul to think that he probably didn't. He wanted to burst into the hospital, to hell with regulations, and touch Danny's face, make sure he was all right. But fear held him back, and guilt over so many things. Hinestroza, Danny,

Rachel, Colin. He was caught in a straightjacket of regret, and he couldn't manage to pull his feelings for Danny clear of the tangle.

THIS time the park was virtually empty: no joggers, no overworked moms pushing strollers full of screaming children. Just Miller on a desolate wooden bench, the ash-colored sky so low and heavy he imagined he could feel it pressing against the back of his neck, holding him down.

He'd left a hesitant, stuttering message for Danny two days ago on Griff's machine, telling him the FBI investigation into Madrigal's shooting was complete and no one was being charged. He'd asked Danny to call him back. This morning he'd woken up to his own message from Danny, asking Miller to meet him on the park bench where they'd had their first debriefing. Danny had said he'd be there around noon. It was the first time Miller had heard his voice in more than three weeks, and it had brought a lump to his throat so thick he'd felt like he was strangling.

Miller heard the familiar thump of boots against the pavement. He took a deep breath as he turned his head, steadying himself before gazing on Danny again. He stood and watched Danny approach, his steps not as confident as they'd once been. This time Danny's injuries did slow him down, his body still suffering; Miller could tell by the way he held himself tightly as he moved. He'd lost weight, his skin pale, a livid purple scar on the left side of his face just in front of his ear, his broken arm in a full cast half-hidden behind his jacket, which he had draped over one shoulder.

Danny stopped just in front of Miller, not speaking, their eyes locked. Danny looked tired, his face drained, but he was still the most beautiful thing Miller had ever seen. "Danny," he said quietly. And then Danny was against him, Miller's arms closing around his body.

But they didn't fit together the way they had before. Danny's cast denied Miller the contact he craved, Danny's injuries causing him to hold his body stiff and unyielding, anticipating pain. "Miller," Danny whispered against his cheek. Miller turned his head and breathed in the skin of Danny's neck. His smell, at least, remained the same, and the familiar ache of it almost brought Miller to his knees.

"Hey," Danny said gently, pulling back. "Thanks for meeting me out here. I've been inside so much; I just wanted to get some fresh air."

"It's okay," Miller's voice was gruff, his hands still wanting to touch.

"Sorry it took me so long to call you. I'm back at my place, and Griff didn't tell me you'd called right away." Danny gestured at the bench. "Can we sit down? I get tired out."

"Yeah, sure," Miller said. He waited until Danny was seated and then took his own spot on the bench. "How are you?"

"I'm doing okay. The cast will come off in a few more weeks and the gunshot wound is pretty much healed." He wiggled his bandaged fingers. "These will take longer. I keep them covered up so I don't gross people out." He attempted a weak smile. "And I've got a few more scars."

"I heard you lost your kidney."

Danny leaned back against the bench, his eyes on his hands. "Yeah, Griff said he told you. That Madrigal, he sure knew how to pack a punch."

"Not anymore," Miller noted grimly.

"No, not anymore."

Miller squinted at Danny's profile, hearing the heaviness of Danny's words. "You don't feel bad about that, do you? He deserved to die."

"I know he did." Danny turned his eyes to Miller. "But it's still a hard thing, killing a man."

Miller didn't know; he'd never taken a life. But he imagined it would weigh on your soul, no matter how justified.

"I was glad to hear the investigation's closed," Danny said, changing the subject. "You didn't have to take the heat for everything, you know."

"Yes, I did. I couldn't risk them charging you with something because of Madrigal's shooting."

"I remember, Miller. I remember that Hinestroza was there. You let him go, didn't you?"

"Danny."

"How are you going to live with that? I know you. I know what that must have done to you."

The eyes Danny turned on Miller were blinding, so full of guilt that Miller had to look away. He leaned forward, elbows on knees, concentrating his gaze on a smashed pinecone between his shoes. "I'm still figuring that out," he said. "How I'm going to live with it."

"You shouldn't have done it," Danny whispered. "Not for me."

Miller had vowed that he would keep his temper in check, would ignore the anger that had been simmering since the moment Danny had let Madrigal take him away. But he couldn't keep quiet, the horror of those moments rising up in him like it was happening all over again, leaving him broken and helpless.

"What about what you did for me? How could you do that, Danny?" he asked, impotent fury barely hidden behind his words. "How could you have made that deal with Hinestroza?"

"I was trying to save your life."

Miller shook his head. "It wouldn't have saved me. It would have killed me if you'd died that day. Don't you know that by now? It would have killed me."

Danny closed his eyes, his fingers digging into his leg. "I wasn't thinking about that. I was thinking about Ortiz and the debt I owed him. And I was thinking about you, Miller. About finding a way that you could live free and not afraid."

Miller coughed out a breath. "Do you still not get it? Not understand the way I feel about you?"

"Yeah, I get it," Danny said, quiet and gentle. "But I don't deserve it. And pretty soon you're going to realize it too. That you've given up more than you'd be getting in return."

"Oh, Jesus, Danny—"

"It's true, Miller. Look at what you've sacrificed. Rachel, your job—"

"My job's fine," Miller said.

"No, it's not," Danny threw back. "I can tell by your face there's more to that story."

Miller rolled his shoulders forward, hiding from Danny's eyes. "I'm on administrative leave," he said after a long stretch of silence.

"So they're going to fire you."

"You don't know that. It'll be okay."

"None of it's okay!" Danny cried, his voice shaking. "I'm a fucking mess, Miller, and so are you."

Miller didn't deny it, every word Danny said was true. "What are we doing from here?" he asked. "With us?" But he already knew the answer, had known it the moment they'd hugged and Danny had been the first to pull away.

Danny reached out and ran his hand along Miller's jaw, but even that wasn't the same, the white bandages separating Danny's flesh from his. Miller felt only stiff cotton, not warm skin. He closed his eyes, tried to breathe past the pain.

"You make me want to be a better man," Danny said. "You make me want to be worthy of you, Miller. But if that's ever going to stick, if it's ever going to be real, I have to do it for me. I can't do it just because it's who you need me to be. It has to be who I need to be too."

Miller tried to speak but all that came out was a sob, his shoulders shaking with unshed tears. "Danny, please... you don't have to prove anything to me."

"Can you look at me right now, look in my eyes and tell me we can make this work, today?" Danny demanded, his own voice pinched with sorrow.

Miller didn't answer, thoughts of his job, Colin, Rachel, and learning to live with the choices he'd made all floating through his mind in a sticky soup of pain.

"Because right now, I can't say that," Danny continued. "And I can't live with myself if we try and fail because of me. I have to clean up my own life. And I think you need to clean up yours."

"Is this about Griff?"

"God, no," Danny said, yanking lightly on a lock of Miller's hair. "It's never been about Griff, not even before I knew you. It's about you and me. You said you have to learn how to live with letting Hinestroza go. Well, I have to learn how to live with what I did. With who I was and what I made you give up." Danny drew in a shaky breath. "Right now, being near you hurts too much."

Miller wanted to tell Danny that it was all worth it, that everything he'd given up was nothing compared to Danny's life. But he was nursing his own wounds; he didn't know how to heal Danny's too. He'd never been good with offering comfort, always the first to look away from other people's suffering. "What are you going to do?" he asked instead.

"I don't know."

"Is it over, Danny, between us?"

Danny didn't answer, just leaned forward and kissed Miller's eyebrow, his cheek, the corner of his mouth, his trembling lower lip. "I love you," Danny whispered and then he was up and gone. Miller sat on the cold park bench and, for the second time in his life, watched Danny walk away. Only this time, he understood exactly what he was losing.

CHAPTER 16

"MATTHEW?"

"No."

"Jacob?"

"Uh-uh." Miller shifted against Danny's body, drawing Danny's arms tighter across his bare chest. He'd never thought that two men could fit together so easily, had always assumed only a woman could be cradled the way Danny was holding him now. But it wasn't true. His back molded itself to Danny's chest like they were two halves of the same whole, his head resting comfortably on Danny's shoulder, Danny's breath sighing against his temple.

"Just tell me your goddamn middle name. I'm never going to come up with it," Danny said, pushing against Miller's naked thigh with his own.

"Quitter," Miller mocked. "Keep going."

"Bernard?" Danny guessed, chuckling under his breath.

"Jesus, my parents weren't that cruel."

"Hard to tell, judging by your first name."

Miller barked out a laugh, rolling over quickly to pin Danny against the bed, using his hands as gentle shackles over Danny's wrists. "Asshole. It's Edward. And Miller was my mother's maiden name."

Danny smiled, his slow, sexy grin full of white teeth, the grin that made Miller's stomach fall so hard he felt almost sick, the one that made him crazy with wanting, like some teenage boy mooning over his first love.

"Miller Edward Sutton," Danny said quietly. "It's a good name."

He raised his head off the bed, arms still pinned next to his pillow, and kissed Miller. Softly at first, then with more pressure, his tongue sliding hot and wet, taunting a little, pulling back whenever Miller pushed forward until Miller caught that teasing tongue with his own.

Miller released Danny's wrists, bringing his own hands down to run across Danny's chest, thumbing his nipples lightly, then flicking them with his tongue. His own breath hitched at the way Danny moaned, lifting his chest off the bed to get closer to Miller's mouth.

Miller moved lower, his tongue forging a wet trail. He laid his cheek against Danny's stomach for a moment, just breathing him in, rising and falling with Danny's exhales, Danny twining lazy fingers in his hair.

"I'm hungry." Danny's words were punctuated by a stomach rumble, loud in Miller's ear.

"You're always hungry," he noted, resting his chin on Danny's stomach. "I thought we were about to do something besides eat."

"I think I need food first."

"All we have is peanut butter and jelly."

Danny gave a noncommittal grunt.

"I take it peanut butter and jelly is not your favorite," Miller said dryly.

"I should have reminded you to get something else when you were out yesterday."

"I had other things on my mind." Miller's eyes skated over to the box of condoms on the bedside table.

Danny grinned. "At least you've got your priorities straight." He paused, pinching Miller's earlobe playfully. "But seriously, would it have killed you to pick up some turkey?"

Miller tipped his head downward, his laugh muffled by Danny's belly. "Christ, I've never met anybody who bitches about food the way you do."

"What do you mean?" Danny craned his neck to look at Miller.

"You complain about the sandwich selection, my cooking skills, the pizza, the cereal, those stale crackers from the hospital." Miller

tried to sound disgusted, but he couldn't help smiling.

Danny looked at him without speaking.

"What?" Miller asked, suddenly self-conscious.

"You remember all that stuff?"

Miller stared into Danny's eyes. "Yeah," he said. "I do." He wanted to make a joke, but he couldn't back away from what he saw in Danny's eyes, couldn't make light of what was real and alive between them.

"Come here." Danny tugged on Miller's arm, moving him up to cover his body, his legs braiding their way around Miller's. Danny's hands clutched at Miller's ass as they rocked against each other, one finger sliding into the cleft, pushing lightly.

Miller stiffened up—not out of fear exactly, just overcome with the knowledge that this was one more place he was opening up to Danny, giving over another piece of himself to the man beneath him.

"Can I?" Danny whispered.

"Yes." Miller hitched his body upward, giving Danny more room to explore.

Danny's finger slid in smooth. It didn't hurt, the way Miller expected it might. He felt pressure and stretching, but nothing that he would describe as pain.

Danny groaned, moving his finger slowly in and out. Miller curved his back, arching down to kiss Danny with a probing tongue, matching his movements to the thrusts of Danny's finger.

Danny pulled back a little, looking at Miller as he pushed his hips up and his finger deep at the same moment, Danny's question— Someday?—clear in his eyes, and Miller's answer—Yes—clear in his own. He'd never in a million years thought he'd open his body for another man, but for Danny? Yes, he'd do that; he'd do anything.

Danny wrapped his legs over Miller's shoulders as they made love, his head tipped back on the pillow as Miller thrust hard. It was the first time they'd done this face-to-face, and Miller growled through his pleasure, not wanting it to end too soon, wanting to savor every second, every expression gliding across Danny's face, every sound he made, and the way his green eyes flew open wide as he came, allowing Miller to see all the way inside.

When it was over Miller slid out slowly, collapsing onto Danny's body. "Why," he panted into Danny's neck, "why's it so goddamn good?" He was surprised at how full his voice sounded, so close to overflowing its steady banks.

Danny stroked his hair, his lips warm against Miller's cheek. "Because it's us, Miller," he whispered. "Because it's us."

DENIAL. Miller recognized it easily enough, had seen it on the faces of countless suspects, their spouses and children, parents and friends. He'd seen it in the eyes of fellow agents when a jury shuffled back into the courtroom with a "not guilty" verdict, erasing years of work in an instant. And God knew he'd made its personal acquaintance, hiding behind his own mask for a lifetime. So he knew what he was feeling as he turned a slow circle in Danny's empty apartment, furniture cleaned out, a few scraps of crumpled newspaper all that was left behind of Danny's life.

"Did he…." Miller cleared his throat. "Did he say where he was going?"

The apartment manager shrugged, her manner bored and slightly put out. She'd hemmed and hawed about letting Miller inside until he'd told her he was with the FBI, which wasn't technically true while on administrative leave. Given his larger transgressions, he didn't think playing fast and loose with Danny's landlady was going to get him in water any hotter than he was boiling in already. "I heard him say he had a long drive ahead of him, so I'm assuming outside the city. But more than that, I have no idea."

Miller had called Danny every day since Danny had walked away and left him alone on the park bench. Fifteen calls, and the machine had picked up every time. Miller never left a message; he had no idea what to say to make it right again, didn't know what words Danny needed to hear. Then yesterday when he'd called, a familiar electronic voice came over the wire, telling Miller that Danny's number had been disconnected or was no longer in service. Miller had wanted to travel through the telephone and strangle the voice speaking words he could not accept.

And now here he was in Danny's apartment, finally getting off his ass and making a move, and it was too late because Danny was gone. Cleared out and vanished into the world. The ache settling under Miller's ribs, sending its tentacles into his stomach and lungs, sprang not from the fact that he couldn't find Danny. That could be accomplished easily enough. It was because Danny had gone without a word, leaving Miller without even a good-bye. And Miller understood suddenly that Danny's "I love you" on the bench had been his farewell, a final good-bye present.

Miller felt a strange kind of nakedness, not knowing where Danny was or what he was doing. For so long he'd been aware of Danny's every move—what he wore each day, who he saw, what he ate. And then Miller had gained even more intimate knowledge—how Danny tasted, how his skin felt, the way his face softened during sleep. And now it was all gone. Miller's focus for so long had disappeared, had slipped through his fingers when he was looking the other way.

"Can I have a minute?" Miller asked.

"Sure," the woman said. "I'm going back to my office." She handed Miller the key. "Just lock up when you're done and bring the key down."

Miller walked slowly across the living room, the winter light filtering in through half-open blinds. Danny's apartment was housed in an old mansion in the central part of the city, near the art museum. It was considered an up-and-coming neighborhood, charming with just a hint of leftover seediness. The apartment itself was large, lacking the high ceilings of Miller's own place but made airy by the big windows and clean, white paint. Miller wandered into Danny's bedroom and his bathroom just beyond. The medicine cabinet opened with a startled squawk of metal, Miller's heart racing loudly in his ears in the following silence. The cabinet held only a roll of dental floss. Miller cupped it in his hand, slipping it into his pocket without knowing why.

He leaned his hands against the pedestal sink, head hanging low, and counted to ten, willing himself back to neutral. He didn't know if he'd ever hurt this badly before or felt this diminished by loss. Danny had left, moved on, and maybe that was what Miller should do as well—forget about the life that had almost been his and try to be content with the life he'd had before Danny Butler had entered his world.

Miller tried to imagine instead living that new life Danny had shown him—walking through the world as a gay man, not pretending anymore, turning away from his career, loving a man who would probably never outrun his demons and whose face would always remind Miller of his own dark places. He let the fear wash over him, the strong urge to duck away from those truths surging through his blood. And then he thought of Danny. Stepped back from all the heaviness surrounding them both and just conjured up the man—the way he smiled and smelled, the way he laughed and let Miller be, never wanting anything more from him than who he really was. Danny, whose body made Miller forget the world and whose soul, even marked with shadows, made Miller believe in something beyond the stars. Danny... who had traded his life for Miller's without a second thought.

You have to decide the man you want to be from here on out. How long ago had Danny said that to him? And he still hadn't decided. Still had Rachel marooned out in no-man's land, wondering what the hell had happened to her plans for the future. His career still poised on the brink, and he didn't even know if it was worth pulling back. His own darkness hung over him like a guillotine, and time was running out for him to make peace with his choices.

Miller slammed the medicine cabinet hard, eyes like gunmetal in the mirror. They both had to clean up their lives; that's what Danny had told him. Miller didn't know if he had the strength to do that, to face Rachel and Colin with an open heart, to look without flinching at what had become of his life. But cleaning up his mess was the only gift he could give Danny, and he would do it with the hope that, wherever he was, Danny was doing the same.

"YOU planned this, didn't you?" Griff huffed as he staggered through the door with an armful of boxes.

"What are you talking about?"

"Planned this move for when your arm was still in a cast, just so you wouldn't have to help with any of the heavy lifting, you fucker."

Danny laughed, scooting boxes against the walls with his feet. "Is that it?"

"Yeah, that was the last load."

"Well, sit down for a little bit; you've been working like a dog."

"Nice of you to notice." Griff glanced around the living room crowded with boxes. "Where?"

"Just push that shit off the sofa."

Griff cleared a small space and flopped down on the sofa with a groan. "If you come across the cooler, pass me a beer."

"I already put them in the fridge. The pizza guy was here while you were downstairs. It's in the kitchen too."

"I'll get some in a minute," Griff sighed. "Too tired right now."

Danny cut through packing tape with his Swiss Army knife, kicking boxes through the doorway into the kitchen or down the short hall to his bedroom, where they belonged. This apartment was half the size of his old one and in a less-than-ideal area of Chicago, but at six hundred dollars a month it was the most he could afford.

"So, tell me more about this job," Griff said when Danny returned to the living room. He handed Danny a beer and gestured toward the greasy pizza box he'd opened.

Danny shrugged, lowering himself to the floor at Griff's feet. "I don't know much. It's at Legal Aid. Sort of a runner, I guess. Just helping them with whatever needs doing."

Griff threw Danny a skeptical glance. "And they know your record?"

"Yeah. My probation officer was the one who told me about it. He recommended me for the job and they interviewed me over the phone. It was all pretty casual."

"So you work for the whole office?"

"Yeah, but I have a primary attorney I help out. Jill Ward. She seemed nice enough when we talked. I think they're desperate. The job doesn't pay for shit. It's part of a grant, some rehabilitation project"—Danny rolled his eyes—"trying to keep us ex-cons out of the pokey."

"You're going to starve," Griff pointed out.

"I've got some money left. And I sold my bike. I'll be okay." Danny paused to stuff half a slice of pizza in his mouth. "What about you? What are you going to do in St. Louis? Live with your brother?"

"Yeah, Owen said he had room for me and could help me get a job."

"Are you sure hanging around your brother is such a good idea?" Danny asked carefully. Owen Gentry made Griff look like a small-time crook, having spent more of his adult life in prison than out. It made Danny nervous to know Griff was going to be living with the man.

"Sure, I like St. Louis." Griff grinned, knowing that wasn't what Danny meant.

"Yeah, but you know Owen's going to want you to get mixed up in—"

"Danny, stop worrying. I'm a big boy."

"Okay," Danny nodded. "Okay."

"Besides, not all of us are meant for a life on the right side of the law."

"Griff." Danny shifted his position so he could get a better look at Griff's face, wincing as he moved.

"You still hurting?" Griff asked, sliding off the couch to sit next to him.

"Nah, it's nothing," Danny said, waving him off. "Just sore."

"You've got to take better care of yourself, man," Griff said, his face inches from Danny's. Danny saw the feeling in Griff's eyes and wished—God, how he wished—that he could love this man. When Griff left, he would be alone with regret that was eating him from the inside out, with pain he was trying to stifle by keeping busy, by moving his body, moving his life, so that he wouldn't have to face the empty spot where Miller used to stand.

Danny pressed forward quickly, bringing his mouth to Griff's, opening Griff's lips with his tongue, desperate to soothe the ache and fill the emptiness inside. The kiss was familiar, a move they knew by heart, but it wasn't what Danny needed, the shape of Griff's lips not what he craved, the taste of his mouth only reminding Danny of who it was he really wanted.

"Stop," Griff said, untangling himself, giving Danny a gentle shove. "Stop. I'm not him, Danny."

Danny saw the conflict in Griff's face, understood what it cost Griff to turn him away. "God, I'm sorry," he choked out. "I'm sorry."

Griff took a long swallow of beer, his eyes on the ceiling.

"How did you know?" Danny asked. "About Miller and me." Even saying his name hurt, a direct hit to the heart.

"I suspected something when he came to interview me. He was jealous; it was written all over him. He could hardly stand to look at me. Then, when I talked to him that night at the hospital, I knew for sure. And your face, when I told you he'd been there…."

"I'm sorry," Danny repeated. "That wasn't fair to you."

Griff blew out a short breath. "People can't help what they feel, Danny. If they could, I would have been over you a long time ago." He gave Danny a rueful smile. "What happened between you two?"

"It didn't work out for us," Danny said. "He deserved something more than being stuck with me and my shitty past for the rest of his life."

"He didn't seem too worried about your shitty past that night outside the hospital."

Danny shook his head. "He did something for me, something that he's not going to be able to live with."

"Was he forced to do it?" Griff asked, confused.

"No."

"Well then, it was a choice he made, wasn't it? So that just means he loves you more than doing the right thing all the time." The words looked like they hurt Griff as they left his lips, his eyes reading Danny's face as easily as Danny had read his. "You're always putting people up on a pedestal, Danny, people who have more education or better jobs. Shit, don't you ever watch the news? Seems like every day some big-shot head of a company is going to prison because he fucked over his employees and they lost their life savings. Everybody's got a dark side. It's nothing that wasn't already there in Miller."

"Yeah, but I made it come out. He gave up everything for me and I'm—"

"Oh, bullshit!" Griff exclaimed. "There's no talking to you sometimes, you idiot. You have to take the blame for every fucking bad thing that happens in the world? People make their own choices. Whatever it was Miller did, he did it because he thought you were worth it. He chose *you*, Danny. That's what you should be thinking about, not about what he gave up. Jesus." Griff threw up his hands in exasperation.

Danny could hear the wisdom of Griff's words, but it was so hard to believe they applied to him. They seemed such small comfort in the wake of all Miller had sacrificed. Danny had left Miller on the park bench, walked away and then kept on going, because he wanted to give Miller a chance at a life where he could forget what he'd done. And that would never happen with Danny there to remind him.

But Danny's leaving wasn't just about Miller and what Danny believed he deserved. It was about Danny, too, and finding a way to start over. He hadn't expected to live beyond that day in the kitchen with Madrigal, had already released his hold on life and made his peace with death. But now he had to come back from the dead and find a way to live again, to stand tall as his own man, to uncover the true Danny Butler and face whoever he turned out to be.

RACHEL was chewing each bite at least fifty times. Miller wondered if she was counting in her head, forcing the food down after the prescribed number of chews, a trick borrowed from the obsessive-compulsive handbook to get her through this meal. It was the first time they'd seen each other since that night at his apartment almost six weeks ago. They'd talked on the phone a few times—short, awkward conversations with neither of them sure where they stood, Miller always making excuses about why he couldn't see her quite yet. Every time he expected her to curse and shout or slam the receiver down into his ear, but she never did.

Miller had known that when they finally saw each other, he'd have to look within himself and answer her questions honestly in a way he'd never done before. And it was only now that he was ready. With Danny gone from his life, the way before him was no longer clear, but he had to keep walking, take the steps and hope that by doing so the right path would reveal itself.

"How has work been?" Rachel asked, using a gulp of wine to swallow her latest bite of salmon. They'd been making stilted small talk all evening, avoiding the real reason they were sitting across from each other.

The restaurant had been a bad choice on his part—too fancy, too formal, both of them feeling on display in the hushed, rich atmosphere. On the upside, Rachel was hardly going to throw her drink in his face in front of this crowd, but Rachel wasn't the type for public displays anyway.

"Fine," Miller answered, eyes on his plate. *Time to be honest with her about everything, jackass.* "Actually, I'm on administrative leave." It was almost a relief to finally be getting down to it.

"What?" Rachel's fork clattered against her china plate and she glanced around guiltily. She wasn't wearing her ring, and every time she moved her hand, the lack of sparkle hurt Miller's eyes. "When did that happen?" she whispered, her fingers twisting nervous loops in her pearl necklace.

"A few weeks ago."

"You said they cleared you in that shooting."

"They did."

Rachel's brows drew together like magnets, confusion clear in her eyes. "Then why?"

Miller set down his glass, took a deep breath, drawing courage up through his core. He could do this; he had to do this, because if he didn't, all the sacrifice had been for nothing. "There are some unanswered questions about me and an informant." He looked at Rachel. "The man you saw me with at my apartment."

Rachel stared at him. She took her napkin off her lap and placed it across her plate.

"Rachel...."

"I'm not talking about this here. I'm not," she said brokenly, pushing back from the table. Even on the verge of tears she walked with care; no one watching would have suspected anything more than a trip to the ladies' room.

Miller fished a wad of bills out of his wallet and tossed them onto the table. He shoved against the tide in the crowded lobby, shouldering his way past couples who looked happy for a night out together. Rachel didn't wait for him at the door to the restaurant, the heavy cut-glass and mahogany closing in his face. He caught up with her where she stood shivering against his car, the branches of an ice-burdened tree curling downward to nearly touch her head.

"Rachel, come back inside where it's warm," he coaxed.

"No, I want to go home." She jerked against the door handle. "Open the door."

Miller unlocked her door then moved around to the driver's side, starting the engine and cranking the heater once he was settled behind the wheel. He leaned back in his seat and closed his eyes, listening to Rachel weep beside him.

"I thought you knew after you saw us," he said softly. "I thought that was why you weren't wearing your ring."

"I suspected, but I didn't know for sure," she whispered. "I wanted to believe you were being honest with me. But you lied to me that day at your apartment. You told me it wasn't what it looked like. You said you would explain it all later."

Miller knew that wanting to believe and truly believing were not the same thing at all. Rachel had known the truth from the moment she'd seen him with Danny. She just needed to hear him say the words. "I'm sorry, Rachel." He glanced at her tear-stained face. "I'm so sorry."

"Were you... did you have sex with him?"

The lie was right there against his lips, ready to slingshot out and tell Rachel what she wanted to hear, what it would be so easy for Miller to say: *No, of course not, it never went that far.* But that would be denying Danny, denying what Danny meant to him, and he couldn't do it. He was suddenly hit with a powerful superstition that warned him not to push Danny any further away. He'd vowed to clean up his mess, not just shove it into a corner and pretend not to see. "Yes, we slept together."

Rachel inhaled a shuddering, high-pitched breath. "So you're—You're gay?" she asked, her eyes shifting to her clasped hands.

Was he gay? That's the question he'd spent all his life avoiding, not wanting to hear the answer. Because he knew the answer. He'd known it in high school when he looked a little too long at the lean thigh muscles of the boys who ran track. Had known it at the academy when the sight of sweaty forearms holding a gun made all the spit dry up in his mouth. There had always been such shame and disgust, hating himself for something he could not control, wanting to wipe away a part of himself that was fundamental and refused to be dislodged.

"Yes," he said finally, "I'm gay." He forced the words out through a reluctant throat. He wondered if it got easier to say over time, if he'd ever be able to say it without choking on the admission. He wished Danny were waiting at home for him, thought maybe this would all be easier if he had Danny to share it with—Danny who was never ashamed of being gay and didn't want Miller to be ashamed, either.

Rachel heaved out a sob, pinching the back of her hand with sugar-pink fingernails. "Why didn't you tell me? Were you ever going to tell me?"

He thought about saying he hadn't known, but that would put too much of the blame at Danny's feet, as though Danny's presence had made him gay. And Miller knew that was not the truth. He'd always been gay; Danny had only forced him to face it. "I didn't want to admit it, Rachel. I wanted it to go away."

"How does something like that 'go away'?" Rachel demanded. "I've wasted five years of my life waiting for you, Miller Sutton! Making excuses for why it was taking us so long to get married. And you just let me keep thinking it would happen someday. You didn't even have the guts to be honest!" She snatched her purse off her lap and rooted around inside, thrusting a small velvet box into his hand. "Here, take the ring. It's not mine anymore."

"I want you to have it."

"I don't want it." She crossed her arms over her chest, cradling her elbows, her tears still flowing hard and fast. "Are you with him? That man?"

"His name is Danny," Miller said quietly. "And no, we're not together."

"I don't want to know his name!" Rachel cried. "You said he was an informant. That means he's a criminal, right?" She swiped at her cheeks with a wadded-up Kleenex.

"He has a record, yes." Miller hated handing over Danny's life for her to judge.

"And that's what you really want? Some man, some criminal?" She hissed out the words, trying to transform Danny into something ugly with her voice.

Miller didn't answer, turned his face and looked at the dirty snow covering the sidewalk in misshapen lumps. There was no way to explain to Rachel that Danny was more than he appeared on paper. That somehow that man, with a felony record and no hope for the future, with a body marked with scars, with a brave, strong heart, was the person Miller had been searching for his whole life without even knowing it.

"What happened to the Miller I knew?" Rachel asked, her voice broken. "Where did he go? It's like I'm sitting next to a stranger."

But it was the Miller Rachel had known who was really the stranger—the man who hid behind his badge and his fiancée and his goddamn all-knowing certainty about everything. He remembered the weight he'd carried for so many years, trying to keep himself stiff and rigid, so careful all the time that no one see beyond his cool exterior. But then he'd met Danny, and even burdened with fear about Madrigal, Miller had felt a lightness in his soul, a lifting of the heaviness he'd been shackled with for so long. And as terrified as he was to go forward, he was even more scared to go back.

"This is the real me, Rachel," Miller said, his voice steady. "And I'm not going to hide anymore." It felt good to say the words, for himself... and for Danny, who had recognized the true Miller from the very beginning, had seen through all his flaws and defenses, and loved him anyway.

DANNY was nervous. It had been a long time since he'd started a new job and had to work his way up from the bottom of the ladder with no idea of what he was doing.

Well, at least these people won't kill you if they decide you're not right for the job.

Danny raked through his hair with one hand, still not used to having both arms at his disposal. He'd spent ten minutes just scratching when they'd finally cut the damn cast off. He pulled open the glass door of the Legal Aid building, a nondescript brick one-story house between a sandwich shop and a bank, a ten-minute L ride from his apartment.

"Um... yeah, hi, I'm Danny Butler," he said to a bored-looking girl barely out of her teens who was flipping through a gossip magazine at the front desk. She raised her eyebrow at him, saying *So?* without even opening her mouth.

"He's mine! He's mine!" a voice yelled from down the hall. "Don't you dare give him to anyone else." A tall, thin woman with long waves of chestnut-colored hair flying around her face came barreling in his direction, her hand extended for his before she got close enough to touch. "Hi, I'm Jill," she said, giving him a quick handshake, her whole body crackling with energy.

"I'm Danny."

Jill flashed a big, stretch-your-face smile. She was younger than he'd expected—Danny guessed he had at least a few years on her—and pretty in a sharp, no-nonsense way, the only concession to cosmetics a wide swath of scarlet lipstick.

"Come with me." She motioned him forward. "I'm so swamped right now. You have no idea how much I need your help."

Danny followed her back down the hall from where she'd appeared, stepping around banker's boxes stacked against the walls.

"Did you all just move here?"

"What? No." Jill glanced over her shoulder, following his gaze. "Those are just case files we don't have room for anywhere else."

Jill ducked into the last office on the left. "Okay, here," she said, thrusting a huge mountain of papers into Danny's hands. "I need you to put these pleadings in order, most recent on top. Here's a two-hole punch and here's a file folder to put them in."

"Where…." Danny looked around the cramped office, every inch covered with stacks of papers, books, files split at the bindings and spilling their contents onto the floor. He felt momentarily overwhelmed; he'd had no idea he'd be tossed into the meat of the job less than five minutes after walking through the door.

"Oh, shit, yeah. Come across the hall with me." Jill pointed him into a small room crowded with three desks. "This one's yours. Feel free to bring stuff in if you want, pictures and crap like that."

There was an older black man sitting at one of the desks, his silver hair close-cropped, a pair of glasses that seemed too small for his wide face perched on the end of his nose.

"Danny Butler, meet Ellis Campbell."

"Hi," Danny said, setting down his load of papers.

"Nice to meet you," Ellis said in an easy baritone.

"Ellis is retiring in… what? A month?" Jill asked, her brow furrowed.

"Six weeks."

"Right, I knew that. Six weeks. He'll help show you the ropes before he goes. He's been here a long time."

"Eighteen years," Ellis supplied.

"You all set?" Jill asked, her eyes back on Danny.

"Yeah, I guess."

"Sorry things are so crazy around here. I'd like to tell you it will settle down later, but that would be a lie."

"It's okay," Danny smiled. "Crazy I think I can handle."

"Marie, our HR person, will track you down sometime today and give you a ton of forms to fill out and explain your nonexistent salary and all that good stuff."

Danny laughed. "So everyone knows how much I won't be making?"

"Don't feel bad, it's only slightly less than my paycheck." Jill glanced at her watch as she brought her hands up, twisting her hair into a knot on top of her head. "Shit. Client's going to be here in twenty minutes. Holler if you need anything."

"That girl needs to watch her language," Ellis said as Jill retreated to her office. From the good-natured tone of his voice Danny guessed it wasn't the first time he'd expressed that particular lament. "Her momma should have taken some soap to her mouth a long time ago."

"She seems like she'd be pretty hard to catch," Danny observed.

Ellis laughed, long and low. "Good point, good point," he mused, tipping back slightly in his chair. "So you're the new ex-con." It wasn't a question.

Danny's back stiffened as he pulled out his chair. But what was the point of getting bent out of shape? He was an ex-con and always would be. "Yep. That's me."

Ellis was watching him with thoughtful eyes. "Don't get offended. I'm one myself."

"You?" Danny asked, surprised. The glasses and cardigan sweater and the face like a favorite grandfather didn't bring "felon" instantly to mind.

"Before I came to work here. Served twenty-one years for murder."

"Shit," Danny muttered, not sure if it was the admission of murder or the length of the sentence that hit him hardest.

"When I started here, it was a big risk for them. But I worked out okay, so now the office applies for a grant every year to hire someone who's trying to go straight. Sometimes we get the grant, sometimes we don't. But this year we did. This is a good place to be, if you don't mind working hard for no pay."

Ellis smiled, but Danny knew what he was really saying. *Don't fuck this up, kid, because it might be your last, best chance to be something more than what you've been so far.*

"DANNY, you can go home if you want. You've worked late every night for the past three weeks."

Danny looked up from the trial transcript he was reading, marking his place with a green highlighter. "Don't you have a client coming in?"

Jill nodded, yawning behind her hand. "Yeah, but you don't have to stay for that."

"It's okay." Danny stretched his arms above his head, working out the kinks in his neck. "I don't like the idea of you being here alone."

Jill rolled her eyes. "I've got mace in my desk drawer and I know some killer kung-fu moves." She demonstrated a sharp, off-balance kick that sent her careening into the wall.

"Yeah," Danny said dryly. "That's some pretty scary heat you're packing there."

"I was just warming up."

"Uh-huh."

"Well, if you're going to stick around, can you make sure the Lawrence file is organized? I've got a suppression hearing in the morning."

"Sure. Trying to keep the gun out?"

"Yeah. And don't tell me 'good luck' in that sarcastic tone of yours, please."

Danny smiled, keeping his lips pressed firmly together.

Jill eyed him with raised eyebrows. "If you have to say something, say, 'Jill, I know you'll work a legal miracle'. Show a little faith."

"Jill, I know you'll work a legal miracle," Danny intoned.

"Thank you," she said, turning back toward her office.

"You're welcome. But you're still not keeping that gun out of evidence."

"Jerk," Jill's voice floated in from the hallway.

Danny laughed, turning his attention back to the transcript in front of him. But he couldn't concentrate; it felt like tiny grains of sand were stuck under his eyelids. Jill was right: he should go home, relax, get a change of scenery. But being alone these days was the worst sort of torture, and even late nights at work for no extra pay were better than sitting in his empty apartment.

Miller was the reason Danny had been working every night since he'd started at the Legal Aid office, trying to stay one step ahead of his memories. It was too depressing, too fucking lonely, to go back to his quiet apartment and eat cold cereal on the sofa. He didn't even have canned TV laughter to keep him company because he couldn't afford cable and couldn't get any reception without it. He hated sleeping, too, because Miller was always waiting behind his closed eyelids, and waking up alone after having Miller with him in his dreams was an agony Danny could hardly bear.

He'd thought the longing, the need for Miller, would lessen with each day that passed. But the opposite had proven true. With each sunset he wanted Miller more, missed him with a fierceness that came from his soul, a bone-deep ache of wanting. That Danny's feelings for Miller grew stronger by the day went against all logic. They'd been apart now for longer than they'd ever been together. But Danny had discovered that logic wasn't a part of loving someone, and he was slowly coming to accept that being without Miller was an unhealed wound he'd carry for eternity.

"Hey, anybody here?" a voice called from the front of the building, rising above the bell that notified them they had a visitor.

Danny stood in the doorway of his office as Jill escorted her client down the hall; he wanted to let the man know Jill was not alone. The client was young, startlingly so, greasy hair pulled back into a ponytail, his thin body cloaked in teenage swagger.

"How are you doing?" Danny asked as he passed.

The kid gave him a quick up-and-down glance, his eyes distant and cold. "Just fine, man," he said, with a knowing little grin. Danny recognized his posing for what it was: a way to push back the fear and pretend this was all part of his master plan, as though going to prison was only a tiny bump in the road instead of the pothole that would sink him. Danny had been this boy more than once.

It was after eight o'clock when the kid finally left. Danny could hear Jill talking to him in the lobby and then the jingling bell as the front door opened and closed. "So, what's his deal?" Danny asked as he pulled on his jacket in anticipation of the snarling Chicago wind.

"Drugs. What else?" Jill looked tired, her energy down to a low boil. "It's his first offense, but he had quite a stash. It's going to be a tough introduction into the system for him."

"How old is he?"

"Almost twenty. It's always a deadly combination: young, cocky, and desperate to please."

They both moved out onto the sidewalk. "You need a ride?" Jill asked as she locked the door behind them.

"No. I'm going to take the L."

"Okay," she smiled. "See you tomorrow."

Danny waited until Jill was behind the wheel of her tiny Toyota before he turned toward the train station. He could see the kid sauntering along in front of him, probably headed to the same destination.

It was hard to believe he'd been even younger than this kid when he'd fallen in with Hinestroza. The boy seemed hardly older than a child, more a product of his youth than of his own choices. It didn't seem right that someone so unformed could be held solely responsible for his bad decisions. He wanted to catch up to the kid and tell him it wasn't too late, that with someone like Jill in his corner and a change of attitude, he might avoid making a train wreck of his life. Danny saw his own reflection in every inch of the boy.

It hit Danny suddenly that he felt compassion for this kid that he'd never offered himself, that maybe some of his own bad choices had sprung, at least in part, from having been little more than a child when he'd made them, from having no one in the world who gave a shit about helping him do better. And maybe it would be okay if he started to forgive himself for the boy he had been. He would always have to live with the consequences of his choices, even the ones made in the haste and ignorance of youth, but maybe he could try forgiving himself for the choices themselves. Maybe it would be all right with Ortiz or God or whoever was watching if he showed himself just that little bit of mercy, allowed himself to believe that forgiveness might be something he deserved after all.

CHAPTER 17

ELLIS CAMPBELL had been using the same desk for fourteen years and it showed. Danny had volunteered to empty out the lower right-hand drawer, and so far he'd thrown more stuff into the trash can than into the banker's box Ellis had placed on his chair.

"I thought you were neat," Danny commented, pointing to the clean desktop Ellis took such pride in.

"I am. It all goes in that drawer."

Danny smiled, shaking his head as he tossed a mangled paper-clip chain into the trash. He fished out four staplers from under a pile of ancient telephone books and lined them up on the desk. "Are you going to miss this place?"

"Sure. I've been here for a long time. It will be strange to wake up and not have anywhere I'm supposed to be," Ellis said, heaving himself up with a steadying hand on Danny's shoulder. "But Rita will be glad to have me around the house more."

Danny had met Ellis's wife, Rita, a couple of times at the office. She was a regal-looking woman with a fluff of black hair and a quick laugh. Every time Ellis saw her, his eyes burned bright like charcoal on a fire, and his face left a decade behind.

"Hey, Danny, can you come in here for a minute?" Jill called, her voice carrying easily across the narrow hall.

"I'll be right back." Danny wiped his dusty hands on the seat of his jeans as he picked his way gingerly across Jill's land mine of a floor. "What's up?"

Jill pointed to a three-inch-thick stack of paper perched on the corner of her desk. "I need you to read these cases and give me a memo on them. I want to know if any of them are helpful on the Lawrence suppression issue." Just as Danny had predicted, Jill had lost the battle to keep the gun out of evidence at the Lawrence suppression hearing, but she wasn't conceding the war.

Danny picked up the cases, testing their weight in his hands. Jill hadn't asked him to do anything like this before. "I've never read a case," Danny reminded her.

"Oh, yeah." Jill bit her bottom lip as she scanned her crowded workspace. "Ah, there it is." She tossed him a *Black's Law Dictionary*. "You can look up any words you're not familiar with in here."

Danny didn't move, his eyes on Jill's shiny hair as she returned to her work, her head bent over whatever she was reading. "Jill? Maybe somebody else should do this. I mean, I never even went to college, I'm not sure—"

"You're smart, Danny. You'll figure it out." She didn't even look up, not giving him any room to argue or back away, expecting more from him than he would ever have dared to expect from himself.

Danny returned to his desk, stopping for another cup of coffee first—gritty, black sludge they made every morning in the small kitchen at the back of the building. As nasty as the stuff was, he figured this assignment required more than his usual dose of caffeine. He sat down and took the first case off the pile; his heart hammering in his throat reminded him in some small way of those early days with Hinestroza, when the fear of fucking up had been a looming giant breathing hot fire down his neck. After a solid hour of reading, Danny's brain hurt, his mind so overtaxed he swore the roots of his hair were throbbing with the effort of trying to make sense of the words in front of him. He'd made it through one page. One page of a seventy-page Supreme Court opinion. The pure hell of it made him want to punch something. Couldn't these fucking people speak English? He'd never felt so stupid or out of his element.

Danny tossed down his highlighter, blowing out angry puffs of air, fighting his body's urge to simply slam out the door without looking back. He didn't need this shit.

"I see she's got you reading cases," Ellis said from across the room, his voice mild.

Danny looked over his shoulder. "Yeah."

"It's hard, I know. Took me a long time before I could figure out what they were saying."

"I think I'm giving up," Danny said, rubbing his forehead.

"Nah," Ellis chided. "You've barely started. Keep at it. By the end of this week it'll be easier."

Danny couldn't imagine it would ever get easier, any of it: being the dumbest one in the room instead of the man Hinestroza counted on to help run things; being so poor he couldn't afford a pizza instead of having money to blow on motorcycles and leather jackets; being alone instead of with Miller. Miller, who never left Danny's thoughts, only circling above when Danny was busy, landing with a life-consuming thud the moment Danny let down his guard.

"I won't make it to the end of the week."

Something in Danny's voice gave Ellis pause. He stopped packing up his desk and crossed to Danny's chair. "She believes you can do this, Danny, otherwise she wouldn't ask. Jill doesn't waste her time, you know that."

"I know," Danny sighed. "But why me? There have to be people here who can do this in their sleep."

Ellis clucked his tongue impatiently. "Because she wants you to see what you can do. You're not here to get coffee and staple papers. She wants you to use your brain." Ellis tapped his own temple in demonstration. "Keep at it," Ellis repeated, this time not urging but commanding.

"Okay," Danny agreed wearily. "But how about a five-minute break first?"

Ellis nodded. "Let's make use of those young arms of yours. Come on and help me carry a couple of these boxes to my car."

The bright sunshine when they opened the back door was deceiving, failing to cancel out the bitter late-January wind that swirled around Danny's head, turning the tips of his ears to numb bands of flesh within seconds. "Damn," he muttered as they hurried to Ellis's car.

Danny deposited the boxes into Ellis's trunk and stuffed his frozen hands into his pockets, waiting as Ellis slammed the trunk lid.

"Ellis, who did you kill?" he blurted out, his curiosity finally getting the best of him now that it was Ellis's last week before his retirement. Danny's time for answers was running short.

Ellis shot Danny a look he couldn't decipher, his steps falling into time with Danny's as they turned away from the car. "How long have you been wanting to ask me that?"

Danny shrugged. "For a while."

"Not many people have the guts to ask flat-out like that." Ellis hunched his shoulders against the wind. "It was my wife. I killed my wife," he said after a heavy beat of silence.

"But—"

"My first wife."

"And you managed to get a second one?"

Ellis glanced at him sharply, a short, surprised laugh exploding from his belly.

"Sorry," Danny said, embarrassed. "I didn't mean—"

"No, it's okay. I've been married to Rita for seventeen years, and there are days I still can't believe she was willing."

"What happened with your first wife?"

"We were both young, messed-up kids, not even close to being adults, not in any way that counted. I was a junkie when I could afford it, an alcoholic when I couldn't. Just bulldozing my way through my life and through my marriage. We had one of those relationships that's doomed from the first moment you lay eyes on each other." Ellis let out a strangled sigh. "I came home drunk and drugged-up, and she wasn't in much better shape. We started fighting. To this day I can't remember what the fight was about." Ellis's voice sounded old for the first time since Danny had met him.

"Christ," Danny murmured.

"I was sorry the second it happened; couldn't believe I'd done it. But it was too late by then. Too late to change any of it."

Ellis held open the back door of the building and they both ducked inside, escaping the stinging cold. Ellis didn't head straight for their office, instead leaning up against the wall, his eyes on Danny.

"Do you ever...." Danny looked down at his feet, shifting nervously from side to side. "Do you ever think about her, what she would think knowing you've got a life now when you took hers away?"

Ellis smiled, a small, pained curve of his lips. "All the time, Danny, all the time. But her forgiveness is something I'll never have. Probably don't deserve it anyway." Ellis's voice dropped, low and soothing. "What do you want to hear? That someday you're going to be able to look in the mirror and not see every bad thing you've ever done, every mistake you've made, staring right back at you?"

Danny's eyes met Ellis's across the small hall. He could feel the pleading in his own without even needing to see.

"'Cause that's not going to happen," Ellis said, not softening the words. "It's always our mistakes, the things we aren't proud of, that are the first ones to stand up, ready to be counted. That's human nature and it's not going to change, not for me or for you, either."

"Then what's the point?" Danny demanded. "What's the point of trying to do anything different?"

Ellis took off his glasses, hiking his sweater up to polish them with the white T-shirt he wore underneath. "The point is...." His voice trailed off, his eyes focused somewhere distant, like he was trying to pull a memory out of a thick fog. "It's like this old patchwork quilt my momma used to have. It came from her grandma or maybe her great-grandma, I can't remember; anyway, it was sort of a family scrapbook, I guess. Each piece on that quilt meant something. And some of those pieces were the damn ugliest things you've ever seen—old brown corduroy worn to the nub or stained pieces of cotton you wouldn't want to use as a rag to clean your bathroom floor. But some of the pieces were so beautiful they almost hurt my eyes to look at when I was a kid. White silk from a wedding dress or the red velvet from a baby's first Christmas coat." Ellis paused, perching his glasses back on his nose. "That's the best you can hope for, Danny. That your life turns out like that patchwork quilt. That you can add some bright, sparkling pieces to the dirty, stained ones you've got so far. That in the end, the bright

264 | Brooke McKinley

patches might take up more space on your quilt than the dark ones."
Ellis stared at Danny, making sure he was listening. "That's the point."

When Ellis had started talking, Danny had almost tuned him out.
He didn't see what a quilt had to do with the question he was asking.
But the thing was, as he listened, he could see *his* quilt, the inky black
and bruised purple patches spreading out like some dark and
treacherous ocean. But tucked in among all that swallowing darkness
there was a tiny speck of silver, from an essay contest he'd won in tenth
grade, so proud of his cheap, plastic plaque; a small crimson patch from
those first months with Amanda, when her laugh had sparkled with joy;
a crisp flash of yellowy-green that marked his friendship with Griff;
and the brightest piece of all, shimmering golden silk threaded with
starlight… Miller.

"Yeah," Danny said quietly. "I think I get it."

Ellis nodded, then reached out and patted Danny's shoulder with
a gentle hand. "Come on. Time to get back to your cases."

DANNY had made it through a whopping ten pages of the Supreme
Court case when he finally hung it up for the night at nine o'clock. He
was the only one left in the building; Jill had given him her key to lock
up with when she'd left at seven. Danny turned off lights as he went,
making sure the coffeemaker was unplugged and the back door was
locked before he left through the main entrance.

As he fought the wind, heading toward the L station, his stomach
gnawed at him, reminding him he'd skipped dinner. He mentally
reviewed what he had at home in his kitchen, resigned to the fact that it
was probably going to be another cereal night, unless he went all out
and made himself some macaroni and cheese.

"Hey, you," a voice called from a shadowy doorway as he passed.

Danny glanced to his left, his eyes picking up a skinny figure
beckoning him closer. He kept on walking, hoping to make it to the
station just as a train pulled in; he wasn't in the mood to wait.

"Hey, you want anything? I got some good stuff," the doorway-
lurker urged, leaving his position to walk alongside Danny, his smile

revealing a row of rotted teeth.

"No, not interested," Danny responded, keeping up his quick clip until he left the man behind on his patch of sidewalk.

Danny wasn't tempted to buy any drugs. That had never been his weakness. But he felt like an addict all the same, shot through with sharp, electric cravings when his thoughts turned to walking into his cold, quiet apartment at the end of this long day, his fingers itching to make the call. Dial the number he still had memorized and probably always would—his insurance against the future, his own dark and terrible safety net. Maybe Hinestroza would be glad to hear from him. Maybe he could fall right back into the slot he used to occupy, all these months just a hiccup in his rightful life. There would be such relief in being the Danny he knew so well, the one who let people down and didn't have a future and knew exactly what tomorrow held because it was never anything better than the day that had come before.

But it was more difficult to disappoint people when they expected something of you, expected more from you than to show them your worst at every turn. Danny didn't want to betray Jill's trust, her matter-of-fact faith that he had it inside him to change. And if he returned to his old life, what would that say to Miller about the sacrifice he'd made—that he'd given up everything for a man who didn't give a damn, a man who, after everything they'd been through, would still choose Hinestroza and a life in the shadows.

Danny stomped his feet against the concrete platform, trying to keep warm as he waited for his train, listening for the distant rumble that would carry him home. He wanted to make a promise to himself, to Miller, and to Jill that he would never make that call, never jump into that safety net riddled with jagged holes. But such a promise felt too big for him, beyond what he was capable of giving. Its very vastness made him feel smothered and weighed down with leaden expectations.

So, instead, he blew into his cupped hands, heating his icy fingers with steamy breaths, and swore that at least for tonight he would not disappoint anyone who was trying so hard to believe in him. He'd go home, eat his solitary dinner, and fall into bed. His phone would remain in his pocket, silent and dark. Not tonight, he vowed, not tonight.

MILLER'S right hook connected with a dull thud, the impact traveling up his arm to explode in his shoulder. He ignored the throb and struck out again, harder this time, grunting when his fist connected.

"Shit, Miller, you working out or trying to kill that bag?"

Miller wiped a forearm across his sweat-streaked brow. "I took too much time off from this place," he told Ben, the manager of the gym where he had worked out regularly before Danny. Ben had owned the place for years, and as far as Miller could tell, he'd never put a cent into the dump beyond installing two boxing rings, a dozen bags, and a couple of run-down treadmills that no one ever used. If you wanted a massage or herbal tea, you went elsewhere. "I've got to get back into the swing of it."

"Fair enough. But don't break your fist while you're at it."

Miller gave Ben what passed for a smile these days and went back to punching the bag. He wondered what exactly he was trying to get back into the swing of—his old life, his hiding from the world, his guilt?

He'd had such high hopes for himself that night with Rachel, as though one moment of courage would reverse a lifetime of cowardice. And what a fucking joke that had turned out to be; since that night he'd not taken one more step forward, had let his mess sit untouched and filthy while life went on without him, while Danny went on without him. Just that thought alone warranted a half-dozen hard hits to the bag, sweat flying from Miller's hair as he gritted his teeth through the final punches.

Virtually every part of his life was in limbo. He'd been on administrative leave for months now. He knew Nash was dragging out the investigation as a form of punishment because, although he could feel that there was something more to the story of Danny Butler and Miller Sutton, he couldn't put his hands on it. Since official censure would likely not be coming, Nash was handing down his own vigilante sentence.

And Nash had been running his mouth, too; Miller was convinced. The few times he'd been to the office, the other agents had given him a wide berth, everyone looking at him with wary eyes, pity just below the surface of their smiles. He still wasn't sure he wanted his job back, but he felt stuck in place, his FBI badge a form of concrete shoes he wasn't sure how to shed.

Miller stopped for a few groceries on the way home, knocking back a bottle of Gatorade on the short walk from his car to his building's fire escape. He was already at a loss as to how he was going to fill the long hours until night, watching TV and staring at a book without reading it having both lost their allure weeks ago. When he turned the corner of the building, he found Colin waiting against the metal railing, his eyes hidden behind his own pair of mirrored shades.

"Hi," Miller said cautiously. "What are you doing here?"

Colin pulled off his sunglasses, tucking them into the interior pocket of his suit jacket. "Nash closed the investigation. You were cleared of any wrongdoing." Colin's voice was heavy, relief absent from his tone. "We need to talk."

"Okay." Miller led the way, Colin's footsteps clanging behind him on the steps, shushing lightly at his heels as they walked down the carpeted hall. Miller unlocked his front door and tossed his keys onto the table, gesturing Colin toward a seat while he put his milk and beer in the fridge.

Colin sat down in the chair nearest the door. He leaned forward and rested his elbows on his knees, clasping his hands. He looked like he was steeling himself for something unpleasant, and Miller's stomach contracted into a small, cold ball.

"Have you talked to Danny Butler lately?" Colin asked.

Miller's whole body jerked, nothing he could control. His insides reacted to the sound of Danny's name like a beehive poked with a stick, the nerve endings under his skin buzzing with anticipation. "No." He paused, sitting down across from Colin. "Why?"

"I heard he's in Chicago. He got a job at Legal Aid."

Chicago. "What kind of job?"

Colin shrugged. "Part of some grant. He helps out around the office; I don't know any details."

"How did you find out?"

"Patterson. She's the one who recommended him for the job, through his probation officer."

"Patterson," Miller repeated, dumbfounded. He couldn't have been more shocked if Colin had told him Nash was responsible for Danny's new employment. Now that Miller's eyes were opening to the infinite variations within people who seemed so one-dimensional on the surface, he wondered if he'd ever stop being surprised by them, by their capacity for conflicting emotions and deeds. "Well, I guess she owed him," Miller said, "after cutting him loose the way she did."

"Could be she did you a favor when she cut him loose," Colin said.

"What?" Miller asked in surprise. "What are you talking about?"

"You tell me," Colin said, pointing at him with a stabbing finger, and Miller realized exactly how angry Colin was, how hard he was pulling back on his own fury. "If we had gone ahead to trial, would Butler have made it off the witness stand without being ripped to shreds? I know something was going on between you two. Christ, Nash never even saw you and Butler in the same room together and he knew it too. You think any defense attorney worth a shit wasn't going to be able to sniff that out in under five minutes? Give me a fucking break."

"Colin, I—"

"So just lay off Patterson, would you? Because the Hinestroza case was sunk long before she fucked over Butler. What the *hell* were you thinking?"

Miller slumped back on the sofa and pressed the heels of his hands against his eyes, hard. This felt different than facing Rachel, worse in some way he couldn't define. People cheated on their lovers every day, screwed up their relationships. Maybe not because they were gay, but still. But putting your own desires ahead of justice? That was embracing a darkness he hadn't known lived within him.

"I didn't mean for it to happen. We just… the feelings were real, Colin." Miller spoke against his wrists, his eyes still hidden behind his hands.

"I don't care if he was the goddamn love of your life! You threw away years of work, Miller, and not just your own efforts."

Miller pulled in a deep breath, the air stinging in his throat. "I'm sorry," he managed. He almost laughed at how pathetic it sounded. "I know you've been covering for me."

Colin's voice softened slightly. "I don't want to be a jackass about this. But the bottom line is, you got involved with an informant, a witness. You got involved. And that cannot happen. I don't think there's any way back from a mistake like that. I don't think the FBI is where you belong anymore," he continued, his voice tired. "And I think you know it too."

"Am I being fired?" Miller asked, meeting Colin's eyes.

"No. But do the right thing here, please."

"It's hard," Miller said. "Hard to walk away from the job, even when you know it's not the place for you."

"You were a good agent, Miller, damn good. But sometimes life gets in the way of the job and you have to make a choice. You made yours; now you've got to follow it through."

"Are you going to tell Nash?"

"No. If I thought it was going to make a difference in the Hinestroza case, I already would have. But telling him doesn't change anything. It only gets us both in trouble." Colin sighed. "They expect you at work Monday. Why don't you come back for a little while, just until you figure out what you're going to do. They won't assign you to anything major at first, so that gives you a window."

Miller nodded. "Okay."

Colin looked back down at his hands, his fingers lacing together and then apart. "Miller, why aren't you with Butler? I know you well enough to know you're not a guy who acts on a whim. You said what you felt for him was real. You put your whole career on the line for him, so why the hell aren't you with him?"

Miller turned his face away, looking out the ceiling-high windows. It had started snowing in the minutes since they'd come inside, fat, lazy flakes taking their sweet time falling from the sky. Just one more reminder of Danny. "Something happened that day with Madrigal." Miller's voice sounded hazy and far away, as though he were outside in the snow, speaking through the winter-cold panes of glass. "Hinestroza was—"

"No!" Colin exclaimed. "No. Don't tell me that!"

Miller's eyes moved back to Colin, taking in the thumping vein in his temple, his hands laced again, the knuckles tight with tension. "The time for telling me that has come and gone. It's too late. What can I do with something like that now?" Colin demanded. "I don't want to know! Jesus!"

Miller thinned his lips against the urge to keep talking, to speak the truth in the hope that Colin would say he'd made the right decision, that his choice had been the one any man would have made. But like so much of what had passed between Danny and him, this was their secret, their burden to shoulder, and the weight couldn't be shared by an outsider.

"All right." Miller nodded. "All right. I'll be at work on Monday."

"Fine." Colin stood up, shoving his hands into his pockets as Miller walked him to the door.

"Thanks for what you did," Miller said. "I know you risked a lot."

Colin glanced at Miller over his shoulder, gave him a sharp nod. And Miller understood his friendship with Colin had come to an end.

THE back door banged loudly as Danny let himself out into the mild night air. According to the calendar it was still winter, but they'd gotten lucky this St. Patrick's Day and the temperature was hovering somewhere in the fifties, even this close to midnight. Jesus, he was tired all of a sudden. Earlier today they'd tromped all the way down Michigan Avenue to the bridges over the river, just to watch dirty, fake-green water rush by. At the time it had seemed like a good idea. That's what five beers with lunch will do to you.

Danny lowered himself to the steps, digging his cigarettes out of his jacket pocket. The party was still going full swing inside—Lauren, one of the attorneys from work, and her husband were inaugurating their new house in appropriate Irish style.

The door behind Danny opened swiftly, crashing into his back. "Shit," he griped, scooting forward as Jill inched out.

"Sorry." Jill sighed as she plopped down next to him, holding out her hand for a drag.

"I didn't know you smoked." Danny passed over his cigarette, which she inhaled with gusto.

"I don't, really. Not since college. But it's like riding a bike."

Danny laughed, leaning his elbows on the step behind him. "Pretty rowdy crowd in there. Somehow I expected a more sedate party from a bunch of attorneys."

"Nah—get a bunch of lawyers together with some booze and all hell breaks loose." Jill passed him back his cigarette, hunching over with her arms curled around her jean-clad knees. "Did you hear Taylor got into law school?"

"Yeah, she told me at work today. That's great."

"It means come September we'll need a new paralegal." Jill tipped her face toward him, her long hair falling forward like a curtain.

"Okay," Danny said, unsure of her point.

"You should apply for it, Danny."

Danny coughed on his inhale, blowing smoke out his nostrils. "Me? I don't think so."

"Why not?"

"Because... because I'm not qualified. Don't you have to go to school for that?"

Jill shrugged. "Nowadays most people do, but it didn't used to be that way. You can do the job. Shit, you already practically do it for me. Reading cases, writing memos, outlining witness testimony, arranging trial exhibits. It's nothing you don't do every day. And you'd get paid more. It would be a permanent position."

Danny hadn't thought beyond the end of his year-long stint at the Legal Aid office. He didn't know what kind of commitment he was willing to make to Chicago, to this job, to this new type of life. "I'll think about it," he said, tapping ash off against the side of the steps.

"Okay," Jill said, not pushing. "You have a while before you need to decide." She shivered slightly in the breeze, wrapping her arms more closely around her knees.

"Here," Danny said, shrugging out of his jacket. "Take this."

"Thanks." She put her arms through the sleeves, practically disappearing inside the black leather. "Danny?"

"Hmmm?"

"Would you like to go to dinner with me sometime?" Her question came out in a rush, sounding like one long, single phrase. It took him a moment to break it up into separate words.

Danny tossed his half-smoked cigarette to the concrete and crushed it under his heel. "Jill, I'm gay."

She stared at him. "No, you're not," she said after a moment, pushing against him with her shoulder.

"Yes, I am."

"But your ex-wife called that day."

"Amanda. Yeah, I was married. I'm still gay, though."

"Oh. *Oh*," Jill breathed. "Fuck. Now I feel really stupid."

"Don't feel stupid." Danny smiled. "It's not like I advertise it."

"No, you don't," Jill agreed. "Obviously, or I wouldn't have asked you out."

"Are you even supposed to do that? Since we work together?"

"Eh, it's pretty casual around that place. I don't think going to dinner would have been crossing any lines."

"Why would you want to go out with me anyway?"

"What do you mean?" Jill asked, her brow furrowed. She twisted her hair up on top of her head as she spoke.

"I mean, you're an attorney, you could have your pick of guys. I'm an ex-con, Jill, with a high school education. I'm not quite in your league."

"You're not doing anything illegal now, are you? Not selling crack out behind the building on your lunch hour?"

"No." Danny grinned with a shake of his head.

"You've got a real job, right? You're trying to turn things around. And you aren't half bad to look at, Danny Butler." Jill flashed her own wide grin. "Why wouldn't I want to go out with you?"

Danny didn't answer right away, listening to the thumping beats of music vibrating from the house. "You really believe people can change?" he asked. "That they deserve second chances?"

Jill took his hand in hers, but there was nothing sexual in the touch; it was a sister's caress, meant to ease suffering, not kindle lust. "Of course I do. Otherwise I'm sort of wasting my life, right? I mean, look at what I do all day, every day. If I don't believe people can change, that a second chance might be all someone needs to get their act together, then why am I doing this shit-for-pay, thankless job?"

Danny squeezed Jill's hand, her fingers so small and delicate in his own. He'd only stopped wearing the bandages over his fingertips recently and it was nice to touch someone else's skin.

"Are you seeing anybody, Danny?" Jill asked after several minutes of easy silence. "Because you could have brought him tonight."

"No, I'm not with anyone." He could feel Jill watching him.

"I hear a broken heart in your voice," she said gently. "I've had some experience in that department."

"It's a long story." Danny withdrew his hand, using it to light a new cigarette.

"Does this long story have a name?"

Danny sucked so hard against the filter he thought he might inhale the entire cigarette down his throat. "Miller," he managed.

"Miller. Now that's a name you don't hear every day."

"Nope." Danny choked out a sad little laugh.

"Do you want to talk about it?"

"Not tonight."

"Okay." Jill nodded. "And I hope you appreciate how difficult that is for me to say, because I'm naturally such a nosy bitch."

Danny laughed, a real one this time. "Maybe someday."

"Deal." She dragged herself up off the step, using both hands around the railing as leverage. "I'm going in. Need anything?" She stripped off his jacket and handed it back.

"No, I'm good. Jill?"

"Yeah?" She paused, her hand on the screen door handle.

"I like that thing you do with your hair, the knot."

Jill smiled, her face lit with genuine joy. She let go of the door and bent down to kiss him lightly on the cheek. Even after smoking, she smelled like flowers. "Thanks, Danny."

The party sounds grew louder as she opened the door, receding again when she shut it behind her, leaving Danny to man the back stoop alone. The edges of Lauren's backyard were dense with bushes, the interior lights failing to reach the shadowy corners. Danny crushed out his cigarette and stood, wandering into the dark. He could see a few stars, the city lights not obscuring their dim glow. Nothing like a prairie sky, but he'd take it.

Miller was heavy on his mind tonight. More than three months had passed since he'd seen Miller's face, touched his hair, or heard his low voice, and it still hurt to say his name. It was too long and yet not long enough, because the guilt still burned in Danny's heart, a brand on the inside that wasn't going away. He wondered what Miller was doing tonight, if he was moving on, if he was healing. Danny hoped so, had hope for Miller he was still trying to find for himself.

"Miller," he breathed, lifting his face to the stars.

Danny didn't believe in ghosts or conjuring people's spirits, even when they were still alive, but as he spoke Miller's name he felt warmth against his back, a man's strength behind him, holding him tight. He could have sworn he smelled the spice of Miller's skin, his soft lips murmuring words of comfort against Danny's neck. For the first time since he'd walked away from Miller, Danny knew peace.

A single hot tear ran down his cheek, catching on the corner of his mouth. "I miss you," Danny whispered. "I miss you." He felt loved. He felt heard. And for now it was enough. It would have to be.

CHAPTER 18

THE razor made a harsh, scraping sound against Danny's cheek, louder in his ear than in reality. For a moment he was transported somewhere he did not want to travel: a cold warehouse full of death. Funny how that happened; the disposable Bic in his hand was nothing like Madrigal's favored weapon, but the bright scrape of metal was reminder enough. Danny forced his mind back to the small motel bathroom, leaning closer to the mirror as he tucked his top lip over his teeth, shaving the delicate skin underneath his nose.

"You're shaving?" Miller's head poked out from behind the shower curtain, his hair standing up in shampoo-laden tufts.

"Yep."

Miller's head disappeared again and Danny smiled as he listened to Miller rushing his way through the rest of his shower. He couldn't keep from sneaking a peek—or two—when Miller yanked the curtain open, reaching for a towel with a dripping arm. Miller twisted the towel around his waist, coming up to press his damp chest against Danny's bare back.

"Hey," Miller said softly, resting his chin on Danny's shoulder, meeting his eyes in the mirror.

"Hey, yourself. I didn't realize this was so exciting."

"I've never seen you shave before," Miller said, as though that explained it. And maybe it did. Hadn't he stayed awake after Miller fell asleep last night, watching the slow rise and fall of his chest, tracing a random pattern on his arm? Or this morning, hadn't he been fascinated by the way Miller thumbed his way through the paper as he nursed a cup of coffee, every motion slow and deliberate? Maybe they were both storing up memories, tiny moments in time, to sustain them in the bleak, *lonely days that waited just around the corner.*

Miller planted a wet row of kisses along Danny's neck. "When did you get this one?" Miller's fingers trailed a lazy loop around the yin-yang tattoo on Danny's shoulder.

"After Leavenworth. That one was actually my idea, as opposed to Hinestroza's or Amanda's."

"Why did you want it?"

Danny shrugged, pulling the razor down his cheek. "I read about the symbol when I was in prison. I liked the idea of it. Light and dark, two halves making a whole." He met Miller's eyes in the mirror again, setting his razor down on the sink.

"Are you the dark, Danny?" Miller asked quietly.

But Danny didn't want to talk about his mistakes, the shadows that swirled within him and would never go away, having grown accustomed to their dank and fertile home, roots embedded deep in the rich, black soil. So he grabbed Miller's hand and pushed it lower, watching when Miller's mouth opened, a low groan escaping as he pulled Danny's towel away, loosening his own with his free hand, spreading Danny's thighs with strong and demanding knees.

Danny gripped the edge of the sink, arching his back as Miller surged into his body, Miller's hot breaths whistling against his neck. They worked together without speaking, Danny driving back for every thrust forward. Their eyes caught in the mirror, showing faces slack with pleasure.

Miller came with a shout, his fingers carving rough troughs in Danny's hips, and Danny closed his eyes and took what Miller gave him, wishing that somehow a spark from Miller might be left behind, a tiny flicker in the darkness.

"GUILTY."

The judge's voice was calm and even, probably not carrying much beyond the first row of the gallery, which was fine, because the courtroom was practically empty. The reaction was nothing like what you saw on TV; no one screamed in hysterics and the bailiff sat calmly in his seat, not fighting off a distraught defendant or his family. The jurors looked blasé, most of them anxious to be home now that their civic duty was complete.

Danny glanced across the table at Ronnie Jennings, watching as Jill murmured something in his ear. Ronnie nodded, his eyes focused on his hands. To someone who'd never sat in Ronnie's seat and heard the single word, *guilty*, that would dictate his life from now on, it would probably seem as though Ronnie was fine, that he was paying attention, present. But Danny had been in that seat several times, and he suspected Ronnie was retreating further into that space he'd created around himself from the moment he'd been arrested—the safe space that kept him removed from what happened to him and insulated him from thoughts of how his life was no longer his to control. If Ronnie was lucky, he could stay inside that self-made bubble for the length of his prison sentence. The trick was figuring out how to step back into life when the prison doors swung open, how to become a part of the living world again.

Jill gave Ronnie a quick pat on the upper arm as the bailiff led him away, his hands shackled behind his back, a chain securing his ankles together. Ronnie kept his gaze straight ahead as he shuffled through the door that would take him to the holding room down the hall, and from there to his new home.

"How are you doing?" Danny asked as they gathered up their clutter from the defense table, plastic tubs filled with numbered exhibits, scores of yellow legal pads, highlighters and pens, half-empty water bottles, a box of Kleenex, and several tins of Altoids, which Jill refused to enter the courtroom without.

"Me?" Jill smiled at Danny across the table. "I'm fine."

"Are you upset about the verdict?"

"Not really." Jill shrugged. "I expected it."

"But you worked so hard."

"I did," she agreed. "But he was guilty, Danny. He robbed that store. How can I be mad when the jury made the right decision? He should have taken the plea."

"But...." Danny stopped, at a rare loss for words.

"Let me guess, you want to know why I worked so hard if I knew he was guilty, right? Or how I could represent him in the first place?" Jill didn't wait for Danny's response, stuffing the last of the legal pads into her battered briefcase with a sigh. "I did it because it's my job. I can't go into it thinking about guilt or innocence or what my client deserves. Those kinds of judgments are beyond me. Everyone's entitled to a good defense and that's my job. Fighting for a fair sentence, that's my job too. But as far as the verdict, the system usually works the way it's supposed to. Innocent men are convicted and guilty men go free, but not as often as people think."

Danny stared at her and Jill laughed. "Bet you weren't expecting a speech, were you? I've got more where that came from. Someday, ask to hear the one on three-strikes laws. It's a doozy."

"How do you do it?" Danny asked. "How do you do this job every day?"

Jill looked up at him. "Because I love it. And because I'm one of those pathetic bleeding hearts who really does believe that everyone deserves a decent defense. Sad, but true."

"It's not sad."

Jill smiled as she hoisted a box of exhibits onto her hip. "Hey, a few of us are going out for a beer. Want to come?"

"Nah," Danny shook his head. "I'm beat. I'm going to head home." He knew Jill's invitation was genuine, just as the friendly greeting he'd received every morning from the prosecutor and bailiff, the judge and his clerk were truly meant. But he still felt uncomfortable around this courthouse crowd.

The first day he'd shown up here in his new black slacks and white button-down shirt, his heart had threatened to burst out of his chest, his feet dragging with thoughts of setting foot in a courtroom again. He'd only done it for Jill, because she'd needed help with this trial, and she'd promised him it would be three days or less. His anxiety must have shown on his face because Jill had pulled him aside and told him to relax, he wasn't a defendant anymore. He didn't know how many of the people working in the courtroom knew his history, but even if they all did, no one acted like it mattered. It still mattered to Danny, though, and he was pretty sure it always would.

"See you on Monday," Jill said as they parted ways on the courthouse steps, waving with her briefcase. "You did a good job, Danny."

"Thanks." Danny smiled. "See you later."

The St. Patrick's Day weather had held for more than a week now, and Danny took advantage of the unseasonable warmth, getting off the L one stop early to swing by a local sandwich shop for dinner. He got a turkey club to go, knowing the sandwich wasn't in his budget but for one night not caring.

The warmer temperature brought a hint of spring to the air, but the deep twilight pushing in by six o'clock told a different story. Danny let himself into his apartment, shedding his shirt before he'd even switched on the living room lamp. Thank God Jill hadn't made him wear a tie, at least. More comfortable in old jeans and a T-shirt, he grabbed a beer and his sandwich, settling himself on the couch to eat. It was so quiet in the room he could hear each crunch of the lettuce, the lonely sounds of his meal shriveling his appetite into nothing.

He knew what he was going to do—had known from the minute he'd turned down Jill's invitation for beers. It was one of those nights. He could feel Miller rising up in him, swamping him with need. He put his plate, complete with half-finished sandwich, down on the floor and lay back on the couch, resting his head on a chenille throw pillow Amanda had picked out a lifetime ago.

He closed his eyes, searching for the right image, trying to decide which one he'd dole out tonight. Only one—that was the most he could handle and the most he could afford to use up. It reminded him of being a kid, when his dad had always received a tiny box of chocolates for Christmas from his sister-in-law. Danny was allowed to have one, just one, and he had to pick carefully because if he chose wrong and ended up with the maple nougat or the raspberry cream, that was his own tough luck.

Danny felt like that boy as he sifted through his memories, trying to put his fingers on just the right vision for tonight, one he could savor, one that would melt slowly on his tongue like chocolate and caramel, sweet and rich, one that couldn't be swallowed down too quickly, disappearing in a single ravenous gulp.

His mind closed around the memory in a greedy clutch, but Danny slowed himself down, easing his fingers off the vision, letting it unfold slowly. He pictured rolling over, his body limp with sleep and satisfaction, and seeing Miller's face above his, those gray eyes warm and peaceful, hearing the faint, almost imagined, snap of snow against the windows. Miller's face had been soft and easy that morning after they'd first made love, for once not carrying any weight around his eyes, his mouth loose and relaxed. Whatever else Danny had fucked up between them, he'd done something right that day because Miller had been happy, lit up from the inside.

It was a good memory. One that was worth the bittersweet sting of remembering.

WAITING until morning was the smart thing to do, get a decent night's sleep and head out when the sun was up. But Miller had spent his whole life doing the smart thing, the safe thing, and now he couldn't wait for daylight. He wanted to look at his watch in an hour, on the dark and deserted highway, and know he was getting closer to Danny with each ticking second.

He'd waited all week for Colin to call him back, impatience robbing him of appetite, longing stealing his rest. He'd promised himself he'd give Colin five days, one hundred and twenty hours, before he'd simply head to Chicago without any clear plan, just show up on Danny's doorstep with no idea what he'd do in that strange city. But in the end Colin had come through, and Miller could go to Danny with more than just a wish for their future.

He packed quickly; he didn't need much. He'd have to come back here soon, no matter what happened. Either to pick up the pieces of this life or to gather his things and move them to his new life with Danny. He didn't allow himself to think beyond the drive, beyond rolling over the miles separating them. Nine hours, give or take, and he'd see Danny's face again.

Miller zipped up his duffel bag and laced up his battered tennis shoes. He stood in the doorway of his apartment for a moment, the moon high and bright through the window. Going after what he really wanted, reaching for it with both hands, was unfamiliar to Miller. He'd lived his life waiting patiently for what would come to him. But Danny had changed all that. Miller thought that maybe Danny's walking away that day in the park had been a blessing in disguise. By letting go, Danny had freed him to pursue, had forced Miller to find the courage to follow.

THE sun woke Danny before he was ready. He'd planned on sleeping in, taking advantage of his work-free Saturday. He tried putting the pillow over his head but couldn't settle back into sleep, the sun hitting right between his bare shoulder blades, heating the skin to an itchy tingle.

"Shit," he muttered, squinting at his bedside clock. Eight o'clock. The "real job" schedule he kept during the week was wreaking havoc with his lazy mornings in bed. He needed to shower, and, judging from the sorry state of his kitchen, a trip to the grocery store was definitely in order. Maybe this week he'd branch out and get something besides cereal and Hamburger Helper.

When he opened his living room window, the breeze hitting his face was warm, ruffling his shower-damp hair. He figured he probably still needed his jacket, the Chicago wind capable of chilling the mildest-looking day. As he jogged down the stairs to the front door of his building, he sent up a quick prayer that his car would be where he'd left it, three blocks away. He hadn't driven it in over a week; parking in Chicago was such a bitch he walked or took the L if at all possible.

The sun hit Danny's eyes in a blinding glare as he stepped out onto the sidewalk. He patted his jacket pockets for his sunglasses, too late remembering them sitting on his kitchen counter. Fuck it—he wasn't going back up four flights of stairs. There was a brown Jeep parked at the curb, its bumper flush against the car in front. Danny smiled to himself. Someone was going to be pissed when they woke up and couldn't move their car because of that Jeep's snug embrace. He turned left, toward his own car, his rapid pace slowing suddenly… that brown Jeep.

Danny pivoted and stared. He knew that Jeep. He'd almost died in that car, he and Miller both. Miller.

No, it's a different Jeep. There are thousands of brown ones just like that. You're imagining it.

But Danny knew he wasn't. Because the license plate was the same. He never forgot details like that, never forgot details about Miller. Danny moved closer, peering into the passenger window, seeing nothing but a clean interior. From a distance he heard the faint tinkling of the bell on the door of the corner shop, the one that sold newspapers, stale doughnuts, and day-old coffee. Without even looking, he knew who had come out of that store. Even from five car lengths away, Danny could feel him.

Danny straightened up slowly, almost scared to see, scared that if he turned his head Miller would disappear, a figment of his starved imagination. Danny turned his head, eyes drawn to the lanky man standing on the sidewalk, a Styrofoam cup of coffee clutched in his hand, his eyes camouflaged by mirrored shades.

They stared at each other, neither one moving. And then Miller pulled off his sunglasses, hooking them through the neck of his army-green T-shirt, closing the distance between them in long strides. Danny stood frozen in place as his mind clicked off facts in a detached, distant voice: he needs a haircut, he's not smiling, he's getting closer, the freckles on his nose are darker.

Miller stopped in front of him, his eyes sweeping over Danny then locking on his face, not moving.

"That coffee sucks," Danny croaked, because he couldn't find his voice to ask the important questions, the *why* and *how* and *what does it mean* of Miller's presence on this sunny Saturday morning.

Miller's mouth curved upward, the very beginnings of a smile, and then he opened his fingers, the cup thudding down onto the pavement. Coffee soaked into the concrete in a muddy stain as the lid gave way.

Their bodies came together hard, the force of Miller's lunge driving the air from Danny's chest, the mirrored sunglasses sacrificed between them. Danny's arms wrapped around Miller's back, one hand fisting in his hair, threatening to never let go, tugging against the soft strands. "Miller," Danny whispered, closing his eyes, swallowing past a throat crowded with tears.

"Danny, Danny." Miller's voice was thick, his lips moving against Danny's neck. "God, Danny."

Danny pulled him closer, his arms ratcheting tight. He didn't know what the future held or why Miller was there, but for a single endless moment, standing with Miller in a warm March breeze, Danny had everything he'd ever wanted, and he didn't want to lose his grip.

MILLER wasn't sure he was going to make it up the stairs. He concentrated on Danny climbing steadily in front of him, ignoring his trembling knees and shaking fingers that registered an internal earthquake. He followed Danny down the narrow hall to the apartment at the far end of the building, waited while Danny fiddled with the multiple inner-city locks.

"Come on in," Danny said, hoarse and breathless.

The apartment was small and plain but clean, Danny's furniture too nice for its new home. Miller watched as Danny locked the door behind them, bracing himself for Danny's weight against his body. But Danny skirted his way around him, throwing his jacket onto the couch as he passed. Danny took a seat on the edge of the far windowsill, his eyes on the floor. The silence between them was laced with tension, the lack of words as loud as any scream. Miller cleared his throat, moving a little closer to Danny, unsure how to begin. In his imaginings it had all been easier, this awkwardness between them something he'd never anticipated. "I heard you got a job," he blurted out.

"Yeah," Danny nodded. "At Legal Aid."

"How's it going?"

"Fine. They want me to apply for a paralegal job that's opening up."

"That's great, Danny. That would be really good—"

"What are you doing here, Miller?" Danny's voice was flat, cutting Miller's words short.

Miller blinked. "I wanted to see you," he said, even though he didn't think it needed saying.

"Why?"

"Why?" Miller repeated. He felt mired in uncertainty, off balance since they'd entered the apartment, the atmosphere so different from their greeting on the sidewalk.

"Yeah, Miller, why?"

"Because... because I did what you said. I cleaned up my life. I told Rachel the truth, I quit my job—"

"I hope you didn't do all that for me." Danny grasped the windowsill with white knuckles.

"I—I thought I was doing it for both of us." Miller exhaled a shaky breath, ran one hand through his hair. "What's going on? You seem angry."

Danny looked away and Miller could see how hard he was fighting back his emotions, his throat muscles straining beneath the skin. "What did you expect?"

What had he expected? Danny to fall into his arms and thank him for coming, to be so happy to see him that they could avoid all the tough questions? Yeah, if he was being honest, that was about what he'd envisioned.

"Did you hear I had a new job and think I was a new man? I told you I wanted to be a better person, Miller, and I meant it. But there's no quick fix for me. I'm not there yet, not by a long shot."

"I don't... I didn't...." Miller blew out a tongue-tied breath. Why was this so damn hard? Why couldn't he say in words what he held in his heart? Everything he wanted Danny to know, to hope for, was stuck in a bottle with a broken cork blocking the neck. "I'm not there yet, either, Danny. I'm just trying to live a more honest life, trying to get my shit together, like we talked about."

Danny let out a ragged sigh, hiding his face from Miller. "I hate to break it to you, but I'm still the same fucked-up mess I've always been. Maybe a little shinier on the outside, but the inside is still an ugly place." Danny's words zinged between them like wild bullets, Miller not sure who or what the intended target.

"I don't believe that, Danny. This life you're living now, it's proof that you are changing."

"Oh, yeah?" Danny challenged. "Well, every day I walk home from work, back to this shitty apartment, and I pass guys selling crack on street corners and I think about calling him, about asking for my job back. I wonder what he might say if I made that call. I think about it, Miller, and I probably always will."

"You think you're the only one who has thoughts like that? I still wake up some days and wish I wasn't gay, wish I could have that life with Rachel that I planned out for myself. And I doubt those thoughts will ever go away for me, either." He took a step toward Danny. "So what if you think about calling Hinestroza. You haven't actually done it, have you?"

Danny shook his head, his eyes floating down to the floor.

"We all have our demons, Danny. Yours aren't worse than anybody else's."

"That's a load of crap, Miller, and you know it. Look at what you did... because of me. You let Hinestroza walk away. Before me, you would never have done something like that."

"It doesn't matter what I would have done before!" Miller nearly shouted. "Don't you see? Because by that day in the kitchen, I was already a different man. What we found together had already changed me. In a good way, in the best way. It opened my eyes to the crap life I'd been living. I made the deal with Hinestroza because I had to. There was no other possible choice for me." Miller threw up his hands, fishing for some way to make Danny understand, willing to open his soul if that's what it took. "Do you remember that day on the park bench, when you asked me how I was going to live with letting Hinestroza go?"

Danny nodded, still not looking at him. "Yeah, I remember."

Miller caught Danny's eyes as they tried to glide past. "Well, it turned out living with it wasn't as hard as I thought it would be. Because I realized living without you was the alternative. I wouldn't change it. Not even if I could."

"How can you say that?"

"I can say it because you were the trade. Your life. And saving you was worth any price."

"Miller." Danny shook his head, moving to stand against the wall. Miller felt a moment of frustration so huge it threatened to eclipse his hope. What if he couldn't convince Danny? What if Danny didn't want to believe?

Then you keep trying, Miller. You keep trying.

And maybe that was the simple secret: not giving up. Pushing forward, no matter the odds. He stepped up, right in front of Danny, where he couldn't look away.

"I don't have all the answers, Danny. I never have. But I know I want to be with you."

"I didn't think I'd ever see you again," Danny said, almost to himself, as if Miller hadn't spoken. "I walked away. I thought you'd move on, find a way to be happy."

Miller stared at him. "Is that what you're doing? Are you happy now, are you moving on?" The thought tore at him, left him feeling gutted, hollowed out with loss.

Danny shook his head, his face marked with grief. "No. No, I'm not happy, and you're always on my mind."

"What makes you think it's any different for me?"

"I don't... I still don't deserve you." Danny sounded like a starving man turning away from a meal, a tortured man refusing relief.

Keep trying.

"What makes you think I deserve *you*, Danny? You think my life was rosy, so fucking perfect before you came along and screwed it up? Is that what you think? Well, it wasn't. I was so lonely and closed off, and scared to take a good look at myself. And then you showed me a way it could be different. A way *I* could be different. You saw right through all my bullshit, and you made me see through it too. And yeah, you're right, bad things happened, but Jesus, look at all the good there was too. Can't you see how good it was? Don't you remember?"

Miller's voice broke and he lowered his head, pressing his thumbs into his closed eyelids, exhausted by the effort of giving voice to what was private within him. "I don't know if you deserve me or I deserve you. How about we just deserve each other? How about that?" Miller let his hands fall and stared into Danny's eyes, willing him to see the truth, offering up the best he had to give. "I love you, Danny," he said. "I love you."

Danny's eyelids fluttered down. He reached out blindly to clutch at Miller's T-shirt, bunching the cotton in his palm. He didn't pull Miller closer, simply held him that way, tight and captive. Miller could feel the heat from Danny's skin, and it took everything he had not to reach out and touch, fighting so damn hard to give Danny the space to decide.

Danny's fingers and eyes opened at the same moment, his gaze rising to fix on Miller's. "I need you to be sure, Miller," he said, his voice rough. "Because this is who I am. All the ugly parts of me are here to stay. I'm never going to outrun my past, not all of it. It's a package deal. So be sure, because this is who I am."

Miller leaned forward, bracing his hands on the wall on either side of Danny's face. "I like who you are. And I like who we are together." He spoke each word carefully, a promise unfurling between them. Miller understood that Danny's past was part of the package. And that past held dirty secrets, but it was also what made Danny the man who fit with Miller the way no other human being ever had. That past had shaped Danny into the person Miller was meant to be with, the man Miller knew he was meant to love.

They stared at each other for long seconds. Miller's skin felt electric, buzzing with need under the hot weight of Danny's gaze. "Can I touch you?" Miller asked gently. "Because I think I might die if I don't." They weren't words he'd ever imagined saying, but they sounded right against his lips. He wasn't ashamed of them.

"Yes," Danny nodded, his voice a breathless sigh. "Yes."

Miller moved his hands from the wall to cradle Danny's face, his fingers still dancing a nervous tune. "Danny," he whispered as he brought his mouth forward, going slow. He wanted to taste and touch, he didn't want to rush. Danny lips were warm and soft under his, opening to allow his tongue inside, the wet heat of Danny's mouth wringing a moan from Miller's throat.

"I love you," Danny murmured. His voice sounded watery, full to the brim.

Miller's hands moved down Danny's chest, working their way underneath his shirt, spreading flat across his stomach. "Say it again," he urged.

He felt Danny smile into his mouth. "I love you, Miller Sutton."

Miller yanked on Danny's T-shirt, tugging it over his head, feeling Danny do the same to his, and then they were back against each other, bare skin coming together as their arms clutched tight. Miller took a moment to just breathe against the warmth of Danny's body, his heart so full he thought his chest might crack wide open, joy spilling out like blood.

Danny buried his face in Miller's neck, not speaking, his breathing ragged. Miller pulled back a little, running his fingers down Danny's chest, pushing Danny away when he tried to touch in return. "Just let me… let me look at you," he said.

Danny leaned back against the wall, the breath whistling out of him in stunted gasps as his eyes followed Miller's hands down his body. Miller stopped at the small purple scar on his abdomen, raising questioning eyes.

"My kidney," Danny explained.

"I thought the scar would be in the back."

"No, they take it out from the front."

Miller dropped down to his knees, his face buried in Danny's stomach. He wished he could make it all go away, but that would mean he and Danny would not have been, so the regret would have to be part of it, forever a part of them. Miller ran his fingers along the scar, following the path with his mouth, his hands moving to loosen Danny's jeans, easing them down over his hips, Danny's feet slipping out of his shoes.

When Danny was naked, Miller sat back on his heels, taking his time looking, letting his eyes have their fill. He'd thought he remembered how beautiful Danny was, but he hadn't, not really. His latest battle wounds only added to his appeal, new paths for Miller to explore. The scars reminded Miller of how strong and beautiful Danny was on the inside, where it mattered most of all.

"Come here," Danny whispered, pulling at him with both hands.

"Wait." Miller brought his mouth to Danny's thigh, licking the old scar the way he'd tried to once before. He felt the muscles harden under his tongue and held his breath, waiting to see what Danny would allow. But then Danny's legs spread slightly, the skin softening against his mouth as Danny released a sobbing moan that might have been Miller's name.

He traveled his way up Danny's body, leaving a glistening path in his wake. When he reached Danny's mouth again, it was demanding, sucking hard against Miller's tongue, nibbling light vampire kisses along his bottom lip. Danny reached down and took Miller's hands in his, walking backward into the bedroom, pulling Miller along with him, their mouths never losing contact as they moved.

The small bedroom was sun-dappled, the wind casting tree-branch shadows against the creamy walls. Danny sat on the edge of the unmade bed and positioned Miller between his knees. Miller noticed he wasn't the only one with uncooperative fingers, Danny's trembling hands interfering with his task of removing Miller's jeans.

Danny finally managed to pull the buttons free, tugging the denim and cotton down together. Miller stepped out of the bunched material, flinging his jeans and shorts away from the bed with one foot after kicking off his shoes. He looked down at Danny's bent head, wishing he could see his face. But Danny was concentrating on other things, running both hands up Miller's thighs, his fingers kneading lightly as they moved. He smoothed the backs of his fingers over Miller's hard length, his thumb flicking against the tip.

"Did you think about me?" Danny asked, breaking the silence of their shattered breaths.

"All the time." Miller raked his fingers through Danny's dark hair, tipping his head upward, tracing along the new scar partially hidden beneath Danny's rough stubble.

"What would you do, when you thought about me?" Danny's voice was low, almost a growl, and the eyes he raised to Miller's revealed a wild and reckless freedom Miller had never seen there before. But he thought he understood it. They were released, different men than they had been the last time they were together this way.

"I'd close my eyes and remember you. How you looked and smelled. How you tasted."

"Let me see," Danny coaxed. "Show me what you would do."

Miller reached down and wrapped his fingers around himself, pumped his hand slowly, doing this with Danny watching so much more erotic than he could have imagined. He didn't feel any shame, not for what he was letting Danny see, not for standing naked in the daylight with another man. Not for any of it. Danny put his hands on Miller's hips, his mouth coming forward. Miller's slick fingers bumped against Danny's lips as he fisted his hand up and down, increasing the pace as Danny sucked harder.

"Christ, Danny," Miller gasped. He pulled his hand away and Danny took more of him into his mouth, causing Miller's hips to thrust forward, his orgasm already thundering into view. "Danny, stop," he cried, tangling his fingers in Danny's hair. "Stop...."

Danny pulled back, their eyes catching as Miller slid out from between Danny's lips. Miller pushed forward with a snarl, knocking Danny back onto the bed, landing across his body with a muffled groan. Before Danny could move, Miller reached between them, taking Danny in his hand, doing to Danny what he'd just done to himself. Danny whimpered low in his throat, twisting his face into the curve of Miller's neck.

"I like touching you better," Miller panted.

Danny moved his head so they could look at each other. "I don't know," he teased on a whisper, his hips bucking against Miller's hand. "It was pretty sexy watching you do that. You'll have to do it all the way some day."

"We've got time," Miller said, his hand stilling, his eyes serious on Danny's. "Lots of time."

Danny reached up and ran his finger along Miller's jaw in his old, familiar way. The heat from his touch tunneled under Miller's skin, sprinting along his nerve endings. It felt like fire might shoot out of his fingertips, lightning radiate from his skin.

"I want you inside me," Danny murmured, his finger still stroking against Miller's cheek.

Miller's stomach flew to his throat, crashing back down like an elevator with a severed cable. Danny smiled that wide grin that Miller had been waiting for since the moment they'd seen each other on the sidewalk. The one that made Miller wish they could have back every second they'd been apart.

Danny rolled Miller over onto his back, reaching across his chest to fumble on the nightstand. He squirted lotion into his hand, heating it in his circling palms before he smoothed it on Miller in long, firm strokes. Miller arched his back against the bed, closing his eyes and chewing on the inside of his cheek, fighting for control as Danny straddled his body.

Miller opened his eyes and reached for the lotion himself while Danny lifted up onto his knees. Miller pushed into Danny with one finger, his eyes never leaving Danny's face. "More," Danny demanded, and Miller complied, a second finger joining the first, Danny's guttural moan making Miller's hips jerk against the bed.

Miller pulled his hand away, leveraging himself up to a sitting position, Danny resting on his thighs. "Like this… I want to be able to kiss you."

"Yeah." Danny leaned forward, his mouth quiet and soft but his tongue making different demands. "This way."

Danny lifted himself up and then lowered back down, slowly drawing Miller into his body. "Oh, God," Danny moaned, his hands gripping Miller's shoulders when Miller was all the way inside. "I missed you. Missed you so much."

Miller groaned, his breath hitching in his chest. The pleasure of having Danny again and the anguish of knowing what they'd almost lost knotted the air in his lungs, his breathing labored and full of sorrow.

"Miller?" Danny questioned quietly, his body still.

"It's just so much more." Miller's voice was choked, his words barely making it past his lips as he tried to explain what he could hardly put into words, hoping Danny would understand. "It's so much more than I ever thought I'd have."

"I know, baby," Danny soothed. "I know."

Miller felt Danny's tender kisses against his closed eyelids, gentle fingers running along his eyebrows, and then Danny was moving on him in the rhythm they'd found so easily in the past, their bodies remembering the way of it as if they'd never been apart, as if they'd only been waiting to find each other again.

"TURN over," Miller mumbled, barely raising his head from Danny's chest.

Danny looked down at him with raised eyebrows and Miller made a rolling motion with his hand. "Onto your side," he prompted.

Danny didn't want to move, his body sated and peaceful, but he turned onto his side, facing away from Miller.

"*Ahhh*," Miller breathed, like a man who'd just discovered buried treasure, his fingers stroking feather-light against the snake tattoo.

Danny laughed, bringing one foot back to rub Miller's calf. "I'm going to start thinking you only want me for that tattoo."

"Not true," Miller rumbled against his skin. "But it's still about the sexiest thing in the world."

Danny flipped onto his other side so he could see Miller's face. He didn't know if now was the time to continue speaking truths, but he wanted them to start out honest, to not shy away from the hard questions and the even harder answers. "What happened with the FBI?"

Miller sighed, the playfulness fading out of his eyes as he found Danny's fingers and squeezed tight. "I knew it was time for me to leave. I couldn't do that job anymore. Colin suggested I find something else, and I agreed with him. It started to go bad for me even before you, Danny. Meeting you only sped up the inevitable."

"Have you found a new job?"

Miller shook his head. "Not yet. But I have an interview next week with a firm that handles private investigations. The investigators are primarily ex-FBI agents; they take all kinds of cases, from the little domestic stuff to overflow from big court cases, both prosecution and defense. Colin recommended me for the job."

"Is that something you want to do?"

"The smaller cases don't sound like my type of thing. But some of the bigger ones, they could be interesting."

Danny kissed the hard knob of Miller's shoulder bone. "I hate to see you settle for something."

"Who gets everything they want, Danny, exactly how they want it? You have to decide the most important thing and go from there."

"Where is this job?" Danny asked, his stomach cramping in anticipation. He knew in his heart that sacrifices would have to be made if he and Miller wanted to be together, but he didn't know if he was ready to pull up stakes again; everything felt too new and raw for him to start over.

"Here," Miller said, meeting his eyes. "In Chicago."

"Do you... do you even like this city? Do you want to live here?"

Miller shrugged. "I like Chicago fine. I've only been here a couple of times before. But you're settled here, so I think this is where we should be, at least for now. You have a good job, right? Why mess with that?"

Danny smiled. "Well, depends on your definition of good. If by good you mean nice people, interesting work, then yeah, it's good. If you mean a paycheck big enough to cover the rent, then no."

"I meant a job you like, one you're happy with." Miller's voice was serious. "And you must be doing well, or they wouldn't want you to apply for the paralegal position."

"Jill, the attorney I do most of my work for, seems happy with me. She thinks I'd be good at the paralegal job. And it's more money, more responsibility."

They watched each other in the quiet, Danny lulled by the sound of Miller's even breaths.

"So, are you going to apply for the job or not?" Miller asked eventually.

"Christ, you can take the man out of the FBI...."

"Shut up, dumbass," Miller laughed. "Answer the question."

"I don't know. I'll probably apply."

"Why wouldn't you?"

"It just... it feels like I'm tempting fate, you know?"

Miller cocked his head, his brow furrowing. "What do you mean?"

"I worry about setting myself up to fail, about letting people down. If I don't try for a better life, then I don't have to worry about disappointing anybody."

Miller's rubbed a soft circle on Danny's thigh. "You'd be disappointing yourself, though, wouldn't you, by not taking the chance?"

"Yeah, I guess so," Danny sighed. He knew his fear of failure, of not living up to expectations, was something he would have to conquer alone. But with Miller by his side, he thought he might be strong enough to start believing, to begin asking for more than life had given him so far. "But I'm not so sure about this job. A male paralegal? Isn't that kind of like a male nurse?" He was only half-joking. "It just seems kind of weird."

"Oh, Jesus." Miller rolled his eyes. "I can't believe I'm in love with such a fucking idiot."

Danny moved swiftly, pinning Miller to the bed with his full weight, groaning helplessly when their naked bodies came together. He took a deep breath, steadying himself, forcing his hips to stop their slow glide against Miller's.

"Danny?"

"Yeah?"

"What you said earlier, about being the same mess you've always been. Do you really believe that?"

Danny raised his eyes to Miller's. "I don't know. It depends on the day." He sighed, worrying a corner of the sheet between his fingers. "Sometimes it depends on the hour." He looked down at Miller's smooth chest, studying the few freckles sprinkled there. He hadn't realized until this moment how much he'd missed them.

Miller touched his face, stroking a lazy line down his cheek. "Do you remember in the apartment how you were always on me about seeing everything in black and white? You kept telling me people are more complicated than that."

"Yeah."

"It applies to you, too, you know. You've got to start cutting yourself the same slack you offer everyone else."

"I just… I didn't want you to have to give up everything," Danny said quietly.

"Oh, Danny," Miller breathed, holding Danny's face with gentle hands. "Look at what I got in its place."

Danny's first instinct was to protest, but there was no denying the happiness he saw in Miller's eyes, the hard planes of his face smoothed out with contentment as they stared at each other. He remembered the easy way Miller's body had moved just now when they'd made love, no holding back. And he could still hear the sparkle in Miller's laugh, picture the loose curves of his smile. Maybe Danny Butler, with all his faults and failings, had something worth giving after all.

"Do you see?" Miller asked, his eyes never leaving Danny's, one hand stroking his arm in a whisper-light caress.

"Yes," Danny's voice was low, his tears so close now. "I see." He attempted a wobbly smile, rubbing the tips of his fingers against the stubble on Miller's jaw. "I'm glad you came here," he said. "I'm glad you came to find me."

Miller's eyes clouded over a little. "I wasn't sure. You didn't seem happy at first."

Danny rested his forehead on Miller's collarbone. "It's always going to be hard for me, Miller. To believe in myself, to believe I can really change. But I'm trying; I'll keep trying." He paused. "I've hurt everyone who's ever cared about me. Ruined them. It's hard not to think about that."

"You didn't ruin me, Danny," Miller whispered against his temple. "I'm fine and I'm right here."

Danny drew in a shuddering breath, a lone tear spilling over onto Miller's skin.

"How do you feel about me?" Miller murmured against his hair.

Danny inhaled, rough and deep. "I love you."

"Is it strong?" As he spoke, Miller ran a warm hand down Danny's back.

"God, yes." Danny felt that strength, that bond, that love for Miller in all parts of himself—heart, mind, body, and soul.

"Look at me," Miller said, and Danny did, tilting his face until his chin rested on Miller's shoulder. "That's how I feel about you, Danny. Just as strong, just as real, and it's not going to go away."

"So we're in this together." Danny's voice shook but he didn't look away.

Miller smiled, his eyes calm and steady and sure. "Yeah, Danny Butler, we're in this together."

"OKAY, seriously, you guys, shut up! I'm trying to give a toast!" Jill's voice carried beyond their oversized corner booth, causing the bartender across the room to glance in her direction with an indulgent smile.

"I think that bartender likes you," Danny noted, pointing with his beer bottle.

Jill glanced over her shoulder. "Shit, Danny, he has a mullet! I'm not that desperate."

Danny laughed mid-swallow, threatening to snort beer out of his nose.

"Attractive," Jill said dryly. She shot Miller a sympathetic look. "I don't know how you put up with him."

Miller smiled, pushing Danny's foot with his own. Jill tapped hard against her wineglass with a fork. "Okay, everybody raise your glasses. Come on, come on," she urged. "To Danny, our newest paralegal."

"Hear, hear!" Ellis called, clinking his glass against Danny's.

"Way to go!" Taylor hooted from across the table. "You're going to do great, Danny."

The ring of faces around the table were all smiling, cheeks flushed from one too many beers, the rising laughter drowning out the warbling jukebox. It felt good to be sitting here among the people he thought of as his friends. Danny felt a finger brush against his hand, underneath the table. He glanced down and then up, catching Miller's eye.

"Congratulations, Danny," Miller said solemnly, but his eyes were smiling. "You are now the legal equivalent of a male nurse."

"Shut up, asshole," Danny laughed, threading his fingers through Miller's where no one could see. No one at the table would care, but Miller was still skittish in public. He usually didn't touch Danny unless they were alone. But tonight he held Danny's hand and moved it onto his thigh, his warm leg heating Danny's fingers.

Jill smiled at Danny from across the table as she looked from him to Miller and back again, raising her wineglass in a tiny, private toast. "Hey, Ellis," she said. "Tell Miller the story about that dickhead FBI agent we worked with on the Compton case, remember that guy?"

"Oh, Jesus," Miller protested, leaning forward to rest his free elbow on the table. "Haven't you already told me that one, Jill? I'm pretty sure—"

"Ellis tells it better," Jill grinned.

Miller sighed good-naturedly, giving Danny a sideways smile. Danny was struck with a jolt of déjà vu when he saw Miller's face happy and peaceful, like it had been that very first time they'd made love in the snow-shrouded apartment, like it had been on so many days since they'd come together again.

You're doing that, Danny. You're making him happy.

That look on Miller's face was something Danny could believe in, more than words or promises. He could believe in the joy he saw in Miller when they were together. And he could feel it inside himself, too, the tiny spark growing stronger with each day he spent next to Miller Sutton.

Danny knew he still carried his darkness and it would never go quietly, always waiting for its moment, whispering of other choices in the cold hours of night, beckoning Danny with a traitor's fingers. He thought the same was true of Miller, who was too quiet some days, avoiding Danny's eyes; Danny suspected he was mourning the life that was no longer his, struggling to accept his choices. But so far their love had proved deeper than their doubts, their faith in each other more unshakeable than the fear.

And for today they were happy. Danny didn't know about tomorrow. But he could live with the uncertainty, because what they had right now was pretty goddamn good.

"Hey," Jill called. "Earth to Danny! You've got to hear this story."

Danny leaned forward with a smile, resting his shoulder against Miller's, and listened.

BROOKE MCKINLEY has always been practical. So after college she continued on to law school, instead of pursuing her lifelong dream of writing novels. She didn't stop writing but confined it to scribbles on the edges of yellow legal pads and hurried paragraphs during late-night coffee breaks. After ten interesting and challenging years as a criminal defense attorney, Brooke left the practice of law to try something new. She now divides her time between corralling her children and giving voice to the endless characters in her head. And she has decided that practicality is vastly overrated.

E-mail Brooke at brookemckinley@earthlink.net.

LaVergne, TN USA
14 July 2010
189482LV00009B/64/P